THE LEOPARD'S SPOTS

"TWO THOUSAND MEN WENT MAD."

Can the Ethiopian change his skin or the leopard his spots?

THE
LEOPARD'S SPOTS

A ROMANCE OF THE WHITE
MAN'S BURDEN — 1865 – 1900

BY

THOMAS DIXON, JR.

ILLUSTRATED BY C. D. WILLIAMS

A FIREBIRD PRESS BOOK

Gretna 2001

Manufactured in the United States of America
Published by Pelican Publishing Company, Inc.
1000 Burmaster Street, Gretna, Louisiana 70053

Historical Note

IN answer to hundreds of letters, I wish to say that all the incidents used in Book I., which is properly the prologue of my story, were selected from authentic records, or came within my personal knowledge.

The only serious liberty I have taken with history is to tone down the facts to make them credible in fiction. The village of "Hambright" is my birthplace, and is located near the center of "Military District No. 2," comprising the Carolinas, which were destroyed as States by an Act of Congress in 1867. It will be a century yet before people outside the South can be made to believe a literal statement of the history of those times.

I tried to write this book with the utmost restraint.

THOMAS DIXON, JR.

MAY 9, 1902.
ELMINGTON MANOR,
DIXONDALE, VA.

LIST OF ILLUSTRATIONS

LEADING CHARACTERS OF THE STORY

Scene: The Foothills of North Carolina—Boston—New York
Time: From 1865 to 1900

CHARLES GASTON.........Who dreams of a Governor's Mansion
SALLIE WORTH...........A daughter of the old fashioned South
GEN. DANIEL WORTH.............................Her father
MRS. WORTH.................. ....Sallie's mother
THE REV. JOHN DURHAM....A preacher who threw his life away
MRS. DURHAM....Of the Southern Army that never surrendered
TOM CAMP..................A one-legged Confederate soldier
FLORA......................................Tom's little daughter
SIMON LEGREE.......Ex-slave driver and Reconstruction leader
ALLAN McLEOD....................................A Scalawag
HON. EVERETT LOWELL........Member of Congress from Boston
HELEN LOWELL.................................His daughter
MISS SUSAN WALKER.....................A maiden of Boston
MAJOR STUART DAMERON............Chief of the Ku Klux Klan
HOSE NORMAN....................A dare-devil poor white man
NELSE.........................A black hero of the old régime
AUNT EVE..................His wife—" a respectable woman."
HON. TIM SHELBY.................Political boss of the new era
HON. PETE SAWYER.......Sold seven times, got the money once
GEORGE HARRIS, JR.............An Educated Negro, son of Eliza
DICK..An unsolved riddle

CONTENTS

BOOK I

Legree's Regime

BOOK II

Love's Dream

BOOK III

The Trial by Fire

LEGREE'S REGIME

THE LEOPARD'S SPOTS

Book One—Legree's Regime

CHAPTER I

A HERO RETURNS

O N the field of Appomattox General Lee was waiting the return of a courier. His handsome face
was clouded by the deepening shadows of defeat. Rumours of surrender had spread like wildfire, and
the ranks of his once invincible army were breaking into
chaos.

Suddenly the measured tread of a brigade was heard
marching into action, every movement quick with the
perfect discipline, the fire, and the passion of the first days
of the triumphant Confederacy.

" What brigade is that? " he sharply asked.

" Cox's North Carolina," an aid replied.

As the troops swept steadily past the General, his eyes
filled with tears, he lifted his hat, and exclaimed,

" God bless old North Carolina! "

The display of matchless discipline perhaps recalled to
the great commander that awful day of Gettysburg when
the Twenty-sixth North Carolina infantry had charged
with 820 men rank and file and left 704 dead and wounded
on the ground that night. Company F from Campbell
county charged with 91 men and lost every man killed

3

and wounded. Fourteen times their colours were shot down, and fourteen times raised again. The last time they fell from the hands of gallant Colonel Harry Burgwyn, twenty-one years old, commander of the regiment, who seized them and was holding them aloft when instantly killed.

The last act of the tragedy had closed. Johnston surrendered to Sherman at Greensboro on April 26th, 1865, and the Civil War ended,—the bloodiest, most destructive war the world ever saw. The earth had been baptized in the blood of five hundred thousand heroic soldiers, and a new map of the world had been made.

The ragged troops were straggling home from Greensboro and Appomattox along the country roads. There were no mails, telegraph lines or railroads. The men were telling the story of the surrender. White-faced women dressed in coarse homespun met them at their doors and with quivering lips heard the news.

Surrender!

A new word in the vocabulary of the South—a word so terrible in its meaning that the date of its birth was to be the landmark of time. Henceforth all events would be reckoned from this; " before the Surrender," or " after the Surrender."

Desolation everywhere marked the end of an era. Not a cow, a sheep, a horse, a fowl, or a sign of animal life save here and there a stray dog, to be seen. Grim chimneys marked the site of once fair homes. Hedgerows of tangled blackberry briar and bushes showed where a fence had stood before war breathed upon the land with its breath of fire and harrowed it with teeth of steel.

These tramping soldiers looked worn and dispirited. Their shoulders stooped, they were dirty and hungry. They looked worse than they felt, and they felt that the end of the world had come.

They had answered those awful commands to charge without a murmur; and then, rolled back upon a sea of blood, they charged again over the dead bodies of their comrades. When repulsed the second time and the mad cry for a third charge from some desperate commander had rung over the field, still without a word they pulled their old ragged hats down close over their eyes as though to shut out the hail of bullets, and, through level sheets of blinding flame, walked straight into the jaws of hell. This had been easy. Now their feet seemed to falter as though they were not sure of the road.

In every one of these soldier's hearts, and over all the earth hung the shadow of the freed Negro, transformed by the exigency of war from a Chattel to be bought and sold into a possible Beast to be feared and guarded. Around this dusky figure every white man's soul was keeping its grim vigil.

North Carolina, the typical American Democracy, had loved peace and sought in vain to stand between the mad passions of the Cavalier of the South and the Puritan fanatic of the North. She entered the war at last with a sorrowful heart but a soul clear in the sense of tragic duty. She sent more boys to the front than any other state of the Confederacy—and left more dead on the field. She made the last charge and fired the last volley for Lee's army at Appomattox.

These were the ragged country boys who were slowly tramping homeward. The group whose fortunes we are to follow were marching toward the little village of Hambright that nestled in the foothills of the Blue Ridge under the shadows of King's Mountain. They were the sons of the men who had first declared their independence of Great Britain in America and had made their country a hornet's nest for Lord Cornwallis in the darkest days of the cause of Liberty. What tongue can tell the tragic story of their humble home coming?

In rich Northern cities could be heard the boom of guns, the scream of steam whistles, the shouts of surging hosts greeting returning regiments crowned with victory. From every flag-staff fluttered proudly the flag that our fathers had lifted in the sky—the flag that had never met defeat.

It is little wonder that in this hour of triumph the world should forget the defeated soldiers who without a dollar in their pockets were tramping to their ruined homes.

Yet Nature did not seem to know of sorrow or death. Birds were singing their love songs from the hedgerows, the fields were clothed in gorgeous robes of wild flowers beneath which forget-me-nots spread their contrasting hues of blue, while life was busy in bud and starting leaf reclothing the blood-stained earth in radiant beauty.

As the sun was setting behind the peaks of the Blue Ridge, a giant negro entered the village of Hambright. He walked rapidly down one of the principal streets, passed the court house square unobserved in the gathering twilight, and three blocks further along paused before a law-office that stood in the corner of a beautiful lawn filled with shrubbery and flowers.

"Dars de ole home, praise de Lawd! En now I'se erfeard ter see my Missy, en tell her Marse Charles's daid. Hit'll kill her! Lawd hab mussy on my po black soul! How kin I!"

He walked softly up the alley that led toward the kitchen past the "big" house, which after all was a modest cottage boarded up and down with weatherstrips nestling amid a labyrinth of climbing roses, honeysuckles, fruit bearing shrubbery and balsam trees. The negro had no difficulty in concealing his movements as he passed.

"Lordy, dars Missy watchin' at de winder! How pale she look! En she wuz de purties' bride in de two counties! God-der-mighty, I mus' git somebody ter he'p me! I nebber tell her! She drap daid right 'fore my eyes, en hant me twell I die. I run fetch de Preacher, Marse John Durham, he kin tell her."

A few moments later he was knocking at the door of the parsonage of the Baptist church.

"Nelse! At last! I knew you'd come!"

"Yassir, Marse John, I'se home. Hit's me."

"And your Master is dead. I was sure of it, but I never dared tell your Mistress. You came for me to help you tell her. People said you had gone over into the promised land of freedom and forgotten your people; but Nelse, I never believed it of you and I'm doubly glad to shake your hand to-night because you've brought a brave message from heroic lips and because you have brought a braver message in your honest black face of faith and duty and life and love."

"Thankee Marse John, I wuz erbleeged ter come home."

The Preacher stepped into the hall and called the servant from the kitchen.

"Aunt Mary, when your Mistress returns tell her I've received an urgent call and will not be at home for supper."

"I'll be ready in a minute, Nelse," he said, as he disappeared into the study. When he reached his desk, he paused and looked about the room in a helpless way as though trying to find some half forgotten volume in the rows of books that lined the walls and lay in piles on his desk and tables. He knelt beside the desk and prayed. When he rose there was a soft light in his eyes that were half filled with tears.

Standing in the dim light of his study he was a striking man. He had a powerful figure of medium height, deep piercing eyes and a high intellectual forehead. His hair was black and thick. He was a man of culture, had graduated at the head of his class at Wake Forest College before the war, and was a profound student of men and books. He was now thirty-five years old and the acknowledged leader of the Baptist denomination in the state. He was eloquent, witty, and proverbially good natured. His voice in the pulpit was soft and clear, and full of a magnetic quality that gave him hypnotic power over an audience. He had the prophetic temperament and was more of poet than theologian.

The people of this village were proud of the man as a citizen and loved him passionately as their preacher. Great churches had called him, but he had never accepted. There was in his make-up an element of the missionary that gave his personality a peculiar force.

He had been the college mate of Colonel Charles Gaston whose faithful slave had come to him for help, and they had always been bosom friends. He had performed the marriage ceremony for the Colonel ten years before when he had led to the altar the beautiful daughter of the richest planter in the adjoining county. Durham's own heart was profoundly moved by his friend's happiness and he threw into the brief preliminary address so much of tenderness and earnest passion that the trembling bride and groom forgot their fright and were melted to tears. Thus began an association of their family life that was closer than their college days.

He closed his lips firmly for an instant, softly shut the door and was soon on the way with Nelse. On reaching the house, Nelse went directly to the kitchen, while the Preacher walking along the circular drive approached the front. His foot had scarcely touched the step when Mrs. Gaston opened the door.

" Oh, Dr. Durham, I am so glad you have come! " she exclaimed. " I've been depressed to-day, watching the soldiers go by. All day long the poor foot-sore fellows have been passing. I stopped some of them to ask about Colonel Gaston and I thought one of them knew something and would not tell me. I brought him in and gave him dinner, and tried to coax him, but he only looked wistfully at me, stammered and said he didn't know. But some how I feel that he did. Come in Doctor, and say something to cheer me. If I only had your faith in God! "

" I have need of it all to-night, Madam! " he answered with bowed head.

" Then you have heard bad news? "

" I have heard news,—wonderful news of faith and love, of heroism and knightly valour, that will be a priceless heritage to you and yours. Nelse has returned—"

" God have mercy on me! "—she gasped covering her face and raising her arm as though cowering from a mortal blow.

" Here is Nelse, Madam. Hear his story. He has only told me a word or two." Nelse had slipped quietly in the back door.

" Yassum, Missy, I'se home at las'."

She looked at him strangely for a moment. " Nelse, I've dreamed and dreamed of your coming, but always with him. And now you come alone to tell me he is dead. Lord have pity! there is nothing left! " There was a far-away sound in her voice as though half dreaming.

" Yas, Missy, dey is, I jes seed him—my young Marster—dem bright eyes, de ve'y nose, de chin, de mouf! He walks des like Marse Charles, he talks like him, he de ve'y spit er him, en how he hez growed! He'll be er man fo you knows it. En I'se got er letter fum his Pa fur him, an er letter fur you, Missy."

At this moment Charlie entered the room, slipped past Nelse and climbed into his mother's arms. He was a sturdy little fellow of eight years with big brown eyes and sensitive mouth.

"Yassir—Ole Grant wuz er pushin' us dar afo' Richmon'. Pear ter me lak Marse Robert been er fightin' him ev'y day for six monts. But he des keep on pushin' en pushin' us. Marse Charles say ter me one night atter I been playin' de banjer fur de boys, 'Come ter my tent Nelse fo turnin' in—I wants ter see you.' He talk so solemn like, I cut de banjer short, en go right er long wid him. He been er writin' en done had two letters writ. He say, 'Nelse, we gwine ter git outen dese trenches ter-morrer. It twell be my las' charge. I feel it. Ef I falls, you take my swode, en watch en dese letters back home to your Mist'ess and young Marster, en you promise me, boy, to stan' by em in life ez I stan' by you.' He know I lub him bettern any body in dis worl', en dat I'd rudder be his slave dan be free if he's daid! En I say, 'Dat I will, Marse Charles.'

"De nex day we up en charge ole Grant. Pears ter me I nebber see so many dead Yankees on dis yearth ez we see layin' on de groun' whar we brake froo dem lines! But dey des kep fetchin' up annudder army back er de one we breaks, twell bymeby, dey swing er whole millyon er Yankees right plum behin' us, en five millyon er fresh uns come er swoopin' down in front. Den yer otter see my Marster! He des kinder riz in de air— pear ter me like he wuz er foot taller en say to his men —''Bout face, en charge de line in de rear!' Wall sar, we cut er hole clean froo dem Yankees en er minute, end den bout face ergin en begin ter walk backerds er fightin' like wilecats ev'y inch. We git mos back ter de trenches, when Marse Charles drap des lak er flash! I runned up to him, en dar wuz er big hole in his breas'

whar er bullet gone clean froo his heart. He nebber
groan. I tuk his head up in my arms en cry en take on
en call him! I pull back his close en listen at his heart.
Hit wuz still. I takes de swode an de watch en de letters
outen de pockets en start on—when bress God, yer cum
dat whole Yankee army ten hundred millyons, en dey
tromple all over us!

"Den I hear er Yankee say ter me 'Now, my man,
you'se free.' 'Yassir, sezzi, dats so,' en den I see a hole
ter run whar dey warn't no Yankees, en I run spang
into er millyon mo. De Yankees wuz ev'y whar. Pear
ter me lak dey riz up outer de groun'. All dat day I try
ter get away fum 'em. En long 'bout night dey 'rested
me en fetch me up fo er Genr'l, en he say,

"What you tryin' ter get froo our lines fur, nigger?
Doan yer know yer free now, en if you go back you'd be
a slave ergin?"

"Dats so, sah," sezzi, "but I'se 'bleeged ter go
home."

"What fur?" sezze.

"Promise Marse Charles ter take dese letters en swode
en watch back home to my Missus en young Marster,
en dey waitin' fur me—I'se 'bleeged ter go."

"Den he tuk de letters en read er minute, en his eyes
gin ter water en he choke up en say, 'Go-long!'

"Den I skeedaddled ergin. Dey kep on ketchin' me
twell bimeby er nasty stinkin low-life slue-footed Yankee
kotched me en say dat I wuz er dang'us nigger, en sont
me wid er lot er our prisoners way up ter ole Jonson's
Islan' whar I mos froze ter deaf. I stay dar twell one
day er fine lady what say she from Boston cum er long,
en I up en tells her all erbout Marse Charles and my
Missus, en how dey all waitin' fur me, en how bad I want
ter go home, en de nex news I knowed I wuz on er train
er whizzin' down home wid my way all paid. I get wid

our men at Greensboro en come right on fas' ez my legs'd carry me."

There was silence for a moment and then slowly Mrs. Gaston said, " May God reward you, Nelse! "

" Yassum, I'se free, Missy, but I gwine ter wuk for you en my young Marster."

Mrs. Gaston had lived daily in a sort of trance through those four years of war, dreaming and planning for the great day when her lover would return a handsome bronzed and famous man. She had never conceived of the possibility of a world without his will and love to lean upon. The Preacher was both puzzled and alarmed by the strangely calm manner she now assumed. Before leaving the home he cautioned Aunt Eve to watch her Mistress closely and send for him if anything happened.

When the boy was asleep in the nursery adjoining her room, she quietly closed the door, took the sword of her dead lover-husband in her lap and looked long and tenderly at it. On the hilt she pressed her lips in a lingering kiss.

" Here his dear hand must have rested last! " she murmured. She sat motionless for an hour with eyes fixed without seeing. At last she rose and hung the sword beside his picture near her bed and drew from her bosom the crumpled, worn letters Nelse had brought. The first was addressed to her.

" *In the Trenches Near Richmond, May* 4, 1864.

" SWEET WIFIE:—I have a presentiment to-night that I shall not live to see you again. I feel the shadows of defeat and ruin closing upon us. I am surer day by day that our cause is lost and surrender is a word I have never learned to speak. If I could only see you for one hour, that I might tell you all I have thought in the lone watches of the night in camp, or marching

over desolate fields. Many tender things I have never
said to you I have learned in these days. I write this last
message to tell you how, more and more beyond the power
of words to express, your love has grown upon me, until
your spirit seems the breath I breathe. My heart is so full
of love for you and my boy, that I can't go into battle now
without thinking how many hearts will ache and break in
far away.homes because of the work I am about to do. I
am sick of it all. I long to be at home again and walk
with my sweet young bride among the flowers she loves
so well, and hear the old mocking bird that builds each
spring in those rose bushes at our window.

If I am killed, you must live for our boy and rear
him to a glorious manhood in the new nation that will
be born in this agony. I love you,—I love you unto the
uttermost, and beyond death I will live, if only to love
you forever.

Always in life or death your own,

CHARLES."

For two hours she held this letter open in her hands
and seemed unable to move it. And then mechanically
she opened the one addressed to " Charles Gaston, jr."

" MY DARLING BOY :—I send you by Nelse my watch
and sword. It will be all I can bequeath to you from
the wreck that will follow the war. This sword was your
great grandfather's. He held it as he charged up the
heights of King's Mountain against Ferguson and helped
to carve this nation out of a wilderness. It was a sorrowful day for me when I felt it my duty to draw that
sword against the old flag in defence of my home and
my people. You will live to see a reunited country. Hang
this sword back beside the old flag of our fathers when
the end has come, and always remember that it was never

drawn from its scabbard by your father, or your grandfather who fought with Jackson at New Orleans, or your
great grandfather in the Revolution, save in the cause
of justice and right. I am not fighting to hold slaves in
bondage. I am fighting for the inalienable rights of my
people under the Constitution our fathers created. It
may be we have outgrown this Constitution. But I
calmly leave to God and history the question as to who
is right in its interpretation. Whatever you do in life,
first, last and always do what you believe to be right.
Everything else is of little importance. With a heart
full of love, Your father,

CHARLES GASTON."

This letter she must have held open for hours, for it
was two o'clock in the morning when a wild peal of
laughter rang from her feverish lips and brought Aunt
Eve and Nelse hurrying into the room.

It took but a moment for them to discover that their
Mistress was suffering from a violent delirium. They
soothed her as best they could. The noise and confusion
had awakened the boy. Running to the door leading
into his mother's room he found it bolted, and with his
little heart fluttering in terror he pressed his ear close
to the key-hole and heard her wild ravings. How strange
her voice seemed! Her voice had always been so soft
and low and full of soothing music. Now it was sharp
and hoarse and seemed to rasp his flesh with needles.
What could it all mean? Perhaps the end of the world,
about which he had heard the Preacher talk on Sundays.
At last unable to bear the terrible suspense longer he
cried through the key-hole,

"Aunt Eve, what's the matter? Open the door quick."

"No, honey, you mustn't come in. Yo Ma's awful
sick. You run out ter de barn, ketch de mare, en fly for

de doctor while me en Nelse stay wid her. Run honey, day's nuttin' ter hurt yer."

His little bare feet were soon pattering over the long stretch of the back porch toward the barn. The night was clear and sky studded with stars. There was no moon. He was a brave little fellow, but a fear greater than all the terrors of ghosts and the white sheeted dead with which Negro superstition had filled his imagination, now nerved his child's soul. His mother was about to die! His very heart ceased to beat at the thought. He must bring the doctor and bring him quickly.

He flew to the stable not looking to the right or the left. The mare whinnied as he opened the door to get the bridle.

"It's me Bessie. Mama's sick. We must go for the doctor quick!"

The mare thrust her head obediently down to the child's short arm for the bridle. She seemed to know by some instinct his quivering voice had roused that the home was in distress and her hour had come to bear a part.

In a moment he led her out through the gate, climbed on the fence, and sprang on her back.

"Now, Bess, fly for me!" he half whispered, half cried through the tears he could no longer keep back. The mare bounded forward in a swift gallop as she felt his trembling bare legs clasp her side, and the clatter of her hoofs echoed in the boy's ears through the silent streets like the thunder of charging cavalry. How still the night! He saw shadows under the trees, shut his eyes and leaning low on the mare's neck patted her shoulders with his hands and cried,

"Faster, Bessie! Faster!" And then he tried to pray. "Lord don't let her die! Please, dear God, and I will always be good. I am sorry I robbed the bird's nests last summer—I'll never do it again. Please, Lord I'm such a wee boy and I'm so lonely. I can't lose my Mama! "—and the voice choked and became a great sob. He looked across the square as he passed the court house in a gallop and saw a light in the window of the parsonage and felt its rays warm his soul like an answer to his prayer.

He reached the doctor's house on the further side of the town, sprang from the mare's back, bounded up the steps and knocked at the door. No one answered. He knocked again. How loud it rang through the hall! May be the doctor was gone! He had not thought of such a possibility before. He choked at the thought. Springing quickly from the steps to the ground he felt for a stone, bounded back and began to pound on the door with all his might.

The window was raised, and the old doctor thrust his head out calling,

"What on earth's the matter? Who is that?"

"It's me, Charlie Gaston—my Mama's sick—she's awful sick, I'm afraid she's dying—you must come quick!"

"All right, sonny, I'll be ready in a minute."

The boy waited and waited. It seemed to him hours, days, weeks, years! To every impatient call the doctor would answer,

"In a minute, sonny, in a minute!"

At last he emerged with his lantern, to catch his horse. The doctor seemed so slow. He fumbled over the harness.

"Oh! Doctor you're so slow! I tell you my Mama's sick—!"

"Well, well, my boy, we'll soon be there," the old man kindly replied.

When the boy saw the doctor's horse jogging quickly toward his home he turned the mare's head aside as he reached the court house square, roused the Preacher, and between his sobs told the story of his mother's illness. Mrs. Durham had lost her only boy two years before. Soon Charlie was sobbing in her arms.

"You poor little darling, out by yourself so late at night, were you not scared?" she asked as she kissed the tears from his eyes.

"Yessum, I was scared, but I had to go for the doctor. I want you and Dr. Durham to come as quick as you can. I'm afraid to go home. I'm afraid she's dead, or I'll hear her laugh that awful way I heard to-night."

"Of course we will come, dear, right away. We will be there almost as soon as you can get to the house."

He rode slowly along the silent street looking back now and then for the Preacher and his wife. As he was passing a small deserted house he saw to his horror a ragged man peering into the open window. Before he had time to run, the man stepped quickly up to the mare and said,

"Who lived here last, little man?"

"Old Miss Spurlin," answered the boy.

"Where is she now?"

"She's dead."

The man sighed, and the boy saw by his gray uniform that he was a soldier just back from the war, and he quickly added,

"Folks said they had a hard time, but Preacher Durham helped them lots when they had nothing to eat."

"So my poor old mother's dead. I was afraid of it." He seemed to be talking to himself. "And do you know where her gal is that lived with her?"

"She's in a little house down in the woods below town.

They say she's a bad woman, and my Mama would never let me go near her."

The man flinched as though struck with a knife, steadied himself for a moment with his hands on the mare's neck and said,

" You're a brave little one to be out alone this time o'night,—what's your name? "

" Charles Gaston."

" Then you're my Colonel's boy—many a time I followed him where men were fallin' like leaves—I wish to God I was with him now in the ground! Don't tell anybody you saw me,—them that knowed me will think I'm dead, and it's better so."

" Good-bye, sir," said the child " I'm sorry for you if you've got no home. I'm after the doctor for my Mama, —she's very sick. I'm afraid she's going to die, and if you ever pray I wish you'd pray for her."

The soldier came closer. " I wish I knew how to pray, my boy. But it seemed to me I forgot everything that was good in the war, and there's nothin' left but death and hell. But I'll not forget you, good-bye! "

When Charlie was in bed, he lay an hour with wide staring eyes, holding his breath now and then to catch the faintest sound from his mother's room. All was quiet at last and he fell asleep. But he was no longer a child. The shadow of a great sorrow had enveloped his soul and clothed him with the dignity and fellowship of the mystery of pain.

CHAPTER II

A LIGHT SHINING IN DARKNESS

IN the rear of Mrs. Gaston's place, there stood in the midst of an orchard a log house of two rooms, with hallway between them. There was a mud-thatched wooden chimney at each end, and from the back of the hallway a kitchen extension of the same material with another mud chimney. The house stood in the middle of a ten acre lot, and a woman was busy in the garden with a little girl, planting seed.

"Hurry up Annie, less finish this in time to fix up a fine dinner er greens and turnips an 'taters an a chicken. Yer Pappy 'll get home to-day sure. Colonel Gaston's Nelse come last night. Yer Pappy was in the Colonel's regiment an' Nelse said he passed him on the road comin' with two one-legged soldiers. He ain't got but one leg, he says. But, Lord, if there's a piece of him left we'll praise God an' be thankful for what we've got."

"Maw, how did he look? I mos' forgot—'s been so long sence I seed him?" asked the child.

"Look! Honey! He was the handsomest man in Campbell county! He had a tall fine figure, brown curly beard, and the sweetest mouth that was always smilin' at me, an' his eyes twinklin' over somethin' funny he'd seed or thought about. When he was young ev'ry gal around here was crazy about him. I got him all right, an' he got me too. Oh me! I can't help but cry, to think he's been gone so long. But he's comin' to-day! I jes feel it in my bones."

19

"Look a yonder, Maw, what a skeer-crow ridin' er ole hoss!" cried the girl, looking suddenly toward the road.

"Glory to God! It's Tom!" she shouted, snatching her old faded sun-bonnet off her head and fairly flying across the field to the gate, her cheeks aflame, her blond hair tumbling over her shoulders, her eyes wet with tears.

Tom was entering the gate of his modest home in as fine style as possible, seated proudly on a stack of bones that had once been a horse, an old piece of wool on his head that once had been a hat, and a wooden peg fitted into a stump where once was a leg. His face was pale and stained with the red dust of the hill roads, and his beard, now iron grey, and his ragged buttonless uniform were covered with dirt. He was truly a sight to scare crows, if not of interest to buzzards. But to the woman whose swift feet were hurrying to his side, and whose lips were muttering half articulate cries of love, he was the knightliest figure that ever rode in the lists before the assembled beauty of the world.

"Oh! Tom, Tom, Tom, my ole man! You've come at last!" she sobbed as she threw her arms around his neck, drew him from the horse and fairly smothered him with kisses.

"Look out, ole woman, you'll break my new leg!" cried Tom when he could get breath.

"I don't care,—I'll get you another one," she laughed through her tears.

"Look out there again you're smashing my game shoulder. Got er Minie ball in that one. "

"Well your mouth's all right I see," cried the delighted woman, as she kissed and kissed him.

"Say, Annie, don't be so greedy, give me a chance at my young one." Tom's eyes were devouring the excited girl who had drawn nearer.

"Come and kiss your Pappy and tell him how glad

you are to see him!" said Tom, gathering her in his arms
and attempting to carry her to the house.

He stumbled and fell. In a moment the strong arms
of his wife were about him and she was helping him into
the house.

She laid him tenderly on the bed, petted him and cried
over him. "My poor old man, he's all shot and cut to
pieces. You're so weak, Tom—I can't believe it. You
were so strong. But we'll take care of you. Don't you
worry. You just sleep a week and then rest all summer
and watch us work the garden for you!"

He lay still for a few moments with a smile playing
around his lips.

"Lord, ole woman, you don't know how nice it is to
be petted like that, to hear a woman's voice, feel her
breath on your face and the touch of her hand, warm
and soft, after four years sleeping on dirt and living with
men and mules, and fightin' and runnin' and diggin'
trenches like rats and moles, killin' men, buryin' the
dead like carrion, holdin' men while doctors sawed their
legs off, till your turn came to be held and sawed! You
can't believe it, but this is the first feather bed I've
touched in four years."

"Well, well!—Bless God it's over now," she cried.
"S'long as I've got two strong arms to slave for you—
as long as there's a piece of you left big enough to hold
on to—I'll work for you," and again she bent low over
his pale face, and crooned over him as she had so often
done over his baby in those four lonely years of war and
poverty.

Suddenly Tom pushed her aside and sprang up in bed.

"Geemimy, Annie, I forgot my pardners—there's two
more peg-legs out at the gate by this time waiting for
us to get through huggin' and carryin' on before they
come in. Run, fetch 'em in quick!"

Tom struggled to his feet and met them at the door.

"Come right into my palace, boys. I've seen some fine places in my time, but this is the handsomest one I ever set eyes on. Now, Annie, put the big pot in the little one and don't stand back for expenses. Let's have a dinner these fellers 'll never forget."

It was a feast they never forgot. Tom's wife had raised a brood of early chickens, and managed to keep them from being stolen. She killed four of them and cooked them as only a Southern woman knows how. She had sweet potatoes carefully saved in the mound against the kitchen chimney. There were turnips and greens and radishes, young onions and lettuce and hot corn dodgers fit for a king; and in the centre of the table she deftly fixed a pot of wild flowers little Annie had gathered. She did not tell them that it was the last peck of potatoes and the last pound of meal. This belonged to the morrow. To-day they would live.

They laughed and joked over this splendid banquet, and told stories of days and nights of hunger and exhaustion, when they had filled their empty stomachs with dreams of home.

"Miss Camp, you've got the best husband in seven states, did you know that?" asked one of the soldiers, a mere boy.

"Of course she'll agree to that, sonny," laughed Tom.

"Well it's so. If it hadn't been for him, M'am, we'd a been peggin' along somewhere way up in Virginny 'stead o' bein' so close to home. You see he let us ride his hoss a mile and then he'd ride a mile. We took it turn about, and here we are."

"Tom, how in this world did you get that horse?" asked his wife.

"Honey, I got him on my good looks," said he with a wink. "You see I was a settin' out there in the sun the day o' the surrender. I was sorter cryin' and wonderin' how I'd get home with that stump of wood instead of a foot, when along come a chunky heavy set Yankee General, looking as glum as though his folks had surrendered instead of Marse Robert. He saw me, stopped, looked at me a minute right hard and says, " Where do you live? "

" Way down in ole No'th Caliny," I says, " at Hambright, not far from King's Mountain."

" How are you going to get home? " says he.

" God knows, I don't, General. I got a wife and baby down there I ain't seed fer nigh four years, and I want to see 'em so bad I can taste 'em. I was lookin' the other way when I said that, fer I was purty well played out, and feelin' weak and watery about the eyes, an' I didn't want no Yankee General to see water in my eyes."

" He called a feller to him and sorter snapped out to him, " Go bring the best horse you can spare for this man and give it to him."

" Then he turns to me and seed I was all choked up and couldn't say nothin' and says:

" I'm General Grant. Give my love to your folks when you get home. I've known what it was to be a poor white man down South myself once for awhile."

" God bless you, General. I thanks you from the bottom of my heart," I says as quick as I could find my tongue, " if it had to be surrender I'm glad it was to such a man as you.

" He never said another word, but just walked slow along smoking a big cigar. So ole woman, you know the reason I named that hoss, ' General Grant.' It may be I have seen finer hosses than that one, but I couldn't recollect anything about 'em on the road home."

Dinner over, Tom's comrades rose and looked wistfully down the dusty road leading southward.

" Well, Tom, ole man, we gotter be er movin'," said the

older of the two soldiers. "We're powerful obleeged to you fur helpin' us along this fur."

"All right, boys, you'll find yer train standin' on the side o' the track eatin' grass. Jes climb up, pull the lever and let her go."

The men's faces brightened, their lips twitched. They looked at Tom, and then at the old horse. They looked down the long dusty road stretching over hill and valley, hundreds of miles south, and then at Tom's wife and child, whispered to one another a moment, and the elder said:

"No, pardner, you've been awful good to us, but we'll get along somehow—we can't take yer hoss. It's all yer got now ter make a livin' on yer place."

"All I got?" shouted Tom, "man alive, ain't you seed my ole woman, as fat and jolly and han'some as when I married her 'leven years ago? Didn't you hear her cryin' an' shoutin' like she's crazy when I got home? Didn't you see my little gal with eyes jes like her daddy's? Don't you see my cabin standin' as purty as a ripe peach in the middle of the orchard when hundreds of fine houses are lyin' in ashes? Ain't I got ten acres of land? Ain't I got God Almighty above me and all around me, the same God that watched over me on the battlefields? All I got? That old stack o' bones that looks like er hoss? Well I reckon not!"

"Pardner, it ain't right," grumbled the soldier, with more of cheerful thanks than protest in his voice.

"Oh! Get off you fools," said Tom good-naturedly, "ain't it my hoss? Can't I do what I please with him?"

So with hearty hand-shakes they parted, the two astride the old horse's back. One had lost his right leg, the other his left, and this gave them a good leg on each side to hold the cargo straight.

"Take keer yerself, Tom!" they both cried in the same breath as they moved away.

"Take keer yerselves, boys. I'm all right!" answered Tom, as he stumped his way back to the home. "It's all right, it's all right," he muttered to himself. "He'd a come in handy, but I'd a never slept thinkin' o' them peggin' along them rough roads."

Before reaching the house he sat down on a wooden bench beneath a tree to rest. It was the first week in May and the leaves were not yet grown. The sun was pouring his hot rays down into the moist earth, and the heat began to feel like summer. As he drank in the beauty and glory of the spring his soul was melted with joy. The fruit trees were laden with the promise of the treasures of the summer and autumn, a cat-bird was singing softly to his mate in the tree over his head, and a mocking-bird seated in the topmost branch of an elm near his cabin home was leading the oratorio of feathered songsters. The wild plum and blackberry briars were in full bloom in the fence corners, and the sweet odour filled the air. He heard his wife singing in the house.

"It's a fine old world after all!" he exclaimed leaning back and half closing his eyes, while a sense of ineffable peace filled his soul. "Peace at last! Thank God! May I never see a gun or a sword, or hear a drum or a fife's scream on this earth again!"

A hound came close wagging his tail and whining for a word of love and recognition.

"Well, Bob, old boy, you're the only one left. You'll have to chase cotton-tails by yourself now."

Bob's eyes watered and he licked his master's hand apparently understanding every word he said.

Breaking from his master's hands the dog ran toward the gate barking, and Tom rose in haste as he recognised the sturdy tread of the Preacher, Rev. John Durham, walking rapidly toward the house.

Grasping him heartily by the hand the Preacher said,

"Tom, you don't know how it warms my soul to look into your face again. When you left, I felt like a man who had lost one hand. I've found it to-day. You're the same stalwart Christian full of joy and love. Some men's religion didn't stand the wear and tear of war. You've come out with your soul like gold tried in the fire. Colonel Gaston wrote me you were the finest soldier in the regiment, and that you were the only Chaplain he had seen that he could consult for his own soul's cheer. That's the kind of a deacon to send to the front! I'm proud of you, and you're still at your old tricks. I met two one-legged soldiers down the road riding your horse away as though you had a stable full at your command. You needn't apologise or explain, they told me all about it."

"Preacher, it's good to have the Lord's messenger speak words like them. I can't tell you how glad I am to be home again and shake your hand. I tell you it was a comfort to me when I lay awake at night on them battlefields, a wonderin' what had become of my ole woman and the baby, to recollect that you were here, and how often I'd heard you tell us how the Lord tempered the wind to the shorn lamb. Annie's been telling me who watched out for her them dark days when there was nothin' to eat. I reckon you and your wife knows the way to this house about as well as you do to the church."

Tom had pulled the Preacher down on the seat beside him while he said this.

"The dark days have only begun, Tom. I've come to see you to have you cheer me up. Somehow you always seemed to me to be closer to God than any man in the church. You will need all your faith now. It seems

to me that every second woman I know is a widow.
Hundreds of families have no seed even to plant, no
horses to work crops, no men who will work if they had
horses. What are we to do? I see hungry children in
every house."

"Preacher, the Lord is looking down here to-day and
sees all this as plain as you and me. As long as He is
in the sky everything will come all right on the earth."

"How's your pantry?" asked the Preacher.

"Don't know. 'Man shall not live by bread alone,'
you know. When I hear these birds in the trees an' see
this old dog waggin' his tail at me, and smell the breath
of them flowers, and it all comes over me that I'm done
killin' men, and I'm at home, with a bed to sleep on, a
roof over my head, a woman to pet me and tell me I'm
great and handsome, I don't feel like I'll ever need anything more to eat! I believe I could live a whole month
here without eatin' a bite."

"Good. You come to the prayer meeting to-night
and say a few things like that, and the folks will believe
they have been eating three square meals every day."

"I'll be there. I ain't asked Annie what she's got,
but I know she's got greens and turnips, onions and col-
lards, and strawberries in the garden. Irish taters 'll be
big enough to eat in three weeks, and sweets comin' right
on. We've got a few chickens. The blackberries and
plums and peaches and apples are all on the road. Ah!
Preacher, it's my soul that's been starved away from my
wife and child!"

"You don't know how much I need help sometimes
Tom. I am always giving, giving myself in sympathy
and help to others, I'm famished now and then. I feel
faint and worn out. You seem to fill me again with
life."

"I'm glad to hear you say that, Preacher. I get down-hearted sometimes, when I recollect I'm nothin' but a poor white man. I'll remember your words. I'm goin' to do my part in the church work. You know where to find me."

"Well, that's partly what brought me here this morning. I want you to help me look after Mrs. Gaston and her little boy. She is prostrated over the death of the Colonel and is hanging between life and death. She is in a delirious condition all the time and must be watched day and night. I want you to watch the first half of the night with Nelse, and Eve and Mary will watch the last half."

"Of course, I'll do anything in the world I can for my Colonel's widder. He was the bravest man that ever led a regiment, and he was a father to us boys. I'll be there. But I won't set up with that nigger. He can go to bed."

"Tom, it's a funny thing to me that as good a Christian as you are should hate a nigger so. He's a human being. It's not right."

"He may be human, Preacher, I don't know. To tell you the truth, I have my doubts. Anyhow, I can't help it. God knows I hate the sight of 'em like I do a rattlesnake. That nigger Nelse, they say is a good one. He was faithful to the Colonel, I know, but I couldn't bear him no more than any of the rest of 'em. I always hated a nigger since I was knee high. My daddy and my mammy hated 'em before me. Somehow, we always felt like they was crowdin' us to death on them big plantations, and the little ones too. And then I had to leave my wife and baby and fight four years, all on account of their stinkin' hides, that never done nothin' for me except make it harder to live. Every time I'd go into battle and hear them Minie balls begin to sing over us, it seemed to me I could see their black ape faces grin-

nin' and makin' fun of poor whites.   At night when
they'd detail me to help the ambulance corps carry off
the dead and the wounded, there was a strange smell on
the field that came from the blood and night damp and
burnt powder.   It always smelled like a nigger to me!
It made me sick.   Yes, Preacher, God forgive me, I hate
'em!   I can't help it any more than I can the color of my
skin or my hair."

"I'll fix it with Nelse, then.   You take the first part
of the night 'till twelve o'clock.   I'll go down with you
from the church to-night," said the Preacher, as he shook
Tom's hand and took his leave.

CHAPTER III

DEEPENING SHADOWS

ON the second day after Mrs. Gaston was stricken a forlorn little boy sat in the kitchen watching Aunt Eve get supper. He saw her nod while she worked the dough for the biscuits.

"Aunt Eve, I'm going to sit up to-night and every night with my Mama, 'till she gets well. I can't sleep for hours and hours. I lie awake and cry when I hear her talking 'till I feel like I'll die. I must do something to help her."

"Laws, honey, you'se too little. You can't keep 'wake 'tall. You get so lonesome and skeered all by yer-self."

"I don't care, I've told Tom to wake me to-night if I'm asleep when he goes, and I'll sit up from twelve 'till two o'clock and then call you."

"All right, Mammy's darlin' boy, but you git tired en can't stan' it."

So that night at midnight he took his place by the bed-side. His mother was sleeping, at first. He sat and gazed with aching heart at her still, white face. She stirred, opened her eyes, saw him, and imagined he was his father.

"Dearie, I knew you would come," she murmured. "They told me you were dead; but I knew better. What a long, long time you have been away. How brown the sun has tanned your face, but it's just as handsome. I think handsomer than ever. And how like you is little Charlie! I knew you would be proud of him!"

While she talked, her eyes had a glassy look, that seemed to take no note of anything in the room.

The child listened for ten minutes, and then the horror of her strange voice, and look and words overwhelmed him. He burst into tears and threw his arms around his mother's neck and sobbed.

"Oh! Mama dear, it's me, Charlie, your little boy, who loves you so much. Please, don't talk that way. Please look at me like you used to. There! Let me kiss your eyes 'till they are soft and sweet again!"

He covered her eyes with kisses.

The mother seemed dazed for a moment, held him off at arm's length, and then burst into laughter.

"Of course, you silly, I know you. You must run to bed now. Kiss me good night."

"But you are sick, Mama, I am sitting up with you."

Again she ignored his presence. She was back in the old days with her Love. She was kissing her hand to him as he left her for his day's work. Charlie looked at the clock. It was time to give her the soothing drops the doctor left. She took it, obedient as a child, and went on and on with interminable dreams of the past, now and then uttering strange things for a boy's ears. But so terrible was the anguish with which he watched her, the words made little impression on his mind. It seemed to him some one was strangling him to death, and a great stone was piled on his little prostrate body.

When she grew quiet, at last, and dosed, how still the house seemed! How loud the tick of the clock! How slowly the hands moved! He had never noticed this before. He watched the hands for five minutes. It seemed each minute was an hour, and five minutes were as long as a day. What strange noises in the house! Suppose

a ghost should walk into the room! Well, he wouldn't
run and leave his Mama; he made up his mind to that.

Some nights there were other sounds more ominous.
The town was crowded with strange negroes, who were
hanging around the camp of the garrison. One night a
drunken gang came shouting and screaming up the alley
close beside the house, firing pistols and muskets. They
stopped at the house, and one of them yelled,

"Burn the rebel's house down! It's our turn now!"

The terrified boy rushed to the kitchen and called
Nelse. In a minute, Nelse was on the scene. There was
no more trouble that night.

"De lazy black debbels," said Nelse, as he mopped the
perspiration from his brow, "I'll teach 'em what freedom
is."

The next day when the Rev. John Durham had an interview with the Commandant of the troops, he succeeded
in getting a consignment of corn for seed, and to meet
the threat of starvation among some families whose condition he reported. This important matter settled, he
said to the officer,   ·

"Captain, we must look to you for protection. The
town is swarming with vagrant negroes, bent on mischief. There are camp followers with you organizing
them into some sort of Union League meetings, dealing
out arms and ammunition to them; and what is worse,
inflaming the worst passions against their former masters, teaching them insolence and training them for
crime."

"I'll do the best I can for you, Doctor, but I can't control the camp followers who are organising the Union
League. They live a charmed life."

That night, as the Preacher walked home from a visit
to a destitute family, he encountered a burly negro on
the sidewalk, dressed in an old suit of Federal uniform,

evidently under the influence of whiskey. He wore a belt around his waist, in which he had thrust, conspicuously, an old horse pistol.

Standing squarely across the pathway, he said to the Preacher,

" Git outer de road, white man, you'se er rebel, I'se er Loyal Union Leaguer! "

It was his first experience with Negro insolence since the emancipation of his slaves. Quick as a flash, his right arm was raised. But he took a second thought, stepped aside, and allowed the drunken fool to pass. He went home wondering in a hazy sort of way through his excited passions what the end of it all would be. Gradually in his mind for days this towering figure of the freed Negro had been growing more and more ominous, until its menace overshadowed the poverty, the hunger, the sorrows and the devastation of the South, throwing the blight of its shadow over future generations, a veritable Black Death for the land and its people.

CHAPTER IV

MR. LINCOLN'S DREAM

EVERY morning before the Preacher could finish his breakfast, callers were knocking at the door —the negro, the poor white, the widow, the orphan, the wounded, the hungry, an endless procession.

The spirit of the returned soldiers was all that he could ask. There was nowhere a slumbering spark of war. There was not the slightest effort to continue the lawless habits of four years of strife. Everywhere the spirit of patience, self-restraint and hope marked the life of the men who had made the most terrible soldiery. They were glad to be done with war, and have the opportunity to rebuild their broken fortunes. They were glad, too, that the everlasting question of a divided Union was settled and settled forever. There was now to be one country and one flag, and deep down in their souls they were content with it.

The spectacle of this terrible army of the Confederacy, the memory of whose battle cry yet thrills the world, transformed in a month into patient and hopeful workmen, has never been paralleled in history.

Who destroyed this scene of peaceful rehabilitation? Hell has no pit dark enough, and no damnation deep enough for these conspirators when once history has fixed their guilt.

The task before the people of the South was one to tax the genius of the Anglo-Saxon race as never in its history, even had every friendly aid possible been extended by the victorious North. Four million negroes had suddenly been freed, and the foundations of economic order destroyed. Five billions of dollars worth of property were wiped out of existence, banks closed, every dollar of money worthless paper, the country plundered by victorious armies, its cities, mills and homes burned, and the flower of its manhood buried in nameless trenches, or worse still, flung upon the charity of poverty, maimed wrecks. The task of organising this wrecked society and marshalling into efficient citizenship this host of ignorant negroes, and yet to preserve the civilisation of the Anglo-Saxon race, the priceless heritage of two thousand years of struggle, was one to appal the wisdom of ages. Honestly and earnestly the white people of the South set about this work, and accepted the Thirteenth amendment to the Constitution abolishing slavery without a protesting vote.

The President issued his proclamation announcing the method of restoring the Union as it had been handed to him from the martyred Lincoln, and endorsed unanimously by Lincoln's Cabinet. This plan was simple, broad and statesmanlike, and its spirit breathed Fraternity and Union with malice toward none and charity toward all. It declared what Lincoln had always taught, that the Union was indestructible, that the rebellious states had now only to repudiate Secession, abolish slavery, and resume their positions in the Union, to preserve which so many lives had been sacrificed.

The people of North Carolina accepted this plan in good faith. They elected a Legislature composed of the noblest men of the state, and chose an old Union man, Andrew Macon, Governor. Against Macon was pitted the man who was now the President and organiser of a federation of secret oath-bound societies, of which the

Union League, destined to play so tragic a part in the
drama about to follow was the type. This man, Amos
Hogg, was a writer of brilliant and forceful style. Before the war, a virulent Secessionist leader, he had justified
and upheld slavery, and had written a volume of poems
dedicated to John C. Calhoun. He had led the movement for Secession in the Convention which passed the
ordinance. But when he saw his ship was sinking, he
turned his back upon the " errors " of the past, professed
the most loyal Union sentiments, wormed himself into
the confidence of the Federal Government, and actually
succeeded in securing the position of Provisional Governor of the state! He loudly professed his loyalty, and
with fury and malice demanded that Vance, the great
war Governor, his predecessor, who, as a Union man had
opposed Secession, should now be hanged, and with him
his own former associates in the Secession Convention,
whom he had misled with his brilliant pen.

But the people had a long memory. They saw through
this hollow pretense, grieved for their great leader, who
was now locked in a prison cell in Washington, and
voted for Andrew Macon.

In the bitterness of defeat, Amos Hogg sharpened his
wits and his pen, and began his schemes of revengeful
ambition.

The fires of passion burned now in the hearts of hosts
of cowards, North and South, who had not met their
foe in battle. Their day had come. The times were
ripe for the Apostles of Revenge and their breed of statesmen.

The Preacher threw the full weight of his character
and influence to defeat Hogg and he succeeded in carrying the county for Macon by an overwhelming majority.
At the election only the men who had voted under the old
regime were allowed to vote. The Preacher had not ap-

peared on the hustings as a speaker, but as an organizer and leader of opinion he was easily the most powerful man in the county, and one of the most powerful in the state.

CHAPTER V

THE OLD AND THE NEW CHURCH

IN the village of Hambright the church was the centre of gravity of the life of the people. There were but two churches, the Baptist and the Methodist. The Episcopalians had a building, but it was built by the generosity of one of their dead members. There were four Presbyterian families in town, and they were working desperately to build a church. The Baptists had really taken the county, and the Methodists were their only rivals. The Baptists had fifteen flourishing churches in the county, the Methodists six. There were no others.

The meetings at the Baptist church in the village of Hambright were the most important gatherings in the county. On Sunday mornings everybody who could walk, young and old, saint and sinner, went to church, and by far the larger number to the Baptist church.

You could tell by the stroke of the bells that the two were rivals. The sextons acquired a peculiar skill in ringing these bells with a snap and a jerk that smashed the clapper against the side in a stroke that spoke defiance to all rival bells, warning of everlasting fire to all sinners that should stay away, and due notice to the saints that even an apostle might become a castaway unless he made haste.

The men occupied one side of the house, the women the other. Only very small boys accompanying their mothers were to be seen on the woman's side, together with a few young men who fearlessly escorted thither their sweethearts.

Before the services began, between the ringing of the first and second bells, the men gathered in groups in the church yard and discussed grave questions of politics and weather. The services over the men lingered in the yard to shake hands with neighbours, praise or criticise the sermon, and once more discuss great events. The boys gathered in quiet, wistful groups and watched the girls come slowly out of the other door, and now and then a daring youngster summoned courage to ask to see one of them home.

The services were of the simplest kind. The Singing of the old hymns of Zion, the Reading of the Bible, the Prayer, the Collection, the Sermon, the Benediction.

The Preacher never touched on politics, no matter what the event under whose world import his people gathered. War was declared, and fought for four terrible years. Lee surrendered, the slaves were freed, and society was torn from the foundations of centuries, but you would never have known it from the lips of the Rev. John Durham in his pulpit. These things were but passing events. When he ascended the pulpit he was the Messenger of Eternity. He spoke of God, of Truth, of Righteousness, of Judgment, the same yesterday, to-day and forever.

Only in his prayers did he come closer to the inner thoughts and perplexities of the daily life of the people. He was a man of remarkable power in the pulpit. His mastery of the Bible was profound. He could speak pages of direct discourse in its very language. To him it was a divine alphabet, from whose letters he could compose the most impassioned message to the individual hearer before him. Its literature, its poetic fire, the epic sweep of the Old Testament record of life, were inwrought into the very fibre of his soul. As a preacher he spoke with authority. He was narrow and dogmatic in his interpretations of the Bible, but his very narrowness and dogmatism were of his flesh and blood, elements of his power. He never stooped to controversy. He simply announced the Truth. The wise received it. The fools rejected it and were damned. That was all there was to it.

But it was in his public prayers that he was at his best. Here all the wealth of tenderness of a great soul was laid bare. In these prayers he had the subtle genius that could find the way direct into the hearts of the people before him, realise as his own their sins and sorrows, their burdens and hopes and dreams and fears, and then, when he had made them his own, he could give them the wings of deathless words and carry them up to the heart of God. He prayed in a low soft tone of voice; it was like an honest earnest child pleading with his father. What a hush fell on the people when these prayers began! With what breathless suspense every earnest soul followed him!

Before and during the war, the gallery of this church, which was built and reserved for the negroes, was always crowded with dusky listeners that hung spellbound on his words. Now there were only a few, perhaps a dozen, and they were growing fewer. Some new and mysterious power was at work among the negroes, sowing the seeds of distrust and suspicion. He wondered what it could be. He had always loved to preach to these simple hearted children of nature, and watch the flash of resistless emotion sweep their dark faces. He had baptised over five hundred of them into the fellowship of the churches in the village and the county during the ten years of his ministry.

He determined to find out the cause of this desertion

of his church by the negroes to whom he had ministered so many years.

At the close of a Sunday morning's service, Nelse was slowly descending the gallery stairs leading Charlie Gaston by the hand, after the church had been nearly emptied of the white people. The Preacher stopped him near the door.

"How's your Mistress, Nelse?"

"She's gettin' better all de time now praise de Lawd. Eve she stay wid er dis mornin', while I fetch dis boy ter church. He des so sot on goin'."

"Where are all the other folks who used to fill that gallery, Nelse?"

"You doan tell me, you aint heard about dem?" he answered with a grin.

"Well, I haven't heard, and I want to hear."

"De laws-a-massy, dey done got er church er dey own! Dey has meetin' now in de school house dat Yankee 'oman built. De teachers tell 'em ef dey aint good ernuf ter set wid de white folks in dere chu'ch, dey got ter hole up dey haids, and not 'low nobody ter push em up in er nigger gallery. So dey's got ole Uncle Josh Miller to preach fur 'em. He 'low he got er call, en he stan' up dar en holler fur 'em bout er hour ev'ry Sunday mawnin' en night. En sech whoopin', en yellin', en bawlin'! Yer can hear 'em er mile. Dey tries ter git me ter go. I tell 'em, Marse John Durham's preachin's good ernuf fur me, gall'ry er no gall'ry. I tell 'em dat I spec er gall'ry nigher heaven den de lower flo' enyhow—en fuddermo', dat when I goes ter church, I wants ter hear sumfin' mo' dan er ole fool nigger er bawlin'. I can holler myself. En dey low I gwine back on my colour. En den I tell 'em I spec I aint so proud dat I can't larn fum white folks. En dey say dey gwine ter lay fur me yit."

"I'm sorry to hear this," said the Preacher thoughtfully.

"Yassir, hits des lak I tell yer. I spec dey gone fur good. Niggers aint got no sense nohow. I des wish I own 'em erbout er week! Dey gitten madder'n madder et me all de time case I stay at de ole place en wuk fer my po' sick Mistus. Dey sen' er Kermittee ter see me mos' ev'ry day ter 'splain ter me I'se free. De las' time dey come I lam one on de haid wid er stick er wood erfo dey leave me lone."

"You must be careful, Nelse."

"Yassir, I nebber hurt 'im. Des sorter crack his skull er little ter show 'im what I gwine do wid 'im nex' time dey come pesterin' me."

"Have they been back to see you since?"

"Dat dey aint. But dey sont me word dey gwine git de Freeman's Buro atter me. En I sont 'em back word ter sen Mr. Buro right on en I land 'im in de middle er a spell er sickness, des es sho es de Lawd gimme strenk."

"You can't resist the Freedman's Bureau, Nelse."

"What dat Buro got ter do wid me, Marse John?"

"They've got everything to do with you, my boy. They have absolute power over all questions between the Negro and the white man. They can prohibit you from working for a white person without their consent, and they can fix your wages and make your contracts."

"Well, dey better lemme erlone, or dere'll be trouble in dis town, sho's my name's Nelse."

"Don't you resist their officer. Come to me if you get into trouble with them," was the Preacher's parting injunction.

Nelse made his way out leading Charlie by the hand, and bowing his giant form in a quaint deferential way to the white people he knew. He seemed proud of his association in the church with the whites, and the position of inferiority assigned him in no sense disturbed his pride. He was muttering to himself as he walked slowly along looking down at the ground thoughtfully. There was infinite scorn and defiance in his voice.

"Bu-ro! Bu-ro! Des let 'em fool wid me! I'll make 'em see de seben stars in de middle er de day!"

CHAPTER VI

THE PREACHER AND THE WOMAN OF BOSTON

THE next day the Preacher had a call from Miss Susan Walker of Boston, whose liberality had built the new Negro school house and whose life and fortune was devoted to the education and elevation of the Negro race. She had been in the village often within the year, running up from Independence where she was building and endowing a magnificent classical college for negroes. He had often heard of her, but as she stopped with negroes when on her visits he had never met her. He was especially interested in her after hearing incidentally that she was a member of a Baptist church in Boston.

On entering the parlour the Preacher greeted his visitor with the deference the typical Southern man instinctively pays to woman.

"I am pleased to meet you, Madam," he said with a graceful bow and kindly smile, as he led her to the most comfortable seat he could find.

She looked him squarely in the face for a moment as though surprised and smilingly replied,

"I believe you Southern men are all alike, woman flatterers. You have a way of making every woman believe you think her a queen. It pleases me, I can't help confessing it, though I sometimes despise myself for it. But I am not going to give you an opportunity to feed my vanity this morning. I've come for a plain face to

44

face talk with you on the one subject that fills my heart, my work among the Freedmen. You are a Baptist minister. I have a right to your friendship and co-operation."

A cloud overshadowed the Preacher's face as he seated himself. He said nothing for a moment, looking curiously and thoughtfully at his visitor.

He seemed to be studying her character and to be puzzled by the problem. She was a woman of prepossessing appearance, well past thirty-five, with streaks of grey appearing in her smoothly brushed black hair. She was dressed plainly in rich brown material cut in tailor fashion, and her heavy hair was drawn straight up pompadour style from her forehead with apparent carelessness and yet in a way that heightened the impression of strength and beauty in her face. Her nose was the one feature that gave warning of trouble in an encounter. She was plump in figure, almost stout, and her nose seemed too small for the breadth of her face. It was broad enough, but too short, and was pug tipped slightly at the end. She fell just a little short of being handsome and this nose was responsible for the failure. It gave to her face when agitated, in spite of evident culture and refinement, the expression of a feminine bull dog.

Her eyes were flashing now, and her nostrils opened a little wider and began to push the tip of her nose upward. At last she snapped out suddenly,

" Well, which is it, friend or foe? What do you honestly think of my work? "

" Pardon me, Miss Walker, I am not accustomed to speak rudely to a lady. If I am honest, I don't know where to begin."

" Bah! Lay aside your Don Quixote Southern chivalry this morning and talk to me in plain English. It doesn't matter whether I am a woman or a man. I am an idea,

a divine mission this morning.   I mean to establish a
high school in this village for the negroes, and to build
a Baptist church for them.   I learn from them that
they have great faith in you.   Many of them desire your
approval and co-operation.   Will you help me?"

"To be perfectly frank, I will not.   You ask me for
plain English.   I will give it to you.   Your presence
in this village as a missionary to the heathen is an insult
to our intelligence and Christian manhood.   You come
at this late day a missionary among the heathen, the
heathen whose heart and brain created this Republic with
civil and religious liberty for its foundations, a missionary among the heathen who gave the world Washington,
whose giant personality three times saved the cause of
American Liberty from ruin when his army had melted
away.   You are a missionary among the children of Washington, Jefferson, Monroe, Madison, Jackson, Clay and
Calhoun!   Madam, I have baptised into the fellowship
of the church of Christ in this county more negroes than
you ever saw in all your life before you left Boston.

"At the close of the war there were thousands of
negro members of white Baptist churches in the state.
Your mission is not to proclaim the gospel of Jesus
Christ.   Your mission is to teach crack-brained theories
of social and political equality to four millions of ignorant negroes, some of whom are but fifty years removed
from the savagery of African jungles.   Your work is to
separate and alienate the negroes from their former
masters who can be their only real friends and guardians.   Your work is to sow the dragon's teeth of an
impossible social order that will bring forth its harvest
of blood for our children."

He paused a moment, and, suddenly facing her continued, "I should like to help the cause you have at heart;
and the most effective service I could render it now would

be to box you up in a glass cage, such as are used for rattlesnakes, and ship you back to Boston."

"Indeed! I suppose then it is still a crime in the South to teach the Negro?" she asked this in little gasps of fury, her eyes flashing defiance and her two rows of white teeth uncovering by the rising of her pugnacious nose."

"For you, yes. It is always a crime to teach a lie."

"Thank you. Your frankness is all one could wish!"

"Pardon my apparent rudeness. You not only invited, you demanded it. While about it, let me make a clean breast of it. I do you personally the honour to acknowledge that you are honest and in dead earnest, and that you mean well. You are simply a fanatic."

"Allow me again to thank you for your candour!"

"Don't mention it, Madam. You will be canonised in due time. In the meantime let us understand one another. Our lives are now very far apart, though we read the same Bible, worship the same God and hold the same great faith. In the settlement of this Negro question you are an insolent interloper. You're worse, you are a wilful spoiled child of rich and powerful parents playing with matches in a powder mill. I not only will not help you, I would, if I had the power seize you, and remove you to a place of safety. But I cannot oppose you. You are protected in your play by a million bayonets and back of these bayonets are banked the fires of passion in the North ready to burst into flame in a moment. The only thing I can do is to ignore your existence. You understand my position."

"Certainly, Doctor," she replied good naturedly.

She had recovered from the rush of her anger now and was herself again. A curious smile played round her lips as she quietly added:

"I must really thank you for your candour. You have

helped me immensely. I understand the situation now perfectly. I shall go forward cheerfully in my work and never bother my brain again about you, or your people, or your point of view. You have aroused all the fighting blood in me. I feel toned up and ready for a life struggle. I assure you I shall cherish no ill feeling toward you. I am only sorry to see a man of your powers so blinded by prejudice. I will simply ignore you."

" Then, Madam, it is quite clear we agree upon establishing and maintaining a great mutual ignorance. Let us hope, paradoxical as it may seem, that it may be for the enlightenment of future generations ! "

She arose to go, smiling at his last speech.

" Before we part, perhaps never to meet again, let me ask you one question," said the Preacher still looking thoughtfully at her.

" Certainly, as many as you like."

" Why is it that you good people of the North are spending your millions here now to help only the negroes, who feel least of all the sufferings of this war? The poor white people of the South are your own flesh and blood. These Scotch Covenanters are of the same Puritan stock, these German, Huguenot and . English people are all your kinsmen, who stood at the stake with your fathers in the old world. They are, many of them, homeless, without clothes, sick and hungry and broken hearted. But one in ten of them ever owned a slave. They had to fight this war because your armies invaded their soil. But for their sorrows, sufferings and burdens you have no ear to hear and no heart to pity. This is a strange thing to me."

" The white people of the South can take care of themselves. If they suffer, it is God's just punishment for their sins in owning slaves and fighting against the flag. Do I make myself clear? " she snapped.

"Perfectly, I haven't another word to say."

"My heart yearns for the poor dear black people who have suffered so many years in slavery and have been denied the rights of human beings. I am not only going to establish schools and colleges for them here, but I am conducting an experiment of thrilling interest to me which will prove that their intellectual, moral, and social capacity is equal to any white man's."

"Is it so?" asked the Preacher.

"Yes, I am collecting from every section of the South the most promising specimens of negro boys and sending them to our great Northern Universities where they will be educated among men who treat them as equals, and I expect from the boys reared in this atmosphere, men of transcendent genius, whose brilliant achievements in science, art and letters will forever silence the tongues of slander against their race. The most interesting of these students I have at Harvard now is young George Harris. His mother is Eliza Harris, the history of whose escape over the ice of the Ohio River fleeing from slavery thrilled the world. This boy is a genius, and if he lives he will shake this nation."

"It may be, Miss Walker. There are more ways than one to shake a nation. And while I ignore your work, as a citizen and public man,—privately and personally, I shall watch this experiment with profound interest."

"I know it will succeed. I believe God made us of one blood," she said with enthusiasm.

"Is it true, Madam, that you once endowed a home for homeless cats before you became interested in the black people?" With a twinkle in his eye the Preacher softly asked this apparently irrelevant question.

"Yes, sir, I did,—I am proud of it. I love cats. There are over a thousand in the home now, and they are well cared for. Whose business is it?"

"I meant no offense by the question. I love cats too. But I wondered if you were collecting negroes only now, or, whether you were adding other specimens to your menagerie for experimental purposes."

She bit her lips, and in spite of her efforts to restrain her anger, tears sprang to her eyes as she turned toward the Preacher whose face now looked calmly down upon her with ill-concealed pride.

"Oh! the insolence of you Southern people toward those who dare to differ with you about the Negro!" she cried with rage.

"I confess it humbly as a Christian, it is true. My scorn for these maudlin ideas is so deep that words have no power to convey it. But come," said the Preacher in the kindliest tone. "Enough of this. I am pained to see tears in your eyes. Pardon my thoughtlessness. Let us forget now for a little while that you are an idea, and remember only that you are a charming Boston woman of the household of our own faith. Let me call Mrs. Durham, and have you know her and discuss with her the thousand and one things dear to all women's hearts."

"No, I thank you! I feel a little sore and bruised, and social amenities can have no meaning for those whose souls are on fire with such antagonistic ideas as yours and mine. If Mrs. Durham can give me any sympathy in my work I'll be delighted to see her, otherwise I must go."

The Preacher laughed aloud.

"Then let me beg of you, never meet Mrs. Durham. If you do, the war will break out again. I don't wish to figure in a case of assault and battery. Mrs. Durham was the owner of fifty slaves. She represents the bluest of the blue blood of the slave-holding aristocracy of the South. She has never surrendered and she never will. Wars, surrenders, constitutional amendments and such little things make no impression on her mind whatever. If you think I am difficult, you had better not puzzle your brain over her.   I am a mildly constructive man of progress.   She is a Conservative."

"Then we will say good-bye," said Miss Walker, extending her small plump hand in friendly parting.   "I accept your challenge which this interview implies.   I will succeed if God lives," and she set her lips with a snap that spoke volumes.

"And I will watch you from afar with sorrow and fear and trembling," responded the Preacher.

CHAPTER VII

THE HEART OF A CHILD

MRS. GASTON'S recovery from the brain fever which followed her prostration was slow and painful. For days she would be quite herself as she would sit up in bed and smile at the wistful face of the boy who sat tenderly gazing into her eyes, or with swift feet was running to do her slightest wish.

Then days of relapse would follow when the child's heart would ache and ache with a dumb sense of despair as he listened to her incoherent talk, and heard her meaningless laughter. When at length he could endure it no longer, he would call Aunt Eve, run from the house, as fast as his little legs could carry him, and in the woods lie down in the shadows and cry for hours.

"I wonder if God is dead?" he said one day as he lay and gazed at the clouds sweeping past the openings in the green foliage above.

"I pray every day and every night, but she don't get well. Why does He leave her like that, when she's so good!" and then his voice choked into sobs, and he buried his face in the leaves.

He was suddenly roused by the voice of Nelse who stood looking down on his forlorn figure with tenderness.

"What you doin' out in dese woods, honey, by yo' se'f?"

"Nothin', Nelse."

"I knows. You'se er crying 'bout yo Ma."

The boy nodded without looking up.

"Doan do dat way, honey. You'se too little ter cry lak dat. Yer Ma's gittin' better ev'ry day, de doctor done tole me so."

"Do you think so, Nelse?" There was an eagerness and yearning in the child's voice, that would have moved the heart of a stone.

"Cose I does. She be strong en well in little while when cole wedder comes. Fros' 'll soon be here. I see whar er ole rabbit been er eatin' on my turnip tops. Dat's er sho sign. I gwine make you er rabbit box termorrer ter ketch dat rabbit."

"Will you, Nelse?"

"Sho's you bawn. Now des lemme pick you er chune on dis banjer 'fo I goes ter my wuk."

Of all the music he had ever heard, the boy thought Nelse's banjo was the sweetest. He accompanied the music in a deep bass voice which he kept soft and soothing. The boy sat entranced. With wide open eyes and half parted lips he dreamed his mother was well, and then that he had grown to be a man, a great man, rich and powerful. Now he was the Governor of the state, living in the Governor's palace, and his mother was presiding at a banquet in his honour. He was bending proudly over her and whispering to her that she was the most beautiful mother in the world. And he could hear her say with a smile,

"You dear boy!"

Suddenly the banjo stopped, and Nelse railed with mock severity, "Now look at 'im er cryin' ergin, en me er pickin' de eens er my fingers off fur 'im!"

"No, I aint cryin'. I am just listenin' to the music. Nelse, you're the greatest banjo player in the world!"

"Na, honey, hits de banjer. Dats de Jo-bloin'est ban-

jer! En des ter t'ink—er Yankee gin 'er to me in de wah!
Dat wuz the fus' Yankee I ebber seed hab sense ernuf
ter own er banjer. I kinder hate ter fight dem Yankees
atter dat."

"But Nelse, if you were fighting with our men how
did you get close to any Yankees?"

"Lawd child, we's allers slippin' out twixt de lines
atter night er carryin' on wid dem Yankees. We trade
'em terbaccer fur coffee en sugar, en play cyards, en
talk twell mos' day sometime. I slip out fust in er patch
er woods twix' de lines, en make my banjer talk. En den
yere dey come! De Yankees fum one way en our boys
de yudder. I make out lak I doan see 'em tall, des playin'
ter myself. Den I make dat banjer moan en cry en talk
about de folks way down in Dixie. De boys creep up
closer en closer twell dey right at my elbow en I see 'em
cryin', some un 'em—den I gin 'er' a juk! en way she go
pluckety plunck! en dey gin ter dance and laugh! Sometime dey cuss me lak dey mad en lam me on de back.
When dey hit me hard den I know dey ready ter gimme
all dey got."

"But how did you get this banjo, Nelse?"

"Yankee gin 'er ter me one night ter try 'er, en when
he hear me des fairly pull de insides outen 'er, he 'low
dat hit 'ed be er sin ter ebber sep'rate us. Say he nebber
know what 'uz in er banjer."

Nelse rose to go.

"Now, honey, doan you cry no mo, en I make you
dat rabbit box sho, en erlong 'bout Chris'mas I gwine
larn you how ter shoot."

"Will you let me hold the gun?" the boy eagerly
asked.

"I des sho you how ter poke yo gun in de crack er
de fence en whisper ter de trigger. Den look out birds
en rabbits!"

The boy's face was one great smile.

It was late in September before his mother was strong enough to venture out of the house—six terrible months from the day she was stricken. What an age it seemed to a sensitive boy's soul. To him the days were weeks, the weeks months, the months, long weary years. It seemed to him he had lived a life-time, died, and was born again the day he saw her first walking on the soft grass that grew under the big trees at the back of the house. He was gently holding her by the hand.

"Now, Mama dear, sit here on this seat—you mustn't get in the sun."

"But, Charlie, I want to see the flowers on the front lawn."

"No, no, Mama, the sun is shinin' awful on that side of the house!"

A great fear caught the boy's heart. The lawn had grown up a mass of weeds and grass during the long hot summer and he was afraid his mother would cry when she saw the ruin of those flowers she loved so well.

How impossible for his child's mind to foresee the gathering black hurricane of tragedy and ruin soon to burst over that lawn!

Skillfully and firmly he kept her on the seat in the rear where she could not see the lawn. He said everything he could think of to please her. She would smile and kiss him in her old sweet way until his heart was full to bursting.

"Do you remember, Mama, how many times when you were so sick I used to slip up close and kiss your mouth and eyes?"

"I often dreamed you were kissing me."

"I thought you would know. I'll soon be a man. I'm going to be rich, and build a great house and you are going to live in it with me, and I am to take care of you as long as you live."

" I expect you will marry some pretty girl, and almost forget your old Mama who will be getting grey."

" But I'll never love anybody like I love you, Mama dear ! "

His little arms slipped around her neck, held her close for a moment, and then he tenderly kissed her.

After supper he sought Nelse.

" Nelse, we must work out the flowers in the lawn. Mama wants to see them. It was all I could do to keep her from going out there to-day."

" Lawd chile, hit'll take two niggers er week ter clean out dat lawn. Hits gone fur dis year. Yer Ma'll know dat, honey."

The next morning after breakfast the boy found a hoe, and in the piercing sun began manfully to work at those flowers. He had worked perhaps, a half hour. His face was red with heat and wet with sweat. He was tired already and seemed to make no impression on the wilderness of weeds and grass.

Suddenly he looked up and saw his mother smiling at him.

" Come here, Charlie! " she called.

He dropped his hoe and hurried to her side. She caught him in her arms and kissed the sweat drops from his eyes and mouth.

" You are the sweetest boy in the world! "

What music to his soul these words to the last day of his life !

" I was afraid when you saw all these weeds you would cry about your flowers. Mama."

" It does hurt me, dear, to see them, but it's worth all their loss to see you out there in the broiling sun working so hard to please me. I've seen the most beautiful flower this morning that ever blossomed on my lawn!—and its perfume will make sweet my whole life. I am going to be brave and live for you now."

And she kissed him fondly again.

CHAPTER VIII

AN EXPERIMENT IN MATRIMONY

NELSE was informed by the Agent of the Freedman's Bureau when summoned before that tribunal that he must pay a fee of one dollar for a marriage license and be married over again.

"What's dat? Dis yer war bust up me en Eve's marryin'?"

"Yes," said the Agent. "You must be legally married."

Nelse chucked on a brilliant scheme that flashed through his mind.

"Den I see you ergin 'bout dat," he said as he hastily took his leave.

He made his way homeward revolving his brilliant scheme. "But won't I fetch dat nigger Eve down er peg er two! I gwine ter make her t'ink I won' marry her nohow. I make 'er ax my pardon fur all dem little disergreements. She got ter talk mighty putty now sho nuf!" And he smiled over his coming triumph.

It was four o'clock in the afternoon when he reached his cabin door on the lot back of Mrs. Gaston's home. Eve was busy mending some clothes for their little boy now nearly five years old.

"Good evenin', Miss Eve!"

Eve looked up at him with a sudden flash of her eye. "What de matter wid you nigger?"

"Nuttin' tall. Des drapped in lak ter pass de time

er day, en ax how's you en yer son stanin' dis hot wedder!" Nelse bowed and smiled.

"What ail you, you big black baboon?"

"Nuttin' tall M'am, des callin' roun' ter see my frien's." Still smiling Nelse walked in and sat down.

Eve put down her sewing, stood up before him, her arms akimbo, and gazed at him steadily till the whites of her eyes began to shine like two moons.

"You wants me ter whale you ober de head wid dat poker?"

"Not dis evenin', M'am."

"Den what ail you?"

"De Buro des inform me, dat es I'se er young han'-some man en you'se er gittin' kinder ole en fat, dat we aint married nohow. En dey gimme er paper fur er dollar dat allow me ter marry de young lady er my choice. Dat sho is er great Buro!"

"We aint married?"

"Nob-um."

"Atter we stan' up dar befo' Marse John Durham en say des what all dem white folks say?"

"Nob-um."

Eve slowly took her seat and gazed down the road thoughtfully.

"I t'ink I drap eroun' ter see you en gin you er chance wid de odder gals fo' I steps off," explained Nelse with a grin.

No answer.

"You 'member dat night I say sumfin' 'bout er gal I know once, en you riz en grab er poun' er wool outen my head fo' I kin move?"

No answer yet.

"Min' dat time, you bust de biscuit bode ober my head, en lam me wid de fire-shovel, en hit me in de burr er de year wid er flatiron es I wuz makin' fur de do'?"

"Yas, I min's dat sho!" said Eve with evident **satisfaction.**

"Doan you wish you nebber done dat?"

"You black debbil!"

"Dat's hit! I'se er bad nigger, M'am,—bad nigger fo'
de war. En I'se gittin' wuss en wuss," Nelse chuckled.

She looked at him with gathering rage and contempt.

"En den fudder mo, M'am, I doan lak de way you
talk ter me sometimes. Yo voice des kinder takes de
skin off same's er file. I laks ter hear er 'oman's voice
lak my Missy's, des es sof' es wool. Sometime one word
from her keep me warm all winter. De way you talk
sometime make me cole in de summer time."

Nelse rose while Eve sat motionless.

"I des call, M'am, ter drap er little intment inter dem
years er yourn, dat'll percerlate froo you min', en when
I calls ergin I hopes ter be welcome wid smiles."

Nelse bowed himself out the door in grandiloquent
style.

All the afternoon he was laughing to himself over
his triumph, and imagining the welcome when he returned that evening with his marriage license and the
officer to perform the ceremony. At supper in the kitchen
he was polite and formal in his manners to Eve. She
eyed him in a contemptuous sort of way and never spoke
unless it was absolutely necessary.

It was about half past eight when Nelse arrived at
home with the license duly issued and the officer of the
Bureau ready to perform the ceremony.

"Des wait er minute here at de corner, sah, twell I
kinder breaks de news to 'em,"said Nelse to the officer.
He approached the cabin door and knocked.

It was shut and fastened. He got no response.

He knocked loudly again.

Eve thrust her head out the window.

" Who's dat ? "

" Hits me, M'am, Mister Nelson Gaston, I'se call ter see you."

" Den you hump yo'se'f en git away from dat do, you rascal."

" De Lawd. honey, I'se des been er foolin' you ter day. I'se got dem licenses en de Buro man right out dar now ready ter marry us. You know yo ole man nebber gwine back on you—I des been er foolin'."

" Den you been er foolin' wid de wrong nigger ! "

" Lawd, honey, doan keep de bridegroom er waitin'."

" Git er way from dat do ! "

" G'long chile, en quit yer projeckin'."   Nelse was using his softest and most persuasive tones now.

" G'way from dat do ! "

" Come on, Eve, de man waitin' out dar fur us ! "

" Git away I tells you er I scald you wid er kittle er hot water ! "

Nelse drew back slightly from the door.

" But, honey, whar yo ole man gwine ter sleep ? "

" Dey's straw in de barn, en pine shatters in de dog house ! " she shouted slamming the window.

" Eve, honey ! "—

" Doan you come honeyin' me, I'se er spec'able 'oman I is. Ef you wants ter marry me you got ter come cotin' me in de day time fust, en bring me candy, en ribbins en flowers and sich, en you got ter talk purtier'n you ebber talk in all yo born days. Lots er likely lookin' niggers come settin up ter me while you gone in dat wah, en I keep studin' 'bout you, you big black rascal. Now you got ter hump yo'se'f ef you eber see de inside er dis cabin ergin."

Crestfallen Nelse returned to the officer.

" Wall sah, deys er kinder hitch in de perceedins."

" What's the matter? "

" She 'low I got ter come cotin' her fust. En I spec
I is."

The officer laughed and returned to his home. She
made Nelse sleep in the barn for three weeks, court her
an hour every day, and bring her five cents worth of red
stick candy and a bouquet of flowers as a peace offering
at every visit. Finally she made him write her a note and
ask her to take a ride with him. Nelse got Charlie
to write it for him, and made his own boy carry it to
his mother. After three weeks of humility and attention
to her wishes, she gave her consent, and they were duly
married again.

CHAPTER IX

A MASTER OF MEN

THE first Monday in October was court day at Hambright, and from every nook and corner of Campbell county, the people flocked to town. The court house had not yet been transformed into the farce-tragedy hall where jail birds and drunken loafers were soon to sit on judge's bench and in attorney's chair instead of standing in the prisoner's dock. The merciful stay laws enacted by the Legislature had silenced the cry of the auctioneer until the people might have a moment to gird themselves for a new life struggle.

But the black cloud was already seen on the horizon. The people were restless and discouraged by the wild rumours set afloat by the Freedman's Bureau, of coming confiscation, revolution and revenge. A greater crowd than usual had come to town on the first day. The streets were black with negroes.

A shout was heard from the crowd in the square, as the stalwart figure of General Daniel Worth, the brigade commander of Colonel Gaston's regiment was seen shaking hands with the men of his old army.

The General was a man to command instant attention in any crowd. An expert in anthropology would have selected his face from among a thousand as the typical man of the Caucasian race. He was above the average height, a strong muscular and well-rounded body, crowned by a heavy shock of what had once been raven

63

black hair, now iron grey. His face was ruddy with the glow of perfect health and his full round lips and the twinkle of his eye showed him to be a lover of the good things of life. He wore a heavy moustache which seemed a fitting ballast for the lower part of his face against the heavy projecting straight eyebrows and bushy hair.

As he shook hands with his old soldiers his face was wreathed in smiles, his eyes flashed with something like tears and he had a pleasant word for all.

Tom Camp was one of the first to spy the General and hobble to him as fast as his peg-leg would carry him.

" Howdy, General, howdy do! Lordy it's good for sore eyes ter see ye! " Tom held fast to his hand and turning to the crowd said,

" Boys, here's the best General that ever led a brigade, and there wasn't a man in it that wouldn't a died for him. Now three times three cheers! " And they gave it with a will.

" Ah! Tom you're still at your old tricks," said the General. " What are you after now? "

" A speech General! "—" A speech! A speech! " the crowd echoed.

The General slapped Tom on the back and said,

" What sort of a job is this you're putting up on me— I'm no orator! But I'll just say to you, boys, that this old peg-leg here was the finest soldier that I ever saw carry a musket and the men who stood beside him were the most patient, the most obedient, the bravest men that ever charged a foe and crowned their General with glory while he safely stood in the rear."

Again a cheer broke forth. The General was hurrying toward the court house, when he was suddenly surrounded by a crowd of negroes. In the front ranks were a hundred of his old slaves who had worked on his

Campbell county plantation. They seized his hands and laughed and cried and pleaded for recognition like a crowd of children. Most of them he knew. Some of their faces he had forgotten.

" Hi dar, Marse Dan'l, you knows me! Lordy, I'se your boy Joe dat used ter ketch yo hoss down at the plantation! "

" Of course, Joe! Of course."

" I know Marse Dan'l aint forget old Uncle Rube," said an aged negro pushing his way to the front.

" That I haven't Reuben! and how's Aunt Julie Ann? "

" She des tollable, Marse Dan'l. We'se bof un us had de plumbago. How is you all sence de wah? "

" Oh! first rate, Reuben. We manage somehow to get enough to eat and if we do that nowadays we can't complain."

" Dats de God's truf, Marster sho! En now Marse Dan'l, we all wants you ter make us er speech en 'splain erbout dis freedom ter us. Dey's so many dese yere Buroers en Leaguers round here tellin' us niggers what's er coming', twell we des doan know nuttin' fur sho. "

" Yassir dat's hit! You tell us er speech Marse Dan'l! "

The white men crowded up nearer and joined in the cry. There was no escape. In a few moments the court house was filled with a crowd.

When he arose a cheer shook the building, and strange as it may seem to-day, it came with almost equal enthusiasm from white and black.

" I thank you, my friends," said the General, " for this evidence of your confidence. I was a Whig in politics. I reckon I hated a Democrat as God hates sin. I was a Union man and fought Secession. My opponents won. My state asked me to defend her soil. As an obedient son I gave my life in loyal service.

" I need not tell you as a Union man that I am glad

this war is over. I have always felt as a business man, a cotton manufacturer as well as farmer, in touch with the free labour of the North as well as the slave labour of the South, that free labour was the most economical and efficient. I believe that terrible as the loss of four billions of dollars in slaves will be to the South, if the South is only let alone by the politicians and allowed to develop her resources, she will become what God meant her to be, the garden of the world. I say it calmly and deliberately, I thank God that slavery is a thing of the past."

A whirlwind of applause arose from the negroes. Uncle Reuben's voice could be heard above the din.

"Hear dat! You niggers! Dat's my ole Marster talkin' now!"

"Let me say to the negroes here to-day, this war was not fought for your freedom by the North, and yet in its terrific struggle, God saw fit to give you freedom. Life, liberty and the pursuit of happiness are now yours and the birthright of your children.

"We need your labour. Be honest, humble, patient, industrious and every white man in the South will be your friend. What you need now is to go to work with all your might, build a roof over your head, get a few acres of land under your feet that is your own, put decent clothes on your back, and some money in the bank, and you will become indispensable to the people of the South. They will be your best friends and give you every right and privilege you are prepared to receive.

"The man who tells you that your old Master's land will be divided among you, is a criminal, or a fool, or both. If you ever own land, you will earn it in the sweat of your brow like I got mine."

"Hear dat now, niggers!" cried old Reuben.

"The man who tells you that you are going to be

given the ballot indiscriminately with which you can rule
your old masters is a criminal or a fool, or both. It is
insanity to talk about the enfranchisement of a million
slaves who can not read their ballots. Mr. Lincoln who
set you free was opposed to any such measure.

"Let me read an extract from a letter Mr. Lincoln
wrote me just before the war."

The General drew from his pocket a letter in the handwriting of the President and read:—

"MY DEAR WORTH:—You must hold the Union men
of the South together at all hazards. The one passion
of my soul is to save the Union. In answer to the
question you ask me about the equality of the races I
enclose you a newspaper clipping reporting my reply to
Judge Douglas at Charleston, Sept. 18, 1858. I could
not express myself more plainly. Have this extract published in every paper in the South you can get to print it."

The General paused and turning toward the negroes
said,

"Now listen carefully to every word. Says Mr. Lincoln,

*I am not, nor ever have been in favour of bringing
about in any way the social and political equality of the
white and black races!* (here is marked applause from a
Northern audience.) *I am not, nor ever have been in
favour of making voters or jurors of negroes, nor of
qualifying them to hold office, nor to intermarry with
white people. I will say in addition to this that there
is a physical difference between the white and black races
which I believe will forever forbid the two races living
together on terms of social and political equality: and in-
asmuch as they can not so live, while they do remain together, there must be the position of the inferior and*

superior, and I am, as much as any other man, in favour
of having the superior position assigned to the white
race.

" This was Lincoln's position and is the position of
nine-tenths of the voters of his party. It is insanity to
believe that the Anglo-Saxon race at the North can ever
be so blinded by passion that they can assume any other
position.

" Slavery is dead for all time. It would have been
destroyed whatever the end of the war. I know some of
the secrets of the diplomatic history of the Confederacy.
General Lee asked the government at Richmond to
enlist 200,000 negroes to defend the South, which he
declared was their country as well as ours, and grant
them freedom on enlistment. General Lee's request was
ultimately accepted as the policy of the Confederacy
though too late to save its waning fortunes. Not only
this, but the Confederate government sent a special ambassador to England and France and offered them the
pledge of the South to emancipate every slave in return
for the recognition of the independence of the Confederacy. But when the ambassador arrived in Europe, the
lines of our army had been so broken, the governments
were afraid to interfere.

" The man who tells you that your old masters are
your enemies and may try to reinslave you is a wilful
and malicious liar. "

" Hear dat, folks ! " yelled old Reuben as he waved
his arm grandly toward the crowd.

" To the white people here to-day, I say be of good
cheer. Let politics alone for awhile and build up your
ruined homes. You have boundless wealth in your soil.
God will not forget to send the rain and the dew and
the sun. You showed yourselves on a hundred fields
ready to die for your country. Now I ask you to do

something braver and harder. Live for her when it is hard to live. Let cowards run, but let the brave stand shoulder to shoulder and build up the waste places till our country is once more clothed in wealth and beauty. "

The General bowed in closing to a round of applause. His soldiers were delighted with his speech and his old slaves revelled in it with personal pride. But the rank and file of the negroes were puzzled. He did not preach the kind of doctrine they wished to hear. They had hoped freedom meant eternal rest, not work. They had dreamed of a life of ease with government rations three times a day, and old army clothes to last till they put on the white robes above and struck their golden harps in paradise. This message the General brought was painful to their newly awakened imaginations.

As the General passed through the crowd he met the Ex-Provisional Governor, Amos Hogg, busy with the organising work of his Leagues.

" Glad to see you General," said Hogg extending his hand with a smile on his leathery face.

" Well, how are you, Amos, since Macon pulled your wool? "

" Never felt better in my life, General. I want a few minutes' talk with you."

" All right, what is it? "

" General, you're a progressive man. Come, you're flirting with the enemy. The truly loyal men must get together to rescue the state from the rebels who have it again under their heel."

" So Macon's a rebel because he licked you? "

" You know the rebel crowd are running this state," said Hogg.

" Why, Hogg you were the biggest fool Secessionist I ever saw, and Macon and I were staunch Union men.

We had to fight you tooth and nail. You talk about the truly loyal!"

"Yes but, General, I've repented. I've got my face turned toward the light."

"Yes, I see,—the light that shines in the Governor's Mansion."

"I don't deny it. 'Great men choose greater sins, ambition's mine.' Come into this Union movement with me, Worth, and I'll make you the next Governor."

"I'll see you in hell first. No, Amos, we don't belong to the same breed. You were a Secessionist as long as it paid. When the people you had misled were being overwhelmed with ruin, and it no longer paid, you deserted and became 'loyal' to get an office. Now you're organising the negroes, deserters, and criminals into your secret oath-bound societies. Union men when the war came fought on one side or the other, because a Union man was a man, not a coward. If he felt his state claimed his first love, he fought for his native soil. The gang of plugs you are getting together now as 'truly loyal' are simply cowards, deserters, and common criminals who claim they were persecuted as Union men. It's a weak lie."

"We'll win," urged Hogg.

"Never!" the General snorted, and angrily turned on his heel. Before leaving he wheeled suddenly, faced Hogg and said,

"Go on with your fool societies. You are sowing the wind. There'll be a lively harvest. I am organising too. I'm organising a cotton mill, rebuilding our burned factory, borrowing money from the Yankees who licked us to buy machinery and give employment to thousands of our poor people. That's the way to save the state. We've got water power enough to turn the wheels of the world."

" You'll need our protection in the fight that's coming," replied Hogg, with a straight look that meant much.

The General was silent a moment. Then he shook his fist in Hogg's face and slowly said,

" Let me tell you something. When I need protection I'll go to headquarters. I've got Yankee money in my mills and I can get more if I need it. You lay your dirty claws on them and I'll break your neck. "

CHAPTER X

THE MAN OR BRUTE IN EMBRYO

TWO months later General Worth, while busy rebuilding his mills at Independence, had served on him a summons to appear before the Agent of the Freedman's Bureau at Hambright and answer the charge of using " abusive language " to a freedman.

The particular freedman who desired to have his feelings soothed by law was a lazy young negro about sixteen years old whom the General had ordered whipped and sent from the stables into the fields on one occasion during the war while on a visit to his farm. Evidently the boy had a long memory.

" Now don't that beat the devil! " exclaimed the General.

" What is it? " asked his foreman.

" I've got to leave my work, ride on an old freight train thirty miles, pull through twenty more miles of red mud in a buggy to get to Hambright, and lose four days, to answer such a charge as that before some little wizeneyed skunk of a Bureau Agent. My God, it's enough to make a Union man remember Secession with regrets! "

" My stars, General, we can't get along without you now when we are getting this machinery in place. Send a lawyer," growled the foreman.

" Can't do it, John—I'm charged with a crime."

" Well, I'll swear! "

" Do the best you can, I'll be back in four days, if

I don't kill a nigger!" said the General with a smile.
" I've got a settlement to make with the farm hands anyhow."

There was no help for it. When the court convened,
and the young negro saw the face of his old master red
with wrath, his heart failed him. He fled the town and
there was no accusing witness.

The General gazed at the Agent with cold contempt
and never opened his mouth in answer to expressions
of regret at the fiasco.

A few moments later he rode up to the gate of his
farm house on the river hills about a mile out of town.
A strapping young fellow of fifteen hastened to open
the gate.

" Well, Allan, my boy, how are you? "

" First rate, General. We're glad to see you! but we
didn't make a half crop, sir, the niggers were always
in town loafing around that Freedman's Bureau, holding
meetings all night and going to sleep in the fields."

" Well, show me the books," said the General as they
entered the house.

The General examined the accounts with care and then
looked at young Allan McLeod for a moment as though
he had made a discovery.

" Young man, you've done this work well."

" I tried to, sir. If the niggers dispute anything, I
fixed that by making the store-keepers charge each item
in two books, one on your account, and one on an account
kept separate for every nigger."

" Good enough. They'll get up early to get ahead of
you."

" I'm afraid they are going to make trouble at the
Bureau, sir. That Agent's been here holding Union
League meetings two or three nights every week, and
he's got every nigger under his thumb."

"The dirty whelp!" growled the General.

"If you can see me out of the trouble, General, I'd like to jump on him and beat the life out of him next time he comes out here!"

The General frowned.

"Don't you touch him,—any more than you would a pole cat. I've trouble enough just now."

"I could knock the mud out of him in two minutes, if you say the word," said Allan eagerly.

"Yes, I've no doubt of it." The General looked at him thoughtfully.

He was a well knit powerful youth just turned his fifteenth birthday. He had red hair, a freckled face, and florid complexion. His features were regular and pleasing, and his stalwart muscular figure gave him a handsome look that impressed one with indomitable physical energy. His lips were full and sensuous, his eyebrows straight, and his high forehead spoke of brain power as well as horse power.

He had a habit of licking his lips and running his tongue around inside of his cheeks when he saw anything or heard anything that pleased him that was far from intellectual in its suggestiveness. When he did this one could not help feeling that he was looking at a young well fed tiger. There was no doubt about his being alive and that he enjoyed it. His boisterous voice and ready laughter emphasised this impression.

"Allan, my boy," said the General when he had examined his accounts, "if you do everything in life as well as you did these books, you'll make a success."

"I'm going to do my best to succeed, General. I'll not be a poor white man. I'll promise you that."

"Do you go to church anywhere?"

"No sir, Maw's not a member of any church, and it's so far to town I don't go."

"Well, you must go.   You must go to the Sunday
School too, and get acquainted with all the young folks.
I'll speak to Mrs. Durham and get her to look after you."

"All right, sir, I'll start next Sunday."   Allan was
feeling just then in a good humour with himself and all
the world.   The compliment of his employer had so elated
him, he felt fully prepared to enter the ministry if the
General had only suggested it.

The following day was appointed for a settlement of
the annual contract with the negroes.   The Agent of the
Freedman's Bureau was the judge before whom the General, his overseer, and clerk of account, and all the negroes
assembled.

If the devil himself had devised an instrument for
creating race antagonism and strife he could not have
improved on this Bureau in its actual workings.   Had
clean handed, competent agents been possible it might
have accomplished good.   These agents were as a rule
the riff-raff and trash of the North.   It was the supreme
opportunity of army cooks, teamsters, fakirs, and broken
down preachers who had turned insurance agents.   They
were lifted from penury to affluence and power.   The possibility of corruption and downright theft were practically
limitless.

The Agent at Hambright had been a preacher in Michigan who lost his church because of unsavory rumours
about his character.   He had eked out a living as a book
agent, and then insurance agent.   He was a man of some
education and had a glib tongue which the negroes readily
mistook for inspired eloquence.   He assumed great dignity and an extraordinary judicial tone of voice when
adjusting accounts.

General Worth submitted his accounts and they showed
that all but six of the fifty negroes employed had a little
overdrawn their wages in provisions and clothing.

"I think there is a mistake, General, in these accounts," said the Rev. Ezra Perkins the Agent.

"What?" thundered the General.

"A mistake in your view of the contracts," answered Ezra in his oiliest tone.

The negroes began to grin and nudge one another, amid exclamations of "Dar now!" "Hear dat!"

"What do you mean? The contracts are plain. There can be but one interpretation. I agreed to furnish the men their supplies in advance and wait until the end of the year for adjustment after the crops were gathered. As it is, I will lose over five hundred dollars on the farm." The General paused and looked at the Agent with rising wrath.

"It's useless to talk. I decide that under this contract you are to furnish supplies yourself and pay your people their monthly wages besides. I have figured it out that you owe them a little over fifteen hundred dollars."

"Fifteen hundred dollars! You thief!"——

"Softly, softly!—I'll commit you for contempt of court!"

The General turned on his heel without a word, sprang on his horse, and in a few minutes alighted at the hotel. He encountered the assistant agent of the Bureau on the steps.

"Did you wish to see me, General?" he asked.

"No! I'm looking for a man—a Union soldier not a turkey buzzard!" He dashed up to the clerk's desk.

"Is Major Grant in his room?"

"Yes, sir."

"Tell him I want to see him."

"What can I do for you, General Worth?" asked the Major as he hastened to meet him.

"Major Grant, I understand you are a lawyer. You

"YOU THIEF!"

are a man of principle, or you wouldn't have fought. When I meet a man that fought us I know I am talking to a man, not a skunk. This greasy sanctified Bureau Agent, has decided that I owe my hands fifteen hundred dollars. He knows it's a lie. But his power is absolute. I have no appeal to a court. He has all the negroes under his thumb and he is simply arranging to steal this money. I want to pay you a hundred dollars as a retainer and have you settle with the Lord's anointed, the Rev. Ezra Perkins for me."

"With pleasure, General. And it shall not cost you a cent."

"I'll be glad to pay you, Major. Such a decision enforced against me now would mean absolute ruin. I can't borrow another cent."

"Leave Ezra with me."

"Why couldn't they put soldiers into this Bureau if they had to have it, instead of these skunks and wolves?" snorted the General.

"Well, some of them are a little off in the odour of their records at home, I'll admit," said the Major with a dry smile. "But this is the day of the carrion crow, General. You know they always follow the armies. They attack the wounded as well as the dead. You have my heartfelt sympathy. You have dark days ahead! The death of Mr. Lincoln was the most awful calamity that could possibly have befallen the South. I'm sorry. I've learned to like you Southerners, and to love these beautiful skies, and fields of eternal green. It's my country and yours. I fought you to keep it as the heritage of my children."

The General's eyes filled with tears and the two men silently clasped each other's hands.

"Send in your accounts by your clerk. I'll look them

over to-night and I've no doubt the Honourable Reverend
Ezra Perkins will see a new light with the rising of to-
morrow's sun."

And Ezra did see a new light. As the Major cursed
him in all the moods and tenses he knew, Ezra thought
he smelled brimstone in that light.

"I assure you, Major, I'm sorry the thing happened.
My assistant did all the work on these papers. I hadn't
time to give them personal attention," the Agent apologised in his humblest voice.

"You're a liar. Don't waste your breath."

Ezra bit his lips and pulled his Mormon whiskers.

"Write out your decision now—this minute—confirm-
ing these accounts in double quick order, unless you are
looking for trouble."

And Ezra hastened to do as he was bidden.

The next day while the General was seated on the porch
of the little hotel discussing his campaigns with Major
Grant, Tom Camp sent for him.

Tom took the General round behind his house, with
grave ceremony.

"What are you up to, Tom?"

"Show you in a minute! I wish I could make you a
handsomer present, General, to show you how much I
think of you. But I know yer weakness anyhow. There's
the finest lot er lightwood you ever seed. "

Tom turned back some old bagging and revealed a
pile of fat pine chips covered with rosin, evidently
chipped carefully out of the boxed place of live pine
trees.

The General had two crochets, lightwood and water-
power. When he got hold of a fine lot of lightwood
suitable for kindling fires, he would fill his closet with it,
conceal it under his bed, and sometimes under his mat-

tress. He would even hide it in his bureau drawers and wardrobe and take it out in little bits like a miser.

"Lord Tom, that beats the world!"

"Ain't it fine? Just smell?"

"Rosin on every piece! Tom, you cut every tree on your place and every tree in two miles clean to get that. You couldn't have made me a gift I would appreciate more. Old boy, if there's ever a time in your life that you need a friend, you know where to find me."

"I knowed ye'd like it!" said Tom with a smile.

"Tom, you're a man after my own heart. You're feeling rich enough to make your General a present when we are all about to starve. You're a man of faith. So am I. I say keep a stiff upper lip and peg away. The sun still shines, the rains refresh, and water runs down hill yet. That's one thing Uncle Billy Sherman's army couldn't do much with when they put us to the test of fire. He couldn't burn up our water power. Tom, you may not know it, but I do—we've got water power enough to turn every wheel in the world. Wait till we get our harness on it and make it spin and weave our cotton,—we'll feed and clothe the human race. Faith's my motto. I can hardly get enough to eat now, but better times are coming. A man's just as big as his faith. I've got faith in the South. I've got faith in the good will of the people of the North. Slavery is dead. They can't feel anything but kindly toward an enemy that fought as bravely and lost all. We've got one country now and it's going to be a great one."

"You're right, General, faith's the word."

"Tom, you don't know how this gift from you touches me."

The General pressed the old soldier's hand with feeling. He changed his orders from a buggy to a two-horse team that could carry all his precious lightwood.

He filled the vehicle, and what was left he packed carefully in his valise.

He stopped his team in front of the Baptist parsonage to see Mrs. Durham about Allan McLeod.

"Delighted to see you, General Worth. It's refreshing to look into the faces of our great leaders, if they are still outlawed as rebels by the Washington government."

"Ah, Madam, I need not say it is refreshing to see you, the rarest and most beautiful flower of the old South in the days of her wealth and pride! And always the same!" The General bowed over her hand.

"Yes, I haven't surrendered yet."

"And you never will," he laughed.

"Why should I? They've done their worst. They have robbed me of all. I've only rags and ashes left."

"Things might still be worse, Madam."

"I can't see it. There is nothing but suffering and ruin before us. These ignorant negroes are now being taught by people who hate or misunderstand us. They can only be a scourge to society. I am heart-sick when I try to think of the future!"

There was a mist about her eyes that betrayed the deep emotion with which she uttered the last sentence.

She was a queenly woman of the brunette type with full face of striking beauty surmounted by a mass of rich chestnut hair. The loss of her slaves and estate in the war had burned its message of bitterness into her soul. She had the ways of that imperious aristocracy of the South that only slavery could nourish. She was still uncompromising upon every issue that touched the life of the past.

She believed in slavery as the only possible career for a negro in America. The war had left her cynical on the future of the new "Mulatto" nation as she called it, born in its agony. Her only child had died during the war, and this great sorrow had not softened but rather hardened her nature.

Her husband's career as a preacher was now a double cross to her because it meant the doom of eternal poverty. In spite of her love for her husband and her determination with all her opposite tastes to do her duty as his wife, she could not get used to poverty. She hated it in her soul with quiet intensity.

The General was thinking of all this as he tried to frame a cheerful answer. Somehow he could not think of anything worth while to say to her. So he changed the subject.

" Mrs. Durham, I've called to ask your interest in your Sunday School in a boy who is a sort of ward of mine, young Allan McLeod."

" That handsome red-headed fellow that looks like a tiger, I've seen playing in the streets ? "

" Yes, I want you to tame him."

" Well, I will try for your sake, though he's a little older than any boy in my class. He must be over fifteen."

" Just fifteen. I'm deeply interested in him. I am going to give him a good education. His father was a drunken Scotchman in my brigade, whose loyalty to me as his chief was so genuine and touching I couldn't help loving him. He was a man of fine intellect and some culture. His trouble was drink. He never could get up in life on that account. I have an idea that he married his wife while on one of his drunks. She is from down in Robeson county, and he told me she was related to the outlaws who have infested that section for years. This boy looks like his mother, though he gets that red hair and those laughing eyes from his father. I want you to take hold of him and civilise him for me."

" I'll try, General. You know, I love boys."

" You will find him rude and boisterous at first, but I think he's got something in him."

" I'll send for him to come to see me Saturday."

" Thank you, Madam. I must go. My love to Dr. Durham."

The next Saturday when Mrs. Durham walked into her little parlour to see Allan, the boy was scared nearly out of his wits. He sprang to his feet, stammered and blushed, and looked as though he were going to jump out of the window.

Mrs. Durham looked at him with a smile that quite disarmed his fears, took his outstretched hand, and held it trembling in hers.

" I know we will be good friends, won't we? "

" Yessum," he stammered.

" And you won't tie any more tin cans to dogs like you did to Charlie Gaston's little terrier, will you? I like boys full of life and spirit, just so they don't do mean and cruel things."

The boy was ready to promise her anything. He was charmed with her beauty and gentle ways. He thought her the most beautiful woman he had ever seen in the world.

As they started toward the door, she gently slipped one arm around him, put her hand under his chin and kissed him.

Then he was ready to die for her. It was the first kiss he had ever received from a woman's lips. His mother was not a demonstrative woman. He never recalled a kiss she had given him. His blood tingled with the delicious sense of this one's sweetness. All the afternoon he sat out under a tree and dreamed and watched the house where this wonderful thing had happened to him.

CHAPTER XI

SIMON LEGREE

IN the death of Mr. Lincoln, a group of radical politicians, hitherto suppressed, saw their supreme opportunity to obtain control of the nation in the crisis of an approaching Presidential campaign.

Now they could fasten their schemes of proscription, confiscation, and revenge upon the South.

Mr. Lincoln had held these wolves at bay during his life by the power of his great personality. But the Lion was dead, and the Wolf, who had snarled and snapped at him in life, put on his skin and claimed the heritage of his power. The Wolf whispered his message of hate, and in the hour of partisan passion became the master of the nation.

Busy feet had been hurrying back and forth from the Southern states to Washington whispering in the Wolf's ear the stories of sure success, if only the plan of proscription, disfranchisement of whites, and enfranchisement of blacks were carried out.

This movement was inaugurated two years after the war, with every Southern state in profound peace, and in a life and death struggle with nature to prevent famine. The new revolution destroyed the Union a second time, paralysed every industry in the South, and transformed ten peaceful states into roaring hells of anarchy. We have easily outlived the sorrows of the war. That was a surgery which healed the body. But the child has not yet been born whose children's children will live to see the healing of the wounds from those four years of chaos, when fanatics blinded by passion, armed millions of ignorant negroes and thrust them into mortal combat with the proud, bleeding, half-starving Anglo-Saxon race of the South. Such a deed once done, can never be undone. It fixes the status of these races for a thousand years, if not for eternity.

The South was now rapidly gathering into two hostile armies under these influences, with race marks as uniforms—the Black against the White.

The Negro army was under the command of a triumvirate, the Carpet-bagger from the North, the native Scalawag and the Negro Demagogue.

Entirely distinct from either of these was the genuine Yankee soldier settler in the South after the war, who came because he loved its genial skies and kindly people.

Ultimately some of these Northern settlers were forced into politics by conditions around them, and they constituted the only conscience and brains visible in public life during the reign of terror which the " Reconstruction " régime inaugurated.

In the winter of 1866 the Union League at Hambright held a meeting of special importance. The attendance was large and enthusiastic.

Amos Hogg, the defeated candidate for Governor in the last election, now the President of the Federation of " Loyal Leagues," had sent a special ambassador to this meeting to receive reports and give instructions.

This ambassador was none other than the famous Simon Legree of Red River, who had migrated to North Carolina attracted by the first proclamation of the President, announcing his plan for readmitting the state to the Union. The rumours of his death proved a mistake. He had quit drink, and set his mind on greater vices.

In his face were the features of the distinguished ruffian whose cruelty to his slaves had made him unique in infamy in the annals of the South. He was now pre-eminently the type of the "truly loyal". At the first rumour of war he had sold his negroes and migrated nearer the border land, that he might the better avoid service in either army. He succeeded in doing this. The last two years of the war, however, the enlisting officers pressed him hard, until finally he hit on a brilliant scheme.

He shaved clean, and dressed as a German emigrant woman. He wore dresses for two years, did house work, milked the cows and cut wood for a good natured old German. He paid for his board, and passed for a sister, just from the old country.

When the war closed, he resumed male attire, became a violent Union man, and swore that he had been hounded and persecuted without mercy by the Secessionist rebels.

He was looking more at ease now than ever in his life. He wore a silk hat and a new suit of clothes made by a fashionable tailor in Raleigh. He was a little older looking than when he killed Uncle Tom on his farm some ten years before, but otherwise unchanged. He had the same short muscular body, round bullet head, light grey eyes and shaggy eyebrows, but his deep chestnut bristly hair had been trimmed by a barber. His coarse thick lips drooped at the corners of his mouth and emphasised the crook in his nose. His eyes, well set apart, as of old, were bold, commanding, and flashed with the cold light of glittering steel. His teeth that once were pointed like the fangs of a wolf had been filed by a dentist. But it required more than the file of a dentist to smooth out of that face the ferocity and cruelty that years of dissolute habits had fixed.

He was only forty-two years old, but the flabby flesh

under his eyes and his enormous square-cut jaw made him look fully fifty.

It was a spectacle for gods and men, to see him harangue that Union League in the platitudes of loyalty to the Union, and to watch the crowd of negroes hang breathless on his every word as the inspired Gospel of God. The only notable change in him from the old days was in his speech. He had hired a man to teach him grammar and pronunciation. He had high ambitions for the future.

"Be of good cheer, beloved!" he said to the negroes. "A great day is coming for you. You are to rule this land. Your old masters are to dig in the fields and you are to sit under the shade and be gentlemen. Old Andy Johnson will be kicked out of the White House or hung, and the farms you've worked on so long will be divided among you. You can rent them to your old masters and live in ease the balance of your life."

"Glory to God!" shouted an old negro.

"I have just been to Washington for our great leader, Amos Hogg. I've seen Mr. Sumner, Mr. Stevens and Mr. Butler. I have shown them that we can carry any state in the South, if they will only give you the ballot and take it away from enough rebels. We have promised them the votes in the Presidential election, and they are going to give us what we want."

"Hallelujah! Amen! Yas Lawd!" The fervent exclamations came from every part of the room.

After the meeting the negroes pressed around Legree and shook his hand with eagerness—the same hand that was red with the blood of their race.

When the crowd had dispersed a meeting of the leaders was held.

Dave Haley, the ex-slave trader from Kentucky who had dodged back and forth from the mountains of his

native state to the mountains of Western North Carolina and kept out of the armies, was there. He had settled in Hambright and hoped at least to get the post-
office under the new dispensation.

In the group was the full blooded negro, Tim Shelby.
He had belonged to the Shelbys of Kentucky, but had
escaped through Ohio into Canada before the war. He
had returned home with great expectations of revolutions
to follow in the wake of the victorious armies of the
North. He had been disappointed in the programme of
kindliness and mercy that immediately followed the fall
of the Confederacy; but he had been busy day and night
since the war in organising the negroes, in secretly furnishing them arms and wherever possible he had them
grouped in military posts and regularly drilled. He was
elated at the brilliant prospects which Legree's report
from Washington opened.

"Glorious news you bring us, brother!" he exclaimed
as he slapped Legree on the back.

"Yes, and it's straight."

"Did Mr. Stevens tell you so?"

"He's the man that told me."

"Well, you can tie to him. He's the master now that
rules the country," said Tim with enthusiasm.

"You bet he's runnin' it. He showed me his bill to
confiscate the property of the rebels and give it to the
truly loyal and the niggers. It's a hummer. You ought
to have seen the old man's eyes flash fire when he pulled
that bill out of his desk and read it to me."

"When will he pass it?"

"Two years, yet. He told me the fools up North were
not quite ready for it; and that he had two other bills
first, that would run the South crazy and so fire the North
that he could pass anything he wanted and hang old Andy
Johnson besides."

"Praise God," shouted Tim, as he threw his arms around Legree 'and hugged him.

Tim kept his kinky hair cut close, and when excited he had a way of wrinkling his scalp so as to lift his ears up and down like a mule. His lips were big and thick, and he combed assiduously a tiny moustache which he tried in vain to pull out in straight Napoleonic style.

He worked his scalp and ears vigourously as he exclaimed, "Tell us the whole plan, brother!"

"The plan's simple," said Legree. "Mr. Stevens is going to give the nigger the ballot, and take it from enough white men to give the niggers a majority. Then he will kick old Andy Johnson out of the White House, put the gag on the Supreme Court so the South can't appeal, pass his bill to confiscate the property of the rebels and give it to loyal men and the niggers, and run the rebels out."

"And the beauty of the plan is," said Tim with unction, "that they are going to allow the Negro to vote to give himself the ballot and not allow the white man to vote against it. That's what I call a dead sure thing."
Tim drew himself up, a sardonic grin revealing his white teeth from ear to ear, and burst into an impassioned harangue to the excited group. He was endowed with native eloquence, and had graduated from a college in Canada under the private tutorship of its professors. He was well versed in English History. He could hold an audience of negroes spell bound, and his audacity commanded the attention of the boldest white man who heard him.

Legree, Perkins and Haley cheered his wild utterances and urged him to greater flights.

He paused as though about to stop when Legree, evidently surprised and delighted at his powers said, "Go on! Go on!"

" Yes, go on," shouted Perkins. " We are done with race and colour lines."

A dreamy look came to Tim's eyes as he continued,

" Our proud white aristocrats of the South are in a panic it seems. They fear the coming power of the Negro. They fear their Desdemonas may be fascinated again by an Othello! Well, Othello's day has come at last. If he has dreamed dreams in the past his tongue dared not speak, the day is fast coming when he will put these dreams into deeds, not words.

" The South has not paid the penalties of her crimes. The work of the conqueror has not yet been done in this land. Our work now is to bring the proud low and exalt the lowly. This is the first duty of the conqueror.

" The French Revolutionists established a tannery where they tanned the hides of dead aristocrats into leather with which they shod the common people. This was France in the eighteenth century with a thousand years of Christian culture.

" When the English army conquered Scotland they hunted and killed every fugitive to a man, tore from the homes of their fallen foes their wives, stripped them naked, and made them follow the army begging bread, the laughing stock and sport of every soldier and camp follower! This was England in the meridian of Anglo-Saxon intellectual glory, the England of Shakespeare who was writing Othello to please the warlike populace.

" I say to my people now in the language of the inspired Word, ' All things are yours ! ' I have been drilling and teaching them through the Union League, the young and the old. I have told the old men that they will be just as useful as the young. If they can't carry a musket they can apply the torch when the time comes. And they are ready now to answer the call of the Lord ! "

They crowded around Tim and wrung his hand.

*   *   *   *   *   *

Early in 1867, two years after the war, Thaddeus
Stevens passed through Congress his famous bill destroying the governments of the Southern states, and di-
viding them into military districts, enfranchising the
whole negro race, and disfranchising one-fourth of the
whites. The army was sent back to the South to enforce
these decrees at the point of the bayonet. The authority
of the Supreme Court was destroyed by a supplementary
act and the South denied the right of appeal. Mr.
Stevens then introduced his bill to confiscate the property
of the white people of the South. The negroes laid
down their hoes and plows and began to gather in excited meetings. Crimes of violence increased daily. Not
a night passed but that a burning barn or home wrote its
message of anarchy on the black sky.

The negroes refused to sign any contracts to work, to
pay rents, or vacate their houses on notice even from the
Freedman's Bureau.

The negroes on General Worth's plantation, not only
refused to work, or move, but organised to prevent any
white man from putting his foot on the land.

General Worth procured a special order from the headquarters of the Freedman's Bureau for the district located at Independence. When the officer appeared and
attempted to serve this notice, the negroes mobbed
him.

A company of troops were ordered to Hambright, and
the notice served again by the Bureau official accompanied by the Captain of this company.

The negroes asked for time to hold a meeting and discuss the question. They held their meeting and gathered
fully five hundred men from the neighbourhood, all armed
with revolvers or muskets. They asked Legree and Tim
Shelby to tell them what they should do. There was no

uncertain sound in what Legree said. He looked over the
crowd of eager faces with pride and conscious power.

"Gentlemen, your duty is plain. Hold your land. It's
yours. You've worked it for a lifetime. These officers
here tell you that old Andy Johnson has pardoned General
Worth and that you have no rights on the land without
his contract. I tell you old Andy Johnson has no right
to pardon a rebel, and that he will be hung before another
year. Thaddeus Stevens, Charles Sumner and B. F.
Butler are running this country. Mr. Stevens has never
failed yet on anything he has set his hand. He has promised to give you the land. Stick to it. Shake your fist
in old Andy Johnson's face and the face of this Bureau
and tell them so. "

"Dat we will! " shouted a negro woman, as Tim
Shelby rose to speak.

"You have suffered," said Tim. " Now let the white
man suffer. Times have changed. In the old days the
white man said,

"John, come black my boots! "

"And the poor negro had to black his boots. I expect
to see the day when I will say to a white man, " Black my
boots! " And the white man will tip his hat and hurry
to do what I tell him. "

"Yes, Lawd! Glory to God! Hear dat now! "

"We will drive the white men out of this country.
That is the purpose of our friends at Washington.
If white men want to live in the South they can become
our servants. If they don't like their job they can move
to a more congenial climate. You have Congress on
your side, backed by a million bayonets. There is no
President. The Supreme Court is chained. In San Domingo no white man is allowed to vote, hold office, or
hold a foot of land. We will make this mighty South a
more glorious San Domingo. "

A frenzied shout rent the air. Tim and Legree were carried on the shoulders of stalwart men in triumphant procession with five hundred crazy negroes yelling and screaming at their heels.

The officers made their escape in the confusion and beat a hasty retreat to town. They reported the situation to headquarters, and asked for instructions.

CHAPTER XII

RED SNOW DROPS

THE spirit of anarchy was in the tainted air. The bonds that held society were loosened. Government threatened to become organised crime instead of the organised virtue of the community.

The report of crimes of unusual horror among the ignorant and the vicious began now to startle the world.

The Rev. John Durham on his rounds among the poor discovered a little negro boy whom the parents had abandoned to starve. His father had become a drunken loafer at Independence and the Freedman's Bureau delivered the child to his mother and her sister who lived in a cabin about two miles from Hambright, and ordered them to care for the boy.

A few days later the child had disappeared. A search was instituted, and the charred bones were found in an old ash heap in the woods near this cabin. The mother had knocked him in the head and burned the body in a drunken orgie with dissolute companions.

The sense of impending disaster crushed the hearts of thoughtful and serious people. One of the last acts of Governor Macon, whose office was now under the control of the military commandant at Charleston, South Carolina, was to issue a proclamation, appointing a day of fasting and prayer to God for deliverance from the ruin that threatened the state under the dominion of Legree and the negroes.

It was a memorable day in the history of the people.

In many places they met in the churches the night before, and held all-night watches and prayer meetings. They felt that a pestilence worse than the Black Death of the Middle Ages threatened to extinguish civilisation.

The Baptist church at Hambright was crowded to the doors with white-faced women and sorrowful men.

About ten o'clock in the morning, pale and haggard from a sleepless night of prayer and thought, the Preacher arose to address the people. The hush of death fell as he gazed silently over the audience for a moment. How pale his face! They had never seen him so moved with passions that stirred his inmost soul. His first words were addressed to God. He did not seem to see the people before him.

" Lord, Thou hast been our dwelling place in all generations.

" Before the mountains were brought forth or ever Thou hadst formed the earth and the world, even from everlasting to everlasting Thou art God! "

The people instinctively bowed their heads, fired by the subtle quality of intense emotion the tones of his voice communicated, and many of the people were already in tears.

" Thou turnest man to destruction: and sayest, return, ye children of men."

" Who knowest the power of thine anger? "

" Return, O Lord, how long? and let it repent Thee concerning Thy servants."

" Beloved," he continued, " it was permitted unto your fathers and brothers and children to die for their country. You must live for her in the black hour of despair. There will be no roar of guns, no long lines of gleaming bayonets, no flash of pageantry or martial music to stir your souls.

" You are called to go down, man by man, alone, naked and unarmed in the blackness of night and fight with the powers of hell for your civilisation.

" You must look this question squarely in the face. You are to be put to the supreme test. You are to stand at the judgment bar of the ages and make good your right to life. The attempt is to be deliberately made to blot out Anglo-Saxon society and substitute African barbarism.

" A few years ago a Southern Representative in a stupid rage knocked Charles Sumner down with a cane and cracked his skull. Now it is this poor cracked brain, mad with hate and revenge, that is attempting to blot the Southern states from the map of the world and build Negro territories on their ruins. In the madness of party passions, for the first time in history, an anarchist, Thaddeus Stevens, has obtained the dictatorship of a great Constitutional Government, hauled down its flag and nailed the Black Flag of Confiscation and Revenge to its masthead.

" The excuse given for this, that the lawmakers of the South attempted to reinslave the Negro by their enactments against vagrants and provisions for apprenticeship, is so weak a lie, it will not deserve the notice of a future historian. Every law passed on these subjects since the abolition of slavery was simply copied from the codes of the Northern states where free labour was the basis of society.

" Lincoln alone, with his great human heart and broad statesmanship could have saved us. But the South had no luck. Again and again in the war, victory was within her grasp, and an unseen hand snatched it away. In the hour of her defeat the bullet of a madman strikes down the great President, her last refuge in ruin!

" God alone is our help. Let us hold fast to our faith

in Him. We can only cry with aching hearts in the language of the Psalmist of old, ' How long, O Lord? how long ! '

" The voices of three men now fill the world with their bluster—Charles Sumner, a crack-brained theorist; Thaddeus Stevens, a clubfooted misanthrope, and B. F. Butler, a triumvirate of physical and mental deformity. Yet they are but the cracked reeds of a great organ that peals forth the discord of a nation's blind rage. When the storm is past, and reason rules passion, they will be flung into oblivion. We must bend to the storm. It is God's will."

The people left the church with heavy hearts. They were hopelessly depressed. In the afternoon, as the churches were being slowly emptied, groups of negroes stood on the corners talking loudly and discussing the meaning of this new Sunday so strangely observed. It began to snow. It was late in March and this was an unusual phenomenon in the South.

The next morning the earth was covered with four inches of snow, that glistened in the sun with a strange reddish hue. On examination it was found that every snow drop had in it a tiny red spot that looked like a drop of blood ! Nothing of the kind had ever been seen before in the history of the world, so far as any one knew.

This freak of nature seemed a harbinger of sure and terrible calamity. Even the most cultured and thoughtful could not shake off the impression it made.

The Preacher did his best to cheer the people in his daily intercourse with them. His Sunday sermons seemed in these darkest days unusually tender and hopeful. It was a marvel to those who heard his bitter and sorrowful speech on the day of fasting and prayer, that he could preach such sermons as those which followed.

Occasionally old Uncle Joshua Miller would ask him to preach for the negroes in their new church on Sunday afternoons. He always went, hoping to keep some sort of helpful influence over them in spite of their new leaders and teachers. It was strange to watch this man shake hands with these negroes, call them familiarly by their names, ask kindly after their families, and yet carry in his heart the presage of a coming irreconcilable conflict. For no one knew more clearly than he, that the issues were being joined from the deadly grip of that conflict of races that would determine whether this Republic would be Mulatto or Anglo-Saxon. Yet at heart he had only the kindliest feelings for these familiar dusky faces now rising a black storm above the horizon, threatening the existence of civilised society, under the leadership of Simon Legree, and Mr. Stevens.

It seemed a joke sometimes as he thought of it, a huge, preposterous joke, this actual attempt to reverse the order of nature, turn society upside down, and make a thick-lipped, flat-nosed negro but yesterday taken from the jungle, the ruler of the proudest and strongest race of men evolved in two thousand years of history. Yet when he remembered the fierce passions in the hearts of the demagogues who were experimenting with this social dynamite, it was a joke that took on a hellish, sinister meaning.

CHAPTER XIII

DICK

WHEN Charlie Gaston reached his home after a never-to-be-forgotten day in the woods with the Preacher, he found a ragged little dirt-smeared negro boy peeping through the fence into the woodyard.

"What you want?" cried Charlie.

"Nuttin!"

"What's your name?"

"Dick."

"Who's your father?"

"Haint got none. My mudder say she was tricked, en I'se de trick!" he chuckled and walled his eyes.

Charlie came close and looked him over. Dick giggled and showed the whites of his eyes.

"What made that streak on your neck?"

"Nigger done it wid er axe."

"What nigger?"

"Low life nigger name er Amos what stays roun' our house Sundays."

"What made him do it?"

"He low he wuz me daddy, en I sez he wuz er liar, en den he grab de axe en try ter chop me head off."

"Gracious, he 'most killed you!"

"Yassir, but de doctor sewed me head back, en hit grow'd."

"Goodness me!"

" Say ! " grinned Dick.

" What? "

" I likes you."

" Do you? "

" Yassir, en I aint gwine home no mo'. I done run away, en I wants ter live wid you."

" Will you help me and Nelse work? "

" Dat I will. I can do mos' anyting. You ax yer Ma fur me, en doan let dat nigger Nelse git holt er me."

Charlie's heart went out to the ragged little waif. He took him by the hand, led him into the yard, found his mother, and begged her to give him a place to sleep and keep him.

His mother tried to persuade him to make Dick go back to his own home. Nelse was loud in his objections to the new comer, and Aunt Eve looked at him as though she would throw him over the fence.

But Dick stuck doggedly to Charlie's heels.

" Mama dear, see, they tried to cut his head off with an axe," cried the boy, and he wheeled Dick around and showed the terrible scar across the back of his neck.

" I spec hits er pity dey didn't cut hit clean off," muttered Nelse.

" Mama, you can't send him back to be killed! "

" Well, darling, I'll see about it to-morrow."

" Come on Dick, I'll show you where to sleep! "

The next day Dick's mother was glad to get rid of him by binding him legally to Mrs. Gaston, and a lonely boy found a playmate and partner in work, he was never to forget.

CHAPTER XIV

THE NEGRO UPRISING

THE summer of 1867! Will ever a Southern man or woman who saw it forget its scenes? A group of oath-bound secret societies, The Union League, The Heroes of America, and The Red Strings dominating society, and marauding bands of negroes armed to the teeth terrorising the country, stealing, burning and murdering.

Labour was not only demoralised, it had ceased to exist. Depression was universal, farming paralysed, investments dead, and all property insecure. Moral obligations were dropping away from conduct, and a gulf as deep as hell and high as heaven opening between the two races.

The negro preachers openly instructed their flocks to take what they needed from their white neighbours. If any man dared prosecute a thief, the answer was a burned barn or a home in ashes.

The wildest passions held riot at Washington. The Congress of the United States as a deliberative body under constitutional forms of government no longer existed. The Speaker of the House shook his fist at the President and threatened openly to hang him, and he was arraigned for impeachment for daring to exercise the constitutional functions of his office!

The division agents of the Freedman's Bureau in the South sent to Washington the most alarming reports, declaring a famine imminent. In reply the vindictive leaders levied a tax of fifteen dollars a bale on cotton, plunging thousands of Southern farmers into immediate bankruptcy and giving to India and Egypt the mastery of the cotton markets of the world!

Congress became to the desolate South what Attila, the "*Scourge of God*" was to civilised Europe.

The Abolitionists of the North, whose conscience was the fire that kindled the Civil War, rose in solemn protest against this insanity. Their protest was drowned in the roar of multitudes maddened by demagogues who were preparing for a political campaign.

Late in August Hambright and Campbell county were thrilled with horror at the report of a terrible crime. A whole white family had been murdered in their home, the father, mother and three children in one night, and no clue to the murderers could be found.

Two days later the rumour spread over the country that a horde of negroes heavily armed were approaching Hambright burning, pillaging and murdering.

All day terrified women, some walking with babes in their arms, some riding in old wagons and carrying what household goods they could load on them, were hurrying with blanched faces into the town.

By night five hundred determined white men had answered an alarm bell and assembled in the court house. Every negro save a few faithful servants had disappeared. A strange stillness fell over the village.

Mrs. Gaston sat in her house without a light, looking anxiously out of the window, overwhelmed with the sense of helplessness. Charlie, frightened by the wild stories he had heard, was trying in spite of his fears to comfort her.

"Don't cry, Mama!"

"I'm not crying because I'm afraid, darling, I'm only crying because your father is not here to-night. I can't get used to living without him to protect us."

" I'll take care of you, Mama—Nelse and me."

" Where is Nelse? "

" He's cleaning up the shot gun."

" Tell him to come here."

When Nelse approached his Mistress asked,

" Nelse, do you really think this tale is true? "

" No, Missy, I doan believe nary word uf it. Same time I'se gettin' ready fur 'em. Ef er nigger come foolin' roun' dis house ter night, he'll t'ink he's run ergin er whole regiment! I hain't been ter wah fur nuttin'."

" Nelse, you have always been faithful. I trust you implicitly."

" De Lawd, Missy, dat you kin do! I fight fur you en dat boy till I drap dead in my tracks! "

" I believe you would. "

" Yessum, cose I would. En I wants dat swo'de er Marse Charles to-night, Missy, en Charlie ter help me sharpen 'im on de grine stone."

She took the sword from its place and handed it to Nelse. Was there just a shade of doubt in her heart as she saw his black hand close over its hilt as he drew it from the scabbard and felt its edge! If so she gave no sign.

Charlie turned the grindstone while Nelse proceeded to violate the laws of nations by putting a keen edge on the blade.

" Nebber seed no sense in dese dull swodes nohow! "

" Why ain't they sharp, Nelse? "

" Doan know, honey. Marse Charles tell me de law doan 'low it, but dey sho hain't no law now! "

" We'll sharpen it, won't we, Nelse? " whispered the boy as he turned faster.

" Dat us will, honey. En den you des watch me mow niggers ef dey come er prowlin' round dis house! "

" Did you kill many Yankees in the war, Nelse? "

" Doan know, honey, spec I did."

" Are you going to take the gun or the sword? "

" Bofe um 'em chile. I'se gwine ter shoot er pair er niggers fust, en den charge de whole gang wid dis swode. Hain't nuttin' er nigger's feard uf lak er keen edge. Wish ter God I had a razer long es dis swode! I'd des walk clean froo er whole army er niggers wid guns. Man, hit 'ud des natchelly be er sight! Day'd slam dem guns down en bust demselves open gittin' outen my way! "

When the sun rose next morning the bodies of ten negroes lay dead and wounded in the road about a mile outside of town. The pickets thrown out in every direction had discovered their approach about eleven o'clock. They were allowed to advance within a mile. There were not more than two hundred in the gang, dozens of them were drunk, and like the Sepoys of India, they were under the command of a white Scalawag. At the first volley they broke and fled in wild disorder. Their leader managed to escape.

This event cleared the atmosphere for a few weeks; and the people breathed more freely when another company of army regulars marched into the town and camped in the school grounds of the old academy.

CHAPTER XV

THE NEW CITIZEN KING

OF all the elections ever conducted by the English speaking race the one held under the " Reconstruction " act of 1867 in the South was the most unique.

Ezra Perkins the agent of the Freedman's Bureau issued a windy proclamation to the new citizens to come forward on a certain day to register and receive their ' elective franchise.'

The negroes poured into town from every direction from early dawn. Some carried baskets, some carried jugs, and some were pushing wheelbarrows, but most of them had an empty bag. They were packed around the Agency in a solid black mass.

Nelse laughed until a crowd gathered around him.

" Lordy, look at dem bags! " he shouted. " En dars ole Ike wid er jug. He's gwine ter take hisen in licker. En bress God dars er fool wid er wheel-barer! " Nelse lay down and rolled with laughter.

They failed to see the joke, and when the Agency was opened they made a break for the door, trampling each other down in a mad fear that there wouldn't be enough ' elective franchise ' to go round!

The first negro who emerged from the door came with a crestfallen face and an empty bag on his arm.

He was surrounded by anxious inquirers. " What wuz hit? "

" Nuffin. Des stan up dar befo' er man wid big whiskers en he make me swar ter export de Constertution er de Nunited States er Nor'f Calliny.

When Nelse appeared Perkins looked at him a moment and asked,

" Are you a member of the Union League? "

" Dat I hain't."

" Then stand aside and let these men register. If you want to vote you had better join."

Nelse made no reply, but in a short time he returned with the Rev. John Durham by his side. He was allowed to register, but from that day he was a marked man among his race.

When the registration closed Perkins was in high glee.

" We've got 'em, Timothy! It's a dead sure thing! " he cried as he slipped his arm around Tim's shoulder.

" Will the majority be big? " asked Tim.

" If it ain't big enough we'll disfranchise more aristocrats and enfranchise the dogs. " Tim wondered whether this proposition was altogether flattering.

During the progress of the campaign, a committee from the organisation of the " truly loyal," Ezra Perkins and Dave Haley, called on Tom Camp.

" Mr. Camp, we want your help as a leader among the poor white people to save the country from these rebel aristocrats who have ruined it," said Ezra.

" You're barkin' up the wrong tree! " answered Tom dryly.

" The poor men have got to stand together now and get their rights."

" Well if I've got to stand with niggers, have 'em hug me and blow their breath in my face, as you fellers are doin', you can count me out!—and if that's all you want with me, you'll find the door open."

Haley tried his hand.

"Look here, Camp, we ain't got no hard feelin's agin you, but there's agoin' to be trouble for every rebel in this county who don't git on our side and do it quick."

"I'm used to trouble pardner," replied Tom.

"You've got a nice little cabin home and ten acres of land. Fight us, and we will give this house and lot to a nigger."

"I don't believe it," cried Tom.

"Come, come," said Perkins, "you're not fool enough to fight us when we've got a dead sure thing, a majority fixed before the voting begins, Congress and the whole army back of us?"

"I ain't er nigger!" said Tom, doggedly.

"What's the use to be a fool Camp," cried Haley. "We are just using the nigger to stick the votes in the box. He thinks he's goin' to heaven, but we'll ride him all the way up to the gate and hitch him on the outside. Will you come in with us?"

"Don't like your complexion!" he answered rising and going toward the door.

"Then we'll turn you out into the road in less than two years," said Haley as they left.

"All right!" laughed the old soldier, "I slept on the ground four years, boys."

When he came back into the room he met his wife with tears in her eyes. "Oh! Tom, I'm afraid they'll do what they say."

"To tell you the truth, ole woman, I'm afraid so too. But we're in the hands of the Lord. This is His house. If He wants to take it away from me now when I'm crippled and helpless, He knows what's best."

"I wish you didn't have to go agin 'em."

"I ain't er nigger, ole gal, and I don't flock with niggers. If God Almighty had meant me to be one He'd have made my skin black."

On election day no publication of the polling places had been made. Ezra Perkins had in charge the whole county. He consolidated the fifteen voting precincts into three and located these in negro districts. He notified only the members of the secret Leagues where these three voting places were to be found, and other people were allowed to find them on the day of the election as best they could.

Perkins made himself the poll holder at Hambright though he was a candidate for member of the Constitutional Convention, and the poll holders were allowed to keep the ballots in their possession for three days before forwarding to the General in command at Charleston, South Carolina.

Scores of negroes, under the instructions of their leaders, voted three times that day. Every negro boy fairly well grown was allowed to vote and no questions asked as to his age.

Nelse approached the polls attempting to cast a vote against the Rev. Ezra Perkins the poll holder. A crowd of infuriated negroes surrounded him in a moment.

" Kill 'im! Knock 'im in the head! De black debbil, votin' agin his colour ! "

Nelse threw his big fists right and left and soon had an open space in the edge of which lay a half dozen negroes scrambling to get to their feet.

The negroes formed a line in front of him and the foremost one said,

" You try ter put dat vote in de box we bust yo head open ! "

Nelse knocked him down before he got the words well out of him mouth. " Honey, I'se er bad nigger!" he shouted with a grin as he stepped back and started to rush the line.

Perkins ordered the guard to arrest him.

As the guard carried Nelse away a crowd of angry negroes followed grinning and cursing.

"We lay fur you yit, ole hoss!" was their parting word as he disappeared through the jail door.

That night at the supper table in the hotel at Hambright an informal census of the voters was taken. There were present at the table a distinguished ex-judge, two lawyers, a General, two clergymen, a merchant, a farmer, and two mechanics. The only man of all allowed to vote that day was the negro who waited on the table.

Thus began the era of a corrupt and degraded ballot in the South that was to bring forth sorrow for generations yet unborn. The intelligence, culture, wealth, social prestige, brains. conscience and the historic institutions of a great state had been thrust under the hoof of ignorance and vice.

The votes were sent to the military commandant at Charleston and the results announced. The negroes had elected 110 representatives and the whites 10. It was gravely announced from Washington that a "republican form of government" had at last been established in North Carolina.

CHAPTER XVI

LEGREE SPEAKER OF THE HOUSE

THE new government was now in full swing and a saturnalia began. Amos Hogg was Governor, Simon Legree Speaker of the House, and the Hon. Tim Shelby leader of the majority on the floor of the House.

Raleigh, the quaint little City of Oaks, never saw such an assemblage of law-makers gather in the grey stone Capitol.

Ezra Perkins, who was a member of the Senate, was frugal in his habits and found lodgings at an unpretentious boarding house near the Capitol square.

The room was furnished with six iron cots on which were placed straw mattresses and six honourable members of the new Legislature occupied these. They were close enough together to allow a bottle of whiskey to be freely passed from member to member at any hour of the night. They thought the beds were arranged with this in view and were much pleased.

Ezra was the only man of the crowd who arrived in Raleigh with a valise or trunk. He had a carpet bag. The others simply had one shirt and a few odds and ends tied in red bandana handkerchiefs.

Three of them had walked all the way to Raleigh and kept in the woods from habit as deserters. The other two rode on the train and handed their tickets to the first stranger they saw on the platform of the car they boarded.

"What's this for!" said the stranger.

"Them's our tickets. Ain't you the door keeper?"

"No, but there ought to be one to every circus. You'll have one when you get to Raleigh."

The landlady, Mrs. Duke, apologised for the poor beds, when she showed them to their room. "I'm sorry, gentlemen, I can't give you softer beds."

"That's all right M'am! them's fine. Us fellows been sleeping in the woods and in straw stacks so long dodgin' ole Vance's officers, them white sheets is the finest thing we've seed in four years, er more."

They were humble and made no complaints. But at the end of the week they gathered around the Rev. Ezra Perkins for a grave consultation.

"When are we goin' ter draw?" said one.

"Air we ever goin' ter draw?" asked another with sorrow and doubt.

"What are we here fer ef we cain't draw?" pleaded another looking sadly at Ezra.

"Gentlemen," answered Ezra, "it will be all right in a little while. The Treasurer is just cranky. We can draw our mileage Monday anyhow."

At daylight they took their places on the bank's steps, and at ten o'clock when the bank opened, the doors were besieged by a mob of members painfully anxious to draw before it might be too late.

Next morning there was a disturbance at the breakfast table. The morning paper had in blazing head lines an account of one James "Mileage," who was a member of the Legislature from an adjoining county thirty-seven miles distant. He had sworn to a mileage record of one hundred and seven dollars.

"That's an unfortunate mistake, sir," said Perkins.

"Ten' ter yer own business?" answered James "Mileage."

"I call it er purty sharp trick," grinned his partner.

"I call it stealin'," sneered an honourable member, evidently envious.

And James " Mileage " was his name for all time, but " Mileage " shot a malicious look at the member who had called him a thief.

The next morning the paper of the Opposition had another biographical sketch on the front page.

"I see your name in the paper this morning, Mr. Scoggins?" remarked Mrs. Duke, looking pleasantly at the member who had spoken so rudely to James " Mileage " the day before.

"Well I reckon I'll make my mark down here before it's over," chuckled Scoggins with pride. "What do they say about me, M'am?"

"They say you stole a lot of hogs!" tittered the landlady.

Mr. Scoggins turned red.

"Oho, is there another thief in this hon'able body?" sneered James " Mileage."

"That's all a lie, M'am, 'bout them hogs. I didn' steal 'em. I just pressed 'em from a Secessiner."

"Jes so," said James " Mileage," " but they say you were a deserter at the time, and not exactly in the service of your country."

"Ye can't pay no 'tention ter rebel lies ergin Union men!" explained Scoggins, eating faster.

"Yes, that's so," said James " Mileage," " but there's another funny thing in the paper about you."

"What's that?" cried Scoggins with new alarm.

"That Mr. Scoggins met Sherman's army with loud talk about lovin' the Union, but that a mean Yankee officer gave him a cussin' fur not fightin' on one side or the other, took all that bacon he had stolen, hung him up by the heels, gave him thirty lashes and left him hanging in the air. "

"It's a lie! It's a lie!" bellowed Scoggins.

"Gentlemen! Gentlemen! we must not have such behaviour at my table!" exclaimed Mrs. Duke.

And "Hog" Scoggins was his name from that day.

By the end of the week another painful story was printed about one of this group of statesmen. The newspaper brutally declared that he had been convicted of stealing a rawhide from a neighbour's tanyard. It could not be denied. And then a sad thing happened. The moral sentiment of the little community could not endure the strain. It suddenly collapsed. They laughed at these incidents of the sad past and agreed that they were jokes. They began to call each other James "Mileage," "Hog" Scoggins, and "Rawhide" in the friendliest way, and dared a scornful world to make them feel ashamed of anything!

But the Rev. Ezra Perkins was pained by this breakdown. He felt that being safely removed two thousand miles from his own past, he might hope for a future.

"Mrs. Duke," he complained to his landlady, "I will have to ask you to give me a room to myself. I'll pay double. I want quiet where I can read my Bible and meditate occasionally."

"Certainly Mr. Perkins, if you are willing to pay for it."

It was so arranged. But this assumption of moral superiority by Perkins grieved "Mileage," "Hog" and "Rawhide," and a coolness sprang up between them, until they found Ezra one night in his place of meditation dead drunk and his room on fire. He had gone to sleep in his chair with his empty bottle by his side, and knocked the candle over on the bed. Then they agreed that forever after they would all stand together, shoulder to shoulder, until they brought the haughty low and exalted the lowly and the " loyal."

Tim Shelby early distinguished himself in this august assemblage. His wit and eloquence from the first commanded the admiration of his party.

When he had fairly established himself as leader, he rose in his seat one day with unusual gravity. His scalp was working his ears with great rapidity showing his excitement.

He had in his hands a bill on which he had spent months in secret study. He had not even hinted its contents to any of his associates. Under the call for bills his voice rang with deep emphasis.

" Mr. Speaker ! "

Legree gave him instant recognition.

" I desire to introduce the following: " A Bill to be Entitled An Act to Relieve Married Women from the Bonds of Matrimony when United to Felons, and to Define Felony."

A page hurried to the Reading Clerk with his bill.

The hum of voices ceased. The five or six representatives of the white race left their desks and walked quickly toward the Speaker. The Clerk read in a loud clear voice.

" The General Assembly of North Carolina do enact:

I That all citizens of the State who took part in the Rebellion and fought against the Union, or held office in the so called Confederate States of America, shall be held guilty of felony, and shall be forever debarred from voting or holding office."

II " That the married relations of all such felons are hereby dissolved and their wives absolutely divorced, and said felons shall be forever barred from contracting marriage or living under the same roof with their former wives."

Instantly four Carpet-bagger members of some education rushed for Tim's seat. "Withdraw that bill, man, quick! My God, are you mad!" they all cried in a breath.

Tim was dazed by this unexpected turn, and grinned in an obstinate way.

"I can't see it gentlemen. That bill will kill out the breed of rebels and fix the status of every Southern state for five hundred years. It's just what we need to make this state loyal."

"You pass that bill and hell will break loose!"

"How so, brother? Ain't we on top and the rebels on the bottom? Ain't the army here to protect us?" persisted Tim.

There was a brief consultation among the little group in opposition and the leader said,

"Mr. Speaker, I move that the bill be at once printed and laid on the desk of the members for consideration."

Tim was astonished at this move of his enemy. Legree looked at him and waited his pleasure.

"Mr. Speaker, I withdraw that bill for the present," he said at length.

That night the wires were hot between Washington and Raleigh, and the entire power of Congress was hurled upon the unhappy Tim. His bill was not only suppressed but the news agencies were threatened and subsidised to prevent accounts of its introduction being circulated throughout the country.

Tim decided to lay this measure over until Congress was off his hands, and the state's autonomy fully recognised. Then he would dare interference. In the meantime he turned his great mind to financial matters. His success here was overwhelming.

His first measure was to increase the per diem of the

members from three to seven dollars a day. It passed
with a whoop.

Uncle Pete Sawyer a coal-black fatherly looking old
darkey from an Eastern county made himself immortal
in that debate.

"Mistah Speakah!" he bawled drawing himself up
with great dignity, and holding a pen in his left hand
as though he had been writing. "What do dese white
gem'men mean by ezposen dis bill? Ef we doan pay de
members enuf, dey des be erbleeged ter steal. Hit aint
right, sah, ter fo'ce de members er dis hon'able body ter
prowl atter dark when day otter be here 'tendin' ter de
business o' de country. En I moves you, sah, Mistah
Speakah, dat dese rema'ks er mine be filed in de arkibes
er grabity!"

They were filed and embalmed in the archives of
gravity where they will remain a monument to their author and his times.

As Tim's great financial measures made progress, the
members began to wear better clothes, assumed white
linen shirts, had their shoes blacked, and put on the airs
of overworked statesmen.

When they had used up all the funds of the state in
mileage and per diem, they sold and divided the school
fund, railroad bonds worth a half million, for a hundred
thousand ready cash. It was soon found that Simon Legree, the Speaker of the House, was the master of financial
measures and Tim Shelby was his mouthpiece.

Legree organised three groups of thieves composed of
the officials needed to perfect the thefts in every branch
of the government while he retained the leadership of
the federated groups. The Treasurer, who was an honest
man, was stripped of power by a special act.

The Capitol Ring merely picked up the odds and ends
about the Capitol building. They refurnished the Legis-

lative Halls.   They spent over two hundred thousand
dollars for furniture, and when it was appraised, its value
was found to be seventeen thousand dollars at the prices
they actually paid for it.   The Ring stole one hundred
and seventy thousand dollars on this item alone.

An appropriation of three hundred thousand dollars
was made for " supplies, sundries and incidentals." With
this they built a booth around the statue of Washington
at the end of the Capitol and established a bar with fine
liquors and cigars for the free use of the members and
their friends.   They kept it open every day and night
during their reign, and in a suite of rooms in the Capitol
they established a brothel.   From the galleries a swarm
of courtesans daily smiled on their favourites on the
floor.

The printing had never cost the state more than eight
thousand dollars in any one year.   This year it cost four
hundred and eighty thousand.   Legree drew thousands
of warrants on the state for imaginary persons.   There
were eight pages in the House.   He drew pay for one
hundred and fifty-six pages.   In this way he raised an
enormous corruption fund for immediate use in bribing
the lawmakers to carry through his schemes.

The Railroad Ring was his most effective group of
brigands.

They passed bills authorising the issue of twenty-five
millions of dollars in bonds, and actually issued and stole
fourteen millions, and never built one foot of railroad.

When Legree's movement was at its high tide, Ezra
Perkins sought Uncle Pete Sawyer one night in behalf
of a pet measure of his pending in the House.

Peter was seated by his table counting by the light
of a candle three big piles of gold.

His face was wreathed in smiles.

"Peter, you seem well pleased with the world to-night?" said Ezra gleefully.

"Well, brudder, you see dem piles er yaller money?"

"Yes, it is a fine sight."

Uncle Pete smacked his lips and grinned from ear to ear.

"Well, brudder, I tells you. I ben sol' seben times in my life, but 'fore Gawd dat's de fust time I ebber got de money!"

Uncle Pete dreamed that night that Congress passed a law extending the blessings of a "republican form of government" to North Carolina for forty years and that the Legislature never adjourned.

But the Legislature finally closed, and in a drunken revel which lasted all night. They had bankrupted the state, destroyed its school funds, and increased its debt from sixteen to forty-two millions of dollars, without adding one cent to its wealth or power.

Legree then organised a Municipal and County Ring to exploit the towns, cities, and counties, having passed a bill vacating all county and city offices.

This Ring secured the control of Hambright and levied a tax of twenty-five per cent for municipal purposes! Tom Camp's little home was assessed for eighty-five dollars in taxes. Mrs. Gaston's home was assessed for one hundred and sixty dollars. They could have raised a million as easily as the sum of these assessments.

It cost the United States government two hundred millions of dollars that year to pay the army required to guard the Legrees and their "loyal" men while they were thus establishing and maintaining "a republican form of government" in the South.

CHAPTER XVII

THE SECOND REIGN OF TERROR

IT was the bluest Monday the Rev. John Durham ever remembered in his ministry. A long drought had parched the corn into twisted and stunted little stalks that looked as though they had been burnt in a prairie fire. The fly had destroyed the wheat crop and the cotton was dying in the blistering sun of August, and a blight worse than drought, or flood, or pestilence, brooded over the stricken land, flinging the shadow of its Black Death over every home. The tax gatherer of the new "republican form of government," recently established in North Carolina now demanded his pound of flesh.

The Sunday before had been a peculiarly hard one for the Preacher. He had tried by the sheer power of personal sympathy to lift the despairing people out of their gloom and make strong their faith in God. In his morning sermon he had torn his heart open and given them its red blood to drink. At the night service he could not rally from the nerve tension of the morning. He felt that he had pitiably failed. The whole day seemed a failure black and hopeless.

All day long the sorrowful stories of ruin and loss of homes were poured into his ear.

The Sheriff had advertised for sale for taxes two thousand three hundred and twenty homes in Campbell county. The land under such conditions had no value.

It was only a formality for the auctioneer to cry it and knock it down for the amount of the tax bill.

As he arose from bed with the burden of all this hopeless misery crushing his soul, a sense of utter exhaustion and loneliness came over him.

" My love, I must go back to bed and try to sleep. I lay awake last night until two o'clock. I can't eat anything," he said to his wife as she announced breakfast.

" John, dear, don't give up like that."

" Can't help it."

" But you must. Come, here is something that will tone you up. I found this note under the front door this morning."

" What is it ? "

" A notice from some of your admirers that you must leave this county in forty-eight hours or take the consequences."

He looked at this anonymous letter and smiled.

" Not such a failure after all, am I ? " he mused.

" I thought that would help you," she laughed.

" Yes, I can eat breakfast on the strength of that."

He spread this letter out beside his plate, and read and reread it as he ate, while his eyes flashed with a strange half humourous light.

" Really, that's fine, isn't it ? " " You sower of sedition and rebellion, hypocrite and false prophet. The day has come to clean this county of treason and traitors. If you dare to urge the people to further resistance to authority, there will be one traitor less in this county."

" That sounds like the voice of a Daniel come to judgment, don't it ? "

" I think Ezra Perkins might know something about it."

" I am sure of it."

" Well, I'm duly grateful, it's done for you what your wife couldn't do, cheered you up this morning."

" That is so, isn't it? It takes a violent poison sometimes to stimulate the heart's action."

" Now if you will work the garden for me, where I've been watering it the past month, you will be yourself by dinner time."

" I will. That's about all we've got to eat. I've had no salary in two months, and I've no prospects for the next two months."

He was at work in the garden when Charlie Gaston suddenly ran through the gate toward him. His face was red, his eyes streaming with tears, and his breath coming in gasps.

" Doctor, they've killed Nelse! Mama says please come down to our house as quick as you can."

" Is he dead, Charlie? "

" He's most dead. I found him down in the woods lying in a gully, one leg is broken, there's a big gash over his eye, his back is beat to a jelly, and one of his arms is broken. We put him in the wagon, and hauled him to the house. I'm afraid he's dead now. Oh me! " The boy broke down and choked with sobs.

" Run, Charlie, for the doctor, and I'll be there in a minute."

The boy flew through the gate to the doctor's house.

When the Preacher reached Mrs. Gaston's, Aunt Eve was wiping the blood from Nelse's mouth.

" De Lawd hab mussy! My po' ole man's done kilt."

" Who could have done this, Eve? "

" Dem Union Leaguers. Dey say dey wuz gwine ter kill him fur not jinin' 'em, en fur tryin' ter vote ergin 'em."

" I've been afraid of it," sighed the Preacher as he felt Nelse's pulse.

"Yassir, en now dey's done hit.   My po' ole man.   I
wish I'd a been better ter 'im.   Lawd Jesus, help me
now!"

Eve knelt by the bed and laid her face against Nelse's
while the tears rained down her black face.

"Aunt Eve, it may not be so bad," said the Preacher
hopefully.   "His pulse is getting stronger.   He has an
iron constitution.   I believe he will pull through, if
there are no internal injuries."

"Praise God! ef he do git well, I tell yer now, Marse
John, I fling er spell on dem niggers bout dis!"

"I am afraid you can do nothing with them.   The
courts are all in the hands of these scoundrels, and the
Governor of the state is at the head of the Leagues."

"I doan want no cotes, Marse John, I'se cote ennuf.
I kin cunjure dem niggers widout any cote."

The doctor pronounced his injuries dangerous but not
necessarily fatal.   Charlie and Dick watched with Eve
that night until nearly midnight.   Nelse opened his eyes,
and saw the eager face of the boy, his eyes yet red from
crying.

"I aint dead, honey!" he moaned.

"Oh! Nelse, I'm so glad!"

"Doan you believe I gwine die!   I gwine ter git eben
wid dem niggers 'fore I leab dis worl'."

Nelse spoke feebly, but there was a way about his
saying it that boded no good to his enemies, and Eve
was silent.   As Nelse improved, Eve's wrath steadily
rose.

The next day she met in the street one of the negroes
who had threatened Nelse.

"How's Mistah Gaston dis mawnin' M'am?" he asked.

Without a word of warning she sprang on him like a
tigress, bore him to the ground, grasped him by the throat
and pounded his head against a stone.   She would have

choked him to death, had not a man who was passing
come to the rescue.

"Lemme lone, man, I'se doin' de wuk er God!"

"You're committing murder, woman."

When the negro got up he jumped the fence and tore
down through a corn field, as though pursued by a
hundred devils, now and then glancing over his shoulder
to see if Eve were after him.

The Preacher tried in vain to bring the perpetrators
of this outrage on Nelse to justice. He identified six
of them positively. They were arrested, and when put
on trial immediately discharged by the judge who was
himself a member of the League that had ordered Nelse
whipped.

*   *   *   *   *

Tom Camp's daughter was now in her sixteenth year
and as plump and winsome a lassie, her Scotch mother
declared, as the Lord ever made. She was engaged to
be married to Hose Norman, a gallant poor white from
the high hill country at the foot of the mountains. Hose
came to see her every Sunday riding a black mule, gaily
trapped out in martingales with red rings, double girths
to his saddle and a flaming red tassel tied on each side of
the bridle. Tom was not altogether pleased with his
future son-in-law. He was too wild, went to too many
frolics, danced too much, drank too much whiskey and
was too handy with a revolver.

"Annie, child, you'd better think twice before you
step off with that young buck," Tom gravely warned
his daughter as he stroked her fair hair one Sunday morning while she waited for Hose to escort her to church.

"I have thought a hundred times, Paw, but what's
the use. I love him. He can just twist me 'round his
little finger. I've got to have him."

"Tom Camp, you don't want to forget you were not a saint when I stood up with you one day," cried his wife with a twinkle in her eye.

"That's a fact, ole woman," grinned Tom.

"You never give me a day's trouble after I got hold of you. Sometimes the wildest colts make the safest horses."

"Yes, that's so. It's owing to who has the breaking of 'em," thoughtfully answered Tom.

"I like Hose. He's full of fun, but he'll settle down and make her a good husband."

The girl slipped close to her mother and squeezed her hand.

"Do you love him much, child?" asked her father.

"Well enough to live and scrub and work for him and to die for him, I reckon."

"All right, that settles it, you're too many for me, you and Hose and your Maw. Get ready for it quick. We'll have the weddin' Wednesday night. This home is goin' to be sold Thursday for taxes and it will be our last night under our own roof. We'll make the best of it."

It was so fixed. On Wednesday night Hose came down from the foothills with three kindred spirits, and an old fiddler to make the music. He wanted to have a dance and plenty of liquor fresh from the mountain-dew district. But Tom put his foot down on it.

"No dancin' in my house, Hose, and no licker," said Tom with emphasis. "I'm a deacon in the Baptist church. I used to be young and as good lookin' as you, my boy, but I've done with them things. You're goin' to take my little gal now. I want you to quit your foolishness and be a man."

"I will, Tom, I will. She is the prettiest sweetest little thing in this world, and to tell you the truth I'm goin' to settle right down now to the hardest work I ever did in my life."

"That's the way to talk, my boy," said Tom putting his hand on Hose's shoulder. "You'll have enough to do these hard times to make a livin'."

They made a handsome picture, in that humble home, as they stood there before the Preacher. The young bride was trembling from head to foot with fright. Hose was trying to look grave and dignified and grinning in spite of himself whenever he looked into the face of his blushing mate. The mother was standing near, her face full of pride in her daughter's beauty and happiness, her heart all a quiver with the memories of her own wedding day seventeen years before. Tom was thinking of the morrow when he would be turned out of his home and his eyes filled with tears.

The Rev. John Durham had pronounced them man and wife and hurried away to see some people who were sick. The old fiddler was doing his best. Hose and his bride were shaking hands with their friends, and the boys were trying to tease the bridegroom with hoary old jokes.

Suddenly a black shadow fell across the doorway. The fiddle ceased, and every eye was turned to the door. The burly figure of a big negro trooper from a company stationed in the town stood before them. His face was in a broad grin, and his eyes bloodshot with whiskey. He brought his musket down on the floor with a bang.

"My frien's, I'se sorry ter disturb yer but I has orders ter search dis house."

"Show your orders," said Tom hobbling before him.

"Well, deres one un 'em!" he said still grinning as he cocked his gun and presented it toward Tom. "En ef dat aint ennuf dey's fifteen mo' stanin' 'roun' dis house. It's no use ter make er fuss. Come on, boys!"

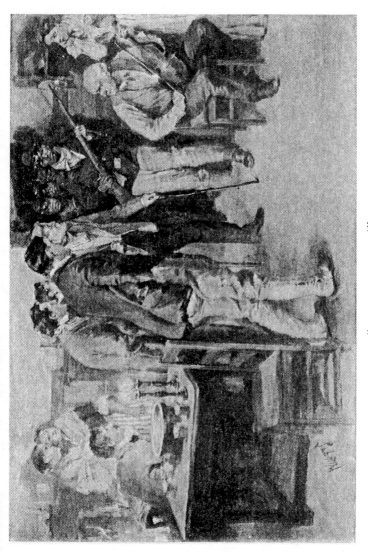

"COME ON BOYS!"

Before Tom could utter another word of protest six more negro troopers laughing and nudging one another crowded into the room. Suddenly one of them threw a bucket of water in the fire place where a pine knot blazed and two others knocked out the candles.

There was a scuffle, the quick thud of heavy blows, and Hose Norman fell to the floor senseless. A piercing scream rang from his bride as she was seized in the arms of the negro who first appeared. He rapidly bore her toward the door surrounded by the six scoundrels who had accompanied him.

" My God, save her! They are draggin' Annie out of the house," shrieked her mother.

" Help! Help! Lord have mercy!" screamed the girl as they bore her away toward the woods, still laughing and yelling.

Tom overtook one of them, snatched his wooden leg off, and knocked him down. Hose's mountain boys were crowding round Tom with their pistols in their hands.

" What shall we do, Tom? If we shoot we may kill Annie."

" Shoot, men! My God, shoot! There are things worse than death!"

They needed no urging. Like young tigers they sprang across the orchard toward the woods whence came the sound of the laughter of the negroes.

" Stop de screechin'!" cried the leader.

" She nebber get dat gag out now."

" Too smart fur de po' white trash dis time sho'!" laughed one.

Three pistol shots rang out like a single report! Three more! and three more! There was a wild scramble. Taken completely by surprise, the negroes fled in confusion. Four lay on the ground. Two were dead, one mortally wounded and three more had crawled away with bullets in their bodies. There in the midst of the heap lay the unconscious girl gagged.

"Is she hurt?" cried a mountain boy.

"Can't tell, take her to the house quick."

They laid her across the bed in the room that had been made sweet and tidy for the bride and groom. The mother bent over her quickly with a light. Just where the blue veins crossed in her delicate temple there was a round hole from which a scarlet stream was running down her white throat.

Without a word the mother brought Tom, showed it to him, and then fell into his arms and burst into a flood of tears.

"Don't, don't cry so Annie! It might have been worse. Let us thank God she was saved from them brutes."

Hose's friends crowded round Tom now with tear-stained faces.

"Tom, you don't know how broke up we all are over this. Poor child, we did the best we could."

"It's all right, boys. You've been my friends to-night. You've saved my little gal. I want to shake hands with you and thank you. If you hadn't been here—My God, I can't think of what would 'a happened! Now it's all right. She's safe in God's hands."

The next morning when Tom Camp called at the parsonage to see the Preacher and arrange for the funeral of his daughter he found him in bed.

"Dr. Durham is quite sick, Mr. Camp, but he'll see you," said Mrs. Durham.

"Thank you, M'am."

She took the old soldier by the hand and her voice choked as she said,

"You have my heart's deepest sympathy in your awful sorrow."

"It'll be all for the best, M'am. The Lord gave and

the Lord has taken away. I will still say, Blessed is the name of the Lord!"

"I wish I had such faith." She led Tom into the room where the Preacher lay.

"Why, what's this, Preacher? A bandage over your eye, looks like somebody knocked you in the head?"

"Yes, Tom, but it's nothing. I'll be all right by to-morrow. You needn't tell me anything that happened at your house. I've heard the black hell-lit news. It will be all over this county by night and the town will be full of grim-visaged men before many hours. Your child has not died in vain. A few things like this will be the trumpet of the God of our fathers that will call the sleeping manhood of the Anglo-Saxon race to life again. I must be up and about this afternoon to keep down the storm. It is not time for it to break."

"But, Preacher, what happened to you?"

"Oh! nothing much, Tom."

"I'll tell you what happened," cried Mrs. Durham standing erect with her great dark eyes flashing with anger.

"As he came home last night from a visit to the sick, he was ambushed by a gang of negroes led by a white scoundrel, knocked down, bound and gagged and placed on a pile of dry fence rails. They set fire to the pile and left him to burn to death. It attracted the attention of Doctor Graham who was passing. He got to him in time to save him."

"You don't say so!"

"I'm sorry, Tom, I'm so weak this morning I couldn't come to see you. I know your poor wife is heartbroken."

"Yes, sir, she is, and it cuts me to the quick when I think that I gave the orders to the boys to shoot. But, Preacher, I'd a killed her with my own hand if I couldn't a saved her no other way. I'd do it over again a thousand times if I had to."

" I don't blame you, I'd have done the same thing. I can't come to see you to-day, Tom, I'll be down to your house to-morrow a few minutes before we start for the cemetery. I must get up for dinner and prevent the men from attacking these troops. They'll not dare to try to sell your place to-day. The public square is full of men now, and it's only nine o'clock. You go home and cheer up your wife. How is Hose?"

" He's still in bed. The Doctor says his skull is broken in one place, but he'll be over it in a few weeks."

Tom hobbled back to his house, shaking hands with scores of silent men on the way.

The Preacher crawled to his desk and wrote this note to the young officer in command of the post,

MY DEAR CAPTAIN,

In the interest of peace and order I would advise you to telegraph to Independence for two companies of white regulars to come immediately on a special, and that you start your negro troops on double quick marching order to meet them. There will be a thousand armed men in Hambright by sundown, and no power on earth can prevent the extermination of that negro company if they attack them. I will do my best to prevent further bloodshed but I can do nothing if these troops remain here to-day. Respectfully,

JOHN DURHAM.

The Commandant acted on the advice immediately.

* * * * *

It was the week following before the sales began. There was no help for it. The town and the county

were doomed to a ruin more complete and terrible than
the four years of war had brought. Independence had
been saved by a skillful movement of General Worth,
who sought an interview with Legree when his council
first issued their levy of thirty per cent for municipal
purposes.

"Mr. Legree, let's understand one another," said the
General.

"All right, I'm a man of reason."

"A bird in hand is worth two in the bush!"

"Every time, General."

"Well, call off your dogs, and rescind your order for
a thirty per cent tax levy, and I'll raise $30,000 in cash
and pay it to you in two days."

"Make it $50,000 and it's a bargain."

"Agreed."

The General raised twenty thousand in the city, went
North and borrowed the remaining thirty thousand.

Legree and his brigands received this ransom and
moved on to the next town.

Poor Hambright was but a scrawny little village on a
red hill with no big values to be saved, and no mills to
interest the commercial world, and the auctioneer lifted
his hammer.

CHAPTER XVIII

THE RED FLAG OF THE AUCTIONEER

THE excitement through which Tom Camp had passed in the death of his daughter, and the stirring events connected with it, had been more than his feeble body could endure. He had been stricken with paroxysms of pain and nausea from his old wounds. For three days and nights he had suffered unspeakable agonies. He had borne his pain with stoical indifference.

"Tom, old man, do look at me! You skeer me," said his wife leaning tenderly over him.

"Oh! I'm all right, Annie."

"What was you studyin' about then?"

"I was just a thinkin' we didn't kill babies in the war. Them was awful times, but they wuz nothin' to what we're goin' through now. The Lord knows best, but I can't understand it."

"Well, don't talk any more. You're too weak."

"I must git up, Annie. Got to git out anyhow. The Sheriff's goin' to sell us out to-day, and I want to sorter look 'round once before we go."

So, leaning on his wife's arm, he hobbled around the place saying good-bye to its familiar objects. They stopped before the garden gate.

"Don't go in there, Tom, I can't stand it," cried his wife. "When I think of leavin' that garden I've worked so hard on all these years, and that's give us so many good things to eat, and never failed us the year round, I just feel like it'll tear my heart out."

"Do you mind the day we set out these trees, Annie, an' you, my own purty gal holdin' em fur me while I packed the dirt around 'em, and told you how sweet you wuz?"

"Yes, and I love every twig of 'em. They've all helped me in times of need. Oh! Lord, it's hard to give it up!" She couldn't keep back the tears.

"Well, now, ole woman, you mustn't break down. You're strong and well and I'm all shot to pieces and crippled and no 'count. But the Lord still lives. We'll get this place back. The Lord's just trying our faith. He thinks mebbe I'll give up."

"You think we can ever get it back?"

"General Worth sent me word he couldn't do anything now, but to let it go and keep a stiff upper lip. The General ain't no fool."

"Surely the Lord can't let us starve."

"Starve! I reckon not! The foxes have holes, the birds of the air nests, but the Son of Man had not where to lay His head, but He never starved. No, God's in Heaven. I'll trust Him."

A mocking bird whose mate had just built her nest to rear a second brood for the season was seated on the topmost branch of a cedar near the house, and singing as though he would fill heaven and earth with the glory of his love.

"Just listen at that bird, Tom!" whispered his wife.

"He does sing sweet, don't he?"

"Oh dear, oh dear, how can I give it all up! I've fed that bird and his mate for years. He knows my voice. I can call him down out of that tree. Many a night when you were away in the war he sat close to my window and sang softly to me all night. When I'd wake, I'd hear

him singin' low like he was afraid he'd wake somebody.
I'd sit down there by the window and cry for you and
dream of your comin' home till he'd sing me to sleep in
the chair. And now we've got to leave him. Oh Lord,
my heart is broken! I can't see the way!"

She buried her face on Tom's shoulder and shook with
sobs.

"Hush, hush, honey, we must face trouble. We are
used to it."

"But not this, Tom. It'll tear my heart out when I
have to leave."

"It can't be helped, Annie. We've got to pay for this
nigger government."

Eleven o'clock was the hour fixed for the sale. At
half past ten a crowd of negroes had gathered. There
were only two or three white men present, the Agent of
the Freedman's Bureau and some of his henchmen.

They began to inspect the place. Tim Shelby was
present, dressed in a suit of broadcloth and a silk hat
placed jauntily on his close-cropped scalp.

"That's a fine orchard, gentlemen," Tim exclaimed.

"Yes, en dats er fine gyarden," said a negro standing
near.

"Let's look at the house," said Tim starting to the
door.

Tom stood up in the doorway with a musket in his hand,
"Put your foot on that doorstep and I'll blow your
brains out, you flat-nosed baboon!"

Tim paused and bowed with a smile.

"Ain't the premises for sale, Mr. Camp?"

"Yes, but my family ain't for inspection by
niggers."

"Just wanted to see the condition of the house, sir,"
said Tim still smiling.

"Well, I'm livin' here yet, and don't you forget it,"

"I'LL KILL THE FIRST NIGGER THAT CROSSES THAT LINE."

answered Tom with quiet emphasis.   Tim walked away laughing.

Tom stepped out of the house, and with his wooden leg marked a dead line around the house about ten feet from each corner.   To the crowd that stood near he said in a clear ringing voice as he stood up in the doorway.

"I'll kill the first nigger that crosses that line."

There was no attempt to cross it.   They did not like the look of Tom's face as he sat there pale and silent. And they could hear the sobs of his wife inside.

The sale was a brief formality.   There was but one bidder, the Honourable Tim Shelby. It was knocked down to Tim for the sum of eighty-five dollars, the exact amount of the tax levy which Legree and his brigands had fixed.

Tim was not buying on his own account.   He was the purchasing agent of the subsidiary ring which Legree had organised to hold the real estate forfeited for taxes until a rise in value would bring them millions of profit. They had stolen from the state Treasury the money to capitalise this company.   Where it was possible to exact a cash ransom, they always took it and cancelled the tax order, preferring the certainty of good gold in their pockets to the uncertainties of politics.

They tried their best to get a cash ransom of ten thousand dollars for the town of Hambright.   But the ruined people could not raise a thousand.   So Tim Shelby as the agent of the "Union Land and Improvement Company," became the owner of farm after farm and home after home.

It was a vain hope that relief could come from any quarter.   The red flag of the Sheriff's auctioneer fluttered from two thousand three hundred and twenty doors in the county.   This was over two-thirds of the total.

Those who were saved, just escaped by the skin of their teeth. They sold old jewelry or plate that had been hidden in the war, or they sold their corn and provisions, trusting to their ability to live on dried fruit, berries, walnuts, hickory nuts, and such winter vegetables as they could raise in their gardens.

The Preacher secured for Tom a tumbled-down log cabin on the outskirts of town, with a half-acre of poor red hill land around it, which his wife at once transformed into a garden. She took up the bulbs and flowers that she had tended so lovingly about the door of their old home, and planted them with tears around this desolate cabin. Now and then she would look down at the work and cry. Then she would go bravely back to it. As nobody occupied her old home, she went back and forth until she moved all the jonquils and sweet pinks from the borders of the garden walk, and reset them in the new garden. She moved then her strawberries and rapsberries, and gooseberries, and set her fall cabbage plants. In three weeks she had transformed a desolate red clay lot into a smiling garden. She had watered every plant daily, and Tom had watched her with growing wonder and love.

"Ole woman, you're an angel!" he cried, "if God had sent one down from the skies she couldn't have done any more."

*   *   *   *   *

The problem which pressed heaviest of all on the Preacher's heart in this crisis was how to save Mrs. Gaston's home.

"If that place is sold next week, my dear," he said to his wife, "she will never survive."

"I know it. She is sinking every day. It breaks my heart to look at her."

"What can we do?"

"I'm sure I can't tell. We've given everything we have on earth except the clothes on our back. I haven't another piece of jewelry, or even an old dress."

"The tax and the costs may amount to a hundred and seventy-five dollars. There isn't a man in this county who has that much money, or I'd borrow it if I had to mortgage my body and soul to do it."

"I'll tell you what you might do," his wife suddenly exclaimed. "Telegraph your old college mate in Boston that you will accept his invitation to supply his pulpit those last two Sundays in August. They will pay you handsomely."

"It may be possible, but where am I to get the money for a telegram and a ticket?"

"Surely you can borrow some here!"

"I don't know a man in the county who has it."

"Then go to the young Commandant of the post here. Tell him the facts. Tell him that a widow of a brave Confederate soldier is about to be turned out of her home because she can't pay the taxes levied by this infamous negro government. Ask him to loan you the money for the telegram and the ticket."

The Preacher seized his hat and made his way as fast as possible to the camp. The young Captain heard his story with grave courtesy.

"Certainly, doctor," he said, "I'll loan you the forty dollars with pleasure. I wish I could do more to relieve the distress of the people. Believe me, sir, the people of the North do not dream of the awful conditions of the South. They are being fooled by the politicians. I'll thank God when I am relieved of this job and get home. What has amazed me is that you hot-headed Southern people have stood it thus far. I don't know a Northern community that would have endured it."

"Ah, Captain, the people are heartsick of bloodshed,

They surrendered in good faith. They couldn't foresee this. If they had "——

The Preacher paused, his eyes grew misty with tears, and he looked thoughtfully out on the blue mountain peaks that loomed range after range in the distance until the last bald tops were lost in the clouds.

"If General Lee had dreamed of such an infamy being forced on the South two years after his surrender, as this attempt to make the old slaves the rulers of their masters, and to destroy the Anglo-Saxon civilisation of the South—he would have withdrawn his armies into that Appalachian mountain wild and fought till every white man in the South was exterminated.

"The Confederacy went to pieces in a day, not because the South could no longer fight, but because they were fighting the flag of their fathers, and they were tired of it. They went back to the old flag. They expected to lose their slaves and repudiate the dogma of Secession forever. But, they never dreamed of Negro dominion, or Negro deification, of Negro equality and amalgamation, now being rammed down their throats with bayonets. They never dreamed of the confiscation of the desolate homes of the poor and the weak and the broken-hearted. Over two hundred thousand Southern men fought in the Union army in answer to Lincoln's call—even against their own flesh and blood. But if this program had been announced, every one of the two hundred thousand Southern soldiers who wore the blue, would have rallied around the firesides of the South. This infamy was something undreamed save in the souls of a few desperate schemers at Washington who waited their opportunity, and found it in the nation's blind agony over the death of a martyred leader."

The Preacher pressed the Captain's hand and hastened to tell Mrs. Gaston of his plans. He found her seated pale and wistful at her window looking out on the lawn, now being parched and ruined since Nelse was disabled and could no longer tend it.

Charlie was trying to kiss the tears away from her eyes.

"Mama dear, you mustn't cry any more!"

"I can't help it, darling."

"They can't take our home away from us. I tore the sign down they nailed on the door, and Dick burned it up!"

"But they will do it, Charlie. The Sheriff will sell it at auction next week, and we will never have a home of our own again."

Charlie bounded to the door and showed the Preacher in.

"I have good news for you, Mrs. Gaston! I start to Boston to-night to preach two Sundays. I am going to try to borrow the money there to save your home. We will not be too sure till it's done, but you must cheer up!"

"Oh! doctor, you're giving me a new lease on life!" she cried, looking up at him through tears of gratitude.

That night the Preacher hurried on his way to Boston.

The days dragged slowly one after another, and still no word came to the anxious waiting woman. It was only two days now until the day fixed for the sale.

She asked the Sheriff to come to see her. He was a brutal illiterate henchman of Legree, who had been appointed to the office to do his bidding. He was a brother of the immortal "Hog" Scoggins, who had represented an adjoining county in the Legislature.

"Mr. Scoggins, I've sent for you to ask you to postpone the sale until Dr. Durham returns from Boston. I expect to get the money from him to pay the tax bill."

"Can't do it, M'um. They's er lot er folks comin' ter bid on the place."

"But I tell you I'm going to pay the tax bill."

"Well, M'um, hit'll have ter be paid afore the time sot, er I'll be erbleeged to sell."

"I'm sure Dr. Durham will get the money."

"Ef he does, hit 'll be the fust time hit's happened in this county sence the sales begun."

In vain she waited for a letter or a telegram from Boston. Charlie went faithfully asking Dave Haley, the postmaster, two or three times on the arrival of each mail.

"I tell ye there's nothin' fur ye!" he yelled as he glared at the boy. "Ef ye don't go way from that winder, I'll pitch ye out the door!"

The scoundrel had recognised the letter in Dr. Durham's handwriting and had hidden it, suspecting its contents.

When the day came for the sale Mrs. Gaston tried to face the trial bravely. But it was too much for her. When she saw a great herd of negroes trampling down her flowers, laughing, cracking vulgar jokes, and swarming over the porches, she sank feebly into her chair, buried her face in her hands and gave way to a passionate flood of tears. She was roused by the thumping of heavy feet in the hall, and the unmistakable odour of perspiring negroes. They had begun to ransack the house on tours of inspection. The poor woman's head drooped and she fell to the floor in a dead swoon.

There was a sudden charge as of an armed host, the sound of blows, a wild scramble, and the house was cleared. Aunt Eve with a fire shovel, Charlie with a broken hoe handle, and Dick with a big black snake whip had cleared the air.

Aunt Eve stood on the front door-step shaking the shovel at the crowd.

"Des put yo big flat hoofs in dis house ergin! I'll split yo heads wide open! You black cattle!"

"Dat we will!" railed Dick as he cracked the whip at a little negro passing.

Charlie ran into his mother's room to see what she was doing, and found her lying across the floor on her face.

"Aunt Eve, come quick, Mama's dying!" he shouted.

They lifted her to the bed, and Dick ran for the doctor. Dr. Graham looked very grave when he had completed his examination.

"Come here, my boy, I must tell you some sad news."

Charlie's big brown eyes glanced up with a startled look into the doctor's face.

"Don't tell me she's dying, doctor, I can't stand it."

The doctor took his hand. "You're getting to be a man now, my son, you will soon be thirteen. You must be brave. Your mother will not live through the night."

The boy sank on his knees beside the still white figure, tenderly clasped her thin hand in his, and began to kiss it slowly. He would kiss it, lay his wet cheek against it, and try to warm it with his hot young blood.

It was about nine o'clock when she opened her eyes with a smile and looked into his face.

"My sweet boy," she whispered.

"Oh! Mama, do try to live! Don't leave me," he sobbed in quivering tones as he leaned over and kissed her lips. She smiled faintly again.

"Yes, I must go, dear. I am tired. Your papa is waiting for me. I see him smiling and beckoning to me now. I must go."

A sob shook the boy with an agony no words could frame.

" There, there, dear, don't," she soothingly said, " you
will grow to be a brave strong man. You will fight this
battle out, and win back our home and bring your own
bride here in the far away days of sunshine and success I see for you. She will love you, and the flowers
will blossom on the lawn again. But I am tired. Kiss
me—I must go."

Her heart fluttered on for a while, but she never spoke
again.

At ten o'clock Mrs. Durham tenderly lifted the boy
from the bedside, kissed him, and said as she led him
to his room,

" She's done with suffering, Charlie. You are going
to live with me now, and let me love you and be your
mother."

*   *   *   *   *

The Preacher had made a profound impression on his
Boston congregation.

They were charmed by his simple direct appeal to the
heart. His fiery emphasis, impassioned dogmatic faith,
his tenderness and the strange pathos of his voice swept
them off their feet. At night the big church was crowded
to the doors, and throngs were struggling in vain to gain
admittance. At the close of the services he was overwhelmed with the expressions of gratitude and heartfelt
sympathy with which they thanked him for his messages.

He was feasted and dined and taken out into the parks
behind spanking teams, until his head was dizzy with
the unaccustomed whirl.

The Preacher went through it all with a heavy heart.
Those beautiful homes with their rich carpets, handsome
furniture, and those long lines of beautiful carriages in
the parks, made a contrast with the agony of universal
ruin which he left at home that crushed his soul.

He hastened to tell the story of Mrs. Gaston to a genial old merchant who had taken a great fancy to him.

A tear glistened in the old man's eye as he quickly rose.

" Come right down to my store. I'll get you a money order before the post-office closes. I've got tickets for you to go to the Coliseum with me to-night and hear the music!—the great Peace Jubilee. We are celebrating the return of peace and prosperity, and the preservation of the Union. It's the greatest musical festival the world ever saw."

The Preacher was dazed with the sense of its sublimity and the pathetic tragedy of the South that lay back of its joy.

The great Coliseum, constructed for the. purpose, seated over forty thousand people. Such a crowd he had never seen gathered together within one building. The soul of the orator in him leaped with divine power as he glanced over the swaying ocean of human faces. There were twelve thousand trained voices in the chorus. He had dreamed of such music in Heaven when countless hosts of angels should gather around God's throne. He had never expected to hear it on this earth. He was transported with a rapture that thrilled and lifted him above the consciousness of time and sense.

They rendered the masterpieces of all the ages. The music continued hour after hour, day after day, and night after night.

The grand chorus within the Coliseum was accompanied by the ringing of bells in the city, and the firing of cannon on the common, discharged in perfect time with the melody that rolled upward from those twelve thousand voices and broke against the gates of Heaven! When every voice. was in full cry, and every instrument of music that man had ever devised, throbbed in harmony, and a hundred anvils were ringing a chorus of steel in perfect time, Parepa Rosa stepped forward on the great stage, and in a voice that rang its splendid note of triumph over all like the trumpet of the archangel, sang the Star Spangled Banner!

Men and women fainted, and one woman died, unable to endure the strain. The Preacher turned his head away and looked out of the window. A soft wind was blowing from the South. On its wings were borne to his heart the cry of the widow and orphan, the hungry and the dying still being trampled to death by a war more terrible than the first, because it was waged against the unarmed, women and children, the wounded, the starving and the defenceless! He tried in vain to keep back the tears. Bending low, he put his face in his hands and cried like a child.

"God forgive them! They know not what they do!" he moaned.

The kindly old man by his side said nothing, supposing he was overcome by the grandeur of the music.

CHAPTER XIX

THE RALLY OF THE CLANSMEN

WHEN the Preacher took the train in Boston for the South, his friendly merchant, a deacon, was by his side.

"Now, you put my name and address down in your note book, William Crane. And don't forget about us."

"I'll never forget you, deacon."

"Say, I just as well tell you," whispered the deacon bending close, "we are not going to allow you to stay down South. We'll be down after you before long—just as well be packing up!"

The Preacher smiled, looked out of the car window, and made no reply.

"Well, good-bye, Doctor, good-bye. God bless you and your work and your people! You've brought me a message warm from God's heart. I'll never forget it."

"Good-bye, deacon."

As the train whirled southward through the rich populous towns and cities of the North, again the sharp contrast with the desolation of his own land cut him like a knife. He thought of Legree and Haley, Perkins and Tim Shelby robbing widows and orphans and sweeping the poverty-stricken Southland with riot, pillage, murder and brigandage, and posing as the representatives of the conscience of the North. And his heart was heavy with sorrow.

On reaching Hambright he was thunderstruck at the

143

news of the sale of Mrs. Gaston's place and her tragic death.

"Why, my dear, I sent the money to her on the first Monday I spent in Boston!" he declared to his wife.

"It never reached her."

"Then Dave Haley, the dirty slave driver, has held that letter. I'll see to this." He hurried to the post-office.

"Mr. Haley," he exclaimed, "I sent a money order letter to Mrs. Gaston from Boston on Monday a week ago."

"Yes, sir," answered Haley in his blandest manner, "it got here the day after the sale."

"You're an infamous liar!" shouted the Preacher.

"Of course! Of course! All Union men are liars to hear rebel traitors talk."

"I'll report you to Washington for this rascality."

"So do, so do. Mor'n likely the President and the Post-Office Department 'll be glad to have this information from so great a man."

As the Preacher was leaving the post-office he encountered the Hon. Tim Shelby dressed in the height of fashion, his silk hat shining in the sun, and his eyes rolling with the joy of living. The Preacher stepped squarely in front of Tim.

"Tim Shelby, I hear you have moved into Mrs. Gaston's home and are using her furniture. By whose authority do you dare such insolence?"

"By authority of the law, sir. Mrs. Gaston died intestate. Her effects are in the hands of our County Administrator, Mr. Ezra Perkins. I'll be pleased to receive you, sir, any time you would like to call!" said Tim with a bow.

"I'll call in due time," replied the Preacher, looking Tim straight in the eye.

Haley had been peeping through the window, watching and listening to this encounter.

"These charmin' preachers think they own this county, brother Shelby," laughed Haley as he grasped Tim's outstretched hand.

"Yes, they are the curse of the state. I wish to God they had succeeded in burning him alive that night the boys tried it. They'll get him later on. Brother Haley, he's a dangerous man. He must be put out of the way, or we'll never have smooth sailing in this county."

"I believe you're right, he's just been in here cussin' me about that letter of the widder's that didn't get to her in time. He thinks he can run the post-office."

"Well, we'll show him this county's in the hands of the loyal!" added Tim.

"Heard the news from Charleston?"

"Heard it? I guess I have. I talked with the commanding General in Charleston two weeks ago. He told me then he was going to set aside that decision of the Supreme Court in a ringing order permitting the marriage of negroes to white women, and commanding its enforcement on every military post. I see he's done it in no uncertain words."

"It's a great day, brother, for the world. There'll be no more colour line. "

"Yes, times have changed," said Tim with a triumphant smile. "I guess our white hot-bloods will sweat and bluster and swear a little when they read that order. But we've got the bayonets to enforce it. They'd just as well cool down."

"That's the stuff," said Haley, taking a fresh chew of tobacco.

"Let 'em squirm. They're flat on their backs. We are on top, and we are going to stay on top. I expect to lead a fair white bride into my house before another year and have poor white aristocrats to tend my lawn." Tim worked his ears and looked up at the ceiling in a dreamy sort of way.

"That'll be a sight won't it!" exclaimed Haley with delight. "Where's that scoundrel Nelse that lived with Mrs. Gaston?"

"Oh, we fixed him," said Tim. "The black rascal wouldn't join the League, and wouldn't vote with his people, and still showed fight after we beat him half to death, so we put a levy of fifty dollars on his cabin, sold him out, and every piece of furniture, and every rag of clothes we could get hold of. He'll leave the country now, or we'll kill him next time."

"You ought to a killed him the first time, and then the job would ha' been over."

"Oh, we'll have the country in good shape in a little while, and don't you forget it."

The news of the order of the military commandant of "District No. 2," comprising the Carolinas, abrogating the decisions of the North Carolina Supreme Court, forbidding the intermarriage of negroes and whites, fell like a bombshell on Campbell county. The people had not believed that the military authorities would dare go to the length of attempting to force social equality.

This order from Charleston was not only explicit, its language was peculiarly emphatic. It apparently commanded intermarriage, and ordered the military to enforce the command at the point of the bayonet.

The feelings of the people were wrought to the pitch of fury. It needed but a word from a daring leader, and a massacre of every negro, scalawag and carpet-bagger in the county might have followed. The Rev. John Durham was busy day and night seeking to allay excitement and prevent an uprising of the white population.

Along with the announcement of this military order,

came the startling news that Simon Legree, whose infamy was known from end to end of the state, was to be the next Governor, and that the Hon. Tim Shelby was a candidate for Chief Justice of the Supreme Court.

Legree was in Washington at the time on a mission to secure a stand of twenty thousand rifles from the Secretary of War, with which to arm the negro troops he was drilling for the approaching election. The grant was made and Legree came back in triumph with his rifles.

Relief for the ruined people was now a hopeless dream. Black despair was clutching at every white man's heart. The taxpayers had held a convention and sent their representatives to Washington exposing the monstrous thefts that were being committed under the authority of the government by the organised band of thieves who were looting the state. But the thieves were the pets of politicians high in power. The committee of taxpayers were insulted and sent home to pay their taxes.

And then a thing happened in Hambright that brought matters to a sudden crisis.

The Hon. Tim Shelby as school commissioner, had printed the notices for an examination of school teachers for Campbell county. An enormous tax had been levied and collected by the county for this purpose, but no school had been opened. Tim announced, however, that the school would be surely opened the first Monday in October.

Miss Mollie Graham, the pretty niece of the old doctor, was struggling to support a blind mother and four younger children. Her father and brother had been killed in the war. Their house had been sold for taxes, and they were required now to pay Tim Shelby ten dollars a month for rent. When she saw that school notice her heart gave a leap. If she could only get the place, it would save them from beggary.

She fairly ran to the Preacher to get his advice.

"Certainly, child, try for it. It's humiliating to ask such a favour of that black ape, but if you can save your loved ones, do it."

So with trembling hand she knocked at Tim's door. He required all applicants to apply personally at his house. Tim met her with the bows and smirks of a dancing master.

"Delighted to see your pretty face this morning, Miss Graham," he cried enthusiastically.

The girl blushed and hesitated at the door.

"Just walk right in the parlour, I'll join you in a moment."

She bravely set her lips and entered.

"And now what can I do for you, Miss Graham?"

"I've come to apply for a teacher's place in the school."

"Ah indeed, I'm glad to know that. There is only one difficulty. You must be loyal. Your people were rebels, and the new government has determined to have only loyal teachers."

"I think I'm loyal enough to the old flag now that our people have surrendered," said the girl.

"Yes, yes, I dare say, but do you think you can accept the new régime of government and society which we are now establishing in the South? We have abolished the colour line. Would you have a mixed school if assigned one?"

"I think I'd prefer to teach a negro school outright to a mixed one," she said after a moment's hesitation.

Tim continued, "You know we are living in a new world. The supreme law of the land has broken down every barrier of race and we are henceforth to be one people. The struggle for existence knows no race or colour. It's a struggle now for bread. I'm in a position to be of great help to you and your family if you will only let me."

The girl suddenly rose impelled by some resistless instinct.

" May I have the place then? " she asked approaching the door.

" Well, now you know it depends really altogether on my fancy. I'll tell you what I'll do. You're still full of silly prejudices. I can see that. But if you will overcome them enough to do one thing for me as a test, that will cost you nothing and of which the world will never be the wiser, I'll give you the place and more, I'll remit the ten dollars a month rent you're now paying. Will you do it? "

" What is it? " the girl asked with pale quivering lips.

" Let me kiss you—once! " he whispered.

With a scream, she sprang past him out of the door, ran like a deer across the lawn, and fell sobbing in her mother's arms when she reached her home.

The next day the town was unusually quiet. Tim had business with the Commandant of the company of regulars still quartered at Hambright. He spent most of the day with him, and walked about the streets ostentatiously showing his familiarity with the corporal who accompanied him. A guard of three soldiers was stationed around Tim's house for two nights and then withdrawn.

The next night at twelve o'clock two hundred white-robed horses assembled around the old home of Mrs. Gaston where Tim was sleeping. The moon was full and flooded the lawn with silver glory. On those horses sat two hundred white-robed silent men whose close-fitting hood disguises looked like the mail helmets of ancient knights.

It was the work of a moment to seize Tim, and bind

him across a horse's back. Slowly the grim procession moved to the court house square.

When the sun rose next morning the lifeless body of Tim Shelby was dangling from a rope tied to the iron rail of the balcony of the court house. His neck was broken and his body was hanging low—scarcely three feet from the ground. His thick lips had been split with a sharp knife and from his teeth hung this placard:

> " The answer of the Anglo-Saxon race to Negro lips that dare pollute with words the womanhood of the South. K. K. K."

And the Ku Klux Klan was master of Campbell county.

The origin of this Law and Order League which sprang up like magic in a night and nullified the programme of Congress though backed by an army of a million veteran soldiers, is yet a mystery.

The simple truth is, it was a spontaneous and resistless racial uprising of clansmen of highland origin living along the Appalachian mountains and foothills of the South, and it appeared almost simultaneously in every Southern state produced by the same terrible conditions.

It was the answer to their foes of a proud and indomitable race of men driven to the wall. In the hour of their defeat they laid down their arms and accepted in good faith the results of the war. And then, when unarmed and defenceless, a group of pot-house politicians for political ends, renewed the war, and attempted to wipe out the civilisation of the South.

This Invisible Empire of White Robed Anglo-Saxon Knights was simply the old answer of organised manhood to organised crime. Its purpose was to bring order out of chaos, protect the weak and defenceless, the widows and orphans of brave men who had died for their country, to drive from power the thieves who were robbing

the people, redeem the commonwealth from infamy, and
reëstablish civilisation.

Within one week from its appearance, life and property were as safe as in any Northern community.

When the negroes came home from their League meeting one night they ran terror stricken past long rows of
white horsemen. Not a word was spoken, but that was
the last meeting the " Union League of America " ever
held in Hambright.

Every negro found guilty of a misdemeanor was
promptly thrashed and warned against its recurrence.
The sudden appearance of this host of white cavalry
grasping at their throats with the grip of cold steel struck
the heart of Legree and his followers with the chill of a
deadly fear.

It meant inevitable ruin, overthrow, and a prison cell
for the " loyal " statesmen who were with him in his
efforts to maintain the new " republican form of government " in North Carolina.

At the approaching election, this white terror could
intimidate every negro in the state unless he could arm
them all, suspend the writ of *Habeas Corpus,* and place
every county under the strictest martial law.

Washington was besieged by a terrified army of the
" loyal " who saw their occupation threatened. They
begged for more troops, more guns for negro militia, and
for the reëstablishment of universal martial law until the
votes were properly counted.

But the great statesmen laughed them to scorn as a
set of weak cowards and fools frightened by negro stories
of ghosts. It was incredible to them that the crushed,
poverty stricken and unarmed South could dare challenge
the power of the National Government. They were sent
back with scant comfort.

The night that Ezra Perkins and Haley got back from

Washington, where they had gone summoned by Legree and Hogg, to testify to the death of Tim Shelby, they saw a sight that made their souls quake.

At ten o'clock, the Ku Klux Klan held a formal parade through the streets of Hambright. How the news was circulated nobody knew, but it seemed everybody in the county knew of it. The streets were lined with thousands of people who had poured in town that afternoon.

At exactly ten o'clock, a bugle call was heard on the hill to the west of the town, and the muffled tread of soft shod horses came faintly on their ears. Women stood on the sidewalks, holding their babies and smiling, and children were laughing and playing in the streets.

They rode four abreast in perfect order slowly through the town. It was utterly impossibly to recognise a man or a horse, so complete was the simple disguise of the white sheet which blanketed the horse fitting closely over his head and ears and falling gracefully over his form toward the ground.

No citizen of Hambright was in the procession. They were all in the streets watching it pass. There were fifteen hundred men in line. But the reports next day all agreed in fixing the number at over five thousand.

Perkins and Haley had watched it from a darkened room.

"Brother Haley, that's the end! Lord I wish I was back in Michigan, jail er no jail," said Perkins mopping the perspiration from his brow.

"We'll have ter dig out purty quick, I reckon," answered Haley.

"And to think them fools at Washington laughed at us!" cried Perkins clinching his fists.

And that night, mothers and fathers gathered their children to bed with a sense of grateful security they had not felt through years of war and turmoil.

CHAPTER XX

HOW CIVILISATION WAS SAVED

THE success of the Ku Klux Klan was so complete, its organisers were dazed. Its appeal to the ignorance and superstition of the Negro at once reduced the race to obedience and order. Its threat against the scalawag and carpet-bagger struck terror to their craven souls, and the " Union League," " Red Strings," and " Heroes of America " went to pieces with incredible rapidity.

Major Stuart Dameron, the chief of the Klan in Campbell county was holding a conference with the Rev. John Durham in his study.

" Doctor, our work has succeeded beyond our wildest dream."

" Yes, and I thank God we can breathe freely if only for a moment, Major. The danger now lies in our success. We are necessarily playing with fire."

" I know it, and it requires my time day and night to prevent reckless men from disgracing us."

" It will not be necessary to enforce the death penalty against any other man in this county, Major. The execution of Tim Shelby was absolutely necessary at the time and it has been sufficient."

" I agree with you. I've impressed this on the master of every lodge, but some of them are growing reckless."

" Who are they? "

" Young Allan McLeod for one. He is a dare devil and only eighteen years old.

"He's a troublesome boy. I don't seem to have any influence with him. But I think Mrs. Durham can manage him. He seems to think a great deal of her, and in spite of his wild habits, he comes regularly to her Sunday School class."

"I hope she can bring him to his senses."

"Leave him to me then a while. We will see what can be done."

*   *   *   *   *

Hogg's Legislature promptly declared the Scotch-Irish hill counties in a state of insurrection, passed a militia bill, and the Governor issued a proclamation suspending the writ of *Habeas Corpus* in these counties.

Fearing the effects of negro militia in the hill districts, he surprised Hambright by suddenly marching into the court house square a regiment of white mountain guerrillas recruited from the outlaws of East Tennessee and commanded by a noted desperado, Colonel Henry Berry. The regiment had two pieces of field artillery.

It was impossible for them to secure evidence against any member of the Klan unless by the intimidation of some coward who could be made to confess. Not a disguise had ever been penetrated. It was the rule of the order for its decrees to be executed in the district issuing the decree by the lodge furthest removed in the county from the scene. In this way not a man or a horse was ever identified.

The Colonel made an easy solution of this difficulty, however. Acting under instructions from Governor Hogg, he secured from Haley and Perkins a list of every influential man in every precinct in the county, and a list of possible turncoats and cowards. He detailed five hundred of his men to make arrests, distributed them throughout the county and arrested without warrants over two hundred citizens in one day.

The next day Berry hand-cuffed together the Rev. John Durham and Major Dameron, and led them escorted by a company of cavalry on a grand circuit of the county, that the people might be terrified by the sight of their chains. An ominous silence greeted them on every hand. Additional arrests were made by this troop and twenty-five more prisoners led into Hambright the next day.

The jail was crowded, and the court house was used as a jail. Over a hundred and fifty men were confined in the court room. Rev. John Durham was everywhere among the crowd, laughing, joking and cheering the men.

" Major Dameron, a jail never held so many honest men before," he said with a smile, as he looked over the crowd of his church members gathered from every quarter of the county.

" Well, Doctor, you've got a quorum here of your church and you can call them to order for business."

" That's a fact, isn't it ? "

" There's old Deacon Kline over there who looks like he wished he hadn't come ! " The Preacher walked over to the deacon.

" What's the matter, brother Kline, you look pensive ? "

The deacon laughed. " Yes, I don't like my bed. I'm used to feathers."

" Well, they say they are going to give you feathers mixed with tar so you won't lose them so easily."

" I'll have company, I reckon," said the deacon with a wink.

" The funny thing, deacon, is that Major Dameron tells me there isn't a man in all the crowd of two hundred and fifty arrested who ever went on a raid. It's too bad you old fellows have to pay for the follies of youth."

" It is tough. But we can stand it, Preacher." They clasped hands.

"Haven't smelled a coward anywhere have you, deacon?"

"I've seen one or two a little fidgety, I thought. Cheer 'em up with a word, Preacher."

Springing on the platform of the judge's desk he looked over the crowd for a moment, and a cheer shook the building.

"Boys, I don't believe there's a single coward in our ranks." Another cheer.

"Just keep cool now and let our enemies do the talking. In ten days every man of you will be back at home at his work."

"How will we get out with the writ suspended?" asked a man standing near.

"That's the richest thing of all. A United States judge has just decided that the Governor of the state cannot suspend the rights of a citizen of the United States under the new Fourteenth Amendment to the Constitution so recently rammed down our throats. Hogg is hoisted on his own petard. Our lawyers are now serving out writs of *Habeas Corpus* before this Federal judge under the Fourteenth Amendment, and you will be discharged in less than ten days unless there's a skunk among you. And I don't smell one anywhere." Again a cheer shook the building.

An orderly walked up to the Preacher and handed him a note.

"What is it?"

"Read it!" The men crowded around.

"Read it, Major Dameron, I'm dumb." said the Preacher.

"A military order from the dirty rascal, Berry, commanding the mountain bummers, forbidding the Rev. John Durham to speak during his imprisonment!"

A roar of laughter followed this announcement.

"That's cruel!   It'll kill him!" cried deacon Kline as he jabbed the Preacher in the ribs.

In a few minutes, the Preacher was back in his place with five of the best singers from his church by his side. He began to sing the old hymns of Zion and every man in the room joined until the building quivered with melody.

"Now a good old Yankee hymn, that suits this hour, written by an an old Baptist preacher I met in Boston the other day!" cried the Preacher.

> "My country 'tis of thee,
> Sweet land of liberty,
> Of thee I sing!"

Heavens, how they sang it, while the Preacher lined it off, stood above them beating time, and led in a clear mighty voice!   Again the orderly appeared with a note.

"What is it now?" they cried on every side.

Again Major Dameron announced "Military order No. 2, forbidding the Rev. John Durham to sing or induce anybody to sing while in prison."

Another roar of laughter that broke into a cheer which made the glass rattle.   When the soldier had disappeared, the Rev. John Durham ascended the platform, looked about him with a humourous twinkle in his eye, straightened himself to his full height and crowed like a rooster! A cheer shook the building to its foundations.   Roar after roar of its defiant cadence swept across the square and made Haley and Perkins tremble as they looked at each other over their conference table with Berry.

"What the devil's the matter now?" cried Haley.

"Do you suppose it's a rescue?" whispered Perkins.

"No, it's some new trick of that damned Preacher.   I'll chain him in a room to himself," growled Berry.

"Better not, Colonel. He's the pet of these white devils. Ye'd better let him alone." Berry accepted the advice.

Five days later the prisoners were arraigned before the United States judge, Preston Rivers, at Independence. Not a scrap of evidence could be produced against them. Governor Hogg was present, with a flaming military escort. He held a stormy interview with Judge Rivers.

"If you discharge these prisoners, you destroy the government of this state, sir!" thundered Hogg.

"Are they not citizens of the United States? Does not the Fourteenth Amendment apply to a white man as well as a negro?" quietly asked the judge.

"Yes, but they are conspirators against the Union. They are murderers and felons."

"Then prove it in my court and I'll hand them back to you. They are entitled to a trial, under our Constitution."

"I'll demand your removal by the President," shouted Hogg.

"Get out of this room, or I'll remove you with the point of my boot!" thundered the judge with rising wrath. "You have suspended the writ of *Habeas Corpus* to win a political campaign. The Ku Klux Klan has broken up your Leagues. You are fighting for your life. But I'll tell you now, you can't suspend the Constitution of the United States while I'm a Federal judge in this state. I am not a henchman of yours to do your dirty campaign work. The election is but ten days off. Your scheme is plain enough. But if you want to keep these men in prison it will be done on sworn evidence of guilt and a warrant, not on your personal whim."

The Governor cursed, raved and threatened in vain. Judge Rivers discharged every prisoner and warned Colonel Berry against the repetition of such arrests within his jurisdiction.

When these prisoners were discharged, a great mass-meeting was called to give them a reception in the public square of Independence. A platform was hastily built in the square and that night five thousand excited people crowded past the stand, shook hands with the men and cheered till they were hoarse. The Governor watched the demonstration in helpless fury from his room in the hotel.

The speaking began at nine o'clock. Every discordant element of the old South's furious political passions was now melted into harmonious unity. Whig and Democrat who had fought one another with relentless hatred sat side by side on that platform. Secessionist and Unionist now clasped hands. It was a White Man's Party, and against it stood in solid array the Black Man's Party, led by Simon Legree.

Henceforth there could be but one issue, are you a White Man or a Negro?

They declared there was but one question to be settled:—

" Shall the future American be an Anglo-Saxon or a Mulatto? "

These determined impassioned men believed that this question was more important than any theory of tariff or finance and that it was larger than the South, or even the nation, and held in its solution the brightest hopes of the progress of the human race. And they believed that they were ordained of God in this crisis to give this question its first authoritative answer.

The state burst into a flame of excitement that fused in its white heat the whole Anglo-Saxon race.

In vain Hogg marched and counter-marched his twenty thousand state troops. They only added fuel to the fire. If they arrested a man, he became forthwith a hero and was given an ovation. They sent bands of music and played at the jail doors, and the ladies filled the jail with every delicacy that could tempt the appetite or appeal to the senses.

Hogg and Legree were in a panic of fear with the certainty of defeat, exposure and a felon's cell yawning before them.

Two days before the election, the prayer meeting was held at eight o'clock in the Baptist church at Hambright. It was the usual mid-week service, but the attendance was unusually large.

After the meeting, the Preacher, Major Dameron, and eleven men quietly walked back to the church and assembled in the pastor's study. The door opened at the rear of the church and could be approached by a side street.

" Gentlemen," said Major Dameron, " I've asked you here to-night to deliver to you the most important order I have ever given, and to have Dr. Durham as our chaplain to aid me in impressing on you its great urgency."

" We're ready for orders, Chief," said young Ambrose Kline, the deacon's son.

" You are to call out every troop of the Klan in full force the night before the election. You are to visit every negro in the county, and warn every one as he values his life not to approach the polls at this election Those who come, will be allowed to vote without molestation. All cowards will stay at home. Any man, black or white, who can be scared out of his ballot is not fit to have one. Back of every ballot is the red blood of the man that votes. The ballot is force. This is simply a test of manhood. It will be enough to show who is fit to rule the state. As the masters of the eleven township lodges of the Klan, you are the sole guardians of society to-day.

When a civilised government has been restored, your work will be done.

"We will do it, sir," cried Kline.

"Let me say, men," said the Preacher, "that I heartily endorse the plan of your chief. See that the work is done thoroughly and it will be done for all time. In a sense this is fraud. But it is the fraud of war. The spy is a fraud, but we must use him when we fight. Is war justifiable?

"It is too late now for us to discuss that question. We are in a war, the most ghastly and hellish ever waged, a war on women and children, the starving and the wounded, and that with sharpened swords. The Turk and Saracen once waged such a war. We must face it and fight it out. Shall we flinch?"

"No! no!" came the passionate answer from every man.

"You are asked to violate for the moment a statutory law. There is a higher law. You are the sworn officers of that higher law."

The group of leaders left the church with enthusiasm and on the following night they carried out their instructions to the letter.

The election was remarkably quiet. Thousands of soldiers were used at the polls by Hogg's orders. But they seemed to make no impression on the determined men who marched up between their fifes and put the ballots in the box.

Legree's ticket was buried beneath an avalanche. The new "Conservative" party carried every county in the state save twelve and elected one hundred and six members of the new Legislature out of a total of one hundred and twenty.

The next day hundreds of carpet-bagger thieves fled to the North, and Legree led the procession.

Legree had on deposit in New York two millions of dollars, and the total amount of his part of the thefts he had engineered reached five millions. He opened an office on Wall Street, bought a seat in the Stock Exchange, and became one of the most daring and successful of a group of robbers who preyed on the industries of the nation.

The new Legislature appointed a Fraud Commission which uncovered the infamies of the Legree régime, but every thief had escaped. They promptly impeached the Governor and removed him from office, and the old commonwealth once more lifted up her head and took her place in the ranks of civilised communities.

CHAPTER XXI

THE OLD AND THE NEW NEGRO

NELSE was elated over the defeat and dissolution of the Leagues that had persecuted him with such malignant hatred. When the news of the election came he was still in bed suffering from his wounds. He had received an internal injury that threatened to prove fatal.

"Dar now!" he cried, sitting up in bed, "Ain't I done tole you no kinky-headed niggers gwine ter run dis gov'ment!"

"Keep still dar, ole man, you'll be faintin' ergin," worried Aunt Eve.

"Na honey, I'se feelin' better. Gwine ter git up and meander down town en ax dem niggers how's de Ku Kluxes comin' on dese days."

In spite of all Eve could say he crawled out of bed, fumbled into his clothes and started down town, leaning heavily on his cane. He had gone about a block, when he suddenly reeled and fell. Eve was watching him from the door, and was quickly by his side. He died that afternoon at three o'clock. He regained consciousness before the end, and asked Eve for his banjo.

He put it lovingly into the hands of Charlie Gaston who stood by the bed crying.

"You keep 'er, honey. You lub 'er talk better'n any body in de worl', en 'member Nelse when you hear 'er moan en sigh. En when she talk short en sassy en make

163

'em all gin ter shuffle, dat's me too.   Dat's me got back
in 'er. "

   Charlie Gaston rode with Aunt Eve to the cemetery.
He walked back home through the fields with Dick.

   " I wouldn' cry 'bout er ole nigger ! " said Dick looking into his reddened eyes.

   " Can't help it.   He was my best friend."

   " Haint I wid you ? "

   " Yes, but you ain't Nelse."

   " Well, I stan' by you des de same."

CHAPTER XXII

THE DANGER OF PLAYING WITH FIRE

THE following Saturday the Rev. John Durham preached at a cross roads school house in the woods about ten miles from Hambright. He preached every Saturday in the year at such a mission station. He was fond of taking Charlie with him on these trips. There was an unusually large crowd in attendance, and the Preacher was much pleased at this evidence of interest. It had been a hard community to impress. At the close of the services, while the Preacher was shaking hands with the people, Charlie elbowed his way rapidly among the throng to his side.

"Doctor, there's a nigger man out at the buggy says he wants to see you quick," he whispered.

"All right, Charlie, in a minute."

"Says to come right now. It's a matter of life and death, and he don't want to come into the crowd."

A troubled look flashed over the Preacher's face and he hastily followed the boy, fearing now a sinister meaning to his great crowd.

"Preacher," said the negro looking timidly around, "de Ku Klux is gwine ter kill ole Uncle Rufus Lattimore ter night. I come ter see ef you can't save him. He aint done nuthin' in God's worl' 'cept he would'n' pull his waggin clear outen de road one day fur dat redheaded Allan McLeod ter pass, en he cussed 'im black and blue en tole 'im he gwine git eben wid 'im."

" How do you know this? "

" I wuz huntin' in de woods en hear a racket en clim' er tree. En de Ku Kluxes had der meetin' right under de tree. En I hear ev'ry word."

" Who was leading the crowd? "

" Dat Allan McLeod, en Hose Norman."

" Where are they going to meet? "

" Right at de cross-roads here at de school house at mid-night. Dey sont er man atter plenty er licker en dey gwine ter git drunk fust. I was erfeered ter come ter de meetin' case I see er lot er de boys in de crowd. Fur de Lawd sake, Preacher, do save de ole man. He des es harmless ez er chile. En I'm gwine ter marry his gal, en she des plum crazy. We'se got five men ter fight fur 'im but I spec dey kill 'em all ef you can't he'p us."

" Are you one of General Worth's negroes? "

" Yassir. I run erway up here, 'bout dat Free'mens Bureau trick dey put me up ter, but I'se larned better sense now."

" Well, Sam, you go to Uncle Rufus and tell him not to be afraid. I'll stop this business before night."

The negro stepped into the woods and disappeared.

" Charlie, we must hurry," said the Preacher springing in his buggy. He was driving a beautiful bay mare, a gift from a Kentucky friend. Her sleek glistening skin and big round veins showed her fine blood.

" Well, Nancy, it's your life now or a man's, or maybe a dozen. You must take us to Hambright in fifty minutes over these rough hills! " cried the Preacher. And he gave her the reins.

The mare bounded forward with a rush that sent four spinning circles of sand and dust from each wheel. She had seldom felt the lines slacken across her beautiful back except in some great emergency. She swung past buggies and wagons without a pause. The people wondered why the Preacher was in such a hurry. Over long sand stretches of heavy road the mare flew in a cloud of dust. The Preacher's lips were firmly set, and a scowl on his brow. They had made five miles without slackening up.

The mare was now a mass of white foam, her big-veined nostrils wide open and quivering, and her eyes flashing with the fire of proud ancestry. The slackened lines on her back seemed to her an insufferable insult!

"Doctor, you'll kill Nancy!" pleaded Charlie.

"Can't help it, son, there's a lot of drunken devils, masquerading as Ku Klux, going to kill a man to-night. If we can't reach Major Dameron's in time for him to get a lot of men and stop them there'll be a terrible tragedy."

On the mare flew lifting her proud sensitive head higher and higher, while her heart beat her foaming flanks like a trip hammer. She never slackened her speed for the ten miles, but dashed up to Major Dameron's gate at sundown, just forty-nine minutes from the time she started. The Preacher patted her dripping neck.

"Good, Nancy! good! I believe you've got a soul!"

She stood with her head still high, pawing the ground.

"Major Dameron, I've driven my mare here at a killing speed to tell you that young McLeod and Hose Norman have a crowd of desperadoes organised to kill old Rufus Lattimore to-night. You must get enough men together, and get there in time to stop them. Sam Worth overheard their plot, knows every one of them, and there will be a battle if they attempt it."

"My God!" exclaimed the Major.

"You haven't a minute to spare. They are already loading up on moonshine whiskey."

"Doctor Durham, this is the end of the Ku Klux Klan in this county. I'll break up every lodge in the next forty-eight hours. It's too easy for vicious men to abuse it. Its power is too great. Besides its work is done."

" I was just going to ask you to take that step, Major. And now for God's sake get there in time to-night. I'd go with you but my mare can't stand it."

" I'll be there on time. Never fear," replied the Major, springing on his horse already saddled at the door.

The Preacher drove slowly to his home, the mare pulling steadily on her lines. She walked proudly into her stable lot, her head high and fine eyes flashing, reeled and fell dead in the shafts! The Preacher couldn't keep back the tears. He called Dick and left him and Charlie the sorrowful task of taking off her harness. He hurried into the house and shut himself up in his study.

That night when the crowd of young toughs assembled at their rendezvous it was barely ten o'clock.

Suddenly a pistol shot rang from behind the school-house, and before McLeod and his crowd knew what had happened fifty white horsemen wheeled into a circle about them. They were completely surprised and cowed.

Major Dameron rode up to McLeod.

" Young man, you are the prisoner of the Chief of the Ku Klux Klan of Campbell county. Lift your hand now and I'll hang you in five minutes. You have forfeited your life by disobedience to my orders. You go back to Hambright with me under guard. Whether I execute you depends on the outcome of the next two days' conferences with the chiefs of the township lodges."

The Major wheeled his horse and rode home. The next day he ordered every one of the eleven township chiefs to report in person to him, at different hours the same day. To each one his message was the same. He dissolved the order and issued a perpetual injunction against any division of the Klan ever going on another raid.

There were only a few who could see the wisdom of such hasty action. The success had been so marvellous, their power so absolute, it seemed a pity to throw it all away. Young Kline especially begged the Major to postpone his action.

" It's impossible Kline. The Klan has done its work. The carpet-baggers have fled. The state is redeemed from the infamies of a negro government, and we have a clean economical administration, and we can keep it so as long as the white people are a unit without any secret societies."

" But, Major, we may be needed again."

" I can't assume the responsibility any longer. The thing is getting beyond my control. The order is full of wild youngsters and revengeful men. They try to bring their grudges against neighbours into the order, and when I refuse to authorise a raid, they take their disguises and go without authority. An archangel couldn't command such a force."

Within two weeks from the dissolution of the Klan by its Chief, every lodge had been reorganised. Some of the older men had dropped out, but more young men were initiated to take their places. Allan McLeod led in this work of prompt reorganisation, and was elected Chief of the county by the younger element which now had a large majority.

He at once served notice on Major Dameron, the former Chief, that if he dared to interfere with his work even by opening his mouth in criticism, he would order a raid, and thrash him.

When the Major found this note under his door one morning, he read and re-read it with increasing wrath. Springing on his horse he went in search of McLeod. He saw him leisurely crossing the street going from the hotel to the court house.

Throwing his horse's rein to a passing boy, he walked rapidly to him and, without a word, boxed his ears as a father would an impudent child. McLeod was so astonished, he hesitated for a moment whether to strike or to run. He did neither, but blushed red and stammered,

"What do you mean, sir?"

"Read that letter, you young whelp!" The Major thrust the letter into his hand.

"I know nothing of this."

"You're a liar. You are its author. No other fool in this county would have conceived it. Now, let me give you a little notice. I am prepared for you and your crowd. Call any time. I can whip a hundred puppies of your breed any time by myself with one hand tied behind me, and never get a scratch. Dare to lift your finger against me, or any of the men who refused to go with your new fool's movement, and I'll shoot you on sight as I would a mad dog." Before McLeod could reply, the Major turned on his heels and left him.

McLeod made no further attempt to molest the Major, nor did he allow any raids bent on murder. The sudden authority placed in his hands in a measure sobered him. He inaugurated a series of petty deviltries, whipping negroes and poor white men against whom some of his crowd had a grudge, and annoying the school teachers of negro schools.

CHAPTER XXIII

THE BIRTH OF A SCALAWAG

THE overwhelming defeat of their pets in the South, and the toppling of their houses of paper built on Negro supremacy, brought to Congress a sense of guilt and shame, that required action. Their own agents in the South were now in the penitentiary or in exile for well established felonies, and the future looked dark.

They found the scapegoat in these fool later day Ku Klux marauders. Once more the public square at Hambright saw the bivouac of the regular troops of the United States Army. The Preacher saw the glint of their bayonets with a sense of relief.

With this army came a corps of skilled detectives, who set to work. All that was necessary, was to arrest and threaten with summary death a coward, and they got all the information he could give. The jail was choked with prisoners and every day saw a squad depart for the stockade at Independence. Sam Worth gave information that led to the immediate arrest of Allan McLeod. He was the first man led into the jail.

The officers had a long conference with him that lasted four hours.

And then the bottom fell out. A wild stampede of young men for the West! Somebody who held the names of every man in the order had proved a traitor.

Every night from hundreds of humble homes might
be heard the choking sobs of a mother saying good-bye in
the darkness to the last boy the war had left her old age.
When the good-bye was said, and the father, waiting in
the buggy at the gate, had called for haste, and the boy
was hurrying out with his grip-sack, there was a moan, the
soft rush of a coarse homespun dress toward the gate
and her arms were around his neck again.

"I can't let you go, child! Lord have mercy! He's
the last!" And the low pitiful sobs!

"Come, come, now Ma, we must get away from here
before the officers are after him!"

"Just a minute!"

A kiss, and then another long and lingering. A sigh,
and then a smothered choking cry from a mother's broken
heart and he was gone.

Thus Texas grew into the Imperial Commonwealth of
the South.

*   *   *   *   *

To save appearance McLeod was removed to Independence with the other prisoners, and in a short time released, with a number of others against whom insignifi-
cant charges were lodged.

When he returned to Hambright the people looked at
him with suspicion.

"How is it, young man," asked the Preacher, "that
you are at home so soon, while brave boys are serving
terms in Northern prisons?"

"Had nothing against me," he replied.

"That's strange, when Sam Worth swore that you organised the raid to kill Rufe Lattimore."

"They didn't believe him."

"Well, I've an idea that you saved your hide by puking.
I'm not sure yet, but information was given that only

the man in command of the whole county could have possessed."

"There were a half-dozen men who knew as much as I did. You mustn't think me capable of such a thing, Dr. Durham!" protested McLeod with heightened colour.

"It's a nasty suspicion. I'd rather see a child of mine transformed into a cur dog, and killed for stealing sheep, than fall to the level of such a man. But only time will prove the issue."

"I've made up my mind to turn over a new leaf," said McLeod. "I'm sick of rowdyism. I'm going to be a law-abiding, loyal citizen."

"That's just what I'm afraid of!" exclaimed the Preacher with a sneer as he turned and left him.

And his fears were soon confirmed. Within a month the Independence Observer contained a dispatch from Washington announcing the appointment of Allan Mc-Leod a Deputy United States Marshal for the District of Western North Carolina, together with the information that he had renounced his allegiance to his old disloyal associates, and had become an enthusiastic Republican; and that henceforth he would labour with might and main to establish peace and further the industrial progress of the South.

"I knew it. The dirty whelp!" cried the Preacher, as he showed the paper to his wife.

"Now don't be too hard on the boy, Doctor Durham," urged his wife. "He may be sincere in his change of politics. You never did like him."

"Sincere! yes, as the devil is always sincere. He's dead in earnest now. He's found his level, and his success is sure. Mark my words the boy's a villain from the crown of his head to the soles of his feet. He has bartered his soul to save his skin, and the skin is all that's left."

" I'm sorry to think it. I couldn't help liking him."

" And that's the funniest freak I ever knew your fancy to take, my dear,—I never could understand it."

When McLeod had established his office in Hambright, he made special efforts to allay the suspicions against his name. His indignant denials of the report of his treachery convinced many that he had been wronged. Two men alone, maintained toward him an attitude of contempt, Major Dameron and the Preacher.

He called on Mrs. Durham, and with his smooth tongue convinced her that he had been foully slandered. She urged him to win the Doctor. Accordingly he called to talk the question over with the Preacher and ask him for a fair chance to build his character untarnished in the community.

The Preacher heard him through patiently, but in silence. Allan was perspiring before he reached the end of his plausible explanation. It was a tougher task than he thought, this deliberate lying, under the gaze of those glowing black eyes that looked out from their shaggy brows and pierced through his inmost soul.

" You've got an oily tongue. It will carry you a long way in this world. I can't help admiring the skill with which you are fast learning to use it. You've fooled Mrs. Durham with it, but you can't fool me," said the Preacher.

" Doctor, I solemnly swear to you I am not guilty."

" It's no use to add perjury to plain lying. I know you did it. I know it as well as if I were present in that jail and heard you basely betray the men, name by name, whom you had lured to their ruin."

" Doctor, I swear you are mistaken ! "

" Bah ! Don't talk about it. You nauseate me ! "

The Preacher sprang to his feet, paced across the floor, sat down on the edge of his table and glared at McLeod for a moment. And then with his voice low and quivering with a storm of emotion he said,

"The curse of God upon you—the God of your fathers! Your fathers in far-off Scotland's hills, who would have suffered their tongues torn from their heads and their skin stripped inch by inch from their flesh sooner than betray one of their clan in distress. You have betrayed a thousand of your own men, and you, their sworn chieftain! Hell was made to consume such leper trash!"

McLeod was dazed at first by this outburst. At length he sprang to his feet livid with rage.

"I'll not forget this, sir!" he hissed.

"Don't forget it!" cried the Preacher trembling with passion as he opened the door. "Go on and live your lie."

CHAPTER XXIV

A MODERN MIRACLE

"MRS. DURHAM, the Doctor wants you," said Charlie when McLeod's footfall had died away.

"Charlie, dear, why don't you call me 'Mama'—surely you love me a little wee bit, don't you?" she asked, taking the boy's hand tenderly in hers.

"Yes'm," he replied hanging his head.

"Then do say Mama. You don't know how good it would be in my ears."

"I try to but it chokes me," he half whispered, glancing timidly up at her. "Let me call you Aunt Margaret, I always wanted an aunt and I think your name Margaret's so sweet," he shyly added.

She kissed him and said, "All right, if that's all you will give me." She passed on into the library where the Preacher waited her.

"My dear, I've just given young McLeod a piece of my mind. I wanted to say to you that you are entirely mistaken in his character. He's a bad egg. I know all the facts about his treachery. He's as smooth a liar as I've met in years."

"With all his brute nature, there's some good in him," she persisted.

"Well, it will stay in him. He will never let it get out."

"All right, have your way about it for the time. We'll

see who is right in the long run. Now I've a more pressing and tougher problem for your solution."

" What is it? "

" Dick."

" What's he done this time? "

" He steals everything he can get his hands on."

" He is a puzzle."

" He's the greatest liar I ever saw," she continued. " He simply will not tell the truth if he can think up a lie in time. I'd say run him off the place. but for Charlie. He seems to love the little scoundrel. I'm afraid his influence over Charlie will be vicious, but it would break the child's heart to drive him away. What shall we do with him? "

The Preacher laughed. " I give it up, my dear, you've got beyond my depth now. I don't know whether he's got a soul. Certainly the very rudimentary foundations of morals seem lacking. I believe you could take a young ape and teach him quicker. I leave him with you. At present it's a domestic problem."

" Thanks, that's so encouraging."

Dick was a puzzle and no mistake about it. But to Charlie his rolling mischievous eyes, his cunning fingers and his wayward imagination were unfailing fountains of life. He found every bird's nest within two miles of town. He could track a rabbit almost as swiftly and surely as a hound. He could work like fury when he had a mind to, and loaf a half day over one row of the garden when he didn't want to work, which was his chronic condition.

When the revival season set in for the negroes in the summer, the days of sorrow began for householders. Every negro in the community became absolutely worthless and remained so until the emotional insanity attending their meetings wore off.

Aunt Mary, Mrs. Durham's cook, got salvation over again every summer with increasing power and increasing degeneration in her work. Some nights she got home at two o'clock and breakfast was not ready until nine. Some nights she didn't get home at all, and Mrs. Durham had to get breakfast herself.

It was a hard time for Dick who had not yet experienced religion, and on whom fell the brunt of the extra work and Mrs. Durham's fretfulness besides.

" I tell you what less do, Charlie!" he cried one day. "Less go down ter dat nigger chu'ch, en bus' up de meetin'! I'se gettin' tired er dis."

" How'll you do it?"

" I show you somefin'?" He reached under his shirt next to his skin, and pulled out Dr. Graham's sun glass.

" Where'd you get that, Dick?"

" Foun' it whar er man lef' it." He walled his eyes solemnly.

" Des watch here when I turns 'im in de sun. I kin set dat pile er straw er fire wid it!"

" You mustn't set the church afire!" warned Charlie.

" Naw, chile, but I git up in de gallery, en when ole Uncle Josh gins ter holler en bawl en r'ar en charge, I fling dat blaze er light right on his bal' haid, en I set him afire sho's you bawn!"

" Dick, I wouldn't do it," said Charlie, laughing in spite of himself.

Charlie refused to accompany him. But Dick's mind was set on the necessity of this work of reform. So in the afternoon he slipped off without leave and quietly made his way into the gallery of the Negro Baptist church.

The excitement was running high. Uncle Josh had preached one sermon an hour in length, and had called up the mourners. At least fifty had come forward. The benches had been cleared for five rows back from the pulpit to give plenty of room for the mourners to crawl over the floor, walk back and forth and shout when they "came through," and for their friends to fan them.

This open place was covered with wheat straw to keep the mourners off the bare floor, and afford some sort of comfort for those far advanced in mourning, who went into trances and sometimes lay motionless for hours on their backs or flat on their faces.

The mourners had kicked and shuffled this straw out to the edges and the floor was bare. Uncle Josh had sent two deacons out for more straw.

In the meantime he was working himself up to another mighty climax of exhortation to move sinners to come forward.

"Come on ter glory you po, po sinners, en flee ter de Lamb er God befo de flames er hell swaller you whole! At de last great day de Sperit 'll flash de light er his shinin' face on dis ole parch up sinful worl', en hit 'll ketch er fire in er minute, an de yearth 'll melt wid furvient heat! Whar 'll you be den po tremblin' sinner? Whar 'll you be when de flame er de Sperit smites de moon and de stars wid fire, en dey gin ter drap outen de sky en knock big holes in de burnin' yearth? Whar 'll you be when de rocks melt wid dat heat, en de sun hide his face in de black smoke dat rise fum de pit?"

Moans and groans and shrieks, louder and louder filled the air. Uncle Josh paused a moment and looked for his deacons with the straw. They were just coming up the steps with a great armful over their heads.

"What's de matter wid you breddern! Fetch on dat wheat straw! Here's dese tremblin' souls gwine down inter de flames er hell des fur de lak er wheat straw!"

The brethren hurried forward with the wheat straw, and just as they reached Uncle Josh standing perspiring

in the midst of his groaning mourners, Dick flashed from
the gallery a stream of dazzling light on the old man's
face and held it steadily on his bald head. Josh was too
astonished to move at first. He was simply paralysed
with fear. It was all right to talk about the flame of the
Spirit, but he wasn't exactly ready to run into it. Suddenly he clapped his hands on the top of his head and
sprang straight up in the air yelling in a plain everyday
profane voice,

"God-der-mighty! What's dat?"

The brethren holding the straw saw it and stood dumb
with terror. The light disappeared from Uncle Josh's
head and lit the straw in splendour on one of the deacon's
shoulders. Aunt Mary's voice was heard above the
mourners' din, clear, shrill and soul piercing.

"G-l-o-r-y! G-l-o-r-y ter God! De flame er de
Sperit! De judgment day! Yas Lawd, I'se here! Glory!
Halleluyah!"

Suddenly the straw on the deacon's back burst into
flames! And pandemonium broke loose. A weak-
minded sinner screamed,

"De flames er Hell!"

The mourners smelled the smoke and sprang from the
floor with white staring eyes. When they saw the fire
and got their bearings they made for the open,—they
jumped on each others' back and made for the door like
madmen. Those nearest the windows sprang through,
and when the lower part of the window was jammed, big
buck negroes jumped on the backs of the lower crowd
and plunged through the two upper sashes with a crash
that added new terror to the panic.

In two minutes the church was empty, and the yard
full of crazy, shouting negroes.

Dick stepped from the gallery into the crowd
as the last ones emerged, ran up to the pulpit and

stamped out the fire in the straw with his bare feet. He looked around to see if they had left anything valuable behind in the stampede, and sauntered leisurely out of the church.

"Now dog-gone 'em let 'em yell!" he muttered to himself.

When Uncle Josh sufficiently recovered his senses to think, and saw the church still standing, with not even a whiff of smoke to be seen, instead of the roaring furnace he had expected, he was amazed. He called his scattered deacons together and they went cautiously back to investigate.

"Hit's no use in talkin' Bre'r Josh, dey sho wuz er fire!" cried one of the deacons.

"Sho's de Lawd's in heaben. I feel it gittin' on my fingers fo I drap dat straw!" said another.

"Hit smite me fust right on top er my haid!" whispered Uncle Josh in awe.

They cautiously approached the pulpit and there in front of it lay the charred fragments of the burned straw pile.

They gathered around it in awe-struck wonder. One of them touched it with his foot.

"Doan do dat!" cried Uncle Josh, lifting his hand with authority.

They drew back, Uncle Josh saw the immense power in that heap of charred straw. Some of it was a little damp and it had been only partly burned.

"Dar's de mericle er de Sperit!" he solemnly declared.

"Yas Lawd!" echoed a deacon.

"Fetch de hammer, en de saw, en de nails, en de boards en build right dar en altar ter de Sperit!" were his prophetic commands.

And they did. They got an old show case of glass,

put the charred straw in it, and built an open box work around it just where it fell in front of the pulpit.

Then a revival broke out that completely paralysed the industries of Campbell county. Every negro stopped work and went to that church. Uncle Josh didn't have to preach or to plead. They came in troops towards the magic altar, whose fame and mystery had thrilled every superstitious soul with its power. The benches were all moved out and the whole church floor given up to mourners. Uncle Josh had an easy time walking around just adding a few terrifying hints to trembling sinners, or helping to hold some strong sister when she had "come through," with so much glory in her bones that there was danger she would hurt somebody.

After a week the matter became so serious that the white people set in motion an investigation of the affair. Dick had thrown out a mysterious hint that he knew some things that were very funny.

"Doan you tell nobody!" he would solemnly say to Charlie.

And then he would lie down on the grass and roll and laugh. At length by dint of perseverance, and a bribe of a quarter, the Preacher induced Dick to explain the mystery. He did, and it broke up the meeting.

Uncle Josh's fury knew no bounds. He was heartbroken at the sudden collapse of his revival, chagrined at the recollection of his own terror at the fire, and fearful of an avalanche of backsliders from the meeting among those who had professed even with the greatest glory.

He demanded that the Preacher should turn Dick over to him for correction. The Preacher took a few hours to consider whether he should whip him himself or turn him over to Uncle Josh. Dick heard Uncle Josh's demand. Out behind the stable he and Charlie held a council of war.

" You go see Miss Mar'get fur me, en git up close to her, en tell her taint right ter 'low no low down black nigger ter whip me! "

" All right Dick, I will," agreed Charlie.

" Case ef ole Josh beats me I gwine ter run away. I nebber git ober dat. "

Dick had threatened to run away often before when he wanted to force Charlie to do something for him. Once he had gone a mile out of town with his clothes tied in a bundle, and Charlie trudging after him begging him not to leave.

The boy did his best to save Dick the humiliation of a whipping at the hands of Uncle Josh, but in vain.

When Uncle Josh led him out to the stable lot, his face was not pleasant to look upon. There was a dangerous gleam in Dick's eye that boded no good to his enemy.

" You imp er de debbil! " exclaimed Uncle Josh shaking his switch with unction.

" I fool you good enough, you ole bal' headed ape! " answered Dick gritting his teeth defiantly.

" I make you sing enudder chune fo I'se done wid you. "

" En if you does, nigger, you know what I gwine do fur you? " cried Dick rolling his eyes up at his enemy.

" What kin you do, honey? asked Uncle Josh, humouring his victim now with the evident relish of a cat before his meal on a mouse.

" Ef you hits me hard, I gwine ter burn you house down on you haid some night, en run erway des es sho es I kin stick er match to it," said Dick.

" You is, is you? " thundered Josh with wrath.

" Dat I is. En I burn yo ole chu'ch de same night."

Uncle Josh was silent a moment. Dick's words had chilled his heart. He was afraid of him, but he was afraid to back down from what was now evidently his duty. So without further words he whipped him. Yet to save his life he could not hit him as hard as he thought he deserved.

That night Dick disappeared from Hambright, and for weeks every evening at dusk the wistful face of Charlie Gaston could be seen on the big hill to the south of town vainly watching for somebody. He would always take something to eat in his pockets, and when he gave up his vigil he would place the food under a big shelving rock where they had often played together. But the birds and ground squirrels ate it. He would slip back the next day hoping to see Dick jump out of the cave and surprise him.

And then at last he gave it up, sat down under the rock and cried. He knew Dick would grow to be a man somewhere out in the big world and never come back.

LOVE'S DREAM

CHAPTER I

BLUE EYES AND BLACK HAIR

"SHE'S coming next month, Charlie," said Mrs. Durham, looking up from a letter.

"Who is it now, Auntie, another divinity with which you are going to overwhelm me?" asked Gaston smiling as he laid his book down and leaned back in his chair.

"Some one I've been telling you about for the last month."

"Which one?"

"Oh, you wretch! You don't think about anything except your books. I've been dinning that girl's praises into your ears for fully five weeks, and you look at me in that innocent way and ask which one?"

"Honestly, Aunt Margaret, you're always telling me about some beautiful girl, I get them mixed. And then when I see them, they don't come up to the advance notices you've sent out. To tell you the truth, you are such a beautiful woman, and I've got so used to your standard, the girls can't measure up to it."

"You flatterer. A woman of forty-two a standard of beauty! Well, it's sweet to hear you say it, you handsome young rascal."

"It's the honest truth. You are one of the women who never show the addition of a year. You have spoiled my eyesight for ordinary girls."

"Hush, sir, you don't dare to talk to any girl like you talk to me. They all say you're afraid of them."

"Well, I am, in a sense. I've been disappointed so many times."

"Oh! you'll find her yet and when you do!"—

"What do you think will happen?"

"I'm certain you will be the biggest fool in the state."

"That will make it nice for the girl, won't it?"

"Yes, and I shall enjoy your antics. You who have dissected love with your brutal German philosophy, and found every girl's faults with such ease,—it will be fun to watch you flounder in the meshes at last."

"Auntie, seriously, it will be the happiest day of my life. For four years my dreams have been growing more and more impossible. Who is this one?"

"She is the most beautiful girl I know, and the brightest and the best, and if she gets hold of you she will clip your wings and bring you down to earth. I'll watch you with interest," said Mrs. Durham looking over the letter again and laughing.

"What are you laughing at?"

"Just a little joke she gets off in this letter."

"But who is she? You haven't told me."

"I did tell you—she's General Worth's daughter, Miss Sallie. She writes she is coming up to spend a month at the Springs, with her friend Helen Lowell, of Boston, and wants me to corral all the young men in the community and have them fed and in fine condition for work when they arrive."

"She evidently intends to have a good time."

"Yes, and she will."

"Fortunately my law practice is not rushing me at this season. My total receipts for June last year were two dollars and twenty-five cents. It will hardly go over two-fifty this year."

"I've told her you're a rising young lawyer."

"I have plenty of room to rise, Auntie. If you will just keep on letting me board with you, I hope to work my practice up to ten dollars a month in the course of time."

"Don't you want to hear something about Miss Sallie?"

"Of course, I was just going to ask you if she's as homely as that last one you tried to get off on me."

"I've told you she's a beauty. She made a sensation at her finishing school in Baltimore. It's funny that she was there the last year you were at the Johns Hopkins University. She's the belle of Independence, rich, petted, and the only child of old General Worth, who thinks the sun rises and sets in her pretty blue eyes."

"So she has blue eyes?"

"Yes, blue eyes and black hair."

"What a funny combination! I never saw a girl with blue eyes and black hair."

"It's often seen in the far South. I expect you to be drowned in those blue eyes. They are big, round and child-like, and look out of their black lashes as though surprised at their dark setting. This contrast accents their dreamy beauty, and her eyes seem to swim in a dim blue mist like the point where the sea and sky meet on the horizon far out on the ocean. She is bright, witty, romantic and full of coquetry. She is determined to live her girl's life to its full limit. She is fond of society and dances divinely."

"That's bad. I never even cut the pigeon's wing in my life—and I'm too old to learn."

"She has a full queenly figure, small hands and feet, delicate wrists, a dimple in one cheek only, and a mass of brown-black hair that curls when it's going to rain."

"That's fine, we wouldn't need a barometer on life's voyage, would we?"

"No, but you will be looking for a pilot and a harbour before you've known her a month. Her upper lip is a little fuller and projects slightly over the lower, and they are both beautifully fluted and curved like the petals of a flower, which makes the most tantalising mouth a standing challenge for a kiss."

"Oh! Auntie, you're joking! You never saw such a girl. You're breaking into my heart, stealing glances at my ideal."

"All right, sir, wait and see for yourself. She has pretty shell-like ears, her laughter is full, contagious, and like music. She plays divinely on the piano, can't sing a note, but dresses to kill. You might as well wind up your affairs, and get ready for the first serious work of your life. You will have your hands full after you see her."

"But did I understand you to say she's rich?"

"Yes, they say her father is worth half a million."

"Do you think she could be interested in the poor in this county?"

"Yes, she doesn't seem to know she's an heiress. Her father, the General, is a deacon in the Baptist church at Independence, and hates dudes and fops with all his old-fashioned soul. His idea of a man is one of character, and the capacity of achievement, not merely a possessor of money. Still, I imagine he is going to give any man trouble who tries to take his daughter away from him."

"I'm afraid that money lets me out of the race."

"Nothing of the sort, when you see her you will never allow a little thing like that to worry you."

"It's not her dollars that will worry me. It's the fact that she's got them and I haven't. But, anyhow, Auntie, from your description you can book me for one night at least."

"I'm going to book you for her lackey, her slave, devoted to her every whim while she's here. One night—the idea!"

"Auntie, you're too generous to others. I've no notion all this rigmarole about your Miss Sallie Worth is true. But I'll do anything to please you."

"Very well, I'll see whom you are trying to please later."

"I must go," said Gaston, hastily rising. I have an engagement to discuss the coming political campaign with the Hon. Allan McLeod, the present Republican boss of the state."

"I didn't know you hobnobbed with the enemy."

"I don't. But as far as I can understand him, he purposes to take me up on an exceeding high mountain and offer me the world and the fulness thereof. We all like to be tempted whether we fall or not. The Doctor hates McLeod. I think he holds some grudge against him. What do you think of him, Auntie? He swears by you. I used to dislike him as a boy, but he seems a pretty decent sort of fellow now, and I can't help liking just a little anybody who loves you. I confess he has a fascination for me."

"Why do you ask my opinion of him?" slowly asked Mrs. Durham.

"Because I'm not quite sure of his honesty. He talks fairly, but there's something about him that casts a doubt over his fairest words. He says he has the most important proposition of my life to place before me to-day, and I'm at a loss how to meet him—whether as a well-meaning friend or a scheming scoundrel. He's a puzzle to me."

"Well, Charlie, I don't mind telling you that he is a

puzzle to me. I've always been strangely attracted to him, even when he was a big red-headed brute of a boy. The Doctor always disliked him and I thought, misjudged him. He has always paid me the supremest deference, and of late years the most subtle flattery. No woman, who feels her life a failure, as I do mine, can be indifferent to such a compliment from a man of trained mind and masterful character. This is a sore subject between the Doctor and myself. And when I see him shaking hands a little too lingeringly with admiring sisters after his services, I repay him with a chat with my devoted McLeod. Don't ask me. I like him, and I don't like him. I admire him and at the same time I suspect and half fear him."

"Strange we feel so much alike about him. But your heart has always been very close to mine, since you slipped your arm around me that night my mother died. I know about what he will say, and I know about what I'll do." He stooped and kissed his foster-mother tenderly.

"Charlie, I'm in earnest about my pretty girl that's coming. Don't forget it."

"Bah! You've fooled me before."

CHAPTER II

THE VOICE OF THE TEMPTER

McLEOD was waiting with some impatience in his room at the hotel.

"Walk in Gaston, you're a little late. However, better late than never." McLeod plunged directly into the purpose of his visit.

"Gaston you're a man of brains, and oratorical genius. I heard your speech in the last Democratic convention in Raleigh, and I don't say it to flatter you, that was the greatest speech made in any assembly in this state since the war."

"Thanks!" said Gaston with a wave of his arm.

"I mean it. You know too much to be in sympathy with the old moss-backs who are now running this state. For fourteen years, the South has marched to the polls and struck blindly at the Republican party, and three times it struck to kill. The Southern people have nothing in common with these Northern Democrats who make your platforms and nominate your candidate. You don't ask anything about the platform or the man. You would vote for the devil if the Democrats nominated him, and ask no questions; and what infuriates me is you vote to enforce platforms that mean economic ruin to the South."

"Man shall not live by bread alone, McLeod."

"Sure, but he can't live on dead men's bones. You vote in solid mass on the Negro question, which you settled by the power of Anglo-Saxon insolence when you destroyed the Reconstruction governments at a blow.

Why should you keep on voting against every interest of the South, merely because you hate the name Republican?"

"Why? Simply because so long as the Negro is here with a ballot in his hands he is a menace to civilisation. The Republican party placed him here. The name Republican will stink in the South for a century, not because they beat us in war, but because two years after the war, in profound peace, they inaugurated a second war on the unarmed people of the South, butchering the starving, the wounded, the women and children. God in heaven, will I ever forget that day they murdered my mother! Their attempt to establish with the bayonet an African barbarism on the ruins of Southern society was a conspiracy against human progress. It was the blackest crime of the nineteenth century."

"You are talking in a dead language. We are living in a new world."

"But principles are eternal."

"Principles? I'm not talking about principles. I'm talking about practical politics. The people down here haven't voted on a principle in years. They've been voting on old Simon Legree. He left the state nearly a quarter of a century ago."

"Yes, McLeod, but his soul has gone marching on. The Republican party fought the South because such men as Legree lived in it, and abused the negroes, and the moment they won, turn and make Legree and his breed their pets. Simon Legree is more than a mere man who stole five millions of dollars, alienated the races, and covered the South with the desolation of anarchy. He is an idea. He represents everything that the soul of the South loathes, and that the Republican party has tried to ram down our throats, Negro supremacy in politics, and Negro equality in society."

" You are talking about the dead past, Gaston. I'm surprised at a man of your brain living under such a delusion. How can there be Negro supremacy when they are in a minority? "

" Supremacy under a party system is always held by a minority. The dominant faction of a party rules the party, and the successful party rules the state. If the Negro only numbered one-fifth the population and they all belonged to one party, they could dictate the policy of that party."

" You know that a few white brains really rule that black mob."

" Yes, but the black mob defines the limits within which you live and have your being."

" Gaston, the time has come to shake off this night-mare, and face the issues of our day and generation. We are going to win in this campaign, but I want you. I like you. You are the kind of man we need now to take the field and lead in this campaign."

" How are you going to win? "

" We are going to form a contract with the Farmer's Alliance and break the backbone of the Bourbon Democracy of the South. The farmers have now a compact body of 50,000 voters, thoroughly organised, and combined with the negro vote we can hold this state until Gabriel blows his trumpet."

" That's a pretty scheme. Our farmers are crazy now with all sorts of fool ideas," said Gaston thoughtfully.

" Exactly, my boy, and we've got them by the nose."

" If you can carry through that programme, you've got us in a hole."

" In a hole? I should say we've got you in the bottom-less pit with the lid bolted down. You'll not even rise at the day of judgment. It won't be necessary! " laughed

McLeod, and as he laughed changed his tone in the midst of his laughter.

"And what is the great proposition you have to make to me?" asked Gaston.

"Join with us in this new coalition, and stump the state for us. Your fortune will be made, win or lose. I'll see that the National Republican Committee pays you a thousand dollars a week for your speeches, at least five a week, two hundred dollars apiece. If we lose, you will make ten thousand dollars in the canvass, and stand in line for a good office under the National Administration. If we win, I'll put you in the Governor's Palace for four years. There's a tide in the affairs of men, you know. It's at the flood at this moment for you."

Gaston was silent a moment and looked thoughtfully out of the window. The offer was a tremendous temptation. A group of old fogies had dominated the Democratic party for ten years, and had kept the younger men down with their war cries and old soldier candidates, until he had been more than once disgusted. He felt as sure of McLeod's success as if he already saw it. It was precisely the movement he had warned the old pudding-head set against in the preceding compaign in which they had deliberately alienated the Farmer's Alliance. They had pooh poohed his warning and blundered on to their ruin.

It was the dream of his life to have money enough to buy back his mother's old home, beautify it, and live there in comfort with a great library of books he would gather. The possibility of a career at the state Capital and then at Washington for so young a man was one of dazzling splendour to his youthful mind. For the moment it seemed almost impossible to say no.

McLeod saw his hesitation and already smiled with the

certainty of triumph.   A cloud overspread his face when Gaston at length said,

"I'll give you my answer to-morrow."

"All right, you're a gentleman.   I can trust you.   Our conversation is of course only between you and me."

"Certainly, I understand that."

All that day and night he was alone fighting out the battle in his soul.   It was an easy solution of life that opened before him.   The attainment of his proudest ambitions lay within his grasp almost without a struggle. Such a campaign, with his name on the lips of surging thousands around those speaker's stands, was an idea that fascinated him with a serpent charm.

All that he had to do was to give up his prejudices on the Negro question.   His own party stood for no principle except the supremacy of the Anglo-Saxon.   On the issue of the party platforms, he was in accord with the modern Republican utterances at almost every issue, and so were his associates in the Southern Democracy.   The Negro was the point.   What was the use now of persisting in the stupid reiteration of the old slogan of white supremacy?   The Negro had the ballot.   He was still the ward of the nation, and likely to be for all time, so far as he could see.   The Negro was the one pet superstition of the millions who lived where no negro dwelt. His person and his ballot were held more peculiarly sacred and inviolate in the South than that of any white man elsewhere.

The possibility of a reunion in friendly understanding and sympathy between the masses of the North and the masses of the South seemed remote and impossible in his day and generation.

He asked himself the question, could such a revolution toward universal suffrage ever go backward, no matter how base the motive which gave it birth?   Why not give up impracticable dreams, accept things as they are, and succeed?

He did not confer with the Rev. John Durham on this question, because he knew what his answer would be without asking. A thousand times he had said to him, with the emphasis he could give to words,

"*My boy, the future American must be an Anglo-Saxon or a Mulatto! We are now deciding which it shall be. The future of the world depends on the future of this Republic. This Republic can have no future if racial lines are broken, and its proud citizenship sinks to the level of a mongrel breed of Mulattoes. The South must fight this battle to a finish. Two thousand years look down upon the struggle, and two thousand years of the future bend low to catch the message of life or death!*"

He could see now his drawn face with its deep lines and his eyes flashing with passion as he said this. These words haunted Gaston now with strange power as he walked along the silent streets.

· He walked down past his old home, stopped and leaned on the gate, and looked at it long and lovingly. What a flood of tender and sorrowful memories swept his soul! He lived over again the days of despair when his mother was an invalid. He recalled their awful poverty, and then the last terrible day with that mob of negroes trampling over the lawn and overrunning the house. He saw the white face of his mother whose memory he loved as he loved life. And now he recalled a sentence from her dying lips. He had all but lost its meaning.

"You will grow to be a brave strong man. You will fight this battle out, and win back our home, and bring your own bride here in the far away days of sunshine and success I see for you."

You will fight this battle out—he had almost lost that

sentence in his hunger for that which followed. It came to his soul now ringing like a trumpet call to honour and duty.

He turned on his heel and walked rapidly home. He looked at his watch. It was two o'clock in the morning.

"We will fight it out on the old lines," he said to McLeod next day.

"You will find me a pretty good fighter."

"Unto death, let it be," answered Gaston firmly setting his lips.

"I admire your pluck, but I'm sorry for your judgment. You know you're beaten before you begin."

"Defeat that's seen has lost its bitterness before it comes."

"Then get ready the flowers for the funeral. I hoped you would have better sense. You are one of the men now I'll have to crush first, thoroughly, and for all time. I'm not afraid of the old fools. I'll be fair enough to tell you this," said McLeod.

"Not since Legree's day has the Republican party had so dangerous a man at its head," said Gaston thoughtfully to himself as McLeod strode away across the square. "He has ten times the brains of his older master, and none of his superstitions. He will give me a hard fight."

CHAPTER III

FLORA

HAMBRIGHT had changed but little in the eighteen years of peace that had followed the terrors of Legree's régime. The population had doubled, though but few houses had been built. The town had not grown from the development of industry, but for a very simple reason—the country people had moved into the town, seeking refuge from a new terror that was growing of late more and more a menace to a country home, the roving criminal negro.

The birth of a girl baby was sure to make a father restless, and when the baby looked up into his face one day with the soft light of a maiden, he gave up his farm and moved to town.

The most important development of these eighteen years was the complete alienation of the white and black races as compared with the old familiar trust of domestic life.

When Legree finished his work as the master artificer of the Reconstruction Policy, he had dug a gulf between the races as deep as hell. It had never been bridged. The deed was done and it had crystallised into the solid rock that lies at the basis of society. It was done at a formative period, and it could no more be undone now than you could roll the universe back in its course.

The younger generation of white men only knew the Negro as an enemy of his people in politics and society.

He never came in contact with him except in menial service, in which the service rendered was becoming more and more trifling, and his habits more insolent. He had his separate schools, churches, preachers and teachers, and his political leaders were the beneficiaries of Legree's legacies.

With the Anglo-Saxon race guarding the door of marriage with fire and sword, the effort was being made to build a nation inside a nation of two antagonistic races. No such thing had ever been done in the history of the human race, even under the development of the monarchial and aristocratic forms of society. How could it be done under the formulas of Democracy with Equality as the fundamental basis of law? And yet this was the programme of the age.

Gaston was feeling blue from the reaction which followed his temptation by McLeod. His duty was clear the night before as he walked firmly homeward, recalling the tragedy of the past. Now in the cold light of day, the past seemed far away and unreal. The present was near, pressing, vital. He laid down a book he was trying to read, locked his office and strolled down town to see Tom Camp.

This old soldier had come to be a sort of oracle to him. His affection for the son of his Colonel was deep and abiding, and his extravagant flattery of his talents and future were so evidently sincere they always acted as a tonic. And he needed a tonic to-day.

Tom was seated in a chair in his yard under a big cedar, working on a basket, and a little golden-haired girl was playing at his feet. It was his old home he had lost in Legree's day, but had got back through the help of General Worth, who came up one day and paid back Tom's gift of lightwood in gleaming yellow metal. His long hair and full beard were white now, and his eyes had a soft deep look that told of sorrows borne in patience and faith beyond the ken of the younger man. It was this look on Tom's face that held Gaston like a magnet when he was in trouble.

"Tom, I'm blue and heartsick. I've come down to have you cheer me up a little."

"You've got the blues? Well that is a joke!" cried Tom. "You, young and handsome, the best educated man in the county, the finest orator in the state, life all before you, and God fillin' the world to-day with sunshine and spring flowers, and all for you! You blue! That is a joke." And Tom's voice rang in hearty laughter.

"Come here, Flora, and kiss me, you won't laugh at me, will you?"

The child climbed up into his lap, slipped her little arms around his neck and hugged and kissed him.

"Now, once more, dearie, long and close and hard— oh! That's worth a pound of candy!" Again she squeezed his neck and kissed him, looking into his face with a smile.

"I love you, Charlie," she said with quaint seriousness.

"Do you, dear? Well, that makes me glad. If I can win the love of as pretty a little girl as you I'm not a failure, am I?" And he smoothed her curls.

"Ain't she sweet?" cried Tom with pride as he laid aside his basket and looked at her with moistened eyes.

"Tom, she's the sweetest child I ever saw."

"Yes, she's God's last and best gift to me, to show me He still loved me. Talk about trouble. Man, you're a baby. You ain't cut your teeth yet. Wait till you've seen some things I've seen. Wait till you've seen the light of the world go out, and staggerin' in the

dark met the devil face to face, and looked him in the
eye, and smelled the pit. And then feel him knock you
down in it, and the red waves roll over you and smother
you. I've been there."

Tom paused and looked at Gaston. "You weren't
here when I come to the end of the world, the time when
that baby was born, and Annie died with the little red
bundle sleepin' on her breast. The oldest girl was murdered by Legree's nigger soldiers. Then Annie give me
that little gal. Lord, I was the happiest old fool that
ever lived that day! And then when I looked into
Annie's dead face, I went down, down, down! But I
looked up from the bottom of the pit and I saw the light
of them blue eyes and I heard her callin' me to take
her. How I watched her and nursed her, a mother and
a father to her, day and night, through the long years,
and how them little fingers of hers got hold of my heart!
Now, I bless the Lord for all His goodness and mercy to
me. She will make it all right. She's going to be a lady
and such a beauty! She's goin' to school now, and me
and the General's goin' to take her ter college bye and
bye, and she's goin' to marry some big handsome fellow
like you, and her crippled grey haired daddy'll live in her
house in his old age. The Lord is my shepherd I shall
not want. "

"Tom, you make me ashamed."

"You ought to be, man, a youngster like you to talk
about gettin' the blues. What's all your education for?"

"Sometimes I think that only men like you have ever
been educated."

"G'long with your foolishness, boy. I ain't never had
a show in this world. The nigger's been on my back
since I first toddled into the world, and I reckon he'll ride
me into the grave. They are my only rivals now making
them baskets and they always undersell me."

Gaston started as Tom uttered the last sentence.

" With you, boy, it's all plain sailin'. You're the best looking chap in the county. I was a dandy when I was young. It does me good to look at you if you don't care nothin' about fine clothes. Then you're as sharp as a razor. There ain't a man in No'th Caliny that can stand up agin you on the stump. I've heard 'em all. You'll be the Governor of this state. "

That was always the climax of Tom's prophetic flattery. He could think of no grander end of a human life than to crown it in the Governor's Palace of North Carolina. He belonged to the old days when it was a bigger thing to be the Governor of a great state than to hold any office short of the Presidency,—when men resigned seats in the United States Senate to run for Governor, and when the national government was so puny a thing that the bankers of Europe refused to loan money on United States bonds unless countersigned by the State of Virginia. And that was not so long ago. The bankers sent that answer to Buchanan's Secretary of the Treasury.

" Tom, you've lifted me out of the dumps. I owe you a doctor's fee," cried Gaston with enthusiasm as he placed Flora back on the grass and started to his office.

" All I charge you is to come again. The old man's proud of his young friend. You make me feel like I'm somebody in the old world after all. And some day when you're great and rich and famous and the world's full of your name, I'll tell folks I know you like my own boy, and I'll brag about how many times you used to come to see me."

" Hush, Tom, you make me feel silly," said Gaston as he warmly pressed the old fellow's hand. He went back toward his office with lighter step and more buoyant heart. His mind was as clear as the noonday sun that was now flooding the green fresh world with its splendour. He would stand by his own people. He would sink or swim with them. If poverty and failure were the result, let it be so. If success came, all the better. There were things more to be desired than gold.

CHAPTER IV

THE ONE WOMAN

G 'ASTON called at the post-office to get his mail.
One relief the Cleveland administration had
brought Hambright—a decent citizen in charge
of the post-office. Dave Haley had given place to a
Democrat and was now scheming and working with
McLeod for the " salvation " of the state, which of
course meant for the old slave trader the restoration
of his office under a Republican administration. If
the South had held no other reason for hating the
Republican party, the character of the men appointed
to Federal office was enough to send every honest man
hurrying into the opposite party without asking any questions as to its principles.

Sam Love, the new postmaster was a jovial, honest,
lazy, good-natured Democrat whose ideal of a luxurious
life was attained in his office. He handed Gaston his mail
with a giggle.

" What's the matter with you, Sam? "

" Nuthin' 'tall. I just thought I'd tell you that I like
her handwriting," he laughed.

" How dare you study the handwriting on my letters,
sir! "

" What's the use of being postmaster? There ain't no
big money in it. I just take pride in the office," said
Sam genially. " That's a new one, ain't it? "

Gaston looked at the letter incredulously. It was a

new one,—a big square envelope with a seal on the back of it, addressed to him in the most delicate feminine hand, and postmarked " Independence."

" Great Scott, this is interesting," he cried, breaking the seal.

When the postmaster saw he was going to open it right there in the office, he stepped around in front and looking over his shoulder said,

" What is it, Charlie? "

" It's an invitation from the Ladies' Memorial Association to deliver the Memorial day oration at Independence the 10th of May. That's great. No money in it, but scores of pretty girls, big speech, congratulations, the lion of the hour! Don't you wish you were really a man of brains, Sam? "

" No, no, I'm married. It would be a waste now."

" Sam, I'll be there. Got the biggest speech of my life all cocked and primed, full of pathos and eloquence, —been working on it at odd times for four years. They'll think it a sudden inspiration."

" What's the name of it? "

" The Message of the New South to the Glorious Old."

" That sounds bully, that ought to fetch 'em."

" It will, my boy, and when Dave Haley gets this postoffice away from you in the dark days coming, I'll publish that speech in a pamphlet, and you can peddle it at a quarter and make a good living for your children."

" Don't talk like that, Gaston, that isn't funny at all. You don't think the Radicals have got any chance? "

" Chance! Between you and me they'll win."

Sam went back to the desk without another word, a great fear suddenly darkening the future. McLeod had gotten off the same joke on him the day before. It sounded ominous coming from both sides like that. He took up his party paper, " The Old Timer's Gazette " and read over again the sure prophecies of victory and felt better.

Gaston accepted the invitation with feverish haste. He had it all ready to put in the office for the return mail to Independence. But he was ashamed to appear in such a hurry, so he held the letter over until the next day. He proudly showed the invitation to Mrs. Durham.

" What do you think of that, Auntie? "

" Immense. You will meet Miss Sallie sure. That letter is in her handwriting. She's the Secretary of the Association and signed the Committee's names."

" You don't say that's the great and only one's handwriting! "

" Couldn't be mistaken. It has a delicate distinction about it. I'd know it anywhere."

" It is beautiful," acknowledged Gaston looking thoughtfully at the letter.'

" I wish you had a new suit, Charlie."

" I wouldn't mind it myself, if I had the money. But clothes don't interest me much, just so I'm fairly decent."

" I'll loan you the money, if you will promise me to devote yourself faithfully to Sallie."

" Never. I'll not sell my interest in all those acres of pretty girls just for one I never saw and a suit of clothes. No thanks. I'm going down there with a premonition I may find Her of whom I've dreamed. They say that town is full of beauties."

" You're so conceited. That's all the more reason you should look your best."

" I don't care so much about looks. I'm going to do my best, whatever I look."

" Oh, you know you're good looking and you don't care," said his foster mother with pride.

On the 10th of May Independence was in gala robes. The long rows of beautiful houses, with dark blue grass lawns on which giant oaks spread their cool arms, were gay with bunting, and with flowers, flowers everywhere! Every urchin on the street and every man, woman and child wore or carried flowers.

The reception committee met Gaston at the depot on the arrival of the excursion train that ran from Hambright. He was placed in an open carriage beside a handsome chattering society woman, and drawn by two prancing horses, was escorted to the hotel, where he was introduced to the distinguished old soldiers of the Confederacy.

At ten o'clock the procession was formed. What a sight! It stretched from the hotel down the shaded pavements a mile toward the cemetery, two long rows of beautiful girls holding great bouquets of flowers. This long double line of beauty and sweetness opened, and escorted gravely by the oldest General of the Confederacy present, he walked through this mile of smiling girls and flowers. Behind him tramped the veterans, some with one arm, some with wooden legs.

When they passed through, the double line closed, and two and two the hundreds of girls carried their flowers in solemn procession. Here was the throbbing soul of the South, keeping fresh the love of her heroic dead.

They spread out over the great cemetery like a host of ministering angels. There was a bugle call. They bent low a moment, and flowers were smiling over every grave from the greatest to the lowliest.

And then to a stone altar marked " To the Unknown Dead," they came and heaped up roses. Then a group of sad-faced women dressed in black, with quaint little bonnets wreathing their brows like nuns, went silently over to the National Cemetery across the way and each taking a basket, walked past the long lines of the dead their boys had fought and dropped a single rose on every soldier's grave. They were women whose boys were buried in strange lands in lonely unmarked trenches. They were doing now what they hoped some woman's hand would do for their lost heroes.

The crowd silently gathered around the speakers' stand and took their seats in the benches placed beneath the trees.

Gaston had never seen this ceremony so lavishly and beautifully performed before. He was overwhelmed with emotion. His father's straight soldierly figure rose before him in imagination, and with him all the silent hosts that now bivouacked with the dead. His soul was melted with the infinite pathos and pity of it all.

He had intended to say some sharp epigrammatic things that would cut the chronic moss-backs that cling to the platforms on such occasions. But somehow when he began they were melted out of his speech. He spoke with a tenderness and reverence that stilled the crowd in a moment like low music.

His tribute to the dead was a poem of rhythmic and exalted thoughts. The occasion was to him an inspiration and the people hung breathless on his words. His voice was never strained but was penetrated and thrilled with thought packed until it burst into the flame of speech. He felt with conscious power his mastery of his audience. He was surprised at his own mood of extraordinary tenderness as he felt his being softened by that oldest religion of the ages, the worship of the dead—as old as sorrow and as everlasting as death! He was for the moment clay in the hands of some mightier spirit above him.

He had spoken perhaps fifteen minutes when suddenly,

straight in front of him, he looked into the face of the One Woman of all his dreams!

There she sat as still as death, her beautiful face tense with breathless interest, her fluted red lips parted as if half in wonder, half in joy, over some strange revelation, and her great blue eyes swimming in a mist of tears. He smiled a look of recognition into her soul and she answered with a smile that seemed to say "I've known you always. Why haven't you seen me sooner?" He recognised her instantly from Mrs. Durham's description and his heart gave a cry of joy. From that moment every word that he uttered was spoken to her. Sometimes as he would look straight through her eyes into her soul, she would flush red to the roots of her brown-black hair, but she never lowered her gaze. He closed his speech in a round of applause that was renewed again and again.

His old classmate, Bob St. Clare, rushed forward to greet him.

"Old fellow, you've covered yourself with glory. By George, that was great! Come, here's a hundred girls want to meet you."

He was introduced to a host of beauties who showered him with extravagant compliments which he accepted without affectation. He knew he had outdone himself that day, and he knew why. The One Woman he had been searching the world for was there, and inspired him beyond all he had ever dared before.

He was disappointed in not seeing her among the crowd who were shaking his hand. He looked anxiously over the heads of those near by to see if she had gone. He saw her standing talking to two stylishly dressed young men.

When the crowd had melted away from the rostrum, she walked straight toward him extending her hand with a gracious smile.

He knew he must look like a fool, but to save him he could not help it, he was simply bubbling over with delight as he grasped her hand, and before she could say a word he said,

"You are Miss Sallie Worth, the Secretary of the Association. My foster mother has described you so accurately I should know you among a thousand."

"Yes, I have been looking forward with pleasure to our trip to the Springs when I knew we should meet you. I am delighted to see you a month earlier." She said this with a simple earnestness that gave it a deeper meaning than a mere commonplace.

"Do you know that you nearly knocked me off my feet when I first saw you in the crowd?"

"Why? How?" she asked.

"You startled me."

"I hope not unpleasantly," she said, looking up at him with her blue eyes twinkling.

"Oh! Heavens no! You are such a perfect image of the girl she described that I was so astonished I came near shouting at the top of my voice, "There she is!" And that would have astonished the audience, wouldn't it?"

"It would indeed," she replied blushing just a little.

"But I'm forgetting my mission, Mr. Gaston. Papa sent me to apologise for his absence to-day. He was called out of the city on some mill business. He told me to bring you home to dine with him. I'm the Secretary, you know and exercise authority in these matters, so I've fixed that programme. You have no choice. The carriage is waiting."

CHAPTER V

THE MORNING OF LOVE

TO his dying day Gaston will never forget that ride to her home with Sallie Worth by his side. It was a perfect May day. The leaves on the trees were just grown and flashed in their green satin under the Southern sun, and every flower seemed in full bloom.

A great joy filled his heart with a sense of divine restfulness. He was unusually silent. And then she said something that made him open his eyes in new wonder.

"Don't drive so fast Ben, and go around the longest way, I'm enjoying this." She paused and a mischievous look came into her eyes as she saw his expression. "I've got the lion here by my side. I want to show all the girls in town that I'm the only one here to-day. It isn't often I've a great man tied down fast like this."

"Why did you spoil the first part of that pretty speech with the last?" he said with a frown.

"It was only your vanity that made me pause."

"Could you read me like that?"

"Of course, all men are vain, much **vainer** than women." Again there was a long silence.

They had reached the outskirts of the city now and were driving slowly through the deep shadows of a great forest.

"What beautiful trees!" he exclaimed.

"They are fine. Do you love big trees?"

213

" Yes, they always seem to me to have a soul. It used to make me almost cry to watch them fall beneath Nelse's axe. I'd never have the heart to clear a piece of woods if I owned it."

" I'm so glad to hear you say that. Papa laughed at me when I said something of the sort when he wanted to cut these woods. He left them just to please me. They belong to our place. They hide the house till you get right up to the gate, but I love them."

Again he looked into her eyes and was silent.

" Now, I come to think of it, you're the only girl I've met to-day who hasn't mentioned my speech. That's strange."

" How do you know that I'm not saving up something very pretty to say to you later about it? "

" Tell me now."

" No, you've spoiled it by your vanity in asking." She said this looking away carelessly.

" Then I'll interpret your silence as the highest compliment you can pay me. When words fail we are deeply moved."

" Vanity of vanity, all is vanity saith the preacher! " she exclaimed lifting her pretty hands.

They turned through a high arched iron gateway, across which was written in gold letters, " Oakwood."

On a gently rising hill on the banks of the Catawba river rose a splendid old Southern mansion, its big Greek columns gleaming through the green trees like polished ivory. A wide porch ran across the full width of the house behind the big pillars, and smaller columns supported the full sweep of a great balcony above. The house was built of brick with Portland cement finish, and the whole painted in two shades of old ivory, with moss-green roof and dark rich Pompeian red brick foundations. With its green background of magnolia trees it seemed like a huge block of solid ivory flashing in splendour from its throne on the hill. The drive wound down a little dale, around a great circle filled with shrubbery and flowers and up to the pillared porte-cochere.

"Oh! what a beautiful home!" Gaston exclaimed with feeling.

"It is beautiful, isn't it?" she said with delight. "I love every brick in its walls, every tree and flower and blade of grass."

"I've always dreamed of a home like that. Those big columns seem to link one to the past and add dignity and meaning to life."

"Then you can understand how I love it, when I was born here and every nook and corner has its love message for me from the past that I have lived, as well as its wider meaning which you see."

"The old South built beautiful homes, didn't they? And that was one of the finest things about the proud old days," he said.

"Yes, and the new South of which you spoke to-day will not forget this heritage of the old, when it comes to itself and shakes off its long suffering and poverty!"

Strange to hear that sort of a speech from a girl who loves society, dances divinely and dresses to kill. He thought of the words of his foster mother with a pang. He hoped she was joking about those things. But he had a strong suspicion from the consciousness of power with which she had tried once or twice to tease him that they were going to prove fatally true.

"Mother tells me you were in Baltimore, in that swell girls' school on North Charles Street when I was a student at the University?"

"Yes, and we gave reception after reception to the Hopkins men and you never once honoured us with your presence."

"But I didn't know you were there, Miss Sallie."

"Of course not. If you had, I wouldn't speak to you now. They said you were a recluse. That you never went into society and didn't speak to a woman for four years."

"How did you hear that?"

"Bob St. Clare told me after I came home by way of apology for your bad manners in so shamefully neglecting a young woman from your own state."

"I'll make amends, now."

"Oh! I'm not suffering from loneliness as I did then. You know Bob put us up to inviting you to deliver the address. He said you were the only orator in North Carolina."

"Bob's the best friend I ever had. We entered college together at fifteen, and became inseparable friends."

He helped her from the carriage and she ran lightly up the high stoop.

"Now come here and look at the view of the river before Papa comes and begins to talk about the tremendous water power in the falls."

He followed her to the end of the long porch overlooking the river. Behind the house the hill abruptly plunged downward to the waters' edge in a mountainous cliff. The river wound around this cliff past the house, emerging into a valley where it described a graceful curve almost doubling on itself and rolled softly away amid green overhanging willows and towering sycamores till lost in the distance toward the blue spurs of King's Mountain.

"A glorious view!" said Gaston, looking long and lovingly at the silver surface of the river.

"Do you love the water, Mr. Gaston?"

"Passionately. I was born among the hills, but the first time I saw the ocean sweeping over five miles of sand reefs and breaking in white thundering spray at my feet, I stood there on a sand dune on our wild coast and gazed entranced for an hour without moving. Of all the things God ever made on this earth I love the waters of the sea, and all moving water suggests it to me. That river says, I must hurry to the sea!"

"It is strange we should have such similar tastes," she said seriously. But it did not seem strange to him. Somehow he expected to find her agree with every whim and fancy of his nature.

"Now we will find Mama. She is such an invalid she rarely goes out. Papa will be home any minute."

"We are glad to welcome you Mr. Gaston," said her mother in a kindly manner. "I'm sure you've enjoyed the drive this beautiful day if Sallie hasn't been trying to tease you. The boys say she's very tiresome at times."

"Why Mama, I'm surprised at you. The idea of such a thing! There's not a word of truth in it, is there, Mr. Gaston?"

"Certainly not, Miss Sallie. I'll testify, Mrs. Worth, that your daughter has been simply charming."

She ran to meet her father at the door. There was the sound of a hearty kiss, a little whispering, and the General stepped briskly into the parlour where she had left her guest.

"Pleased to welcome you to our home, young man. They say down town that you made the greatest speech ever heard in Independence. Sorry I missed it. We'll have you to dinner anyway. I knew your brave father in the army. And now I come to think of it, I saw you once when you were a boy. I was struck with your resemblance to your father then, as now. You showed me the way down to Tom Camp's house. Don't you remember?"

"Certainly General, but I didn't flatter myself that you would recall it."

"I never forget a face. I hope you have been enjoying yourself?"

"More than I can express, sir."

"I'll join you bye and bye," said the General, taking leave.

"Now isn't he a dear old Papa?" she said demurely.

"He certainly knows how to make a timid young man feel at home."

"Are you timid?"

"Hadn't you noticed it?"

"Well, hardly." She shook her head and closed her eyes in the most tantalising way. "To see the cool insolence of conscious power with which you looked that great crowd in the face when you arose on that platform, I shouldn't say I was struck with your timidity."

"I was really trembling from head to foot."

"I wonder how you would look if really cool!"

"Honestly, Miss Sallie, I never speak to any crowd without the intensest nervous excitement. I may put on a brave front, but it's all on the surface."

"I can't believe it," she said shaking her head.

She looked at his serious face a moment and was silent.

"It's queer how we run out of something to say, isn't it?" she asked at length.

"I hadn't thought of it."

"Come up to the observatory and I'll show you Lord Cornwallis' look-out when he had his headquarters here during the Revolution."

She lifted her soft white skirts and led the way up the winding mahogany stairs into the observatory from which the surrounding country could be seen for miles.

"Here Lord Cornwallis waited in vain for Colonel

Ferguson to join him with his regiment from King's Mountain."

"Where my great-grandfather was drawing around him his cordon of death with his fierce mountain men!" interrupted Gaston.

"Was your great-grandfather in that battle?"

"Yes, it was fought on his land, and his two-story log house with the rifle holes cut in the chimney jambs still stands."

"Then we will shake hands again," she cried with enthusiasm, "for we are both children of the Revolution!"

Gaston took her beautiful hand in his and held it lingeringly. Never in all his life had the mere touch of a human hand thrilled him with such strange power. How long he held it he could not tell but it was with a sort of hurt surprise he felt her gently withdraw it at last.

They had reached the parlour again, and he slowly fell into an easy chair.

"Do you dance, Miss Sallie?"

"Why yes, don't you dance?"

"Never tried in my life."

"Don't you approve of dancing?"

"I never had time to think about it. It always seemed silly to me."

"It's great fun."

"I'd take lessons if you would agree to teach me, and I could dance with you all the time, and keep all the other fellows away."

"Well, I must say that's doing fairly well for a timid young man's first day's acquaintance. What will you say when you once become fully self-possessed?" She lifted her high arched eyebrows and looked at him with those blue eyes full of tantalising fun until he had to look down at the floor to keep from saying more than he dared. When he looked up again he changed the subject.

"Miss Sallie, I feel like I've known you ever since I was born." She blushed and made no reply.

Dinner was announced, and Gaston was amazed to see Allan McLeod enter chattering familiarly with the General. He seemed on the most intimate terms with the family and his eye lingered fondly on Sallie's face in a way that somehow Gaston resented as an impertinence.

"I didn't even know you were acquainted with the Hon. Allan McLeod, Miss Sallie," said Gaston as they entered the parlour alone.

"Yes, he was a sort of ward of Papa's when he was a boy. Papa hates his politics, but he has always been in and out almost like one of the family since I can remember. I think he's a fascinating man, don't you?"

"I do, but I don't like him."

"Well, he's a great friend of mine, you mustn't quarrel."

Gaston went to the hotel with his brain in a whirl wondering just what she meant. It was nearly twelve o'clock before he left the General's house. How he had passed these eleven hours he could not imagine. They seemed like eleven minutes in one way. In another he seemed to have lived a lifetime that day.

"By George, she's an angel!" he kept saying over and over to himself as he climbed to his room forgetting the elevator.

CHAPTER VI

BESIDE BEAUTIFUL WATERS

WHEN Gaston tried to sleep, he found it impossible. His brain was on fire, every nerve quivering with some new mysterious power and his imagination soaring on tireless wings. He rolled and tossed an hour, then got up, and sat by his open window looking out over the city sleeping in the still white moonlight. He looked into the mirror and grinned.

"What is the matter with me!" he exclaimed. "I believe I'm going crazy."

He sat down and tried to work the thing out by the formulas of cold reason. "It's perfectly absurd to say I'm in love. My wild romancing about a passion that will grasp all life in its torrent sweep is only a boy's day dream. The world is too prosy for that now."

Yet in spite of this argument the room seemed as bright as day, and the moon was only a pale sister light to the radiance from the face of the girl he had seen that day. Her face seemed to him smiling close into his now. The light of her eyes was tender and soothing like the far away memory of his mother's voice.

"It's a passing fancy," he said at last, after he had sat an hour dreaming and dreaming of scenes he dared not frame in words even alone. He stood by the window again.

"What a beautiful old world this is after all!" he thought as he gazed out on the tops of the oaks whose

221

young leaves were softly sighing at the touch of the night winds. Turning his eye downward to the street he saw the men loading the morning papers into the wagons for the early mail.

" I wonder what sort of report of my speech they put in?" he exclaimed. Unable to sleep he hastily dressed, went down and bought a paper.

On the front page was a flattering portrait, two columns in width, with a report of his speech filling the entire page, and an editorial review of a column and a half. He was hailed as the coming man of the state in this editorial, which contained the most extravagant praise. He knew it was the best thing he had ever done, and he felt for the minute proud of himself and his achievement. This contemplation of his own greatness quieted his nerves and he fell asleep. He was awakened by the first rolling of carts on the pavements at dawn. He knew he had not slept more than two hours but he was as wide awake as though he had slept soundly all night.

" I must be threatened with that spell of fever Auntie has been worrying about since I was a boy!" he laughed as he slowly dressed.

" It's now six o'clock, and my train don't leave till nine," he mused. " But am I going on that train, that's the question?"

The fact was, now he came to think of it, there was no need of hurrying home. He would stay a while and look this mystery in the face until he was dis-illusioned. Besides he wanted to find out what McLeod's visit meant. He had a vague feeling of uneasiness when he recalled the way McLeod had assumed about the General's house. He had told Sallie he must hurry home on the morning's train for no earthly reason than that he had intended to do so when he came.

, So after breakfast he wrote her a little note.

" MY DEAR MISS WORTH,

, My train left me. Will you have compassion on a stranger in a strange city and let me call to see you again to-day?   CHARLES GASTON."

He waited impatiently until he heard his train leave, and then told the boy to make tracks for the General's house.

A peal of laughter rang through the hall when Sallie's dancing eyes read that note.

" Oh! the storyteller! " she cried.

And this was the answer she sent back.

" Certainly. Come out at once. I'll take you buggy driving all by myself over a lovely road up the river. I do this in acknowedgment of the gracious flattery you pay me in the story you told about the train. Of course I know you waited till the train left before you sent the note.   SALLIE WORTH."

" Now I wonder if that young rascal of a boy told her I wrote that note an hour ago? I'll wring his neck if he did. Come here boy! "

The negro came up grinning in hopes of another quarter.

" Did you tell that young lady anything about when I wrote that note? "

" Na-sah! Nebber tole her nuffin. She des laugh and laugh fit ter kill herse'f des quick es she reads de note."

Gaston smiled and threw him another tip.

" Yassah, she's a knowin' lady, sho's you bawn, I been dar lots er times fo' dis! "

Gaston was tempted to ask him for whom he carried those former messages. He walked with bounding steps, his being tingling to his finger tips with the joy of living. The avenue leading the full length of the city toward the General's house was two miles long before it reached the woods at the gate. It seemed only a step this morning.

As he passed through the cool shade of the woods a squirrel was playing hide and seek with his mate on the old crooked fence beside the road. His little nimble mistress flew up a great tree to its topmost bough and chattered and laughed at her lover as he scrambled swiftly after her. She waited until he was just reaching out his arm to grasp her, and then with another scream of laughter leaped straight out into the air to another tree top, and then another and another until lost in the heart of the forest.

"I wonder if that's going to be my fate!" he mused as he turned into the gateway.

Again the majestic beauty of that gleaming mass of ivory on the hill with its green background swept his soul with its power. It seemed a different shade of colour now that he saw it with the sun at another angle. Its surface seemed to have the soft sheen of creamy velvet.

He paused and sighed, "Why should I be so poor! If I only had a house like that I'd turn that big banquet hall on the left wing into a library, and I'd ask no higher heaven."

And he fell to wondering if it would really be worth the having without the face and voice of the girl who was there within waiting for him. No, he was sure of it this morning for the first time in his life. The certainty of this conviction brought to his heart a feeling of loneliness and despair. When he thought of his abject poverty and the long years of struggle before him, and of that beautiful accomplished young woman rich, petted, the belle of the city, the gulf that separated their lives seemed impassable.

"I'm playing with fire!" he said to himself as he

looked up at the graceful pillars with their carved and fluted capitals. "Well, let it be so. Let me live life to its deepest depths and its highest reach. It is better to love and lose than never to love at all." And he walked into the cool hall with the ease and assurance of its master.

Sallie greeted him with the kindliest grace.

"I'm so glad you stayed to-day, Mr. Gaston. I should have been really chagrined to think I made so slight an impression on you that you could walk deliberately away on a pre-arranged schedule. I am not used to being treated so lightly."

He tried to make some answer to this half serious banter, but was so absorbed in just looking at her he said nothing.

She was dressed in a morning gown of a soft red material, trimmed with old cream lace. The material of a woman's dress had never interested him before. He knew calico from silk, but beyond that he never ventured an opinion. To colour alone he was responsive. This combination of red and creamy white, with the bodice cut low showing the lines of her beautiful white shoulders and the great mass of dark hair rising in graceful curves from her full round neck heightened her beauty to an extraordinary degree. As she walked, the clinging folds of her dress, outlining her queenly figure, seemed part of her very being and to be imbued with her soul. He was dazzled with the new revelation of her power over him.

"Have you no apology, sir, for pretending that you were going home this morning?" she said seating herself by his side.

"You didn't ask me to stay with fervour."

"It ought not to have been necessary."

"Didn't you really know I was not going?"

" Yes."

" I'm glad."

" Yes, you see I'm twenty-one years old, and I've seen such things happen before!" she purred this slowly and burst into laughter.

" Now, Miss Sallie, that's cruel to throw me down in a heap of dead dogs I don't even know."

" Don't you like dogs?"

" Four legged ones, yes. But I like my friends alive."

" Oh! It didn't kill any of them. They are all strong and hearty. But if you're so domestic in your tastes why haven't you settled in life?"

" Been waiting to find the woman of my dreams."

" And you haven't found her?"

" Not up to yesterday."

" Oh! I forgot," she said archly, " you're so timid."

" Honestly, I was."

" Up to yesterday!" she murmured. " Well, tell me what your dreams demanded? What kind of a creature must she be?"

" I have forgotten."

" What! Forgotten the dreams of your ideal woman?"

" Yes."

" Since when?"

" Yesterday."

" Thanks. We are getting on beautifully, aren't we? You will get over your timidity in time, I'm sure."

He smiled, looked down at the pattern of the carpet and did not speak for some minutes. His soul was thrilled and satisfied in her presence. As he lifted his eyes from the floor they rested on the piano.

" Will you play for me, Miss Sallie? Auntie says you play delightfully."

" Auntie? Who is Auntie?"

" Mrs. Durham, my foster mother, of course. Excuse

my unconscious assumption of your familiarity with all my antecedents. I can't get over the impression that I have known you all my life."

"And that reminds me that I started to say something to you yesterday that was perfectly ridiculous, but caught myself in time."

"I wish you had said it."

"Mrs. Durham is a great flatterer of those she loves. She thinks I can play. But I'm the veriest amateur."

"Let me be the judge."

She was looking over her music, and he had opened the piano.

"I'll play for you with pleasure. Sit there in that big arm chair. I'm sorry I tired you so early in the day with my chatter."

And before he could protest her fingers were touching the piano with the ease of the born musician.

He sat enraptured as he watched the sinuous grace with which her fingers touched the ivory keys and heard their answering cry which seemed the breath of her own soul in echo.

She had an easy apparently careless touch. To old familiar music she gave a charm that was new, adding something indefinable to the musician's thought that gave luminous power to its interpretation. He had no knowledge of the technique of music, but now he knew that she was improvising. The piano was the voice of her own beautiful soul, and it was pulsing with a tenderness that melted him to tears.

Suddenly the music ceased, and she turned her face full on his before he could brush away a big tear that rolled down. She flushed, closed the piano, and quietly resumed her place by his side.

"And, now, you haven't told me how well I played. You're the first young man so careless."

"I have told you."

"How?"

"The way you told me yesterday that you understood me—with a tear."

"I appreciate it more than words."

"So did I," he slowly said. Again there was a long silence.

"But we do love to hear folks say in words what they think sometimes. I confess I was immensely elated over the fine things the paper said about me this morning."

"It's a wonder too. Our editor is a cranky sort of fellow. I was afraid he'd say a lot of mean things about you. But Papa says you swallowed him whole."

"Did you wish him to say kind things about me?"

"Of course," she said, and then the look of mischief came back in her eye. "Were you not our guest? I should have felt like whipping him if he hadn't said nice things."

"Then I'll tell you what I think about your playing. You gave those strings a soul for the first time for me, beautiful, living, throbbing, that spoke a message of its own. The piece you improvised, I shall never forget. Such music seems to me the grasping of the infinite by hands that touch the impalpable and bringing it for a moment within the sphere of matter that a kindred soul may hear and see and feel."

She started to make some reply but her lips quivered and she looked away across the valley at the river and made no answer.

At dinner the General was in his most genial mood, laughing and joking, and drawing out Gaston on politics and cotton-mill developments, and trying with all his might to tease his daughter.

As he took his departure for the mills, he said, "Young man, I'd ask you to go with me and look at the machinery,

but I see it's no use. I heard her twisting you around
her fingers with that piano a while ago."

"Papa, don't be so silly!' cried Sallie, slipping her
arm around him, putting one hand over his mouth, and
kissing him.

"Go on to your work. I'll entertain Mr. Gaston."

"Indeed you will!" he shouted, throwing her another
kiss as he left.

"He's the dearest father any girl ever had in this
world. I know you loved yours, didn't you, Mr. Gaston?"

"Mine was killed in battle, Miss Sallie. I never knew
him. But I had the most beautiful mother that ever
lived. I lost her when a mere boy. And the world has
never been the same since. I envy you."

"I forgot. Forgive me," she softly said, looking up
into his face with tenderness.

"If I had only had a sister! How my heart used to
ache when I'd see other boys playing with a sister! My
poor little starved soul was so hungry, I would go off
in the woods sometimes and cry for hours."

"I wish I had known you when you were a little boy.
—I can't conceive of a dignified orator swaying thousands
running around as a barefooted boy. But you must have
gone barefooted for I think Papa said so, didn't he?"

"Indeed I did, and sometimes I am afraid for the very
good reason I didn't have any shoes."

"Well, you wouldn't have worn them if you had. I
always wanted to be a boy just to go barefooted. I think
girls lose so much of a child's life by having to wear
shoes."

"But you never knew what it meant to want shoes and
not be able to have them," he said, looking at the shining
tips of her slippers peeping from the edge of her
dress.

" No, but I never thought these things made a great difference in our lives after all. I believe it is what we are, not what we have, that gives life meaning."

He looked at her intently.

" I must get ready now for our drive. The horse will be here in ten minutes. Enjoy the view on the porch until I am ready," and she bounded up the stairs to her room.

In a few minutes she was by his side again dressed in spotless white as he had seen her first. She lifted the lines over the sleek horse, and he dashed swiftly down the drive.

Oh! the peace and bliss of that drive along the lonely river road by its cool green banks!

How he poured out to her his inmost thoughts—things he had not dared to whisper alone with himself and God! And then he wondered why he had thus laid bare his secret dreams to this girl he had known but twenty-four hours. Nonsense, down in his soul he knew he had known her forever. Before the world was made, ages and ages ago in eternity he had known her. He turned to her now drawn by a resistless force as a plant turns toward the sunlight for its life. How he could talk that day! All he had ever known of art and beauty, all he knew of the deep truths of life, were on his lips leaping forth in simple but impassioned words. For hours he lay at her feet where she sat on a rock, high up on the cliffs overlooking the river and poured out his heart like a child. And she listened with a dreamy look as though to the music of a master.

At last she sprang to her feet and looked at her watch.

" Oh! Mama will be furious. It will be after sundown before we can get home. We must hurry."

" I'll make it all right with your Mama," he replied as though he were skilled in meeting such emergencies.

"Don't you speak to her. It'll be all I can do to manage her."

The twilight was gathering when they reached the house, and an angry anxious mother was waiting high up on the stoop.

"Watch me smooth every wrinkle out of her brow now!" she whispered as she flew up the steps.

Before her mother could say a word, a white hand was on her mouth and pretty lips were whispering something in her ears she had never heard before. There was the sound of a kiss and he heard Sallie say, " Not a word!"

And the mother greeted him with a smile and a curiously searching look. She chattted pleasantly until her daughter returned from her room, and then left her. Again it was nearly twelve o'clock before he reached the hotel.

The next morning Bob St. Clare broke in on him before he was out of bed.

" Look here, you sly dog, what are you doing slipping and sliding around here yet?"

" Bob, you're the man I want to see. Tell me all you know about the Worths."

" The Worths? Which one?"

" There's only one so far as I can see."

" Well, you may find out there's two if you should happen to collide with the General."

" Does he cut up at times?"

" He's all right till he turns on you, and then you want to find shelter."

" Did you ever run up against him?"

" No, I never got that far. He's hail-fellow-well-met with every youngster in town. He will laugh and joke about his daughter until he thinks she is in earnest about a fellow, and then he swoops down on him like a hawk. I'll bet a hundred dollars he's playing you now for all you're worth against the latest favourite. But Miss Sallie—she's an angel!"

"Look here, Bob, you're not in love with her?"

"Well, I'm convalescing at present my boy. Every boy in the town has been there, but I don't believe she cares a snap for a man of us unless it's that big red-headed McLeod. I can't make his position out exactly."

"Did she jolt you hard when you hit the ground?"

"Easiest thing you ever saw. She has a supreme genius for painless cruelty. When the time comes she can pull your eye-tooth out in such a delicate friendly way you will have to swear she hasn't hurt you."

"You still go?"

"Lord yes, we all do,—sort of a congress of the lost meet down there. They all hang on. She keeps the friendship of every poor devil she kills."

"You know you make the cold chills run down my back when you talk like that."

"Are you in love with her, Gaston?"

"To tell you the truth, I don't know."

"Then what in the thunder have you been doing out there two days and nights, if you haven't made love to her?"

"Just basking in the sun."

"Well, you are a fool. Eleven hours the first day, and fifteen hours yesterday. Confound you, don't you know a dozen fellows in town are cursing you for all they can think of?"

"What about?"

"Why for trying to hog the whole time, day and night. She won't let a mother's son of them come near till you're gone."

"Well, that's immense!" exclaimed Gaston slapping his friend on the back.

" Don't be too sure. She's just sizing you up. She's done the same thing a dozen times before."

" I don't believe it."

And he didn't go home until the end of the week when the last cent of his money was gone.

CHAPTER VII

DREAMS AND FEARS

HE was on the train at last homeward bound. Gazing out of the window of the car he was trying to find where he stood. He must be in love. He faced the remarkable fact that he had spent a whole week in Independence at an expensive hotel, and squandered every cent of the small fee he had received for his address in what would be otherwise a perfectly senseless manner.

Yet he felt rich. He was sure he had never spent money so wisely and economically in his life. Beyond the shadow of a doubt he was in love,—desperately and hopelessly committed to this one girl for life. He said it in his heart with a shout of triumph. Life was not a sterile desert of brute work. It was true. Love the magician of the ages, lived in this world of lost faiths and dead religions.

Now that he was leaving he felt a tingling impulse to leap off the train, cut across the fields and run back to her—and he laughed aloud, just as the train came to a sudden stop, and everybody looked at him and smiled.

A drummer looked up from a novel he was reading and said,

" It is a fine day, partner, isn't it ? "

" Never saw a finer," answered Gaston with another laugh.

He dwelt long and greedily on the consciousness of

this new vitalising secret he felt for the first time throbbing in his soul. He bathed his heart in its warmth until he could feel the red blood rush to the ends of his fingers with its new fever. He breathed its perfume until every nerve quivered. " I have never lived before. No matter now if I die, I have lived!" he said slowly and reverently.

He wondered long and wistfully what was in her heart while this wild tumult was going on in him. He wondered if it were possible she loved him. It seemed too good to be true. He was afraid to believe it. And yet his whole soul with every power of his being cried out that she did. He could not have been mistaken in the message he read in the liquid depths of her eyes, and the delicate tenderness of her voice. Words may say nothing, but these signs are the language of the universal. Still, others had been equally sure, and been deceived. Might not he too make the fatal mistake? It was possible. And there was the pain.

She had not uttered a single word in all the hours they spent together that might not be interpreted in a conventional meaningless way.

Yet he had given to every one of these words a soul meaning that spoke directly to his inner being and not his ear.

He had never spoken a word of shallow love-making to a woman in his life. To him love was too holy a mystery. It would have been the blasphemy of the Holy Ghost—a sin that would not be forgiven in this world or the world to come. His college mates had called him a crank on this subject. But he shut his lips in a way that always closed the argument, and they let him alone with his Idol.

" I am afraid yet to put it to the test!" he said at last. " I must have time to reveal my best self to her. I must see her again, live close to her day by day, and bring to bear on her every power of body and soul I possess."

Mrs. Durham met him with dancing eyes. "Oh, I've heard from you, sir!"

"Kiss me Auntie, and be kind. I'm in the last stages of delirium!"

He took her hands both in his and looked at her long. "How good you've been to me, Auntie, in all the past. You never looked so beautiful as to-day. I want to thank you for every word you've said to Miss Sallie for me. It may have helped just a little **anyway**."

"Well you are in the last stages!" she exclaimed gleefully.

"And you are glad of it?"

"Of course, I am, it will make a man of you."

"But suppose I lose?"

She was silent a moment and then slipped her arm gently about him, drew down his ear and whispered,

"You shall not lose—I've set my heart on it."

He pressed her hands and said, "How like my sweet mother's voice was that!"

And then they fell to discussing plans for giving Miss Sallie and her friend a jolly time at the Springs.

"But Auntie, these plans don't seem to me exactly what I'd like. You see I want to be the whole thing. It may be hopelessly selfish, but I can't help it."

"Well that isn't best."

"Say Auntie, what do I look like anyway? How would you describe my make up? Let's get at the weak spots and splint them up a little. You know, I never seriously cared a rap before about my looks."

"Well"—she answered, slowly regarding him, "I'll be perfectly frank with you.

"You are tall—at least two inches taller than the average man, and your muscular body gives one the impres-

sion of power. You have black hair, dark-brown eyes
that look out from your shaggy straight eye-brows with
a piercing light."

" You think the brows too shaggy ? "

" No, I like them. They suggest reserve power and
brain capacity."

" Good, I never thought of that."

" You have a face that is massive, almost leonine, and
a square-cut determined mouth, that always clean shaven,
sometimes looks too grim."

" I'll remember that and look pleasant."

" You have a big hand and sometimes shake hands too
strongly. You have a handsome aristocratic foot when
you wear decent shoes. You often walk hump-
shouldered, and sit so too."

" I'll brace up."

" You have deep vertical wrinkles between your eyes
just where your straight eyebrows meet."

" Heavens, I didn't know I had wrinkles! "

" Yes, but they mean habits of thought like your
stooping shoulders, I don't object to such wrinkles in a
man's face. But the best feature of all your stock is
your eye. Your big brown eyes are about the only perfect thing about you. There's infinite tenderness in them.
Now and then they gleam with a hidden fire that tells
of enthusiasm, thought, will, character, and dauntless
courage."

She looked and they were misty with tears.

He pressed her hand. " Auntie, I didn't know how
much you've loved me all these years. How love opens
one's eyes! "

" You have a high temper, plenty of pride, and are
given to looking on the dark side of things too quickly.
You lack poise of character and sureness of touch yet,
but with it all, yours is a masterful nature."

"One you think that a perfect woman could love?"

"There are no perfect women; but I'll match you against any woman I know. So there, now, take courage."

"I will," he gravely answered.

He hurried to his office and read his mail. There were two letters retaining his services for jury work in important cases. His heart leaped at the sign of coming success. What a new meaning love gave to every event in life.

He turned to his books, and began immediately a searching study of every question involved in these cases. He would carry the court by storm. He would lead the jury spellbound by his eloquence to a certain verdict. How clear his brain! He felt he was alive to his finger-tips, and argus-eyed.

He worked hour after hour without the slightest fatigue or knowledge of the flight of time. He looked up at last with surprise to find it was night, and was startled by the voice of the Preacher calling him from below.

"What's the matter with you? Mrs. Durham sent me to find you. She was afraid you had gone up on the roof and walked off."

"I'll be ready in a minute, Doctor," he called from the window.

"I haven't known you to take to law so violently in four years. What's up? Got a capital case?"

"Yes, I believe I have. It's a matter of life and death to one poor soul anyhow."

"Now, honour bright haven't you been working all this afternoon on a love-letter that you've just finished and addressed to Independence?"

"No sir. To tell you the fact, I didn't dare to ask her to write to me. I knew I couldn't control a pen."

"My boy, I wish you success with all my heart. It

makes me young again to look into your face. I've had
my supper, when you've finished your confab with your
Auntie, come out here in the square to the seat under
the old oak, I want to talk to you on some important
business."

"What have you been doing," asked Mrs. Durham.

"Building a home for her!" he cried in a whisper.
He went behind the chair where his foster mother sat
pouring his tea, bent low and kissed her high white forehead. "My own Mother! I'll never call you Auntie
again!"

Tears sprang to her eyes, and she kissed his hand,
tenderly holding it to her lips.

"Ah! Love is a wonder worker, isn't he Charlie?"

"Yes, and I can't realise the joy that lifts and inspires
me when I think that I am one of the elect. It's too good
to be true. I have been initiated into the great secret. I
have tasted the water of Life. I shall not see Death."

She looked at him with pride. "I knew you would
make a matchless lover. I envy Sallie her young eyes
and ears!"

"You need not envy her. You will never grow old."

"So much the worse if we miss the dreams that fill
the souls of the young," she said with an accent of sorrowful pride.

CHAPTER VIII

THE UNSOLVED RIDDLE

GASTON found the Preacher quietly smoking, seated on the rustic under a giant oak that stood in the corner of the square.

Under this tree the speakers' stand had always been built for joint debates in political campaigns.

Here, when a boy he had heard the great debate between Zebulon B. Vance and Judge Thomas Settle in the fierce campaign which followed the overthrow of Legree when the Republican party, under the leadership of Judge Settle made its desperate effort for life. Settle, who was a man of masterful personality, eloquent, and in dead earnest in his appeal for a new South, had made a speech of great power to a crowd that were hostile to every idea for which he stood; and yet he dazzled or stunned them into sullen silence.

And then he recalled with flashes of memory vivid as lightning, the miracle that had followed. He could see Vance now as he slowly lifted his big lion-like head, and calmly looked over the sea of faces with eagle eyes that could flash with resistless humour or blaze with the fury of elemental passion. He reviewed the terrible past in which he had played the tragic role of their war Governor, and tore into tatters with the facts of history the logic of his opponent. And then he opened his batteries of wit and ridicule,—wit that cut to the heart's red blood, and yet convulsed the hearer with its unexpected turn. Ridicule that withered and scorched what it touched into ashes. Five thousand people now in breathless suspense as he swung them into heaven on the wings of deathless words, now screaming with laughter, and now hushed in tears!

The scene that followed this triumph! Two stalwart mountain men snatched him from the rostrum and bore him on their shoulders through the shouting, weeping crowd. Women pressed close and kissed his hands, and old men reached forward their hands to touch his garments. Ah! if he could inherit the power of this king among men! To-night as Gaston walked under that tree with his heart beating with the ecstasy of a new-found source of life, he felt that he could do, and that he would do, what the master had done before him!

"Charlie, I've heard some startling news since you left home, and I can't sleep nights thinking about it."

"You've heard of McLeod's scheme."

"Exactly. And it means the ruin of this state and the ruin of the South unless it can be defeated."

"How are you going to do it?"

"It's a puzzle but it's got to be done. Half the farmers in the strongholds of Democracy are crazy over their fool Sub-Treasury and a hundred other fakir dreams. McLeod has promised them everything—Sub-Treasury, pumpkin leaves for money,—anything they want if they will join forces with his niggers and carry the state. You are the man to begin now a quiet but thorough organisation of the young men, and oust the fools from control of the party.

"When the white race begin to hobnob with the Negro and seek his favour, they must grant him absolute equality. That means ultimately social as well as political equality. You can't ask a man to vote for you and kick him down your front doorstep and tell him to come around the back way."

" I think you exaggerate the social danger, but I see the political end of it."

" I don't exaggerate in the least. I am looking into the future. This racial instinct is the ordinance of our life. Lose it and we have no future. One drop of Negro blood makes a negro. It kinks the hair, flattens the nose, thickens the lip, puts out the light of intellect, and lights the fires of brutal passions. The beginning of Negro equality as a vital fact is the beginning of the end of this nation's life. There is enough negro blood here to make mulatto the whole Republic."

" Such a danger seems too remote for serious alarm to me," replied the younger man.

" Ah! there's the tragedy," passionately cried the Preacher. " You younger men are growing careless and indifferent to this terrible problem. It's the one unsolved and unsolvable riddle of the coming century. *Can you build, in a Democracy, a nation inside a nation of two hostile races?* We must do this or become mulatto, and that is death. Every inch in the approach of these races across the barriers that separate them is a movement toward death. You cannot seek the Negro vote without asking him to your home sooner or later. If you ask him to your house, he will break bread with you at last. And if you seat him at your table, he has the right to ask your daughter's hand in marriage."

" It seems to me a far cry to that. But I see the political crisis. What is your plan? "

" This,—organise the young Democracy in every township in the state, and put yourself at its head, control the primaries and down the old crowd. They've got to follow you. Fight the campaign with the desperation of despair. If you are defeated, God have mercy on us, but you will be ready for the next battle."

" I'll do it," said Gaston with emphasis.

"Then I want you to go on a mission to Col. Duke, the President of the National Farmer's Alliance. He's a good Baptist. He means well, but he's crazy. He dreams of the Presidency when he has established the Sub-Treasury for the farmers. He's afraid of the Negro, and is nervous about using him. He knows I am the most influential Baptist preacher in the state. Tell him I say you will win, and that we will give him the nomination for Governor, and put him in line for the Presidency."

"When shall I go to see him?"

"Immediately. Get ready to-night."

The next week McLeod was seated in his office at Hambright receiving reports from his political henchmen at Raleigh.

"I tell you, McLeod, there's a hitch. Something's dropped. Duke's as coy as a maid of sixteen. He says no decision can be made now until he submits a lot of rot to all the lodges of the Alliance and the " Referendum " decides these points. You'd better get hold of him and comb the kinks out of him quick."

McLeod's eyes flashed with anger, as he twisted the points of his red moustache.

"It's that damned Baptist Preacher," he said. "I'll get even with him yet if it's the only thorough job I do on this earth."

CHAPTER IX

THE RHYTHM OF THE DANCE

BEFORE boarding the train he was to take for Raleigh, he lingered with Mrs. Durham talking, talking, talking about the wonder of his love. As he arose to leave he said,

" Now, Mother dear "——

" Charlie, you just say that so beautifully to make me your slave."

" Of course I do. What I was going to say is, I can't write to her. I don't dare. You can. Tell her all about me won't you? Everything that you think will interest and please her, and that will be discreet. Your intuitions will tell you how far to go. Tell her how hard I'm working and what an important mission I've undertaken, and the tremendous things that hang on its outcome. And tell her how impatiently I'm waiting for her to come to the Springs. Be sure to tell her that."

" All right. I'll act as your attorney in your absence. But hurry back, she must not get here first. I want you to be on the spot."

" I'll be here if I have to give up politics and go into business—and you know how I hate that word ' business.' "

" I'll telegraph you if she comes."

" Don't let her come till I get back. Tell her the hotel isn't fit to receive guests yet—it never is for that matter —but anything to give me time to get here."

He worked with indomitable courage for two weeks, visiting the principal towns in the state, and everywhere arousing intense enthusiasm. There was something contagious in his spirit. The young fellows were charmed by his eager intense way of looking at things, they caught the infection and he made hundreds of staunch friends.

" You're just in time! " cried his mother greeting him with radiant face on his return. " She is coming to-morrow. I've a beautiful letter from her. I think one of the sweetest letters a girl ever wrote."

" Let me see it! "

" No."

" Why, Mother, I thought you were all on my side! "

" But I'm not. I'm a woman, and you can't see some things she says."

" Then it's something awfully nice about me."

" Maybe the opposite."

" Then you'd resent it for me."

" I love her too, sir."

" Let me see the tip end of it where she signs her name! "

" You can see that much, there "——

" Doesn't she write a lovely hand! " He looked long and lovingly. " That pretty name!—Sallie! So old-fashioned, and so homelike. It's music, isn't it? "

" I didn't know you could be so silly, Charlie."

" It is funny, isn't it? You know I think after all, we are made out of the same stuff, saint and sinner, philosopher and fool. The differences are only skin deep."

" You don't think she is made out of ordinary clay? "

" Oh! Lord, no, I meant the men. Every woman is something divine to me. I think of God as a woman, not a man—a great loving Mother of all Life. If I ever saw the face of God it was in my mother's face."

"Hush! you will make me do anything you wish."

"No, no, I don't want to see that letter unless you think it best."

"Well, you will not see any more of it, sir."

When Gaston met them at the depot with a carriage to take Sallie, her mother, and Helen Lowell, her Boston schoolmate, to the Springs, the first passenger to alight was Bob St. Clare.

"What in the thunder are you doing here! This town is quarantined against you!" said Gaston.

"Hush!" said Bob in a stage whisper. "She's here. There's her valise."

"That's why you can't land. Two's company, three's a crowd. I like you, Bob. But I won't stand for this."

The crowd were pouring off the train and had cut off Sallie's party in the centre of the car.

"Gaston, I just came up for your sake. I'm looking after Miss Lowell. I'm lost, ruined. Scared to say a word. I thought maybe, you'd help me out. We'll pool chances. I'll talk for you and you talk for me."

"It's a bargain, St. Clare."

"I want a separate carriage,—get me one quick."

In a few moments, the brief introduction over, Gaston was seated in the carriage facing Sallie and her mother whirling along the road, over the long hills toward the Campbell Sulphur Springs in the woods, two miles from the town.

How beautiful and fresh she looked to him even in a dusty travelling dress! He was drinking the nectar from the depths of her eyes.

"Now don't you think Helen the prettiest girl you ever saw, Mr. Gaston?" she asked.

"I hadn't noticed it."

"Where were your eyes?"

" Elsewhere. I'm so glad you are going to spend a month at the Springs, Miss Sallie. I used to go to school there when a little boy. They had a girl's school there in the winter and boys under twelve were admitted. I know every nook and corner of the big forest back of the hotel. I'll see that you don't get lost."

" That will be fine. But you must bring every good-looking boy in the county and make him bow down and worship Helen. She is not used to it, but she is tickled to death over these Southern boys, and I'm going to give her the best time she ever had in her life."

" I'll do everything you command—except bow down myself. Bob's agreed to do that."

She smiled in spite of her effort to look serious, and her mother pinched her arm. She laughed.

" So you and Bob St. Clare were out there plotting before we could get out of the train? "

" Nothing unlawful, I assure you."

The first day she allowed Gaston to monopolise, and then began his torture. She declared there were others with whom she must be friendly. She determined to give a ball to Helen the next week, and began preparations.

It was a new business for Gaston, but he did his best to please her, in a pathetic half-hearted sort of way. He ran all sorts of errands, and executed her orders with tact.

" Oh! Sallie let the ball go. I don't care for it. I can do nothing to ever repay you for the good time I've been having," said Helen as they sat in her room one night.

" We are going to have it. I tell you. I don't care how much Mr. Gaston sulks. I'm not taking orders from him."

" No, but you'd like to—you know it."

" What an idea! "

" You know you like him better than all the others put together."

" Nonsense. I'm as free as a bird."

" Then what are you blushing for?"

" I'm not." But her face was scarlet.

" You Southern girls are so queer. The moment you like a man you're as sly as a cat, and deny that you even know him. When I find the man I love I don't care who knows it, if he loves me."

" What do you think of Bob St. Clare?"

" I like him."

" Hasn't he made love to you yet?"

" No, and the only one of the crowd who hasn't. I don't mind confessing that I never had love made to me before this visit. In Boston it's a serious thing for a young man to call once. The second call, means a family council, and at the third he must make a declaration of his intentions or face consequences. Down here, the boys don't seem to have anything to do except to make their girl friends happy, and feel they are the queens of the earth, and that their only mission is to minister to them. And some of your girls are engaged to six boys at the same time."

" Don't you like it?"

" It's glorious. I feel that if I hadn't come down here to see you I'd have missed the meaning of life."

" Don't our boys make love beautifully?"

" I never dreamed of anything like it. They make it so seriously, so dead in earnest, you can't help believing them."

" And Bob hasn't said a word?"

" Hasn't breathed a hint."

" Then you have him sure. They are hit hard when they are silent like that. Bob made love to me the second day he ever saw me."

"Don't tease me, dear," said Helen as she put her pretty rosy cheek against the dark beauty of the South. "Do you really think he likes me seriously?"

"He's crazy about you, goose!"

There was the sound of a kiss.

"I can't tell stories about it like you, Sallie, I'm afraid I'm in love with him," she whispered.

"Well, I'll make him court you to-morrow or have him thrashed, if you say so."

"Don't you dare!"

"Then do just as I tell you about this ball and get yourself up regardless."

On the night of the ball, Gaston, sitting out on the porch, felt nervous and fidgety, like a fish out of water. He knew he had no business there, and yet he couldn't go away. They had a quarrel about the ball. Sallie had insisted that Gaston honour her by coming in evening dress whether he danced or not.

"But, Miss Sallie, I'll feel like a fool. Everybody in the country knows that I never entered a ball-room."

"Do you care so much what everybody thinks about you?"

"No, but I care what I think of myself."

"Well, if you don't come in full dress suit, I won't speak to you."

He turned pale in spite of his effort at self control. Then a queer steel-like look came into his eyes.

"I shall be more than sorry to fail to please you, but I have no dress suit. I have never had time for social frivolities. I can't afford to buy one for this occasion. I couldn't be nigger enough to hire one, so that's the end of it. I'll have to come dressed in my own fashion or stay at home."

"Then you can stay at home," she snapped.

"I'll not do it," he coolly replied.

" Well, I like your insolence."

" I'm glad you do.   I'll come as I come to all such
functions, an outsider.   I'll sit out here on the porch in
the shadows and see it from afar.   If I could only dance,
I assure you I'd try to fill every number of your card.
Not being able to do so, I simply decline to make a fool
of myself."

" For that compliment, I'll compromise with you.
Wear that big pompous Prince Albert suit you spoke in
at Independence, and I'll come out on the porch and
chat with you a while."

He sat there now in the shadows waiting for this ball
to begin.   It was a clear night the first week in June.
The new moon was hanging just over the tree tops.   His
heart was full to bursting with the thought that the girl
he loved would, in a few minutes, be whirling over that
polished floor to the strains of a waltz, with another
man's arm around her.   He never knew how deeply he
hated dancing before—that rhythmic touch of the human
body, set to the melody of motion, and voiced in the
passionate cry of music.   He felt its challenge to his love
to mortal combat,—his love that claimed this one woman
as his own, body and soul!

The music from the Italian band was in full swing,
its plaintive notes instinct with the passion of sunny
Italy, a music all Southern people love.

He felt that he should choke.   A sudden thought
came to him.   Tearing a sheet of paper from a note
book he scrawled this line upon it.

" Dear Miss Sallie:—Please let me see you a moment
in the parlour before you enter the ball-room.   Gaston."

At least he would see her in her ball costume first.
Yes, and if she should hate him for it, he would beg
her not to dance that night.   He saw McLeod, bowing
and scraping in the ball-room arrayed in faultless full

Sallie

"A DAZZLING VISION OF BEAUTY."

dress, and glancing toward the door. He knew he was waiting for her to ask her to dance. How he would like to wring his handsome neck!

The boy returned immediately and said the lady was waiting in the parlour. He entered with a sense of fear and confusion.

She came to him with her bare arm extended, a dazzling vision of beauty. She was dressed in a creamy white crêpe ball gown, cut modestly decolleté over her full bust and gleaming shoulders, sleeveless, and held with tiny straps across the curve of the upper arm.

He was stunned. She smiled in triumph, conscious of her resistless power.

"Forgive me for my selfishness in keeping you here just a moment from the rest. I wished to see you first."

"What? to inspect like Mama, to see if I look all right?"

"No, with a mad desire to keep you as long as possible from the others."

Then she looked up at him and said slowly and softly,

"Would it please you very much if I were not to dance to-night?"

"I wouldn't dare ask so selfish a thing of you. It is with you a simple habit of polite society, and you enjoy it as a child does play. I understand that, and yet if you do not dance to-night, I feel as though I would crawl round this world on my hands and knees for you if you would ask it. There are men waiting for you in that ball room whom I hate."

She looked at him timidly as though she were afraid he was about to say too much and replied,

"Then I will not dance to-night. I'll just preside over the ball and let Helen be the queen."

"Words have no power to convey my gratitude. I count all my little triumphs in life nothing to this. You promised to join me on the porch. Don't change that part of the programme. I will talk to your mother until you come."

Gaston went down stairs treading on air. He sought her mother and devoted himself to her with supreme tact. He discovered her tastes and prejudices and paid her that knightly deference some young men express easily and naturally to their elders. He had always been a favourite with old people. He prided himself on it. This faculty he regarded as a badge of honour. As he sat there and talked with this frail little woman, his heart went out to her in a great yearning love. She was the mother of the bride of his soul. He would love her forever for that. No matter whether she loved him or hated him. He would love the mother who gave to his thirsty lips the water of Life.

Drawn irresistibly by the magnetism of his mind and manner Mrs. Worth forgot the flight of time and thought but a moment had past when an hour after the ball had opened, Sallie came out leaning on McLeod's arm.

"Mama, have you been monopolising Mr. Gaston for a whole hour?"

"He hasn't been here a half hour, Miss!" cried her mother.

"He's been here an hour and ten minutes. I'm going to tell Papa on you just as soon as I get home."

"Go back to your dancing."

"No, thank you, I have an engagement to take a walk with your beau. Come Mr. Gaston."

They walked to the spring and along the winding path by the brook at the foot of the hill, and found a rustic seat. They were both silent for several moments.

"I saw you were charming Mama, or I would have come sooner."

" I hope she likes me."

" She has been praising you ever since your visit to Independence. I never saw her talk so long to a young man in my life before. You must have hypnotised her."

" I hope so."

A strange happiness filled her heart. She was afraid to look it in the face; and yet she dared to play with the thought.

" Are you enjoying your triumph to-night? I've had war inside."

" I feel like I am the Emperor of the World and that the Evening Star is smiling on my court! "

She smiled, tossed her head, leaned against the tree and said,

" I wonder if you are in the habit of saying things like that to girls? "

" Upon my soul and honour, no."

" Then thanks. I'll dream about that, maybe."

They returned to the hotel and McLeod claimed her. They went back the same walk, and by a freak of fate he chose the same seat she had just vacated with Gaston.

" Miss Sallie, you are of age now. You know that I have loved you passionately since you were a child. I have made my way in life, I am hungry for a home and your love to glorify it. Why will you keep me waiting? "

" Simply because I know now I do not love you, Allan, and I never will. Once and forever, here, to-night I give you my last answer, I will not be your wife."

" Then don't give the answer to-night. I can wait," he interrupted. " I am just on the threshold of a great career. Success is sure. I can offer you a dazzling position. Don't give me such an answer. Leave the old answer—to wait."

" No, I will not. I do not love you. If you were to

become the President, it would not change this fact, and it is everything."

"Then you love another."

"That is none of your business, sir. I have known you since childhood. I have had ample time to know my own mind."

"All right, we will say good-bye for the present. You have made me a laughing stock of young fools, but I can stand it. I'll not give you up, and if I can't have you, no other man shall."

"If you leave my will out of the calculation, you will make a fatal mistake."

"Women have been known to change their wills."

Before leaving her that night Gaston held her hand for an instant as he bade her good-bye and said, "Miss Sallie, I thank you with inexpressible gratitude for the honour you have done me."

"I've just been wondering what you have done to deserve it?"

"Absolutely nothing,—that's why it is so sweet. This has been the happiest day I ever lived. I cannot see you again before you go. I leave to-morrow on urgent business. May I come to Independence to see you?"

"Yes, I'll be delighted to see you. Good-night."

Gaston was the last to return to Hambright. He walked the two miles through the silent starlit woods. He took a short cut his bare feet had travelled as a boy, and with uncovered head walked slowly through the dim aisles of great trees. It was good, this cool silence and the soft mantle of the night about his soul! The stars whispered love. The wind sighed it through the leaves.

He had withdrawn from the church in his college days because he had grown to doubt everything—God, heaven, hell, and immortality. To-night as he walked slowly home he heard that wonderful sentence of the old Bible ringing down the ages, wet with tears and winged with hope,

"*God is love!*"

He said it now softly and reverently, and the tears came unbidden from his soul. He felt close to the heart of things. He knew he was close to the heart of nature. What if nature was only another name for God? And he whispered it again,

"*God is love!*"

"Ah! If I only knew it I would bow down and worship Him forever!" he cried.

When Sallie reached her mother's room that night, Mrs. Worth was seated by her window.

"Why didn't you dance?"

"Didn't care to."

"Sly Miss, you can't fool me. You didn't dance because Mr. Gaston couldn't. That was a dangerously loud way to talk to him."

"How did you like him, Mama?"

"Come here, dear, and sit on the edge of my chair. I wish I knew when you were in earnest about a man. I like him more than I can tell you. He talked to me so beautifully about his mother, I wanted to kiss him. He is charming."

"Why, Mama!"

"I'd like him for a son. There's a wealth of deep tenderness and manly power in him."

"Mama, you're getting giddy!"

But she kissed her mother twice when she said good night.

CHAPTER X

THE HEART OF A VILLAIN

McLEOD had developed into a man of undoubted power. He was but thirty-two years old, and the dictator of his party in the state.

He had the fighting temperament which Southern people demand in their leaders. With this temperament he combined the skill of subtle diplomatic tact. He had no moral scruples of any kind. The problem of expediency alone interested him in ethics.

McLeod's pet aversion was a preacher, especially a Baptist or a Methodist. His choicest oaths he reserved for them. He made a study of their weaknesses, and could tell dozens of stories to their discredit, many of them true. He had an instinct for finding their weak spots and holding them up to ridicule. He bought every book of militant infidelity he could find and memorised the bitterest of it. He took special pride in scoffing at religion before the young converts of Durham's church.

He was endowed with a personal magnetism that fascinated the young as the hiss of a snake holds a bird. His serious work was politics and sensualism. In politics he was at his best. Here he was cunning, plausible, careful, brilliant and daring. He never lost his head in defeat or victory. He never forgot a friend, or forgave an enemy. Of his foe he asked no quarter and gave none.

His ambitions were purely selfish. He meant to climb to the top. As to the means, the end would justify them. He preferred to associate with white people. But when it was necessary to win a negro, he never hesitated to go any length. The centre of the universe to his mind was A. McLeod.

He was fond of saying to a crowd of youngsters whom he taught to play poker and drink whiskey,

"Boys, I know the world. The great man is the man who gets there."

He was generous with his money, and the boys called him a jolly good fellow. He used to say in explanation of this careless habit,

"It won't do for an ordinary fool to throw away money as I do. I play for big stakes. I'm not a spendthrift. I'm simply sowing seed. I can wait for the harvest."

And when they would admire this overmuch he would warn them,

"As a rule my advice is, Get money. Get it fairly and squarely if you can, but whatever you do,—get it. When you come right down to it, money's your first, last, best and only friend. Others promise well but when the scratch comes, they fail. Money never fails."

A boy of fifteen asked him one day when he was mellow with liquor,

"McLeod, which would you rather be, President of the United States or a big millionaire?"

"Boys," he replied, smacking his lips, and running his tongue around his cheeks inside and softly caressing them with one hand, while he half closed his eyes,

"They say old Simon Legree is worth fifty millions of dollars, and that his actual income is twenty per cent on that. They say he stole most of it, and that every dollar represents a broken life, and every cent of it could be painted red with the blood of his victims. Even so, I would rather be in Legree's shoes and have those millions a year than to be Almighty God with hosts of angels singing psalms to me through all eternity."

And the shallow-pated satellites cheered this blasphemy with open-eyed wonder.

The weakest side of his nature was that turned toward women. He was vain as a peacock, and the darling wish of his soul was to be a successful libertine. This was the secret of the cruelty back of his desire of boundless wealth.

He had the intellectual forehead of his Scotch father, large, handsomely modelled features, nostrils that dilated and contracted widely, and the thick sensuous lips of his mother. His eyebrows were straight, thick, and suggested undoubted force of intellect. His hair was a deep red, thick and coarse, but his moustache was finer and it was his special pride to point its delicately curved tips.

His vanity was being stimulated just now by two opposite forces. He was in love, as deeply as such a nature could love, with Sallie Worth. Her continued rejection of his suit had wounded his vanity, but had roused all the pugnacity of his nature to strengthen this apparent weakness.

He had discovered recently that he exercised a potent influence over Mrs. Durham. The moment he was repulsed, his vanity turned for renewed strength toward her. He saw instantly the immense power even the slightest indiscretion on her part woud give him over the Preacher's life. He knew that while he was not a demonstrative man, he loved his wife with intense devotion. He knew, too, that here was the Preacher's weakest spot. In his tireless devotion to his work, he had starved his wife's heart. He had noticed that she always called him " Dr. Durham " now, and that he had gradually fallen into the habit of calling her " Mrs. Durham."

This had been fixed in their habits, perhaps by the change from housekeeping to living at the hotel. Since old Aunt Mary's death, Mrs. Durham had given up her struggle with the modern negro servants, closed her house, and they had boarded for several years.

He saw that if he could entangle her name with his in the dirty gossip of village society, he could strike his enemy a mortal blow. He knew that she had grown more and more jealous of the crowds of silly women that always dog the heels of a powerful minister with flattery and open admiration. He determined to make the experiment.

Mrs. Durham, while nine years his senior, did not look a day over thirty. Her face was as smooth and soft and round as a girl's, her figure as straight and full, and her every movement instinct with stored vital powers that had never been drawn upon.

She was in a dangerous period of her mental development. She had been bitterly disappointed in life. Her loss of slaves and the ancestral prestige of great wealth had sent the steel shaft of a poisoned dagger into her soul. She was unreconciled to it. While she was passing through the anarchy of Legree's régime which followed the war, her unsatisfied maternal instincts absorbed her in the work of relieving the poor and the broken. But when the white race rose in its might and shook off this nightmare and order and a measure of prosperity had come, she had fallen back into brooding pessimism.

She had reached the hour of that soul crisis when she felt life would almost in a moment slip from her grasp, and she asked herself the question, "Have I lived?" And she could not answer.

She found herself asking the reasons for things long accepted as fixed and eternal. What was good, right, truth? And what made it good, right, or true?

And she beat the wings of her proud woman's heart against the bars that held her, until tired, and bleeding she was exhausted but unconquered.

She was furious with McLeod for his open association with negro politicians.

"Allan, in my soul, I am ashamed for you when I see you thus degrade your manhood."

"Nonsense, Mrs. Durham," he replied, "the most beautiful flower grows in dirt, but the flower is not dirt."

"Well, I knew you were vain, but that caps the climax!"

"Isn't my figure true, whether you say I'm dog-fennel or a pink?"

"No, you are not a flower. Will is the soul of man. The flower is ruled by laws outside itself. A man's will is creative. You can make law. You can walk with your head among the stars, and you choose to crawl in a ditch. I am out of patience with you."

"But only for a purpose. You must judge by the end in view."

"There's no need to stoop so low."

"I assure you it is absolutely necessary to my aims in life. And they are high enough. I appreciate your interest in me, more than I dare to tell you. You have always been kind to me since I was a wild red-headed brute of a boy. And you have always been my supreme inspiration in work. While others have cursed and scoffed you smiled at me and your smile has warmed my heart in its blackest nights."

She looked at him with a mother-like tenderness.

"What ends could be high enough to justify such methods?"

"I hate poverty and squalour. It's been my fate. I've sworn to climb out of it, if I have to fight or buy my way through hell to do it. I dream of a palatial home, of soft white beds, grand banquet halls, and music and wine, and the faces of those I love near me. Besides, the work I am doing is the best for the state and the nation."

"But how can you walk arm in arm with a big black negro, as they say you do, to get his vote?"

"Simply because they represent 120,000 votes I need. You can't tell their colour when they get in the box. I use these fools as so many worms. My political creed is for public consumption only. I never allow anybody to impose on me. I don't allow even Allan McLeod to deceive me with a paper platform, or a lot of articulated wind. I'm not a preacher."

She winced at that shot, blushed and looked at him curiously for a moment.

"No, you are not a preacher. I wish you were a better man."

"So do I, when I am with you," he answered in a low serious voice.

"But I can't get over the sense of personal degradation involved in your association with negroes as your equal," she persisted.

"The trouble is you're an unreconstructed rebel. Women never really forgive a social wrong."

"I am unreconstructed," she snapped with pride.

"And you thank God daily for it, don't you?"

"Yes, I do. Human nature can't be reconstructed by the fiat of fools who tinker with laws," she cried.

"These thousands of black votes are here. They've got to be controlled. I'm doing the job."

"You don't try to get rid of them."

"Get rid of them? Ye gods, that would be a task! The Negro is the sentimental pet of the nation. Put him on a continent alone, and he will sink like an iron wedge to the bottomless pit of barbarism. But he is the ward of the Republic—our only orphan, chronic, incapable. That wardship is a grip of steel on the throat of the South. Back of it is an ocean of maudlin sentimental fools. I am simply making the most of the situation. I didn't make it to order. I'm just doing the best I can with the material in hand."

"Why don't you come out like a man and defy this horde of fools?"

"Martyrdom has become too cheap. The preachers have a hundred thousand missionaries now we are trying to support."

"Allan, I thought you held below the rough surface of your nature high ideals,—you don't mean this."

"What could one man do against these millions?"

"Do!" she cried, her face ablaze. "The history of the world is made up of the individuality of a few men. A little Yankee woman wrote a crude book. The single act of that woman's will caused the war, killed a million men, desolated and ruined the South, and changed the history of the world. The single dauntless personality of George Washington three times saved the colonies from surrender and created the Republic. I am surprised to hear a man of your brain and reading talk like that!"

"When I am with you and hear your voice I have heroic impulses. You are the only human being with whom I would take the time to discuss this question. But the current is too strong. The other way is easier, and it serves my ends better. Besides, I am not sure it isn't better from every point of view. We've got the Negro here, and must educate him."

"Hush! Tell that to somebody that hates you, not to me," she cried.

"Don't you think we must educate them?"

"No, I think it is a crime."

"Would you leave them in ignorance, a threat to society?"

"Yes, until they can be moved. When I see these young negro men and women coming out of their schools and colleges well dressed, with their shallow veneer of an imitation culture, I feel like crying over the farce."

"Surely, Mrs. Durham, you believe they are better fitted for life?"

"They are not. They are lifted out of their only possible sphere of menial service, and denied any career. It is simply inhuman. They are led to certain slaughter of soul and body at last. It is a horrible tragedy."

Allan looked at her, smiled, and replied, "I knew you were a bitter and brilliant woman but I didn't think you would go to such lengths even with your pet aversions."

"It's not an aversion, or a prejudice, sir. It's a simple fact of history. Education increases the power of the human brain to think and the heart to suffer. Sooner or later these educated negroes feel the clutch of the iron hand of the white man's unwritten laws on their throat. They have their choice between a suicide's grave or a prison cell. And the numbers who dare the grave and the prison cell daily increase. The South is kinder to the Negro when he is kept in his place."

"You are a quarter of a century behind the times."

"Am I so old?" she laughed.

"The sentiment, not the woman. You are the most beautiful woman I ever saw."

"I like all my boys to feel that way about me."

"You don't class me quite with the rest, do you?"

She blushed the slightest bit. "No, I've always taken a peculiar interest in you. I have quarrelled with everybody who has hated and spoken evil of you. I have always believed you were capable of a high and noble life of great achievement."

"And your faith in me has been my highest incentive to give the lie to my enemies and succeed. And I will. I will be the master of this state within two years. And I want you to remember that I lay it all at your feet. The world need not know it,—you know it." He spoke with intense earnestness.

"But I don't want you to make such a success at the price of Negro equality. I feel a sense of unspeakable degradation for you when I hear your name hissed. At least I was your teacher once. Come Allan, give up Negro politics and devote yourself to an honourable career in law!"

He shook his head with calm persistence.

"No, this is my calling."

"Then take a nobler one."

"To succeed grandly is the only title to nobility here."

"Is the Doctor on speaking terms with you now?"

"Oh! yes, I joke him about his hide-bound Bourbonism, and he tells me I am all sorts of a villain. But we have made an agreement to hate one another in a polite sort of way as becomes a teacher in Israel and a statesman with responsibilities. By the way, I saw him driving to the Springs with a bevy of pretty girls a few hours ago."

"Indeed, I didn't know it!"

"Yes, he seemed to be having a royal time and to have renewed his youth."

An angry flush came to her face and she made no reply. McLeod glanced at her furtively and smiled at this evidence that his shot had gone home.

"Would you drive with me to the Springs? We will get there before this party starts back." She hesitated, and answered, "yes."

CHAPTER XI

THE OLD OLD STORY

WHEN Gaston arrived in Independence he went direct to St. Clare's.

"Where the Dickens have you been, Gaston?"

"Jumping from Murphy to Manteo making love to hayseed statesmen."

"What luck?"

"They're all crazy. They swear they are going to have the United States establish a Sub-Treasury in Raleigh and issue Government script they can use as money on their pumpkins, or they are going to tear the nation to tatters and vote for a nigger for Governor if necessary!"

"Can't you get into their fool heads that an alliance with the Republican party is the last way on earth for them to go about their Sub-Treasury schemes?"

"Can't seem to do a thing with them. McLeod's stuffed them full. I'm sick of it. I've a notion to let them go with the niggers and go to the devil. It's growing on me that there must be another way out. I can't get down in the dirt and prostitute my intellect and lie to these fools. We've got to get rid of the Negro."

"A large job, old man."

"Yes, it is, and thank God I'm done with it for a week. I'm going to heaven now for a few days. I'll see her in an hour. I rise on tireless wings!"

"Look out you don't come down too suddenly. The earth may feel hard."

"Bob, I'm going to risk it. I'm going to look fate squarely in the face and get my answer like a little man, for life or death."

Mrs. Worth met Gaston and greeted him with warmest cordiality.

"We are charmed to welcome you to Oakwood again, Mr. Gaston."

"I assure you, Mrs. Worth, I never saw a home so beautiful. I feel as though I am in paradise when I get here."

"I hope to see more of you this time, I feel that I know you so much better since our talk at the Springs."

"Thank you, Mrs. Worth." He said this so simply and earnestly she could but feel his deep appreciation of her attitude of welcome.

"Sallie will be down in a minute."

Gaston smiled in spite of himself.

"What are you laughing at?"

"I was just thinking how sweetly her name sounded on your lips."

"Do you like these old-fashioned Southern names?"

"I think they are lovely."

"Well, that's my name too."

Sallie suddenly stepped from the hall into the doorway.

"Now, Mama, there you are again carrying on with one of my beaux! I don't know what I will do with you!"

Mrs. Worth actually blushed, sprang up and struck Sallie lightly on the arm with her fan exclaiming, "Oh! you sly thing, to stand out there and listen to what I said! Mr. Gaston I turn her over to you to punish her for such conduct."

"Isn't she a dear?" said Sallie when her mother was gone.

"I was charmed with her at the Springs, but the

gracious way she made me feel at home this morning completely won my heart."

" I can do anything with Mama. She's the dearest mother that ever lived. She always seems to know intuitively my heart's wish, and, if it's best, give it to me, and if it's not, she makes me cease to desire it. I wish I could manage Papa as easily."

" I'm sure he idolises you, Miss Sallie."

" He does, but when he lays the law down, that settles it. I can't move him one inch."

" That's the way with forceful men, who do things in the world."

" Well, I confess I like to have my own way sometimes. I wonder if you are like that?"

" I'll be frank with you. Somehow I never could be anything else if I tried. I don't think a man of strong character will yield to every whim of a woman, whether wife or daughter."

" I heard of a man the other day who whipped his wife," she said in a far away tone of voice. " Come, my horse is ready, go with me for another ride to-day. I am going to take you across the river and show you a pretty drive over there."

They were soon lost in the deep shadows of the stately pine forest that lay beyond the Catawba. The road was a cross-country narrow way that wound in and out around the big trees.

They jogged slowly along while he bathed his soul in the joy of her presence. Oh, to be alone and near her! There seemed to him a magic power in the touch of her dress as she sat in the little buggy so close by his side. For hours, again he lay at her feet and drank the wine of her beauty until his heart was drunk with love.

Once he opened his lips to tell her, and a great fear awed him into silence. He longed to pour out to her his passion, but feared her answer. He had studied her every word and tone and look and hand-pressure since he had known her. He was sure she loved him. And yet he was not sure. She was so skilled in the science of self defence, so subtle a mistress of all the arts of polite society in which the soul's deepest secrets are hid from the world, he was paralysed now as the moment drew near. He put it off another day and gave himself up to the pure delight of her face and form and voice and presence.

That evening when she entered the home her mother caught her hand and softly whispered, " Did he court you to-day, Sallie? "

She shook her head smilingly. " No, but I think he will to-morrow."

St. Clare was sitting on his veranda awaiting Gaston's return.

" What luck, old boy? " he eagerly asked.

" Couldn't say a word. I'll do it to-morrow or die."

" Shake hands partner. I've been there."

" Bob, it's a serious thing to run up against a little answer ' yes ' or ' no,' that means life or death."

" Feel like you'd rather live on hope a while, and let things drift, don't you? "

" Exactly. I think I can understand for the first time in my life that awful look in a prisoner's face on trial for his life, when he watches the lips of the foreman of the jury to catch the first letter of the verdict. I used to think that an interesting psychological study. By George, I feel I am his brother now."

The next day was perfect. The warm life-giving sun of June was tempered by breezes that swept fresh and invigorating over the earth that had been drenched with showers in the night. The woods were ringing with the chorus of feathered throats chanting the old oratorio of

life and love. Again Gaston and Sallie were jogging
along the shady river road they had travelled on the first
day she had taken him driving.

" Do you remember this road? " she asked.

" I'll never forget it. Along this road we hurried in
the twilight to face your angry mother, and just one
kiss smoothed her brow into a welcoming smile for
me."

" Well, I'm going to risk greater trouble to-day, and
take you a mile or two further up the river to the old
mill site at the rapids. It's the most beautiful and romantic spot in the country. The river spreads out a
quarter of a mile in width, and goes plunging and dash-
ing down the rapids through thousands of projecting
rocks, a mass of white foam as far as you can see. It's
full of tiny green islands with ferns and rhododendron
and wild grape vines, and their perfume sweetens the
air for miles along the water. These little islands, some
ten feet square, some an acre, are full of mocking-birds
nesting there, though since the mills were burned during the war nobody has lived near. The songs of these
birds seem tuned to the music of the river."

" It must be a glimpse of fairy-land! " he exclaimed.

" I know you will be thrilled with its romantic beauty.
It's five miles from a house in any direction."

Gaston was silent. He made a resolution in his
soul that he would never leave that spot until he
knew his fate. His heart began to thump now like a
sledge-hammer. He looked down furtively at her and
tried to imagine how she would look and what she would
say when he should startle her first with some word of
tender endearment or the sound of her name he had said
over and over a thousand times in his heart, and aloud
when alone, but never dared to use without its prefix.

She saw his abstraction and divined intuitively the current of emotions with which he was struggling, but pretended not to notice it. He tied the horse at the old mill, and they walked slowly down the bank of the river.

"That is my island," she cried pointing out into the river. "That third one in the group running out from the point. We can step from one rock to another to it."

It was indeed an entrancing spot. The island seemed all alone in the middle of the river when one was on it. It was not more than fifty feet wide and a hundred feet long, its length lying with the swift current. At the lower end of it a fine ash tree spread its dense shade, hanging far over the still waters that stood in smooth eddy at its roots. On the upper side of this tree lay a big boulder resting against its trunk and embedded in a mass of clean white sand the water had filtered and washed and thrown there on some spring flood.

She climbed on this rock, sat down, and leaned her bare head against its trunk.

"This is my throne," she laughingly cried.

He leaned against the rock and looked up at her with eyes through which the yearning, the hunger, the joy, and the fear of all life were quivering. What a picture she made under the dark cool shadows! Her dress was again of spotless white that seemed now to have been woven out of the foam of the river. Her throat was bare, her cheeks flushed, and her wavy hair the wind had blown loose into a hundred stray ringlets about her face and neck. Her lips were trembling with a smile at his speechless admiration.

"You seem to have been struck dumb," she said. "Isn't this glorious?"

"Beyond words, Miss Sallie. I didn't know there was such a spot on the earth."

"This is my favourite perch. Art and wealth could

"THIS IS MY THRONE."

never make anything like this! I could come here and sit and dream all day alone if Mama would let me."

He tried to begin the story of his love, but every time his tongue refused to move. He was trembling with nervous hesitation and began to dig a hole in the sand with his heel.

"What is the matter with you to-day? I never saw you so serious and moody."

Just then a female mocking-bird in her modest dove-coloured dress lit on a swaying limb whose tips touched the still water of the eddy at their feet, and her proud mate with head erect, far up on the topmost twig of the ash struck softly the first note of his immortal love poem, the dropping song.

"Listen, he's going to sing his dropping song!" he cried in a whisper.

And they listened. He sang his first stanza in a low dreamy voice, and then as the sweetness of his love and the glory of his triumph grew on his bird soul, he lifted his clear notes higher and higher until the woods on the banks of the river rang with its melody.

His mate turned her eyes upward and quietly twittered a sweet little answer.

His response rang like a silver trumpet far up in the sky! He sprang ten feet into the air and slowly dropped singing, singing his long trilling notes of melting sweetness. He stopped on the topmost twig, sat a moment, never ceasing his matchless song, and then began to fall downward from limb to limb toward his mate, pouring out his soul in mad abandonment of joy, but growing softer, sweeter, more tender as he drew nearer. They could see her tremble now with pride and love at his approach, as she glanced timidly upward, and answered him with maiden modesty. At last when he reached her side, his song was so low and sweet and dream-like it

could scarcely be heard. He touched the tip of her beak
with a bird kiss, they chirped, and flew away to the woods
together.

Gaston determined to speak or die. His eyes were wet
with unshed tears, and he was trembling from head to
foot. He had meant to pour out his love for her like
that bird in words of passionate beauty, but all he could
do was to say with stammering voice low and tense with
emotion,

"Miss Sallie, I love you!"

He had meant to say "Sallie," but at the last gasp of
breath, as he spoke, his courage had failed. He did not
look up at first. And when she was silent, he timidly
looked up, fearing to hear the answer or read it in her
face. She smiled at him and broke into a low peal of
joyous laughter! And there was a note of joy in her
laughter that was contagious.

"Please don't laugh at me," he stammered, smiling
himself.

She buried her face in her hands and laughed again.
She looked at him with her great blue eyes wide open,
dancing with fun, and wet with tears.

"Do you know, it's the funniest thing in the world,
you are the sixth man who has made love to me on this
rock within a year!" and again she laughed in his face.

"Look here, Miss Sallie, this is cruel!"

"Dear old rock. It's enchanted. It never fails!" and
she laughed softly again, and patted the rock with her
hand.

"Surely you have tortured me long enough. Have
some pity."

"It is a pitiable sight to see a big eloquent man stam-
mer and do silly things isn't it?"

"Please give me your answer," he cried still trembling.

"Oh! it's not so serious as all that!" she said with dancing eyes.

"I'm in the dust at your feet."

"You mean in the sand. Did you know that you dug a hole in that sand deep enough to bury me in? I thought once you were meditating murder by the expression on your face."

"Please give me one earnest look from your eyes," he pleaded.

"You're a terrible disappointment," she answered leaning back and putting her hands behind her head thoughtfully.

His heart stood still at this unexpected speech.

"How?" he slowly asked, looking down at the sand again.

"Because," she said in her old tantalising tone, "I expected so much of you."

"Then you don't class me with the other poor devils at least?" he asked hopefully.

"No, no, they were handsome boys and made me beautiful speeches. But you are distinguished. You are a man that everybody would look at twice in a crowd. You are a famous young orator who can hold thousands breathless with eloquence. I thought you would make me the most beautiful speech. But you acted like a school boy, stammered, looked foolish, and pawed a hole in the ground!" Again she laughed.

"I confess, Miss Sallie, I was never so overwhelmed with terror and nervousness by an audience before."

"And just one girl to hear!"

"Yes, but she counts more with me than all the other millions, and one kind look from her eyes I would hold dearer at this moment than a conquered world's applause."

"That's fine! That's something like it. Say more!" she cried.

His face clouded and he looked earnestly at her.

"Come, come, Miss Sallie, this is too cruel. I have torn my heart's deepest secrets open to you, and tremblingly laid my life at your feet, and you are laughing at me. I have paid you the highest homage one human soul can offer another. Surely I deserve better than this?"

"There, you do. Forgive me. I have seen so much shallow love making, I am never quite sure a boy's in dead earnest." She spoke now with seriousness.

"You cannot doubt my earnestness. I have spoken to you this morning the first words of love that ever passed my lips. One chamber of my soul has always been sacred. It was the throne room of Love, reserved for the One Woman waiting for me somewhere whom I should find. I would not allow an angel to enter it, and I hid it from the face of God. I have opened it this morning. It is yours."

She softly slipped her hand in his, and tremblingly said, while a tear stole down her cheek,

"I do love you!"

He bent over her hand and kissed it, and kissed it, while his frame shook with uncontrollable emotion. Then looking up through his dimmed eyes, he said,

"My darling, that was the sweetest music, that sentence, that I shall ever hear in this world or in all the worlds beyond it in eternity!"

"When did you first begin to love me?" she asked.

"I don't know. But I loved you the first moment you looked into my face while I was speaking that day. And I recognised you instantly as the Dream of my Soul. I have loved you for ever, ages before we were born in this world, somewhere, our souls met and knew and loved. And I've been looking for you ever since. When I saw you there in the crowd that day looking up at me with those beautiful blue eyes, I felt like shouting "I have found her! I have found her!" and rushing to your side lest I should not see you again."

"It is strange—this feeling that we have known each other forever. The moment you touched my hand that first day, a sense of perfect content and joy in living came over me. I couldn't remember the time when I hadn't known you. You seemed so much a part of my inmost thoughts and every day life. I laughed this morning from sheer madness of joy when you told me your love. I knew you were going to tell me to-day. You tried yesterday, but I held you back. I wanted you to tell me here at this beautiful spot, that the music of this water might always sing its chorus with the memory of your words."

"Let me kiss your lips once!" he pleaded.

"No, you shall hold my hand and kiss that. Your touch thrills every nerve of my being like wine. It is enough. I promised Mama I would never allow a man to kiss me without asking her. And we are like loving comrades. I couldn't violate a promise to her. I will, when she says so."

"Then I'll ask her. I know she's on my side."

"Yes, I believe she loves you because I do."

"What did you whisper to her that night, when we came late, and you said she would be angry?"

"Told her I loved you."

"If I could only have caught that whisper then! You don't know how it delights me to think your mother likes me. I couldn't help loving her. It seems to me a divine seal on our lives."

"Yes, and what specially delights me is, you have completely captured Papa, and he's so hard to please."

" You don't say so ! "

" Yes, he's been preaching you at me ever since you came the first time. I pretended to be indifferent to draw him out. He would say, ' Now Sallie, there's a man for you,—no pretty dude, but a man, with a kingly eye and a big brain. That's the kind of a man who does things in the world and makes history for smaller men to read.' " And then I'd say just to aggravate him, ' But Papa he's as poor as Job's turkey ! '

" Then you ought to have heard him, ' Well, what of it ! You can begin in a cabin like your mother and I did. He's got a better start than I had, for he has a better training.' "

" I am certainly glad to hear that ! " Gaston cried with elation.

" You may be. For Papa is a man of such intense likes and dislikes. The first thing that made my heart flutter with fear was that he might not like you. He loves me intensely. And I love him devotedly. I could not marry without his consent. You are so entirely different from any other beau I ever had, I couldn't imagine what Papa would think of you. You wear such a serious face, never go into society, care nothing for fine clothes, and are so careless that you even hung your feet out of the buggy that first day I took you to drive. I was glad to have you in the woods and not in town. The boys would have guyed me to death. In fact you are the contradiction of the average man I have known, and of all the men I thought as a girl I'd marry some day. I am so glad Papa likes you."

That evening when they reached the house, she hurried through the hall to her mother who was standing on the back porch. There was the sudden swish of a dress, a kiss, another ! and another ! And then the low murmur of a mother's voice like the crooning over a baby .

CHAPTER XII

THE MUSIC OF THE MILLS

WHEN Gaston reached his home that night St. Clare had gone to bed. It was one o'clock. He could not sleep yet, so he sat in the window and tried to realise his great happiness, as he looked out on the green lawn with its white gravelled walk glistening in the full moon.

"The world is beautiful, life is sweet, and God is good!" he cried in an ecstasy of joy.

He sat there in the moonlight for an hour dreaming of his love and the great strenuous life of achievement he would live with her to inspire him. It seemed too good to be true. And yet it was the largest living fact. Like throbbing music the words were ringing in his heart keeping time with the rhythm of its beat, "I do love you!"

And then he did something he had not done for years,—not since his boyhood,—he knelt in the silence of the moonlit room and prayed. Love the great Revealer had led him into the presence of God. The impulse was spontaneous and resistless. "Lord, I have seen Thy face, heard Thy voice, and felt the touch of Thy hand to-day! I bless and praise Thee! Forgive my doubts and fears and sins, cleanse and make me worthy of her whom Thou has sent as Thy messenger!" So he poured out his soul.

Next morning he grasped St. Clare's hand as he entered the room. "Bob, I'm the happiest man in the world!"

"Congratulations! You look it."

" She loves me! I'd like to climb up on the top of this
house and shout it until all earth and heaven could hear
and be glad with me!"

" Well, don't do it, my boy.   See her father first!"

" She says he likes me."

" Then you're elected."

" I'm going to tackle him before I go home."

" Don't rush him.   There's a superstition prevalent
here that the old gentleman has no idea of ever letting
his daughter leave that home, and that he will never give
his consent, when driven to the wall, unless his son-in-
law that is to be, will agree to settle down there and
take his place in those big mills.   He has two great loves,
his daughter and his mills, and he don't mean to let
either one of them go if he can help it."

" Do you believe it's true?"

" Yes, I do. How do you like the idea?"

" It's not my style.   I've a pretty clear idea of what
I'm going to do in this world."

" Well, you'd better begin to haul in your silk sails,
and study cotton goods, is my advice."

" I'll manage him."

" I don't know about it, but if you've got her, you're
the first man that ever got far enough to measure himself with the General.   I wish you luck."

" You the same, old chum.   May you conquer Boston
and all the Pilgrim Fathers!"

" Thanks.   The vision of one of them disturbs my
dreams.   One will be enough."

Then followed six golden days on the banks of the
Catawba.   Every day he insisted with boyish enthusiasm
on returning to that rock and seating her on her throne.
He called her his queen, and worshipped at her feet.

He had the friendliest little chat with her mother, and
told her how he loved her daughter and hoped for her

approval. She answered with frankness that she was glad, and would love him as her own son, but that she disapproved of kissing and extravagant love-making until they were ready to be married, and their engagement duly announced.

So he could only hold Sallie's hand and kiss the tips of her fingers and the little dimples where they joined the hand, and sometimes he would hold it against his own cheek while she smiled at him.

But when they rode homeward one evening he dared to put his arm behind her, high on the phaeton's leather cushion, as they were going down a hill, and then lowered it a little as they started up the grade. She leaned back and found it there. At first she nestled against it very timidly and then trustingly. She looked into his face and both smiled.

" Isn't that nice, Sallie? "

" Yes, it is,—I don't think Mama would mind that, do you? "

" Of course not."

" Well, I never promised not to lean back in a phaeton, did I? "

" Certainly not, and it's all right."

Toward the end of the week the General began to show him a grave friendly interest. He invited Gaston to go over the mills with him. The mills were located back of the wooded cliffs a quarter of a mile up the river. There were now four magnificent brick buildings stretching out over the river bottoms at right angles to its current. And there was a big dye house, a ginning house and a cotton-seed oil mill. The General stood on the hill top and proudly pointed it out to him.

" Isn't that a grand sight, young man! We employ 2,000 hands down there, and consume hundreds of bales of cotton a day. We began here after the war without

a cent, except our faith, and this magnificent water
power. Now look!"

"You have certainly done a great work," said Gaston, "I had no idea you had so many industries in the
enclosure."

"Yes, I sit down here on the hill some nights in the
moonlight and look into this valley, and the hum of that
machinery is like ravishing music. The machinery seems
to me to be a living thing, with millions of fingers of
steel and a great throbbing soul. I dream of the day
when those swift fingers will weave their fabrics of gold
and clothe the whole South in splendour!—the South I
love, and for which I fought, and have yearned over
through all these years. Ah! young man, I wish you
boys of brain and genius would quit throwing yourselves
away in law and dirty politics, and devote your powers
to the South's development!"

"Yes, but General, the people of the South had to go
into politics instead of business on account of the enfranchisement of the Negro. It was a matter of life and
death."

"I didn't do it."

"No, sir, but others did for you."

"How?" he asked incredulously, with just a touch of
wounded pride.

"Well how many negroes do you employ in these mills?"

"None. We don't allow a negro to come inside the
enclosure."

"Precisely so. You have prospered because you have
got rid of the Negro."

"I've simply let the Negro alone. Let others do the
same."

"But everybody can't do it. There are now nine millions of them. You've simply shifted the burden on
others' shoulders. You haven't solved the problem."

" If we had less politics and more business, we would be better off."

" But the trouble is, General, we can't have more business until politics have settled some things."

" Bah! You're throwing yourself away in politics, young man! There's nothing in it but dirt and disappointment."

" To me, sir, politics is a religion."

" Religion! Politics! I didn't know you could ever mix 'em. I thought they were about as far apart as heaven is from hell!" exclaimed the General.

" They ought not to be, sir, whatever the terrible facts. I believe that the Government is the organised virtue of the community, and that politics is religion in action. It may be a poor sort of religion, but it is the best we are capable of as members of society."

" Well, that's a new idea."

" It's coming to be more and more recognised by thoughtful men, General. I believe that the State is now the only organ through which the whole people can search for righteousness, and that the progress of the world depends more than ever on its integrity and purity."

" Well, you've cut out a big job for yourself, if that's your ideal. My idea of politics is a pig pen. The way to clean it is to kill the pigs."

Gaston laughed and shook his head.

When they returned from the mills, Mrs. Worth drew the General into her room.

" Did he ask you for Sallie?"

" No, the young galoot never mentioned her name. I thought he would. But I must have scared him."

" You didn't quarrel over anything?"

" No! But I found out he had a mind of his own."

" So have you, sir."

CHAPTER XIII

THE FIRST KISS

"WHY didn't you ask him yesterday?" cried Sallie, as she entered the parlour the next morning.

"Darling, I was scared out of my wits. We got crossways on some questions we were discussing, and he snorted at me once, and every time I tried to screw up my courage to speak, a lump got in my throat and I gave it up. I thought I'd wait a day or two until he should be in a better humour."

"He's gone away to-day," she said with disappointment.

"I'm glad of it, I'll write him a letter."

"If you had asked him yesterday it would have been all right. He told me so when he left this morning, with a very tender tremor in his voice."

"But it will be all right, sweetheart, when I write."

"I wanted my ring," she whispered.

"You shall have it," he said, as he seized her hand and led her to a seat.

"Have you got it with you?" she asked with excitement. "Let me see it quick."

He drew the little box from his pocket, withdrew the ring, concealing it in his hand, slipped it on her finger and kissed it. She threw her hand up into the light to see it.

"Oh! it is glorious! It's the big green diamond Hiddenite I saw at the Exposition! It is the most beautiful stone I ever saw, and the only one of its kind in size and colour in the world. Professor Hidden told me so. I tried to get Papa to buy it for me. But he laughed at me, and said it was childish extravagance. Charlie dear, how could you get it?"

"That's a little secret. But there are to be no secrets between us any more. I had a little hoard saved from my mother's estate for the greatest need of my life. I confess my extravagance."

"You are a matchless lover. I'm the proudest and happiest girl that breathes."

"Nothing is too good for you, I wish I could make a greater sacrifice."

"Wait, till I show it to Mama," and she flew to her mother's room. She returned immediately, looking at the ring and kissing it.

"Couldn't show it to her, she had company," she said. "Allan is talking to her."

"Let's get out of the house, dear. I hate that man like a rattlesnake."

"Don't be silly, I never cared a snap for him."

"I know you didn't, but there is a poison about him that taints the air for me. Get your horse and let's go to our place at the old mill."

They soon reached the spot, and with a laugh she sprang upon the rock and took her seat against the tree.

"Now, dear, humour this whim of mine. I've grown superstitious since you've made me happy. I have a presentiment of evil because that man was in the house. I am going to take the ring off and put it on your hand again out here where only the eyes of our birds will see, and the river we love will hear."

"That will be nicer. I somehow feel that my life is built on this dear old rock," she answered soberly.

He took the ring off her finger, dipped it in the white foam of the river, kissed it, and placed it on her hand.

"Now the spell is broken, isn't it?" she cried, holding it out in the sunlight a moment to catch the flash of its green diamond depth.

"I've another token for you. This, you will not even show to your mother or father." She bent low over a tiny package he unfolded.

"This is the first medal I won at college," he continued—"the first victory of my life. It was the force that determined my character. It gave me an inflexible will. I worked at a tremendous disadvantage. Others were two years ahead of me in study for the contest. I locked myself up in my room day and night for ten months, and took just enough food and sleep for strength to work. I worked seventeen hours a day, except Sundays, for ten months without an hour of play. I won it brilliantly. Every line cut on its gold surface stands for a thousand aches of my body. Every little pearl set in it, grew in a pain of that struggle which set its seal on my inmost life. I came out of those ten months a man. I have never known the whims of a boy since."

"And you engraved something on the back to me!"

"Yes, can't you read it?"

"My eyes are dim," she whispered.

"It is this—*In the hand of manhood's tenderest love I bring to thee my boyhood's brightest dream.* I was a man when I woke, but I have never lived till you taught me. Keep this as a pledge of eternal love. It's the only little trinket I ever possessed. The world will see our ring. Don't let them see this. It is the seal of your sovereignty of my soul in life, in death, and beyond. Will you make me this eternal pledge?"

"Unto the uttermost!" she murmured.

"Unto the uttermost!" he solemnly echoed.

"And now, what can I say or do for you when you show me in this spirit of prodigal sacrifice how dear I am in your eyes?"

"Those words from your lips are enough," he declared.

"I'll give you more. I'm going to give you just a little bit of myself. I haven't asked Mama, but we are engaged now—come closer."

She placed her beautiful arms around his neck and pressed her lips upon his in the first rapturous kiss of love.

"No,—no more. It is enough," she protested.

CHAPTER XIV

A MYSTERIOUS LETTER

HE was at home now, waiting impatiently for the General's answer to his letter. Two weeks had passed and he had not received it. But she had explained in her letters that her father had returned the day he left, had a talk with McLeod, and left on important business. They were expecting his return at any moment.

It was a new revelation of life he found in their first love letters. He never knew that he could write before. He sat for hours at his desk in his law office and poured out to her his dreams, hopes and ambitions. All the poetry of youth, and the passion and beauty of life, he put into those letters.

He wrote to her every day and she answered every other day. She wrote in half tearful apology that her mother disapproved of a daily letter, and she added wistfully, "I should like to write to you twice a day. Take the will for the deed, and as you love me, be sure to continue yours daily."

And on the days the letter came, with eager trembling hands he seized it, without waiting for the rest of his mail or his papers. With set face, and quick nervous step, he would mount the stairs to his office, lock his door and sit down to devour it. He would hold it in his hands sometimes for ten minutes just to laugh and muse over it and try to guess what new trick of phrase she had used to express her love. He was surprised at her brilliance and wit. He had not held her so deep a thinker on the serious things of life as these letters had showed, nor had he noticed how keen her sense of humour. He was so busy looking at her beautiful face, and drinking the love-light from her eyes, he had overlooked these things when with her. Now they flashed on him as a new treasure, that would enrich his life.

At the end of two weeks when the General had not answered his letter he began to grow nervous. A vague feeling of fear grew on him. Something had happened to darken his future. He felt it by a subtle telepathy of sympathetic thought. He was gloomy and depressed all day after he had received and feasted on the wittiest letter she had ever written. What could it mean he asked himself a thousand times—some shadow had fallen across their lives. He knew it as clearly as if the revelation of its misery were already unfolded.

He went to the post-office on the next day he was to receive a letter, crushed with a sense of foreboding. He waited until the mail was all distributed and the general delivery window flung open before he approached his box. He was afraid to look at her letter. He slowly opened the box.

There was nothing in it!

"Sam, you're not holding out my letter to tease me, old boy?" he asked pathetically.

Sam was about to joke him about the uncertainties of love, when his eye rested on his drawn face.

"Lord no, Charlie," he protested, "you know I wouldn't treat you like that."

"Then look again, you may have dropped it."

Sam turned and looked carefully over the floor, over and under his desks and tables and returned.

"No, but it may have been thrown into the wrong bag

by that fool mail clerk on the train. You may get it to-morrow."

He turned away and walked to his office, forgetting his key in the open box. The vague sense of calamity that weighed on his heart for the past two days, now became a reality.

He sat in his office all the afternoon in a dull stupor of suspense. He tried to read her last letter over. But the pages would get blurred and fade out of sight, and he would wake to find he had been staring at one sentence for an hour.

He knew his foster mother would be all sympathy and tenderness if he told her, but somehow he hadn't the heart. She had led him to his love. He had been so boyishly and frankly happy boasting to her of his success, he sickened at the thought of telling her. He went out for a walk in the woods, and lay down alone beside a brook like a wounded animal.

The next day he watched his box again with the hope that Sam's guess might be right, and the missing letter would come. But, instead of the big square-cut envelope he had waited for, he received a bulky letter in an old-fashioned masculine handwriting with the post mark of Independence, and a mill mark in the upper left hand corner.

He did not have to look twice at that letter. It was the sealed verdict of his jury. He locked his office door. It was long and rambling, full of a kindly sympathy expressed in a restrained manner. He could not believe at first that so outspoken a man as the General could have written it. The substance of its meaning, however, was plain enough. He meant to say that as he was not in a position to make a suitable home at present for a wife, and as he disapproved of long engagements, it seemed better that no engagement should be entered into or announced.

He stared at this letter for an hour, trying to grasp the mystery that lay back of its halting, half-contradictory sentences. He did not know till long afterwards that the General had written it with two blue eyes. tearfully watching him, and waiting to read it; that now and then there was the sound of a great sob, and two arms were around his neck, and a still white face lying on his shoulder, and that tears had washed all the harshness and emphasis out of what he had meant to write, and all but blotted out any meaning to what he did write.

But withal it was clear enough in its import. It meant that the General had haltingly but authoritatively denied his suit. He instantly made up his mind to ask an interview at his home, and know plainly all his reasons for this change of attitude. He wrote his letter and posted it immediately by return mail. He knew that the request would precipitate a crisis, and he trembled at the outcome. Either her father would hesitate and receive him, or end it with a crash of his imperious will.

CHAPTER XV

A BLOW IN THE DARK

THE noon mail brought Gaston no answer. At night he felt sure it would come.

When the wagon dashed up to the post-office that night it was fifteen minutes late. He was walking up and down the street on the opposite pavement along the square, keeping under the shadows of the trees. He turned, quickly crossed the street, and stood inside the office, listening with a feeling of strange abstraction to the tramp of the postmaster's feet back and forth as he distributed the mail. He never knew before what a tragedy might be concealed in the thrust of a bit of folded paper into a tiny glass-eyed box. As he waited, fearing to face his fate, he remembered the pathetic figure of a grey-haired old man who stood there one day hanging on that desk softly talking to himself. He was a stranger at the Springs, and they were alone in the office together. Now and then he brushed a tear from his eyes, glanced timidly at the window of the general delivery, starting at every quick movement inside as though afraid the window had opened. Gaston had gone up close to the old man, drawn by the look of anguish in his dignified face. The stranger intuitively recognised the sympathy of the movement, and explained tremblingly: " My son, I am waiting for a message of life or death "—he faltered, seized his hand, adding, " and I'm afraid to see it ! "

Just then the window opened and he clutched his arm and gasped, with dilated staring eyes,

" There, there it's come! You go for me, my son, and ask while I pray!—I'm afraid." How well Gaston remembered now with what trembling eagerness the old man had broken the seal, and then stood with head bowed low, crying,

" I thank and bless thee, oh, Mother of Jesus, for this hour!" And looking up into his face with tear-streaming eyes he cried in a rich low voice like tender music,

" How beautiful are the feet of them that bring glad tidings!"

He could feel now the warm pressure of his hand as he walked out of the office with him.

How vividly the whole scene came rushing over him! He thought he sympathised with his old friend that night, but now he entered into the fellowship of his sorrow. Now he knew.

At last he drew himself up, walked to his box and opened it. His heart leaped. A big square-cut envelope lay in it, addressed to him in her own beautiful hand. He snatched it out and hurried to his office. The moment he touched it, his heart sank. It was light and thin. Evidently there was but a single sheet of paper within.

He tore it open and stared at it with parted lips and half-seeing eyes. The first word struck his soul with a deadly chill. This was what he read:

" My Dear Mr. Gaston:

I write in obedience to the wishes of my parents to say our engagement must end and our correspondence cease. I can not explain to you the reasons for this. I have acquiesced in their judgment, that it is best.

I return your letters by to-morrow's mail, and Mama

requests that you return mine to her at Oakwood immediately.

I leave to-night on the Limited for Atlanta where I join a friend. We go to Savannah, and thence by steamer to Boston where I shall visit Helen for a month.

Sincerely,

SALLIE WORTH."

For a long time he looked at the letter in a stupor of amazement. That her father could coerce her hand into writing such a brutal commonplace note was a revelation of his power he had never dreamed. And then his anger began to rise. His fighting blood from soldier ancestors made his nerves tingle at this challenge.

He took up the letter and read it again curiously studying each word. He opened the folded sheet hoping to find some detached message. There was nothing inside. But he noticed on the other side of the sheet a lot of indentures as though made by the end of a needle. He turned it back and studied these dots under different letters in the words made by the needle points. He spelled,—

" My Darling—Unto the Uttermost! "

And then he covered the note with kisses, sprang to his feet and looked at his watch.

It was now ten-thirty. The Limited left Independence at eleven o'clock and made no stops for the first hundred miles toward Atlanta. But just to the south where the railroad skirted the foot of King's Mountain, there was a water tank on the mountain side where he knew the train stopped for water about midnight.

With a fast horse he could make the eighteen miles and board the Limited at this water station. The only danger was if the sky should cloud over and the starlight be lost it would be difficult to keep in the narrow road that wound over the semi-mountainous hills, densely wooded, that must be crossed to make it.

" I'll try it!" he exclaimed. " Yes, I will do it!" he added setting his teeth. " I'll make that train."

He got the best horse he could find in the livery stable, saw that his saddle girths were strong, sprang on and galloped toward the south. It was a quarter to eleven when he started, and it seemed a doubtful undertaking. The Limited would make the run from Independence, fifty-two miles, in an hour at the most. If she were on time it would be a close shave for him to make the eighteen miles.

The sky clouded slightly before he reached the mountain. In spite of his vigilance he lost his way and had gone a quarter of a mile before a rift in the cloud showed him the north star suddenly, and he found he had taken the wrong road at the crossing and was going straight back home.

Wheeling his horse, he put spurs to him, and dashed at full speed back through the dense woods.

Just as he got within a mile of the tank he heard the train blow for the bridge-crossing at the river near by.

" Now, my boy," he cried to his horse, patting him. " Now your level best!"

The horse responded with a spurt of desperate speed. He had a way of handling a horse that the animal responded to with almost human sympathy and intelligence. He seemed to breathe his own will into the horse's spirit. He flew over the ground, and reached the train just as the fireman cut off the water and the engineer tapped his bell to start.

He flung his horse's rein over a hitching post that stood near the silent little station-house, rushed to the track, and sprang on the day coach as it passed.

He had intended to ride fifty miles on this train, see his

sweetheart face to face—learn the truth from her own
lips—and then return on the up-train. He hoped to ride
back to Hambright before day and keep the fact of his
trip a secret.

Now a new difficulty arose—a very simple one—that he
had not thought of for a moment. She was in a Pullman
sleeper of course, and asleep.

There were three sleepers, one for Atlanta, one for
New Orleans, and one for Memphis. He hoped she was
in the Atlanta sleeper as that was her destination, though
if that were crowded in its lower berths she might be in
either of the others. But how under heaven could he
locate her? The porter probably would not know her.

He was puzzled. The conductor approached and he
paid his fare to the next stop, fifty miles.

" I've an important message for a passenger in one of
these sleepers, Captain," he exclaimed. " I have ridden
across the mountains to catch the train here."

" All right, sir," said the genial conductor. " Go right
in and deliver it. You look like you had a tussle to get
here."

" It was a close shave," Gaston replied.

He stepped into the Atlanta sleeper and encountered
the dusky potentate who presided over its aisles.

The porter looked up from the shoes he was shining
at Gaston's dishevelled hair and gave him no welcome.

Gaston dropped a half dollar into his hand and the
porter dropped the shoes and grinned a royal welcome.

" Any ting I kin do fer ye boss? "

" Got any ladies on your car? "

" Yassir, three un 'em."

" Young, or old? "

" One young un, en two ole uns."

" Did the young lady get on at Independence? "

" Yassir."

" Going to Atlanta? "

" Yassir."

" Is she very beautiful? "

" Boss, she's de purtiess young lady I eber laid my eyes on—but look lak she been cryin'."

" Then I want you to wake her. I must see her."

" Lordy boss, I cain do dat. Hit ergin de rules."

" But, I'm bound to see her. I've ridden eighteen miles across the mountains and scratched my face all to pieces rushing through those woods. I've a message of the utmost importance for her."

" Cain do hit boss, hits ergin de rules. But you can go wake her yoself, ef you'se er mind ter. I cain keep you fum it. She's dar in number seben."

Gaston hesitated. " No, you must wake her," he insisted, dropping another half dollar in the porter's hand.

The porter got up with a grin. He felt he must rise to a great occasion.

" Well, I des fumble roun' de berth en mebbe she wake herse'f, en den I tell her."

Just then the electric bell overhead rang and the index pointed to 7. " Dar now, dat's her callin' me, sho! "

He approached the berth. " What kin I do fur ye M'am? " he whispered.

" Porter, who is that you are talking to? It sounds like some one I know."

" Yassum, hit's young gent name er Gaston, jump on bode at the water station—say he got 'portant message fur you."

" Tell him I will see him in a moment."

The porter returned with the message.

" You des wait in dar, in number one—hits not made up—twell she come," he added.

There was the soft rustle of a dressing gown—he sprang to his feet, clasped her hand passionately, kissed it, and silently she took her seat by his side. He still held her hand, and she pressed his gently in response. He saw that she was crying, and his heart was too full for words for a moment.

He looked long and wistfully in her face. In her dishevelled hair by the dim light of the car he thought her more beautiful than ever. At last she brushed the tears from her eyes and turned her face full on his with a sad smile.

"My own dear love!" she sobbed, "I prayed that I might see you somehow before I left. I was wide awake when I first heard the distant murmur of your voice. Oh! I am so glad you came!" and she pressed his hand.

"I got your letter at ten-thirty"—

"Oh! that awful letter! How I cried over it. Papa made me write it, and read and mailed it himself. But you saw my message between the lines?"

"Yes, and then I covered it with kisses. But what is the cause of this sudden change of the General toward me? What have I done?"

"Please don't ask me. I can't tell you," she sobbed lowering her face a moment to his hand and kissing it. "Don't ask me."

"But, my dear, I must know. There can be no secrets between us."

"My lips will never tell you. There have been a thousand slanders breathed against you. I met them with fury and scorn, and no one has dared repeat them in my hearing. I would not pollute my lips by repeating one of them."

"But who is their author?"

"I can not tell you. I promised Mama I wouldn't. She loves you, and she is on our side, but said it was best. Papa has made up his mind to break our engagement forever. And I defied him. We had a scene. I didn't know I had the strength of will that came to me. I said some terrible things to him, and he said some very cruel things to me. Poor Mama was prostrated. Her heart is weak, and I only yielded at last as far as I have because of her tears and suffering. I could not endure her pleadings. So I promised to do as he wished for the present, leave for Boston, and cease to write to you."

"My love, I must know my enemy to meet him and face the issues he raises. I can not be strangled in the dark like this."

"You will find it out soon enough, I can not tell you," she repeated. "I only ask you to trust me, in this the darkest hour that has ever come to my life. You will trust me, will you not, dear?" she pleaded.

"I have trusted you with my immortal soul. You know this."

"Yes, yes, dear, I do. Then you can love and trust me without a letter or a word between us until Mama is better and I can get her consent to write to you? Oh, I never knew how tenderly and desperately I love you until this shadow came over our lives! No power shall ever separate us when the final test comes, unless you shall grow weary."

"Do not say that," he interrupted. "I love you with a love that has brought me out of the shadows and shown me the face of God. Death shall not bring weariness. But I dread with a sickening fear the efforts they will make to plunge you into the whirl of frivolous society. I shall be a lonely beggar a thousand miles away with not one friendly face near you to plead my cause."

"Hush!" she broke in upon him. "You are for me the one living presence. You are always near—oh so near, closer than breathing!"

The roar of the train became sonorous with the vibration of a great bridge. He started and looked at his watch.

"We are more than half way to the stop where I must leave you and return."

"How long have you been here?"

"Over a half hour. It does not seem two minutes. Only a few minutes more face to face, and all life crowding for utterance! How can I choose what to say, when my tongue only desires to say *I love you!* Bend near and whisper to me again your love vow," he cried in trembling accents.

Close to his ear she placed her lips, holding fast his hand whispering again and again, "My own dear love —unto the uttermost. In life, in death, forever!"

He bent again and pressed his lips on her hand and she felt the hot tears.

"And now, love, comes the hardest thing of all," she sobbed, "I must return to you my ring."

"For God's sake keep it!" he pleaded.

"No, I promised Mama for peace sake I would return it. She is very weak. I could not dare to hurt her now with a broken promise. She may not live long. I could never forgive myself. Keep it for me, dear, until I can wear it."

She placed it in his hand and it burnt like a red hot coal. He placed it in an inside pocket next to his heart. It felt like a huge millstone crushing him. A lump rose in his throat and choked him until he gasped for breath.

She looked at him pathetically and saw his anguish.

"Come, my love," she pleaded reproachfully, "you must not make it harder for me. You are a man. You are stronger than I am. Love is more my whole life than it can be yours. For this cruel thing I have said and done, you may press on my lips another kiss. If I am disobedient to my mother's wishes God will forgive me."

The train blew the long deep call for its hundred mile stop and they both rose. He took her hands in his.

" You have promised not to write to me, dear, but I have made no promise. I will write to you as often as I can send you a cheerful message," he said.

" It is so sweet of you! "

" You have the little love-token still? " he asked.

" Yes, in my bosom. I feel it warm and throbbing with your love, and it shall not be taken from me in the grave! "

" That thought will cheer the darkest hours that can come and now, till we meet again, we must say good-bye," he said huskily.

She could make no response. He placed his arms around her, pressed her close to his heart for a moment, —one long wistful kiss, and he was gone.

He rode slowly back to Hambright. The eastern horizon was fringed with the light of dawn when he reached the town. The more he had thought of his position and the way the General had treated him in attempting to settle his fate by a fiat of his own will without a hearing, the more it roused his wrath, and nerved him for the struggle. They were to measure wills in a contest that on his part had life for its stake.

" I'll give the old warrior the fight of his career! " he muttered as he snapped his square jaw together with the grip of a vise. " My brains, and every power with which nature has endowed me against his will and his money. And for the dastard who has slandered me there will be a reckoning."

He was fighting in the dark but deep down in him he

had a soldier's love for a fight. His soul rose to meet the challenge of this hidden foe armed in the steel of a proud heritage of courage. He went to bed and slept soundly for six hours.

CHAPTER XVI

THE MYSTERY OF PAIN

GASTON awoke next morning at half past ten o'clock with a dull headache, and a sense of hopeless depression. His anger had cooled and left him the pitiful consciousness of his loss. He slowly and mechanically dressed.

When he buttoned his coat he felt something hard press against his heart. It was the ring. He sat down on his bed and drew it from his pocket. To his surprise he found coiled inside it and tied by a tiny ribbon a ringlet of her hair. She had taken off the ring in her mother's presence and promised her to register and mail it in Atlanta. She had bound this little piece of herself with it. He kissed it tenderly.

" My God, it is hard!" he groaned. And all the unshed tears that his eager interest in her presence and his kindling anger the night before had kept back now blinded him.

He did not notice his door softly open, nor know his mother was near until she placed her hand gently on his shoulder. He looked up at her face full of tender sympathy, and poured out to her his trouble in a torrent of hot rebellious words.

" What have I done to be treated like a dog in this way?" he ended with a voice trembling with protest.

" Perhaps you have offended the General in some way?"

"Impossible. I've been the soul of deference to him."

"He's a very proud man when his vanity is touched, are you sure of it?"

"As sure as that I live. No, some scoundrel has interfered between us and in some unaccountable way covered me with infamy in the General's eyes."

"But who could have done it?"

"I used my utmost power of persuasion to get it from her. But she would not tell me. I have been stabbed in the dark."

"Whom do you suspect? She has a dozen suitors."

"There's only one man among them who is capable of it, Allan McLeod."

"Nonsense, child. He is not one of her suitors," she protested warmly.

"Then why does he hang around the house with such dogged persistence?"

"He has always had the run of the house. His father committed him to the General when he died on the battle field."

Her face clouded, and then a great pity for his sorrow filled her heart. She stooped and kissed him.

"Come, Charlie, you must cheer up. If she loves you, it's everything. You will win her."

"But what rankles in my soul is that I have been treated like a dog. If he objected to my poverty that was as evident the first day he welcomed me to his house as the day he dictated to her his brutal message, refusing me a word. He welcomed me to his house, and gave Miss Sallie his approval of our love while I was there. There could be no mistake, for she told me so."

"I can't understand it," she interrupted.

"Now he suddenly shows me the door and refuses to allow me to even ask an explanation. If he thinks he

can settle my life for me in that simple manner, I'll show
him that I'll at least help in the settlement."

" Good. I like to see your eyes flash that fire. Don't
forget your resolution. Your enemies are your best
friends." She said this with a ring of her old aristocratic
pride. " Come," she continued, " I've a nice warm breakfast saved for you. You don't know how much good
you have done me in my lonely life."

" Dear Mother! " he whispered pressing her hand.

After breakfast he went to his office and read over
slowly the letters he had received from Sallie, kissed
them one by one, tied them up and sent them to her
mother. He took the ring out of his pocket and locked
it in one of his drawers.

" I can't work to-day. It's no use trying! " he muttered
looking out of his window. He locked his office and
started down town with no purpose except in the walk
to try to fight his pain. Instinctively he found his way
to Tom Camp's cottage.

" Tom, old boy, I'm in deep water. You've been there.
I just want to feel your hand."

Tom was clearing up his kitchen with one hand and
holding the other tight over the wound near his spinal
column. He had suffered untold agonies through the
night past and was suffering yet, but he never mentioned it.

" You've just got your blues again! " Tom laughed.

" No, a devil has stabbed me in the back in the dark."
And he told Tom of his love and his inexplicable trouble.

" So, so! " Tom mused with dancing eyes, " The General's gal Miss Sallie! My! my! but ain't she a beauty!
Next to my own little gal there she's the purtiest thing
in No'th Caliny. And you're her sweetheart, and she
told you she loved you? "

" Yes."

"Then what ails you? Man, to hear that from such lips as she's got's music enough for a year. You want the whole regimental band to be playin' all the time. If she loves you, that's enough now to give you nerve to fight all earth and hell combined." Tom urged this with an enthusiasm that admitted no reply.

Flora had climbed in his lap, and was going through his pockets to find some candy.

"You didn't bring me a bit this time!" she cried reproachfully.

"Honey, I forgot it," he apologised.

"I don't believe you love me any more, Charlie," she declared placing her hands on his cheeks and looking steadily into his eyes. "Am I your sweetheart yet?" she asked.

"Of course, dearie, and about the only one I can depend on!"

"La, Charlie, your eyes are red!" she cried in surprise. "Do you cry?"

"Sometimes, when my heart gets too full."

"Then, I'll kiss the red away!" she said as she softly kissed his eyes.

"That's good, Flora. It will make them better.'

"Now, Pappy," she said triumphantly, "you say I'm getting too big to cry, and I ain't but eleven years old, and Charlie's big as you and he cries."

Tom took her in his arms and smoothed his hand over her fair hair with a tenderness that had in its trembling touch all the mystery of both mother and father love in which his brooding soul had wrapped her.

Gaston returned home with lighter step. He met, as he crossed the square, the Preacher who was waiting for him.

"Come here and sit down a minute. I've heard of your trouble. You have my sympathy. But you'll come out all right. The oak that's bent by the storm makes a fibre fit for a ship's rib. You can't make steel without white heat. God's just trying your temper, boy, to see if there's anything in you. When he has tried you in the fire, and the pure gold shines, he will call you to higher things."

Gaston nodded his assent to this saying, "And yet, Doctor, none of us like the touch of fire or the smell of the smoke of our clothes."

"You are right. But it's good for the soul. You are learning now that we must face things that we don't like in this world. I am older than you. I will tell you something that you can't really know until you have lived through this. Love seems to you at this time the only thing in the world. But it is not. My deepest sympathy is with Sallie. She's already pure gold. To such a woman love is the centre of gravity of all life. This is not true of a strong normal man. The centre of gravity of a strong man's life as a whole is not in love and the emotions, but in justice and intellect and their expression in the wider social relations."

"And that means that I must brace up for this political fight?"

"Exactly so. And it's the best thing you can do for your love. Become a power and you can coerce even a man of the General's character."

"You are right, Doctor. I had my mind about fixed on that course."

"You will find the County Committee in session in the Clerk's office there now. They want to see you. I tell you to fight this coalition of McLeod and the farmers every inch up to the last hour it is formed, and if McLeod wins them, and the alliance is made, then fight to break it every day and every hour and every minute till the votes are counted out."

Gaston went at once into the consultation with the Democratic county committee.

CHAPTER XVII

IS GOD OMNIPOTENT?

AS Gaston left the Preacher, the Rev. Ephraim Fox approached. He was the pastor of the Negro Baptist church, and had succeeded old Uncle Josh at his death ten years before.

He bowed deferentially, and, hat in hand, stood close to the seat on which Durham was still resting.

"How dis you doan come down ter our chu'ch en preach fur us no mo Brer' Durham? We been er havin' powerful times down dar lately, en de folks wants you ter come en preach some mo."

"I can't do it, Eph."

"What de matter, Preacher? We ain't hu't yo feelin's, is we?"

"No, not in a personal way, but you've got beyond me."

"How's dat?" asked Ephraim rolling his eyes.

"Well, as long as I preach to your folks about heaven and the glory beyond this world, they shout and sweat and sing. And when I jump on the old sinners in the Bible, they are in glee. They like to see the fur fly. But the minute I pounce on them about stealing, and lying, and drinking, and lust,—they don't want to furnish any of the fur."

"De Lawd, Preacher, hit's des de same wid de white folks!" urged Ephraim with a wink.

"That's so. But the difference is your people talk back at me after the meeting."

" How's dat?" Ephraim repeated.

" Why when I preach righteousness and judgment on the thief and accuse them of stealing, I lose my wood, and my corn, and my chickens."

Ephraim was silent a moment and then he smiled as he said,

" Preacher, dey ain't er nigger in dis town doan lub you."

" Yes, I know it. That's why they steal from me so much."

" Go long wid yo fun!" roared Ephraim. " You know you ain't gone back on us des cause some nigger tuck er stick er wood—deys sumfin' else—you cain fool me."

" Well, you are right, that isn't the main reason. There are others. You turned a man out of your church for voting the Democratic ticket."

" Yes, but Preacher," interrupted Eph impatiently, " dat wuz er low-down mean nigger. He didn't hab no salvation nohow!"

" Then you keep a deacon in your church who served two terms in the penitentiary."

" But dat's de bes' deacon I got," pleaded Eph sadly.

" Turn him out I tell you!"

" But dey all does little tings."

" Turn 'em all out!"

" Den we ain't got no chu'ch, en de shepherd ain't got no flock ter tend, er ter shear. You des splain how de Lawd tempers de win' ter de shorn lam'. Den ef I doan shear 'em, de win' mought blow too hard on 'em. En ef I doan keep 'em in de pen, how kin I shear 'em? I axes you dat?"

The Preacher smiled and continued, " Then I've heard some ugly things about you, Eph," suddenly darting a piercing look straight into his face.

" Who, me?"

"Yes, you. And I can't afford to go into the pulpit with you any more. In the old slavery days you were taught the religion of Christ. It didn't mean crime, and lust, and lying, and drinking, whatever it meant. Your religion has come to be a stench. You are getting lower and lower. You will be governed by no one. I can't use force. I leave you alone. You have gone beyond me."

"But de Lawd lub a sinner, en his mercy enduref foreber!" solemnly grumbled Ephraim.

"In the old days," persisted the Preacher, "I used to preach to your people. I saw before me many men of character, carpenters, bricklayers, wheelwrights, farmers, faithful home servants that loved their masters and were faithful unto death. Now I see a cheap lot of thieves and jailbirds and trifling women seated in high places. You have shown no power to stand alone on the solid basis of character."

"Why Brer' Durham," urged Eph in an injured voice, "I baptised inter de kingdom over a hundred precious souls las' year!"

"Yes, but what they needed was not a baptism of water. You negroes need a racial baptism into truth, integrity, virtue, self-restraint, industry, courage, patience, and purity of manhood and womanhood. I used to be hopeful about you, but I'd just as well be frank with you, I've given you up. I've said the grace of God was sufficient for all problems. I don't know now. I'm getting older and it grows darker to me. I have come to believe there are some things God Almighty can not do. Can God make a stone so big He can't lift it? In either event, He is not omnipotent. It looks like He did just that thing when He made the Negro. Leave me out of your calculation, Ephraim."

"Mus' gib de nigger time, Preacher!" Eph muttered as he walked slowly away.

When Gaston emerged from the court house, the Preacher joined him and they walked home to the hotel together.

"What did the two farmers on your committee think of the chances of preventing the Alliance from joining the negroes?"

"Not much of them. They say we can't do anything with them when the test comes, unless we will endorse their scheme of issuing money on corn and pumpkins and potatoes stored in a government barn. If it comes to that, I will not prostitute my intellect by advocating any such measure on the floor of our convention. We stand for one thing at least, the supremacy of Anglo-Saxon civilisation. I had rather be beaten by the negroes and their allies this time on such an issue."

"But, my boy, if McLeod and his negroes get control of this state for four years, they can so corrupt its laws and its electorate, they may hold it a quarter of a century. We must fight to the last ditch."

"I draw the line at pumpkin leaves for money," insisted Gaston.

It was but ten days to the meeting of the Democratic state convention, and they were coming together divided in opinion, and at sea as to their policy, with a united militant Farmers' Alliance demanding the uprooting of the foundations of the economic world, and a hundred thousand negro voters grinning at this opportunity to strike their white foes, while McLeod stood in the background smiling over the certainty of his triumph.

CHAPTER XVIII

THE WAYS OF BOSTON

WHEN Helen Lowell reached Boston from her visit with Sallie Worth, she found her father in the midst of his political campaign. The Hon. Everett Lowell was the representative of Congress from the Boston Highlands district. His home was an old fashioned white Colonial house built during the American Revolution.

He was not a man of great wealth, but well-to-do, a successful politician, enthusiastic student, a graduate of Harvard, and he had always made a specialty of championing the cause of the " freedmen." He was a chronic proposer of a military force bill for the South.

His family was one of the proudest in America. He had a family tree five hundred years old—an unbroken line of unconquerable men who held liberty dearer than life. He believed in the heritage of good honest blood as he believed in blooded horses. His home was furnished in perfect taste, with beautiful old rosewood and mahogany stuff that had both character and history. On the walls hung the stately portraits of his ancestors representative of three hundred years of American life. He never confused his political theories about the abstract rights of the African with his personal choice of associates or his pride in his Anglo-Saxon blood. With him politics was one thing, society another.

His pet hobby, which combined in one his philanthropic

ideals and his practical politics, was of late a patronage he had extended to young George Harris, the bright mulatto son of Eliza and George Harris whose dramatic slave history had made their son famous at Harvard.

This young negro was a speaker of fair ability and was accompanying Lowell on his campaign tours of the district, making speeches for his patron, who had obtained for him a clerk's position in the United States Custom House. Harris was quite a drawing card at these meetings. He had a natural aptitude for politics; modest, affable, handsome, and almost white, he was a fine argument in himself to support Lowell's political theories, who used him for all he was worth as he had at the previous election.

Harris had become a familiar figure at Lowell's home in the spacious library, where he had the free use of the books, and frequently he dined with the family, when there at dinner time hard at work on some political speech or some study for a piece of music.

Lowell had met his daughter at the depot behind his pair of Kentucky thoroughbreds. This daughter, his only child, was his pride and joy. She was a blonde beauty, and her resemblance to her father was remarkable. He was a widower, and this lovely girl, at once the incarnation of his lost love and so fair a reflection of his being, had ruled him with absolute sway during the past few years.

He was laughing like a boy at her coming.

"Oh! my beauty, the sight of your face gives me new life!" he cried smiling with love and admiration.

"You mustn't try to spoil me!" she laughed.

"Did you really have a good time in Dixie?" he whispered.

"Oh! Papa, such a time!" she exclaimed shutting her eyes as though she were trying to live it over again.

" Really ? "

" Beaux, morning, noon and night,—dancing, moon-light rides, boats gliding along the beautiful river and mocking birds singing softly their love-song under the window all night ! "

" Well you did have romance," he declared.

" Yes," she went on " and such people, such hospitality —oh ! I feel as though I never had lived before."

" My dear, you mustn't desert us all like that," he pro-tested.

" I can't help it, I'm a rebel now."

" Then keep still till the campaign's over ! " he warned in mock fear.

" And the boys down there," she continued, " they are such boys ! Time doesn't seem to be an object with them at all. Evidently they have never heard of our uplifting Yankee motto ' *Time is money.*' And such knightly def-erence ! such charming old fashioned chivalrous ways ! "

" But, dear, isn't that a little out of date ? "

" How staid and proper and busy Boston seems ! I know I am going to be depressed by it."

" I know what's the matter with you ! " he whistled.

" What ? " she slyly asked.

" One of those boys."

" I confess. Papa, he's as handsome as a prince."

" What does he look like ? "

" He is tall, dark, with black hair, black eyes, slender, graceful, all fire and energy."

" What's his name ? "

" St. Clare—Robert St. Clare. His father was away from home. He's a politician, I think."

" You don't say ! St. Clare. Well of all the jokes ! His father is my Democratic chum in the House—an old fire-eating Bourbon, but a capital fellow."

" Did you ever see *him?* "

"No, but I've had good times with his father. He used to own a hundred slaves. He's a royal fellow, and pretty well fixed in life for a Southern politician. I don't think though I ever saw his boy. Anything really serious?"

"He hasn't said a word—but he's coming to see me next week."

"Well things are moving, I must say!"

"Yes, I pretended I must consult you, before telling him he could come. I didn't want to seem too anxious. I'm half afraid to let him wander about Boston much, there are too many girls here."

Her father laughed proudly and looked at her. "I hope you will find him all your heart most desires, and my congratulations on your first love!"

"It will be my last, too," she answered seriously.

"Ah! you're too young and pretty to say that!"

"I mean it," she said earnestly with a smile trembling on her lips.

Her father was silent and pressed her hand for an answer. As they entered the gate of the home, they met young Harris coming out with some books under his arm. He bowed gracefully to them and passed on.

"Oh! Papa, I had forgotten all about your fad for that young negro!"

"Well, what of it, dear?"

"You love me very much, don't you?" she asked tenderly. "I'm going to ask you to be inconsistent, for my sake."

"That's easy. I'm often that for nobody's sake. Consistency is only the terror of weak minds."

"I'm going to ask you to keep that young negro out of the house when my Southern friends are here. After my sweetheart comes I expect Sallie and her mother. I wouldn't have either of them to meet him here in our library and especially in our dining-room for anything on earth! "

" Well, you have joined the rebels, haven't you? "

" You know I never did like negroes any way," she continued. " They always gave me the horrors. Young Harris is a scholarly gentleman, I know. He is good-looking, talented, and I've played his music for him sometimes to please you, but I can't get over that little kink in his hair, his big nostrils and full lips, and when he looks at me, it makes my flesh creep."

" Certainly, my darling, you don't need to coax me. The Lowells, I suspect, know by this time what is due to a guest. When your guests come, our home and our time are theirs. If eating meat offends, we will live on herbs. I'll send Harris down to the other side of the district and keep him at work there until the end of the campaign. My slightest wish is law for him."

" You see, Papa," she went on, " they never could understand that negro's easy ways around our house, and I know if he were to sit down at our table with them they would walk out of the dining-room with an excuse of illness and go home on the first train."

" And yet," returned her father lifting her from the carriage, " their homes were full of negroes were they not? "

" Yes, but they know their place. I've seen those beautiful Southern children kiss their old black ' Mammy.' It made me shudder, until I discovered they did it just as I kiss Fido."

" And this a daughter of Boston, the home of Garrison and Sumner! " he exclaimed.

" I've heard that Boston mobbed Garrison once," she observed.

" Yes, and I doubt if we have canonised Sumner yet. All right. If you say so, I'll order a steam calliope stationed at the gate and hire a man to play Dixie for you!"

She laughed, and ran up the steps.

*   *   *   *   *

Sallie determined to keep the secret of her sorrow in her own heart. On the ocean voyage she had cried the whole first day, and then kissed her lover's picture, put it down in the bottom of her trunk, brushed the tears away and determined the world should not look on her suffering.

She had written Helen of her lover's declaration, and of her happiness. She would find a good excuse for her sorrowful face in their separation. She knew he would write to her, for he had said so, and she had slipped the address into his hand as he left the car that night.

At first she was puzzled to think what she could do about answering these letters so Helen would not suspect her trouble. Then she hit on the plan of writing to him every day, posting the letters herself and placing them in her own trunk instead of the post-box.

"He will read them some day. They will relieve my heart," she sadly told herself.

Helen met her on the pier with a cry of girlish joy, and the first word she uttered was,

"Oh! Sallie, Bob loves me! He's been here two weeks, and he's just gone home. I have been in heaven. We are engaged!"

"Then I'll kiss you again, Helen."—She gave her another kiss.

"And I've a big letter at home for you already! It's post-marked 'Hambright.' It came this morning. I know you will feast on it. If Bob don't write me faithfully I'll make him come here and live in Boston."

When Sallie got this letter, she sat down in her room,

and read and re-read its passionate words. There was a tone of bitterness and wounded pride in it. She struggled bravely to keep the tears back. Then the tone of the letter changed to tenderness and faith and infinite love that struggled in vain for utterance.

She kissed the name and sighed. " Now I must go down and chat and smile with Helen. She's so silly about her own love, if I talk about Bob she will forget I live."

CHAPTER XIX

THE SHADOW OF A DOUBT

MRS. WORTH had arrived in Boston a few days after Sallie, coming direct by rail. She was still very weak from her recent attack, and it cut her to the heart to watch Sallie write those letters faithfully, and never mail them out of deference to her wishes.

One night she drew her daughter down and kissed her.

"Sallie, dear, you don't know how it hurts me to see you suffer this way, and write, and write these letters your lover never sees. You may send him one letter a week, I don't care what the General says."

There was a sob and another kiss and, Sallie was crying on her breast.

In answer to her first letter, Gaston was thrilled with a new inspiration. He sat down that night and answered it in verse. All the deep longings of his soul, his hopes and fears, his pain and dreams he set in rhythmic music. Her mother read all his letters after Sallie. And she cried with sorrow and pride over this poem.

"Sallie, I don't blame you for being proud of such a lover. Your life is rich hallowed by the love of such a man. Your father is wrong in his position. If I were a girl and held the love of such a man, I'd cherish it as I would my soul's salvation. Be patient and faithful."

"Sweet mother heart!" she whispered as she smoothed the grey hair tenderly.

Allan McLeod had arrived in Boston the day before and the morning's papers were full of an interview with him on his brilliant achievement in breaking the ranks of the Bourbon Democracy in North Carolina, and the certainty of the success of his ticket at the approaching election.

McLeod sent the paper to Mrs. Worth by a special messenger, lest she might not see it, and that evening called. He asked Sallie to accompany him to the theatre, and when she refused spent the evening.

When her mother had retired McLeod drew his seat near her and again told her in burning words his love.

"Miss Sallie, I have won the battle of life at its very threshold. I shall be a United States Senator in a few months. I want to lead you, my bride, into the gallery of the Senate before I walk down its aisles to take the oath. I have loved you faithfully for years. I have your father's consent to my suit. I asked him before leaving on this trip. Surely you will not say no?"

"Allan McLeod, I do not love you. I do love another. I hate the sight of you and the sound of your voice."

"If you do not marry Gaston, will you give me a chance?"

"If I do not marry the man of my choice, I will never marry. Now go."

McLeod returned to the hotel with the fury of the devil seething in his soul. He determined to return to Hambright, and if possible entrap Gaston in dissipation and destroy his faith in Sallie's loyalty.

He wrote to the General that he had been rejected by his daughter who still corresponded with Gaston. When General Worth received this letter he wrote in wrath to his wife, peremptorily forbidding Sallie to write another line to Gaston and closed saying,

"I had trusted this matter to you, my dear, now I take

it out of your hands.   I forbid another line or word to this man."

Gaston watched and waited in vain for the letter he was to receive next week. Again his soul sank with doubt and fear. What fiend was striking him with an unseen hand? He felt he should choke with rage as he thought of the infamy of such a warfare.

His mother said to him shortly after McLeod's arrival,

" Charlie, I have some bad news for you."

" It can't be any worse than I have, the misery of an unexplained silence of two weeks."

" I feel that I ought to tell you.   It is the explanation of that silence, I fear."

" What is it, Mother? " he asked soberly.

" I hear that Sallie has plunged into frivolous society, is dancing every night at the hotel at Narragansett Pier where they are stopping now, and flirting with a half-dozen young men."

" I don't believe it," growled Gaston.

" I'm afraid it's true, Charlie, and I'm furious with her for treating you like this. I thought she had more character."

" I'll love and trust her to the end! " he declared as he went moodily to his office. But the poison of suspicion rankled in his thoughts. Why had she ceased to write? Was not this mask of society a habit with those who had learned to wear it? Was not habit, after all, life? Could one ever escape it? It seemed to him more than probable that the old habits should re-assert themselves in such a crisis, a thousand miles removed from him or his personal influence. He held a very exaggerated idea of the corruption of modern society. And his heart grew heavier from day to day with the feeling that she was slipping away from him.

CHAPTER XX

A NEW LESSON IN LOVE

McLEOD returned home to find his plans of political success in perfect order. The programme went through without a hitch. In spite of the most desperate efforts of the Democrats, he carried the state by a large majority and made, for the Republican party and its strange allies, the first breach in the solid phalanx of Democratic supremacy since Legree left his legacy of corruption and terror.

The Legislature elected two Senators. To the amazement of the world, the day before the caucus of the Republicans met, McLeod withdrew. He had no opposition so far as anybody knew, but a curious thing had happened. The Rev. John Durham discovered the fact that McLeod kept a still and had established his mother as an illicit distiller years before. One of his deputies who had become an inebriate, confessed this to the doctor who had informed the Preacher.

The Preacher put this important piece of information into the hands of a daring young Republican who had always been one from principle. He went to Raleigh and interviewed McLeod. At first McLeod denied, and blustered, and swore. When he produced the proofs, he gave up, and asked sullenly,

" What do you want? "

" Get out of the race."

" All right. Is that all? You're on top."

" No, give me the nomination."

" Never ! " he yelled with an oath.

" Then I'll expose you in to-morrow morning's paper, and that's the end of you."

McLeod hesitated a moment, and then said, " I'll agree. You've got me. But I'll make one little condition. You must give me the name of your informant."

" The Rev. John Durham."

" I thought as much."

To the amazement of everyone McLeod waived the crown aside and placed it on the head of one of his lieutenants. He returned to Hambright from this dramatic event with an unruffled front. To his cronies he said, " Bah ! I was joking. Never had any idea of taking the office for myself. I'm playing for larger stakes. I make these puppets, and pull the strings."

He devoted himself assiduously in the leisure which followed to Mrs. Durham. He never intimated to Durham that he knew anything about the part he had taken in his withdrawal from the Senatorship. Nor had the Preacher told his wife of his discovery. They had quarrelled several times about McLeod. His wife seemed determined to remain loyal to the boy she had taught.

McLeod in his talk with her intimated that he had withdrawn from a desire vaguely forming in his mind to get out of the filth of politics altogether, sooner or later, influenced by her voice alone.

With subtle skill he played upon her vanity and jealousy, and at last felt that he had entangled her so far he could dare a declaration of his feelings. There was one element only in her mental make-up he feared. She held tenaciously the old-fashioned romantic ideals of love. To her it seemed a divine mystery linking the souls that felt it to the infinite. If he could only destroy this divine mystery idea, he felt sure that her sense of isolation, and her proud rebellion against the disappointments of life would make her an easy prey to his blandishments.

He searched his library over for a book that could scientifically demonstrate the purely physical basis of love. He knew that somewhere in his studies at a medical college in New York he had read it.

At last he discovered it among a lot of old magazines. It was a brief study by a great physician of Paris, entitled "The Natural History of Love." He gave it to her, and asked her to read it and give him her candid opinion of its philosophy.

He waited a week and on a Saturday when the Preacher was absent at one of his county mission stations he called at the hotel for a long afternoon's talk. He determined to press his suit.

"Do you know, Mrs. Durham, what gives a preacher his boasted power of the spirit over his audiences?" he inquired with a curious laugh in the midst of which he changed his tone of voice.

"No, you are an expert on the diseases of preachers, what is it?"

"Very simple. Religion is founded on love, there never was a magnetic preacher who was not a resistless magnet for scores of magnetic women. If you don't believe it, watch how resistless is the impulse of all these good-looking women to shake hands with their preacher, and how fondly they look at him across the pews if the crowd is too dense to reach his hand."

A frown passed over her face, and she winced at the thrust, yet her answer was a surprising question to him.

"Do you really believe in anything, Allan?"

"You ask that?" he said leaning closer. "You whose great dark eyes look through a man's very soul?"

"I begin to think I have never seen yours. I doubt if you have a soul."

" Well, what's the use of a soul? I can't satisfy the wants of my body . "

" Answer my question. Do you believe in anything? "

" Yes," he replied, his voice sinking to a tense whisper, " I believe in Woman,—in love."

" In Woman? "

" Yes, Woman."

" You mean women," she sneered.

He started at her answer, looked intently at her, and said deliberately,

" I mean you, the One Woman, the only woman in the world to me."

" I do not believe one word you have uttered, yet, I confess with shame, you have always fascinated me."

" Why with shame? You have but one life to live. The years pass. Even beauty so rare as yours fades at last. The end is the grave and worms. Why dash from your beautiful lips the cup of life when it is full to the brim? "

" How skillfully you echo the dark thoughts that flit on devil wings through the soul, when we feel the bitterness of life's failure, its contradictions and mysteries! " she exclaimed, closing her eyes for a moment and leaning back in her chair.

" You've often talked to me about the necessity of some sort of slavery for the Negro if he remain in America. I begin to believe that slavery is a necessity for all women."

" I fail to see it, sir."

" All women are born slaves and choose to remain so through life. It is curious to see you, a proud imperious woman, born of a race of unconquerable men, staggering to-day under the chains of four thousand years of conventional laws made by the brute strength of men. And you, if you struggle at all, beat your wings against the bars that the slaveholding male brute has built about your soul, fall back at last and give up to the will of your master. This too, when you hold in your simple will the key that would unlock your prison door and make you free. It's a pitiful sight."

"How shrewd a tempter!"

"There you are again. He who dares to tell you that you are of yourself a living human being, divinely free, is a tempter from the devil. You are thinking about eternity. Well, now is eternity. Live, stand erect, take a deep breath, and dare to be yourself and do what you please. That is what I do. The future is a myth."

"Yes, I know the freedom of which you boast," she quietly observed, "it is the freedom of lust. The return to nature you dream of is simply the fall downward into the dirt out of which a rational and spiritual manhood has grown. I feel and know this in spite of your handsome face and the fine ring of your voice."

"Dirt. Dirt!" he mused. "Yes, I was in the dirt once, was born in it, the dirt of poverty and superstition and fears of laws here and hereafter. But I awoke at last, and shook it off, washed myself in knowledge and stood erect. I am a man now, with the eye of a king, conscious of my power. I look a lying hypocritical world in the face. I have made up my mind to live my own life in spite of fools, and in spite of the laws and conventions of fools."

"And yet I believe you carry a horse-chestnut in your pocket, and will not undertake an important work on Friday?" she returned.

"But I never strangle a normal impulse of my nature that I can satisfy. I am not that big a fool, at least."

She was silent, and then said, "I can never thank you enough for the book you sent me."

McLeod sighed in relief at her change of tone. After all she was just tantalising him!

" Then you liked it? " he cried with glittering eyes.

" I devoured every word of it with a greed you can not understand. A great man wrote it."

" Then we can understand each other better from to-day," he interrupted smilingly.

" Yes, far better. You gave me this book hoping that it might influence my character by destroying my ideal of love, didn't you, now frankly? "

" Honestly, I did hope it would emancipate you from superstitions."

" It has," she declared, but with a curious curve of her lip that chilled him.

" What are you driving at? " he asked suspiciously.

" This book has given me the key that unlocked for me, for the first time, the riddle of my physical being. It has shown me the physical basis of love, just as I knew before there was a physical basis of the soul."

" What did you understand the book to teach? " he asked.

" Simply that love is based in its material life, on the lobe of the brain which develops at the base of a child's head near the age of thirteen. That this lobe of the brain is the sex centre, and love is impossible until it develops. That this centre of new powers at the base of the skull is a physical magnet. That when a man and woman approach each other, who are by nature mates, these mag-netic centres are disturbed by action and reaction, and that this disturbance develops the second elemental pas-sion called love. The first elemental passion, hunger, has for its end the preservation of the individual; while love finds its fulfillment in the preservation of the species. Love finds its satisfaction in the child, its ardour cools, and it dies, unless kept alive by the social conventions of the family, which are not based merely on this violent emotion, but also on unity of tastes, which produce the sense of comradeship. For these reasons it is possible to fall violently in love more than once, and there are dozens of people who possess this magnetic power over us and would respond to it violently if we only came in social contact with them. That the romantic bombast about the possibility of but one love in life, and that of supernatural origin, is twaddle, and leads to false ideals. Have I given the argument?"

"Exactly. But what do you deduce from it?"

"Freedom!"

"Good!" he cried, licking his lips.

"Freedom from superstitions about love," she answered, "and positive knowledge of its elemental beauty which Nature reveals. In short, I no longer wonder and brood over your charm for me. I know exactly what it means, and how it might occur again and again with another and another. I have simply throttled it in a moment by an act of my will, based on this knowledge."

"You amaze me."

"No doubt. One's character centres in the soul, or the appetites. Mine is in the soul, yours in the appetites. I see you to-day as you really are, and I loathe you with an unspeakable loathing. You have opened my eyes with this beautiful little book of Nature. I thank you. Your scientist has convinced me that there are possibly a hundred men in the world who would affect me as you do, were we to meet. And when I looked back into the sweet face of my dead boy, I learned another truth, that in the union of my first great love I was bound in marriage, not simply by a social convention, or a state contract, but for life by Nature's eternal law. The period of infancy of one child extends over twenty-one years, covering the whole maternal life of the woman who marries at the proper age of twenty-four. This union of one man and one woman never seemed so sacred to me as now. It is Nature's law, it is God's law."

McLeod's anger was fast rising.

" Don't fool yourself," he sneered, " You may overwork your maternal intuitions. You remember the kiss you gave me when a boy just fifteen? Well, you fooled yourself then about its maternal quality. The magnet of my red head drew your coal black one down to it with irresistible power."

" Perhaps so, Allan. Your work is done. There is the door. I say a last good-bye, with pity for your shallow nature, and the bitter revelation you have given me of your worthlessness."

Without another word he left, but with a dark resolution of slander with which he would tarnish her name, and wring the Preacher's heart with anguish.

CHAPTER XXI

WHY THE PREACHER THREW HIS LIFE AWAY

WHILE Mrs. Worth and Sallie were still in the North, the Rev. John Durham received a unanimous call to the pastorate of one of the most powerful Baptist churches in Boston, with a salary of five thousand dollars a year. He was receiving a salary of nine hundred dollars at Hambright, which could boast at most a population of two thousand. He declined the call by return mail.

The committee were thunderstruck at this quick adverse decision, refused to consider it final, and wrote him a long urgent letter of protest against such ill-considered treatment. They urged that he must come to Boston, and preach one Sunday, at least, in answer to their generous offer, before rendering a final decision. He consented to do so, and went to Boston. He sought Sallie the day after his arrival.

"Ah, my beautiful daughter of the South, it's good to see you shining here in the midst of the splendours of the Hub, the fairest of them all!" he said shaking her hand feelingly.

"You mean pining, not shining," she protested.

"That's better still. I knew your heart was in the right place!"

"How is he, Doctor?" she asked.

"He's trying to pull himself together with his work, and succeeding. The shock of a great sorrow has steadied his nerves, broadened his sympathies, and it will make him a man."

A look of longing came over her face. " I don't want him to be too strong without me," she faltered.

" Never fear. He's so despondent at times I have to try to laugh him out of countenance."

She smiled and pressed his hand for answer as he rose to go.

" How do you like these Yankees, Miss Sallie? "

" I've been surprised and charmed beyond measure with everything I've seen! "

" You don't say so! How? "

" Well, I thought they were cold-blooded and inhospitable. I never made a more foolish mistake. I have never been more at home, or been treated more graciously in the South. To tell you the truth, they seem like our most cultured people at home, warm-hearted, cordial, sensible and neighbourly. Mama is so pleased she's trying to claim kin with the Puritans, through her Scotch Covenanter ancestry."

" After all, I believe you are right. I never preached in my life to so sensitive an audience. There's an atmosphere of solid comfort, good sense, and intelligence that holds me in a spell here. This is the place in which I've dreamed I'd like to live and work."

" Then you will accept, Doctor? "

" Now listen to you, child! Don't you think I've a heart too? My brain and body longs for such a home, but my heart's down South with mine own people who love and need me."

The committee did their best to bring the Preacher to a favourable decision at once, but he smiled a firm refusal. They refused to report it to the church, and sent Deacon Crane, now a venerable man of seventy-six, the warmest admirer of the Preacher among them all to

Hambright. They authorised him to make an amazing offer of salary, if that would be any inducement, and they felt sure it would.

When the Deacon reached Hambright and saw its poverty and general air of unimportance he felt encouraged.

"A man of such power stay a lifetime in this little hole! Impossible!" he exclaimed under his breath, when he looked out of the bus along the wide deserted looking streets with a straggling cottage here and there on either side.

He stopped at the same hotel with the Preacher and became his shadow for a week. He was seated with him under the oak in the square, threshing over his argument for the hundredth time, in the most good-natured, but everlastingly persistent way.

"Doctor, it's perfect nonsense for a man of your magnificent talents, of your culture and power over an audience, to think of living always in a little village like this!"

"No, deacon, my work is here for the South."

"But, my dear man, in Boston, it would be for the whole nation, North and South. I'll tell you what we will do. Say you will come, and we will make your salary eight thousand a year. That's the largest salary ever offered a Baptist preacher in America. You will pack our church with people, give us new life, and we can afford it. You will be a power in Boston, and a power in the world."

The Preacher smiled and was silent. At length he said, "I appreciate your offer, deacon. You pay me the highest compliment you know how to express. But you prosperous Yankees can't get into your heads the idea that there are many things which money can't measure."

"But we know a good thing when we see it, and we go for it!" interrupted the deacon.

"Believe me," continued the Preacher, "I appreciate the sacrifice, the generosity, and breadth of sympathy this offer shows in your hearts. But it is not for me. My work is here. I don't mind confessing to you that you have vastly pleased me with that offer. I'll brag about it to myself the rest of my life."

"But Doctor, think how much greater power a generous salary will give you in furnishing your equipment for work, and in ministering to any cause you may have at heart," pleaded the deacon.

"I don't know. I have a salary of nine hundred dollars. With five hundred I buy books,—food, clothes, shelter, the companionship for the soul. The balance suffices for the body. I haven't time to bother with money. The man who receives a big salary must live up to its social obligations, and he must pay for it with his life."

"Doctor, there must be some tremendous force that holds you to such a decision in a village. It seems to me you are throwing your life away."

"There is a tremendous force, deacon. It is the overwhelming sense of obligation I feel to my own people who have suffered so much, and are still in the grip of poverty, and threatened with greater trials. I can't leave my own people while they are struggling yet with this unsolved Negro problem. Two great questions shadow the future of the American people, the conflict between Labor and Capital, and the conflict between the African and the Anglo-Saxon race. The greatest, most dangerous, and most hopeless of these, is the latter. My place is here."

The deacon laughed. "You're a crank on that subject. Come to Boston and you will see with a better perspective that the question is settling itself. In fact the war absolutely settled it."

"Deacon," said the Preacher with a quizzical expression about his eyes, " Do you believe in the doctrine of Election? "

" Yes, I do."

" I thought so. You know, I never saw a man who believed in the doctrine of Election who didn't believe he was elected. I never saw a man in my life, except a lying politician, who declared the Negro problem was settled, unless he had removed his family to a place of fancied safety where he would never come in contact with it. And they all believe that the Negro's place is in the South."

The deacon laughed good-naturedly.

" Come with us, and we will show you greater problems. For one, the life and death struggle of Christianity itself with modern materialism. I tell you the Negro problem was settled when slavery was destroyed."

" You never made a sadder mistake. The South did not fight to hold slaves. Our Confederate government at Richmond offered to guarantee to Europe, the freedom of every slave for the recognition of our independence. Slavery was bound of its own weight to fall. Virginia came within one vote in her assembly of freeing her slaves years before the war. But for the frenzy of your Abolition fanatics who first sought to destroy the Union by Secession, and then forced Secession on the South, we would have freed the slaves before this without a war, from the very necessities of the progress of the material world, to say nothing of its moral progress. We fought for the rights we held under the old constitution, made by a slave-holding aristocracy. But we collided with the resistless movement of humanity from the idea of local sovereignty toward nationalism, centralisation, solidarity."

" That's why I say," interrupted the deacon, " your

Negro question has already been settled. The nation has become a reality not a name."

"And that is why I know, deacon," insisted the Preacher, "that we have not only not settled this question,—we haven't even faced the issues. Nationality demands solidarity. And you can never get solidarity in a nation of equal rights out of two hostile races that do not intermarry. *In a Democracy you can not build a nation inside of a nation of two antagonistic races, and therefore the future American must be either an Anglo Saxon or a Mulatto.* And if a Mulatto, will the future be worth discussing?"

"I never thought of it in just that way," answered the deacon.

"It is my work to maintain the racial absolutism of the Anglo-Saxon in the South, politically, socially, economically."

"But can it be done? I see many evidences of a mixture of blood already," said the deacon seriously.

"Yes, we are doing it. This mixture you observe has no social significance, for a simple reason. It is all the result of the surviving polygamous and lawless instincts of the white male. Unless by the gradual encroachments of time, culture, wealth and political exigencies, the time comes that a negro shall be allowed freely to choose a white woman for his wife, the racial integrity remains intact. The right to choose one's mate is the foundation of racial life and of civilisation. The South must guard with flaming sword every avenue of approach to this holy of holies. And there are many subtle forces at work to obscure these possible approaches."

"Well, no matter," broke in the deacon, "come with us, and you will have more power to touch with your ideas the wealth and virtue of the whole nation."

The Preacher was silent a moment and seemed to be musing in a sort of half dream. The deacon looked at him with a growing sense of the hopelessness of his task, but of surprise at this revelation of the secrets of his inner life.

"The South has been voiceless in these later years," he went on, "her voice has been drowned in a din of cat-calls from an army of cheap scribblers and demagogues. But when these children we are rearing down here grow, rocked in their cradles of poverty, nurtured in the fierce struggle to save the life of a mighty race, they will find speech, and their songs will fill the world with pathos and power.

"I've studied your great cities. Believe me the South is worth saving. Against the possible day when a flood of foreign anarchy threatens the foundations of the Republic and men shall laugh at the faiths of your fathers, and undigested wealth beyond the dreams of avarice rots your society, until it mocks at honour, love and God—against that day we will preserve the South!"

The Preacher's voice was now vibrating with deep feeling, and the deacon listened with breathless interest.

"Believe me, deacon, the ark of the covenant of American ideals rests to-day on the Appalachian Mountain range of the South. When your metropolitan mobs shall knock at the doors of your life and demand the reason of your existence, from these poverty-stricken homes, with their old-fashioned, perhaps mediæval ideas, will come forth the fierce athletic sons and sweet-voiced daughters in whom the nation will find a new birth!" The Preacher's eyes had filled with tears and his voice dropped into a low dream-like prophecy.

"You can not understand," he resumed, in a clear voice, "why I feel so profoundly depressed just now because the Republican party, which, with you stands for the virtue, wealth and intelligence of the community, is now in charge of this state. I will tell you why. A Republican administration in North Carolina simply means a Negro oligarchy. The state is now being debauched and degraded by this fact in the innermost depths of its character and life. My place is here in this fight."

"But, Doctor, will not your industrial training of the Negro gradually minimise any danger to your society?"

"No, it will gradually increase it. Industrial training gives power. If the Negro ever becomes a serious competitor of the white labourer in the industries of the South, the white man will kill him, just as your labour Unions do in the North now where the conditions of life are hard, and men fight with tooth and nail for bread. If you train the negroes to be scientific farmers they will become a race of aristocrats, and when five generations removed from the memory of slavery, a war of races will be inevitable, unless the Anglo-Saxon grant this trained and wealthy African equal social rights. The Anglo-Saxon can not do this without suicide. One drop of Negro blood makes a negro."

"I can't tell you how sorry I am, Doctor, that I can't persuade you to become our pastor. But I can understand since this talk something of the larger views of your duty."

The deacon sought Mrs. Durham that evening and laid siege to her resolutely.

"Ah! deacon, you're shrewd—you are going to flatter me, but I can't let you. I'm an old fogy and out of date. I'm not orthodox on the Negro from Boston's point of view."

"Nonsense!" growled the deacon. "We don't care what you or the Doctor either thinks about the Negro, or the Jap, or the Chinaman. We want a preacher imbued with the power of the Holy Ghost to preach the Gospel of Christ."

"Well, you have quite captured me since you have been here. You are a revelation to me of what a deacon might be to a pastor and his wife. To be frank with you, I am on your side. I am tired of the Negro. I don't want to solve him. He is an impossible job from my point of view. I should be delighted to go to Boston now and begin life over again. But I do not figure in the decision. Dr. Durham settles such questions for himself. And I respect him more for it."

Encouraged by this decision of his wife the deacon renewed his efforts to change the Preacher's mind next day in vain. He stayed over Sunday, heard him preach two sermons, and sorrowfully bade him good-bye on Monday. He carried back to Boston his final word declining this call.

As the deacon stepped on the train, he warmly pressed his hand and said, " God bless you, Doctor. If you ever need a friend, you know my name and address."

CHAPTER XXII

THE FLESH AND THE SPIRIT

GASTON tried to wait in patience another week for a word from the woman he loved, and when the last mail came and brought no letter for him, he found himself face to face with the deepest soul crisis of his life.

After all, thoughts are things. The report of her social frivolities at first made little impression on him. But the thought had fallen in his heart, and it was growing a poisoned weed.

It is possible to kill the human body with an idea. The fairest day the spring ever sent can be blackened and turned from sunshine into storm by the flitting of a little cloud of thought no bigger than a man's hand.

So Gaston found this report of dancing and flirting in a gay society by the woman whom he had enthroned in the holy of holies of his soul to be destroying his strength of character, and like a deadly cancer eating his heart out.

He sat down by his window that night, unable to work, and tried to reconcile such a life with his ideal.

"Why should I be so provincial!" he mused. "The thing only shocks me because I am unused to it. She has grown up in this atmosphere. To her it is a harmless pastime."

Then he took out of his desk her picture, lit his lamp and looked long and tenderly at it, until his soul was drunk again with the memory of her beauty, the

337

warm touch of her hand, and the thrill of her full soft lips in the only two kisses he had ever received from the heart of a woman.

Then, the vision of a ball-room came to torture him. He could see her dressed in that delicate creation of French genius he had seen her wear the memorable night at the Springs. The French know so deeply the subtle art of draping a woman's body to tempt the souls of men. How he cursed them to-night! He could see her bare arms, white gleaming shoulders, neck, and back, and round full bosom softly rising and falling with her breathing, as she swept through a brilliant ball-room to the strains of entrancing music.

He knew the dance was a social convention, of course. But its deep Nature significance he knew also. He knew that it was as old as human society, and full of a thousand subtle suggestions,—that it was the actual touch of the human body, with rhythmic movement, set to the passionate music of love. This music spoke in quivering melody what the lips did not dare to say. This he knew was the deep secret of the fascination of the dance for the boy and the girl, the man and the woman. How he cursed it to-night!

His imagination leaped the centuries that separate us from the great races of the past who scorned humbug and hypocrisy, and held their dances in the deep shadows of great forests, without the draperies of tailors. These men and women looked Nature in the face and were not afraid, and did not try to apologise or lie about it. He felt humiliated and betrayed.

He thought too of her wealth with a feeling of resentment and isolation. Taken with this social nightmare it seemed to raise an impossible barrier between them. He knew that in the terrible quarrel she had with her father on their first clash, he had sworn if she disobeyed him to disinherit her. She had answered him in bitter defiance. And yet time often changes these noble visions of poverty and strenuous faith in high ideals. Wealth and all its good things becomes with us at last habit. And habit is life.

Could it be possible she had weakened in resolution of loyalty when brought face to face with the actual breaking of the habits of a lifetime? Might not the three forces combined, the habit of social conventions, the habit of luxury, and the habit of obedience to a masterful and lovable father, be sufficient to crush her love at last? It seemed to him to-night, not only a possibility, but almost an accomplished fact.

At one o'clock he went to bed and tried to sleep. He tossed for an hour. His brain was on fire, and his imagination lit with its glare. He could sweep the world with his vision in the silence and the darkness. Yes, the world that is, and that which was, and is to come!

He arose and dressed. It was half-past two o'clock. He knew that this was to be the first night in all his life when he could not sleep. He was shocked and sobered by the tremendous import of such an event in the development of his character. He had never been swept off his feet before. He knew now that before the sun rose he would fight with the powers and princes of the air for the mastery of life.

He left his room and walked out on the road to the Springs over which he had gone so many times in childhood. The moon was obscured by fleeting clouds, and the air had the sharp touch of autumn in its breath. He walked slowly past the darkened silent houses and felt his brain begin to cool in the sweet air.

The last note he had received from her weeks ago was the brief one announcing the new break in the poor little correspondence she had promised him. The last paragraph of that note now took on a sinister meaning. He recalled it word by word:

" I feel like I can not trifle with you in this way again. It is humiliating to me and to you. I can see no light in our future. I release you from any tie I may have imposed on your life. I feel I have fallen short of what you deserve, but I am so situated between my mother's failing health and my father's will, and my love for them both, I can not help it. I will love you always, but you are free."

Was not this a kindly and final breaking of their pledge to one another? Yet she had not returned the little medal he had given her with that exchange of eternal love and faith. Could she keep this and really mean to break with him finally? He could not believe it.

His whole life had been dominated by this dream of an ideal love. For it he had denied himself the indulgences that his college mates and young associates had taken as a matter of course. He had never touched wine. He had never smoked. He had never learned the difference between a queen and jack in cards. He had kept away from women. He had given his body and soul to the service of his Ideal, and bent every energy to the development of his mind that he might grasp with more power its sweetness and beauty when realised.

Did it pay? The Flesh was shrieking this question now into the face of the Spirit?

He had met the One Woman his soul had desired above all others. There could be no mistake about that. And now she was failing him when he had laid at her feet his life. It made him sick to recall how utter had been his surrender.

Why should he longer deny the flesh, when the soul's dream failed the test of pain and struggle?

Was it possible that he had been a fool and was missing the full expression of life, which is both flesh and spirit?

The world was full of sweet odours. He had delicate and powerful nostrils. Why not enjoy them? The world was full of beauty ravishing to the eye. He had keen eyes trained to see. Why should he not open his eyes and gaze on it all? The world was full of entrancing music. He had ears trained to hear. Why should he stuff them with dreams of a doubtful future, and not hear it all? The world was full of things soft and good to the touch. Why should he not grasp them? His hands were cunning, and every finger tingled with sensitive nerve tips. The world was full of good things sweet to the taste, why should he not eat and drink as others, as old and wise perhaps?

Was a man full-grown until he had seen, felt, smelled, tasted, and heard all life? Was there anything after all, in good or bad? Were these things not names? If not, how could we know unless we tried them? What was the good of good things?

"Am I not a narrow-minded fool, instead of a wise man, to throttle my impulses and deny the flesh for an imaginary gain?" he asked himself aloud.

She had written he was free.

"Well, by the eternal, I will be free!" he exclaimed, "I will sweep the whole gamut of human passion and human emotion. I will drink life to the deepest dregs of its red wine. I will taste, feel, see, touch, hear all! I will not be cheated. I will know for myself what it is to live."

When he woke to the consciousness of time and place, he found he was seated at the Sulphur Spring where it gushed from the foot of the hill, and that the eastern horizon was grey with the dawn.

A sense of new-found power welled up in him. He had regained control of himself.

"Good! I will no longer be a moping love-sick fool. I am a man. To will is to live, to cease to will is to die. I have regained my will,—I live!"

He walked rapidly back to town with vigourous step. His mind was clear.

"I will never write her another line until she writes to me. I will not be a dog and whine at any rich man's door or any woman's feet. The world is large, and I am large. I will be sought as well as seek. Besides, my country needs me. If I am to give myself it will be for larger ends than for the smiles of one woman!"

And then for two weeks he entered deliberately on a series of dissipations. He left Hambright and sought convivial friends on the sea coast. He amazed them by asking to be taught cards.

He swept the gamut of all the senses without reserve, day after day, and night after night.

At the end of two weeks he found himself haunting the post-office oftener, with a vague sense of impending calamity.

"The thing's all over I tell you!" he said to himself again and again. And then he would hurry to the next mail as eagerly as ever. As the excitement began to tire him, the sense of longing for her face, and voice, and the touch of her hand became intolerable.

"My God, I'd give all the world holds of sin to see her and hear one word from her lips!" he exclaimed as he locked himself in his room one night.

"Why didn't she answer my last letter?" he continued. "Ah, that was the best letter I ever wrote her. I put my soul in every word. I didn't believe the woman lived who could read such confessions and such worship without reply. Surely she has a heart!"

When he went to the post-office next day he got a letter forwarded from Hambright by the Preacher. It was postmarked Narragansett Pier, and addressed in a bold masculine hand he had never seen before.

He tore it open, and inside found his last letter to Sallie Worth, returned with the seal unbroken. He sprang to his feet with flashing eyes, trembling from head to foot.

"Ah! they did not dare to let her receive another of my letters! So a clerk returns it unopened," he cried.

And a great lump rose in his throat as he thought of the scenes of the past two weeks. The old fever and the old longing came rushing over his prostrate soul now in resistless torrents: "How dare a strange hand touch a message to her! I could strangle him. We will see now who wins the fight." He set his lips with determination, packed his valise, and took the train for home without a word of farewell to the companions of his revels.

When he reached Hambright he felt sure of a letter from her. A strange joy filled his heart.

"I have either got a letter or she's writing one to me this minute!" he exclaimed.

He went to the post-office in a state of exhilaration. The letter was not there. But it did not depress him.

"It is on the way," he quickly said.

For two days, he remained in that condition of tense nervous excitement and expectation, and on the following day he opened his box and found his letter.

"I knew it!" he said with a thrill of joy that was half awe at the remarkable confirmation he had received of their sympathy.

He hurried to his office and read the big precious message.

How its words burned into his soul! Every line

seemed alive with her spirit. How beautiful the sight of her handwriting! He kissed it again and again. He read with bated breath. The address was double expressive, because it contained the first words of abandoned tenderness with which she had ever written to him, except in the concealed message dotted in the note that broke their earlier correspondence.

" My Precious Darling:—I have gone through deep waters within the last three weeks. I became so depressed and hungry to see you, I felt some awful calamity was hanging over you and over me, and that it was my fault. I could scarcely eat or sleep.

I felt I should go mad if I did not speak and so I told Mama. She sympathised tenderly with me but insisted I should not write. She is so feeble I could not cross her. But Oh! the agony of it! Sometimes I saw you drowning and stretching out your hands to me for help.

Sometimes in my dreams I saw you fighting against overwhelming odds with strong brutal men, whose faces were full of hate, and I could not reach you.

I was nervous and unstrung, but you can never know how real the horror of it all was upon me.

I made up my mind one night to telegraph you. I heard some one talking inside Mama's room. I gently opened the door between our rooms, and she was praying aloud for me. I stood spellbound. I never knew how she loved me before. When at last she prayed that in the end I might have the desire of my heart, and my life be crowned with the joy of a noble man's love, and that it might be yours, and that she should be permitted to see and rejoice with me, I could endure it no longer.

Choking with sobs I ran to her kneeling figure, threw my arms around her neck and covered her dear face with kisses.

I could not send the message I had written after that scene.

The next day Papa came, and she told him in my presence, ' Now, General I have carried out your wishes with Sallie against my judgment. The strain has been more than you can understand. I give up the task. You can manage her now to suit yourself.'

There was a firmness in her voice I had never heard before. He noted it, and was startled into silence by it. He had a long talk with me and repeated his orders with increasing emphasis.

The next day I was unusually depressed. I did not get out of bed all day. At night I went down to supper. The clerk at the desk of the hotel called me and said, ' Miss Worth, I have a terrible sin to confess to you. I'm a lover myself, and I've done you a wrong. I returned to a young man yesterday a letter to you by request of the General. Forgive me for it, and don't tell him I told you.'

That night Papa and I had a fearful scene. I will not attempt to describe it. But the end was, I said to him with all the courage of despair: I am twenty-one years old. I am a free woman. I will write to whom I please and when I please and I will not ask you again. It is your right to turn me out of your house, but you shall not murder my soul!

Then for the first time in his life Papa broke down and sobbed like a child. We kissed and made up, and I am to write to you when I like.

Forgive my long silence. Write and tell me you love me. My heart is sick with the thought that I have been cowardly and failed you. Write me a long letter, and you can not say things extravagant enough for my hungry heart.

I feel utterly helpless when I think how completely you

have come to rule my life. I wish you to rule it. It is all yours "———

And then she said many little foolish things that only the eyes of the one lover should ever see, for only to him could they have meaning.

When he finished reading this letter, and had devoured with eagerness these foolish extravagances with which she closed it, he buried his face in his arms across his desk.

A big strong boastful man whose will had defied the world! Now he was crying like a whipped child.

THE TRIAL BY FIRE

Book Three—The Trial by Fire

CHAPTER I

A GROWL BENEATH THE EARTH

APPARENTLY McLeod's triumph was complete and permanent. The farmers were disappointed in their wild hopes of a sub-treasury, and other socialistic schemes, but the passions of the campaign had been violent, and the offices they had won with their Negro ally had been soothing to their sense of pride.

A Republican farmer was Governor for a term of four years, they had elected two Senators, and three Supreme Court judges, and they had completely smashed the power of the Democratic party in the county governments. Everywhere they were triumphant in the local elections, filling almost every county office with heavy-handed sons of toil from the country districts, and making the town fops who had been drawing these fat salaries get out and work for a living.

Even McLeod was amazed at the thoroughness with which they cleaned the state of every vestige of the invincible Democracy that had ruled with a rod of iron since Legree's flight.

Gaston could see but one weak spot in the alliance. The negroes had demanded their share of the spoils, and were gradually forcing their reluctant allies to grant them. He watched the progress of this movement with thrilling interest. The negroes had demanded the repeal of the county government plan of the Democracy, under which the credit of the forty black counties had been rescued from bankruptcy at the expense of local self-government.

When the lawmakers who succeeded Legree had put this scheme of centralised power in force, these forty counties were immediately lifted from ruin to prosperity. But no negro ever held another office in them.

Now the negroes demanded the return to the principles of pure Democracy and the right to elect all town, township, and county officers direct. They got their demands. They took charge in short order of the great rich counties in the Black Belt, and white men ceased to hold the offices.

A negro college-graduate from Miss Walker's classical institution had started a newspaper at Independence noted for its open demands for the recognition of the economic, social and political equality of the races. Young negro men and women walking the streets now refused to give half the sidewalk to a white man or woman when they met, and there were an increasing number of fights from such causes.

Gaston noted these signs with a growing sense of their import, and began his work for the second great campaign. The election for a legislature alone, he knew was lost already. His party had simply abandoned the fight. The Allied Party had passed new election laws, and under the tutelage of the doubtful methods of the past they had taken every partisan advantage possible within the limits of the Constitution. They could not be overthrown short of a political earthquake, and he knew it. But he thought he heard in the depths of the earth the low rumble of its coming, and he began to prepare for it.

CHAPTER II

FACE TO FACE WITH FATE

THREE weeks before Christmas Gaston began to dream of the visit he was to make to Independence to see Sallie Worth. How long it seemed since she had kissed him in the twilight of that Pullman car and the Limited had rolled away bearing her further and further from his life! He would sit now for an hour reading her last letter, looking at her picture on his desk, and dreaming of what she would say when he sat by her side again in her own home.

And then like a thunderbolt out of a clear sky came a tearful letter announcing another storm at home. Her father had again forbidden her to write. She said, at the last, that Gaston's visit must be postponed indefinitely for the present. He gazed at the letter with a hardened look.

" I *will* go. I'll face General Worth in his own home, and demand his reasons for such treatment. I am a man. I am entitled to the respect of a man." He made this declaration with a quiet force that left no doubt about his doing it.

He wrote Sallie that he could not and would not endure such a fight in the dark with the General, and that he was going to Independence on the day before Christmas as she had planned at first, to have it out with him face to face.

She wrote in reply and begged him under no circum-

stances to come until conditions were more **favourable.**
He got this letter the day before he was to start.

"I'll go and I'll see him if I have to fight my way into
his house, that's all there is to it!" he exclaimed.

When he reached Independence, St. Clare met him
at the depot, and gave him an eager welcome.

"I've been expecting you, you hard-headed fool!" he
said impulsively.

"Well, your words are not equal to your handshake.
What's the matter?" asked Gaston.

"You know what's the matter. Miss Sallie has been
to see me this afternoon, and begged me to chain you
at my house if you came to town to-day."

"Well, you'll need handcuffs, and help to get them
on," replied Gaston with quiet decision.

"Look here, old boy, you're not going down to that
house to-night with the old man threatening to kill you
on sight, and your girl bordering on collapse!"

"I am. I've been bordering on collapse for some time
myself. I'm getting used to it."

"You're a fool."

"Granted, but I'll risk it."

"But, man, I tell you Miss Sallie will be furious with
you if you go after all the messages she has sent you."

"I'll risk her fury too."

"Gaston, let me beg you not to do it."

"I'm going, Bob. It isn't any use for you to waste
your breath."

"You know where my heart is, old chum," said Bob,
yielding reluctantly. "I couldn't go down to that house
to-night under the conditions you are going for the
world."

"Why not? It's the manly thing to do."

"It's a dangerous thing to do. Fathers have killed
men under such conditions."

"Well, I'll risk it. I'm going as soon as I can brush up a little."

Bob walked with him to the outskirts of the city, begging in vain that he should turn back, but he never slacked his pace.

When he turned to go home, Bob pressed his hand and said "Good luck. And may your shadow never grow less."

Gaston walked rapidly on toward Oakwood. As he passed through the shadows of the forest near the gate, a flood of tender memories rushed over him. He was back again by her side on that morning he met her, with the first flush of love thrilling his life. He could see her looking earnestly at him as though trying to solve a riddle. He could hear her laughter full of joy and happiness. As he turned into the gateway the house flashed on him its gleaming windows from the hill top. He felt his heart sink with bitterness as he realised the contrast of his last entrance into that house, its welcomed guest, and his present unbidden intrusion. Once those lights had gleamed only a message of peace and love. Now they seemed signals of war some enemy had set on the hill to warn of his approach.

He paused a moment and wiped the perspiration from his brow. It was Christmas eve, but the air was balmy and spring-like and his rapid walk had tired him. He had eaten nothing all day, had slept only a few hours the night before, and the nerve strain had been more than he knew.

He looked up at the great white pillars softly shining in the starlight, and a sickening fear of a possible tragedy behind those doors crept over him.

"My God!" he exclaimed, "I had rather charge a breastworks in the face of flashing guns than to go into that house to-night and meet one man!"

He recognised the breach of the finer amenities of life involved in forcing his way into a home under such conditions, and it humiliated him for a moment.

"We will not stickle for forms now," he said to himself firmly. "This is war. I am to uncover the batteries of my enemy. I have hesitated long enough. I will not fight in the dark another day."

As he stepped briskly up to the door, he started at a sudden thought. What if the General had ordered the servants to slam the door in his face! The possibility of such an unforeseen insult made the cold sweat break out over his face as he rang the bell. No matter, he was in for it now, he would face hell if need be!

He waited but an instant, and heard the heavy tread of a man approach the door. Instinctively he knew that the General himself was on guard, and would open the door. Evidently he had expected him.

The door opened about two feet and the General glared at him livid with rage. He held one hand on the door and the other on its facing, and his towering figure filled the space.

"Good evening, General!" said Gaston with embarrassment.

"What do you want, sir?" he growled.

"I wish to see you for a few minutes."

"Well, I don't want to see you."

"Whether you wish to or not, you must do it sooner of later," answered Gaston with dignity.

"Indeed! Your insolence is sublime, I must say!"

"The sooner you and I have a plain talk the better for both of us. It can't be put off any longer," Gaston continued with self control. He was looking the General straight in the eyes now, with head and broad shoulders erect and his square-cut jaws were snapping his words with a clean emphasis that was not lost on the older master of men before him.

" Call at my office in the morning at ten o'clock," he said, at length.

" I will not do it. I am going home on the nine o'clock train. To-morrow is Christmas day. The issue between us is of life import to me, and it may be of equal importance to you. I will not put it off another hour! "

The General glared at him. His hands began to tremble, and raising his voice, he thundered,

" I am not accustomed to take orders from young upstarts. How dare you attempt to force yourself into my house when you were told again and again not to attempt it, sir? "

" Your former welcome to me on three occasions when the object of my visits was as well known to you as to me, gives me, at least, the vested rights of a final interview. I demand it," retorted Gaston curtly.

" And I refuse it! " Still there was a note of indecision in his voice which Gaston was quick to catch.

" General," he protested, " you are a soldier and a gentleman. You never fought an enemy with uncivilised warfare. Yet you have allowed some one under your protection to stab me in the dark for the past year. I am entitled to know why I fight and against whom. I ask your sense of fairness as a soldier if I am not right? "

The General hesitated, and finally said, as he opened the door,

" Walk into the parlour."

When they were seated, Gaston plunged immediately into the question he had at heart.

" Now, General, I wish to ask you plainly why you have treated me as you have since I asked you for your daughter's hand? "

"The less said about it, the better. I have good and sufficient reasons, and that settles it."

"But I have the right to know them."

"What right?"

"The right of every man to face his accuser when on trial for his life."

"Bah! men don't die nowadays for love, or women either," the General growled.

"Besides," continued Gaston, "you are under the deepest obligations to tell me fairly your reasons."

"Obligations?"

"The obligations of the commonest justice between man and man. You invited me to your home. I was your welcome guest. You encouraged my suit for your daughter's hand."

"How dare you say such a thing, sir!"

"Because she told me you did. I was led to believe that you not only looked with favour on my suit, but that you were pleased with it. I asked for your daughter. You insulted my manhood by refusing me permission even to seek an interview, and know the reasons for your change of views. Since then you have treated me with plain brutality. Now something caused this change."

"Certainly something caused it, something of tremendous importance," said the General.

"I am entitled to know what it is."

"Simply this. I received information concerning you, your habits, your associates, your character, and your family, that caused me to change my mind."

"Did you inquire as to their truth?"

"It was unnecessary. I love my daughter beyond all other treasures I possess. With her future I will take no risks."

"I have the right to know the charges, General," insisted Gaston. "I demand it."

"Well, sir, if you demand it, you will get it. I learned that you are a man of the most dissolute habits and character, that you are a hard drinker, a gambler, a rake and a spendthrift, and that your family's history is a deplorable one."

"My family history a deplorable one!" cried Gaston, springing to his feet, with trembling clinched fists and scarlet face on which the blue veins suddenly stood out.

"I begged you to spare me and yourself the pain of this," replied the General in a softer voice.

"No, I do not ask to be spared. Give me the particulars. What is the stain on my family name?"

"Not a moral one, but in some respects more hopeless, a physical one. I have positive information that your people on one side are what is known in the South as poor white trash—"

Gaston smiled. "I thank you, General, for your frankness. The only wrong of which I complain, is your withholding the name of the liar."

"There is no use of a fight over such things. I do not wish my daughter's name to be smirched with it."

"Her name is as dear to me as it can possibly be to you. Never fear. You are her father, I honour you as such. I thank you for the information. I scorn to stoop to answer. The humour of it forbids an answer if I could stoop to make one. Now, General, I make you this proposition. I am not in a hurry. I will patiently wait any time you see fit to set for any developments in my life and character about which you have doubts. All I ask is the privilege of writing to the woman I love. Is not this reasonable?"

"No, sir," declared the General, "I will not have it. You are not in a position to make me a proposition of any sort. I have settled this affair. It is not open for discussion."

"You mean to say that I have no standing whatever in the case?" asked Gaston with a smile, rubbing his hand over his smooth shaved lips and chin.

"Exactly. I've settled it. There's nothing more to be said."

"I'll never give her up. She is the one woman God made for me, and you will have to put me under the ground before you have settled my end of it," said Gaston still smiling.

The old man's face clouded for a moment, he wrinkled his brow, drew his bushy eyebrows closer and then turned toward Gaston in a persuasive way.

"Look here, Gaston, don't be a fool. It's amusing to me to hear a youngster talk such drivel. Love is not a fatal disease for a man, or a woman. You will find that out later if you don't know it now. I loved a half dozen girls, and when I got ready to marry, I asked the one handiest, and that seemed most suited to my temper. We married and have lived as happily as the romancers. The world is full of pretty girls. Go on about your business, and quit bothering me and mine."

"There's only one girl for me, General!"

"That's proof positive to my mind that you are a little cracked!" he answered with a smile.

Gaston laughed and shook his head. "I'll never give her up in this world, or the next," he doggedly added.

Again the General frowned. "Look here, young man, did it ever occur to you that your pursuit might be held the work of a low adventurer? My daughter is an heiress. You haven't a dollar. Don't you know that I will disinherit her if she marries without my consent?"

"You can't frighten me on that tack," answered Gaston firmly. "No dollar mark has yet been placed on the doors of Southern society. Manhood, character and achievement are the keys that unlock it. You know that, and I now it. I was poorer and more obscure the day you first invited me here than to-day. And yet you gave me as hearty a welcome as her richest suitor. All I ask is time to prove to you in my life my manhood and worth,—one year, two years, five years, ten years, any time you see fit to name."

"No, sir," firmly snapped the General, "not a day. I don't like long engagements. Yours is ended, once and for all time. I have settled that."

"Can even a father decide the destiny of two immortal souls off hand like that?"

"Now, you are assuming too much. I am not speaking for myself alone. I have laid all the facts carefully before Sallie, and she has agreed to the wisdom of my decision, and asked me to represent her in what I say this evening."

Gaston turned pale, his lips quivered, and turning to the General suddenly, he said,

"That is the only important fact you have laid before me. Just let her come here, stand by your side and say that with her own lips, and I will never cross your path in life again."

The General hung his head and stammered, "No, it is not necessary. It will embarrass and humiliate her. I will not permit it."

"Then I deny your credentials!" exclaimed Gaston.

The General seemed embarrassed by the failure of this fatherly subterfuge, and Gaston could not help smiling at the revelation of his weakness. He decided to press his advantage and try to see her if only for a moment.

"General," protested Gaston persuasively, "I appeal to your sense of courtesy, even to an enemy. After all that has passed between us in this house, is it fair or courteous to show me that door without one word of farewell to the woman to whom I have given my life? Or is it wise from your point of view?"

Again the General hesitated. He was a big-hearted man of generous impulses, and he felt worsted in this interview somehow, but it was hard to deny such a request. He fumbled at his watch chain, arose, and said,

"I will see if she desires it."

Gaston's heart bounded with joy! If *she* desired it! He could feel her soul enveloping him with its love as he sat there conscious that she was somewhere in that house praying for him!

He fairly choked with the pain and the joy of the certainty that in a moment he would be near her, touch her hand, see her glorious beauty and his ears drink the music of her voice.

"Just step this way," said the General, re-appearing at the door.

Gaston walked into the hall and met Sallie as she emerged from the library door opposite. He tried to say something, but his throat was dry and his tongue paralysed with the wonder of her presence! Besides, the General stood grimly by like a guard over a life prisoner.

He looked searchingly into her eyes as he held her hand for a moment and felt its warm impulsive pressure. Oh! the eyes of the woman we love! What are words to their language of melting tenderness, of faith and longing. Gaston felt like shouting in the General's face his triumph. She tried to speak, but only pressed his hand again. It was enough

He bowed to the General, and left without a word.

CHAPTER III

A WHITE LIE

THAT night as he walked back through the streets he was thrilled with a sense of strength and of triumph. He knew his ground now. There was to be war between him and the General to the bitter end. He had never asked her once to oppose her father's or mother's command. Now he would see who was master in a test of strength. And he was eager for the struggle. His mind was alert, and every nerve and muscle tense with energy.

"Heavens, how hungry I am!" he exclaimed when he reached the brilliantly lighted business portion of the city.

He went into a restaurant, ordered a steak, and enjoyed a good meal. He recalled then that he had not eaten for twenty-four hours. The steak was good, and the faces of the people seemed to him lit with gladness. He was singing a battle song in his soul, and the eyes of the woman he loved looked at him with yearning tenderness.

"Now, Bob, I count on you," he cried to his friend next morning. "I am going to have a merry Christmas and you are to aid in the skirmishing."

"I'm with you to the finish!" Bob responded with enthusiasm.

"We must make a feint this morning to deceive the enemy while I turn his flank. I go home on the nine o'clock train. You understand?"

"Yes, over the left. It's dead easy too. There's to be a big Christmas party to-night at the Alexanders'. She's invited. I'll see that she goes to it if I have to drag her."

"Good. Don't tell her I'm in town. I want to surprise her."

The General had a man at the morning train who reported Gaston's departure. He was surprised at Sallie's good spirits but attributed it to the magnificent present he had given her that morning of a diamond ring and an exquisite pearl necklace.

He bustled her off to the party that night and congratulated himself on the certainty of his triumph over an aspiring youngster who dared to set his will against his own.

When the festivities had begun, and the children were busy with their fireworks, Sallie strolled along the winding walks of the big lawn. She was chatting with Bob St. Clare about a young man they both knew, and when they reached the corner furthest from the house, under the shadows of a great magnolia with low overhanging boughs she saw the figure of a man.

She smiled into Bob's face, pressed his hand and said,

"Now, Bob you've done all a good friend could do. Go back. I don't need you."

And Bob answered with a smile and left her. In a moment Gaston was by her side with both her hands in his kissing them tenderly.

"Didn't I surprise you, dear?" he softly asked.

"No. Bob denied you were here, but I knew he was a story. I was sure you would never leave without seeing me. You couldn't, could you?"

"Not after what I saw in your eyes last night!" he whispered.

"It seems a century since I've heard your voice," she

said wistfully. "God alone knows what I have suffered, and I am growing weary of it."

"Do you think I have been treated fairly?" he asked.

"No, I do not."

"Then you will write to me?"

"Yes. I will not starve my heart any longer." And she pressed his hand.

"You have made the world glorious again! When will you marry me, Sallie?" he bent his face close to her, and for an answer she tenderly kissed him.

They stood in silence a moment with clasped hands, and then she said slowly, "You didn't want your freedom did you, dear? That's the third kiss, isn't it? I wonder if kissing will be always as sweet! But you asked me when we can marry? I can't tell now. I can do nothing to shock Mama. She seems to draw closer and closer to me every day. And now that I have determined no power shall separate us, it seems more and more necessary that I shall win Papa's consent. He loves me dearly. I feel that I must have his blessing on our lives. Give me time. I hope to win him."

"And you will never let another week pass without writing to me?"

"Never. Send my letters to Bob. He loves you better than he ever thought he loved me. He will give them to me on Sundays at church, and when he calls."

For two hours the kindly mantle of the magnolia sheltered them while they told the old sweet story over and over again. And somehow that night it seemed to them sweeter each time it was told.

CHAPTER IV

THE UNSPOKEN TERROR

WHEN Gaston reached Hambright the following day, and whispered to his mother the good news, he hastened to tell his friend Tom Camp. The young man's heart warmed toward the white-haired old soldier in this hour of his victory. With sparkling eyes, he told Tom of his stormy scene with the General, of its curious ending, and the hours he spent in heaven beneath the limbs of an old magnolia.

Tom listened with rapture. "Ah, didn't I tell you, if you hung on you'd get her by-and-by? So you bearded the General in his den did you? I'll bet his eyes blazed when he seed you! He's got an awful temper when you rile him. You ought to a seed him one day when our brigade was ordered into a charge where three concealed batteries was cross firin' and men was fallin' like wheat under the knife. Geeminy but didn't he cuss! He wouldn't take the order fust from the orderly, and sent to know if the Major-General meant it. I tell you us fellers that was layin' there in the grass listenin' to them bullets singin' thought he was the finest cusser that ever ripped an oath.

"He reared and he charged, and he cussed, and he damned that man for tryin' to butcher his men, and he never moved till the third order came. That was the night ten thousand wounded men lay on the field, and me in the middle of 'em with a Minie ball in my shoul-

364

TOM CAMP.

der. The Yankees and our men was all mixed up together, and just after dark the full moon came up through the trees and you could see as plain as day. I begun to sing the old hymn, "There is a land of pure delight," and you ought to have heard them ten thousand wounded men sing!

"While we was singing the General came through lookin' up his men. He seed me and said,

"Is that you, Tom Camp?"

"I looked up at him, and he was crying like a child, and he went on from man to man cryin' and cussin the fool that sent us into that hell-hole. The General's a rough man, if you rub his fur the wrong way, but his heart's all right. He's all gold I tell you!"

"Well, I'm in for a tussle with him, Tom."

"Shucks, man, you can beat him with one hand tied behind you if you've got his gal's heart. She's got his fire, and a gal as purty as she is can just about do what she pleases in this world."

"I hope she can bring him around. I like the General. I'd much rather not fight him."

"Where's Flora?" cried Tom looking around in alarm.

"I saw her going toward the spring in the edge of the woods there a minute ago," replied Gaston.

Tom sprang up and began to hop and jump down the path toward the spring with incredible rapidity.

Flora was playing in the branch below the spring and Tom saw the form of a negro man passing over the opposite hill going along the spring path that led in that direction.

"Was you talkin' with that nigger, Flora?" asked Tom holding his hand on his side and trying to recover his breath.

"Yes, I said howdy, when he stopped to get a drink

of water, and he give me a whistle," she replied with a pout of her pretty lips and a frown.

Tom seized her by the arm and shook her. "Didn't I tell you to run every time you seed a nigger unless I was with you!"

"Yes, but he wasn't hurtin' me and you are!" she cried bursting into tears.

"I've a notion to whip you good for this!" Tom stormed.

"Don't Tom, she won't do it any more, will you Flora?" pleaded Gaston taking her in his arms and starting to the house with her. When they reached the house, Tom was still pale and trembling with excitement.

"Lord, there's so many triflin' niggers loafin' round the county now stealing and doin' all sorts of devilment, I'm scared to death about that child. She don't seem any more afraid of 'em than she is of a cat."

"I don't believe anybody would hurt Flora, Tom,— she's such a little angel," said Gaston kissing the tears from the child's face.

"She is cute—ain't she?" said Tom with pride. "I've wished many a time lately I'd gone out West with them Yankee fellers that took such a likin' to me in the war. They told me that a poor white man had a chance out there, and that there wern't a nigger in twenty miles of their home. But then I lost my leg, how could I go?"

He sat dreaming with open eyes for a moment and continued, looking tenderly at Flora, "But, baby, don't you dare go nigh er nigger, or let one get nigh you no more 'n you would a rattlesnake!"

"I won't Pappy!" she cried with an incredulous smile at his warning of danger that made Tom's heart sick. She was all joy and laughter, full of health and bubbling life. She believed with a child's simple faith that all nature was as innocent as her own heart.

Tom smoothed her curls and kissed her at last, and she slipped her arm around his neck and squeezed it tight.

" Ain't she purty and sweet now ? " he exclaimed.

" Tom, you'll spoil her yet," warned Gaston as he smiled and took his leave, throwing a kiss to Flora as he passed through the little yard gate. Tom had built a fence close around his house when Flora was a baby to shut her in while he was at work.

Two days later about five o'clock in the afternoon as Gaston sat in his office writing a letter to his sweetheart, his face aglow with love and the certainty that she was his, as he read and re-read her last glowing words he was startled by the sudden clang of the court house bell. At first he did not move, only looking up from his paper. Sometimes mischievous boys rang the bell and ran down the steps before any one could catch them. But the bell continued its swift stroke seeming to grow louder and wilder every moment. He saw a man rush across the square, and then the bell of the Methodist, and then of the Baptist churches joined their clamour to the alarm.

He snapped the lid of his desk, snatched his hat and ran down the steps.

As he reached the street, he heard the long piercing cry of a woman's voice, high, strenuous, quivering!

" A lost child! A lost child! "

What a cry! He was never so thrilled and awed by a human voice. In it was trembling all the anguish of every mother's broken heart transmitted through the centuries!

At the court house door an excited group had gathered. A man was standing on the steps gesticulating wildly and telling the crowd all he knew about it. Over the din he caught the name,

"Tom Camp's Flora!"

He breathed hard, bit his lips, and prayed instinctively.

"Lord have mercy on the poor old man! It will kill him!" A great fear brooded over the hearts of the crowd, and soon the tumult was hushed into an awed silence.

In Gaston's heart that fear became a horrible certainty from the first. Within a half hour a thousand white people were in the crowd. Gaston stood among them, cool and masterful, organising them in searching parties, and giving to each group the signals to be used.

In a moment the white race had fused into a homogeneous mass of love, sympathy, hate, and revenge. The rich and the poor, the learned and the ignorant, the banker and the blacksmith, the great and the small, they were all one now. The sorrow of that old one-legged soldier was the sorrow of all, every heart beat with his, and his life was their life, and his child their child.

But at the end of an hour there was not a negro among them! By some subtle instinct they had recognised the secret feelings and fears of the crowd and had disappeared. Had they been beasts of the field the gulf between them would not have been deeper.

When Gaston reached Tom's house the crowd was divided into the groups agreed upon and a signal gun given to each. If the child was not dead when found two should be fired—if dead, but one.

He sought Tom to be sure there was no mistake and that the child had not fallen asleep about the house. He found the old man shut up in his room kneeling in the middle of the floor praying.

When Gaston laid his hand gently on his shoulder his lips ceased to move, and he looked at him in a dazed sort of way at first without speaking.

"Oh!—it's you, Charlie!" he sighed.

"Yes, Tom, tell me quick. Are you sure she is no-where in the house?"

"Sure!—Sure?" he cried in a helpless stare. "Yes, yes, I found her bonnet at the spring. I looked every-where for an hour before I called the neighbours!"

"Then I'm off with the searchers. The signal is two guns if they find her alive. One gun if she is dead. You will understand."

"Yes, Charlie," answered the old soldier in a faraway tone of voice, "and don't forget to help me pray while you look for her."

"I've tried already, Tom," he answered as he pressed his hand and left the house. All night long the search continued, and no signal gun was heard. Torches and lanterns gleamed from every field and wood, byway and hedge for miles in every direction.

Through every hour of this awful night Tom Camp was in his room praying—his face now streaming with tears, now dry and white with the unspoken terror that could stop the beat of his heart. His white hair and snow-white beard were dishevelled, as he unconsciously tore them with his trembling hands. Now he was crying in an agony of intensity,

"As thy servant of old wrestled with the angel of the Lord through the night, so, oh God, will I lie at Thy feet and wrestle and pray! I will not let Thee go until Thou bless me! Though I perish, let her live! I have lost all and praised Thee still. Lord, Thou canst not leave me desolate!"

From the pain of his wound and the exhaustion of soul and body he fainted once with his lips still moving in prayer. For more than an hour he lay as one dead. When he revived, he looked at his clock and it was but an hour till dawn.

Again he fell on his knees, and again the broken accents of his husky voice could be heard wrestling with God. Now he would beg and plead like a child, and then he would rise in the unconscious dignity of an immortal soul in combat with the powers of the infinite and his language was in the sublime speech of the old Hebrew seers!

Just before the sun rose the signal gun pealed its message of life, ONE! TWO! in rapid succession.

Tom sprang to his feet with blazing eyes. *One! Two!* echoed the guns from another hill, and fainter grew its repeated call from group to group of the searchers.

"There! Glory to God!" He screamed at the top of his voice, the last note of his triumphant shout breaking into sobs. "God be praised! I knew they would find her—she's not dead, she's alive! *alive!* oh! my soul, lift up thy head!"

The tramp of swift feet was heard at the door and Gaston told him with husky stammering voice,

"She's alive Tom, but unconscious. I'll have her brought to the house. She was found just where your spring branch runs into the Flat Rock, not five hundred yards from here in those woods. Stay where you are. We will bring her in a minute."

Gaston bounded back to the scene.

Tom paid no attention to his orders to stay at home, but sprang after him jumping and falling and scrambling up again as he followed. Before they knew it he was upon the excited tearful group that stood in a circle around the child's body.

Gaston, who was standing on the opposite side from Tom's approach, saw him and shouted,

"My God, men, stop him! Don't let him see her yet!"

But Tom was too quick for them. He brushed aside the boy who caught at him, as though a feather, crying,

"Stand back!"

The circle of men fell away from the body and in a moment Tom stood over it transfixed with horror.

Flora lay on the ground with her clothes torn to shreds and stained with blood. Her beautiful yellow curls were matted across her forehead in a dark red lump beside a wound where her skull had been crushed. The stone lay at her side, the crimson mark of her life showing on its jagged edges.

With that stone the brute had tried to strike the death blow. She was lying on the edge of the hill with her head up the incline. It was too plain, the terrible crime that had been committed.

The poor father sank beside her body with an inarticulate groan as though some one had crushed his head with an axe. He seemed dazed for a moment, and looking around he shouted hoarsely,

"The doctor boys! The doctor quick! For God's sake, quick! She's not dead yet—we may save her—help—help!" he sank again to the ground limp and faint from pain and was soon insensible.

Gaston gathered the child tenderly in his arms and carried her to the house. The men hastily made a stretcher and carried Tom behind him.

CHAPTER V

A THOUSAND-LEGGED BEAST

WHILE Gaston and the men were carrying Flora and Tom to the house, another searching party was formed. There were no women and children among them, only grim-visaged silent men, and a pair of little mild-eyed sharp-nosed blood-hounds. All the morning men were coming in from the country and joining this silent army of searchers.

Doctor Graham came, looked long and gravely at Flora and turned a sad face toward Tom.

The old soldier grasped his arm before he spoke.

"Now, doctor wait—don't say a word yet. I don't want to know the truth, if it's the worst. Don't kill me in a minute. Let me live as long as there's breath in her body—after that! well, that's the end—there's nothin' after that!"

The doctor started to speak.

"Wait," pleaded Tom, "let me tell you something. I've been praying all night. I've seen God face to face. She can't die. He told me so—"

He paused and his grip on the doctor's arm relaxed as though he were about to faint, but he rallied.

The kindly old doctor said gently, "Sit down Tom."

He tried to lead Tom away from the bed, but he held on like a bull dog.

The child breathed heavily and moaned.

Tom's face brightened. "She's comin' to, doctor,— thank God!"

The doctor paid no more attention to him and went on with his work as best he could.

Tom laid his tear-stained face close to hers, and murmured soothingly to her as he used to when she was a wee baby in his arms,

"There, there, honey, it will be all right now! The doctor's here, and he'll do all he can! And what he can't do, God will. The doctor'll save you. God will save you! He loves you. He loves me. I prayed all night. He heard me. I saw the shinin' glory of His face! He's only tryin' His poor old servant."

The broken artery was found and tied and the bleeding stopped. When the wound in her head was dressed the doctor turned to Tom,

"That wound is bad, but not necessarily fatal."

"Praise God!"

"Keep the house quiet and don't let her see a strange face when she regains consciousness," was his parting injunction.

The next morning her breathing was regular, and pulse stronger, but feverish; and about seven o'clock she came out of her comatose state and regained consciousness. She spoke but once, and apparently at the sound of her own voice immediately went into a convulsion, clinching her little fists, screaming and calling to her father for help!

When Tom first heard that awful cry and saw her terrified eyes and drawn face, he tried to cover his own eyes and stop his ears. Then he gathered the little convulsed body into his arms and crooned into her ears,

"There, Pappy's baby, don't cry! Pappy's got you now. Nothin' can hurt you. There, there, nothin' shall come nigh you!"

He covered her face with tears and kisses while he whispered and soothed her to sleep. When the noon train came up from Independence, General Worth arrived. Tom had asked Gaston to telegraph for him in his name.

Tom eagerly grasped his hand. " General I knowed you'd come—you're a man to tie to. I never knowed you to fail me in your life. You're one of the smartest men in the world too. You never got us boys in a hole so deep you didn't pull us out"—

" What can I do for you? " interrupted the General.

" Ah, now's the worst of all, General. I'm in water too deep for me. My baby, the last one left on earth, the apple of my eye, all that holds my old achin' body to this world—she's—about—to—die ! I can't let her. General, you must save her for me. I want more doctors. They say there's a great doctor at Independence. I want 'em all. Tell 'em it's a poor old one-legged soldier who's shot all to pieces and lost his wife and all his children—all but this one baby. And I can't lose her ! They'll come if you ask 'em—" His voice broke.

" I'll do it, Tom. I'll have them here on a special in three hours or maybe sooner," returned the General pressing his hand and hurrying to the telegraph office.

The doctors arrived at three o'clock and held a consultation with Doctor Graham. They decided that the loss of blood had been so great that the only chance to save her was in the transfusion of blood.

" I'll give her the blood, Tom," said Gaston quietly removing his coat and baring his arm.

The old soldier looked up through grateful tears.

" Next to the General, you're the best friend God ever give me, boy ! "

The General turned his face away and looked out of the window. The doctors immediately performed the operation, transfusing blood from Gaston into the child.

The results did not seem to promise what they had hoped. Her fever rose steadily. She became conscious again and immediately went into the most fearful convulsions, breaking the torn artery a second time.

Just as the sun sank behind the blue mountains peaks in the west, her heart fluttered and she was dead.

Tom sat by the bed for two hours, looking, looking, looking with wide staring eyes at her white dead face. There was not the trace of a tear. His mouth was set in a hard cold way and he never moved or spoke.

The Preacher tried to comfort Tom, who stared at him as though he did not recognise him at first, and then slowly began,

"Go away, Preacher, I don't want to see or talk to you now. It's all a swindle and a lie. There is no God!"

"Tom, Tom!" groaned the Preacher.

"I tell you I mean it," he continued. "I don't want any more of God or His heaven. I don't want to see God. For if I should see Him, I'd shake my fist in His face and ask Him where His almighty power was when my poor little baby was screamin' for help while that damned black beast was tearin' her to pieces! Many and many a time I've praised God when I read the Bible there where it said, not a sparrow falleth to the ground without His knowledge, and the very hairs of our head are numbered. Well, where was He when my little bird was flutterin' her broken bleedin' wings in the claws of that stinkin' baboon,—damn him to everlastin' hell!—It's all a swindle I tell you!"

The Preacher was watching him now with silent pity and tenderness.

"What a lie it all is!" Tom repeated. "Scratch my name off the church roll. I ain't got many more days here, but I won't lie. I'm not a hypocrite. I'm going to meet God cursin' Him to His face!"

The Preacher slipped his arm around the old soldier's neck, and smoothed the tangled hair back from his forehead as he said brokenly,

" Tom, I love you ! My whole soul is melted in sympathy and pity for you ! "

The stricken man looked up into the face of his friend, saw his tears and felt the warmth of his love flood his heart, and at last he burst into tears.

" Oh ! Preacher, Preacher ! you're a good friend I know, but I'm done, I can't live any more ! Every minute, day and night, I'll hear them awful screams—her a callin' me for help ! . I can see her lyin' out there in the woods all night alone moanin' and bleedin' ! "

His breast heaved and he paused as if in reverie. And then he sprang up, his face livid and convulsed with volcanic passions, that half strangled him while he shrieked,

" Oh ! if I only had him here before me now, and God Almighty would give me strength with these hands to tear his breast open and rip his heart out !—I—could— eat—it—like—a—wolf ! "

*   *   *   *   *

When they reached the cemetery the next day and the body was about to be lowered into the grave, Tom suddenly spied old Uncle Reuben Worth leaning on his spade by the edge of the crowd. Uncle Reuben was the grave digger of the town and the only negro present.

" Wait ! " said Tom raising his hand. " Don't put her in that grave ! A nigger dug it. I can't stand it." He turned to a group of old soldier comrades standing by and said,

" Boys, humour an old broken man once more. You'll dig another grave for me, won't you ? It won't take long. The folks can go home that don't want to stay. I ain't got no home to go to now but this graveyard."

His comrades filled up the grave that Uncle Reuben had dug, and opened a new one on the other side of the graves where slept his other loved ones.

Gaston took Tom to his home and stayed with him several hours trying to help him. He seemed to have settled into a stupor from which nothing could rouse him. When at length the old man fell asleep, Gaston softly closed the door and returned to his office with a heavy heart.

As he neared the centre of the town, he heard a murmur like the distant moaning of the wind in the hush that comes before a storm. It grew louder and louder and became articulate with occasional words that seemed far away and unreal. What could it be? He had never heard such a sound before. Now it became clearer and the murmur was the tread of a thousand feet and the clatter of horses' hoofs. Not a cry, or a shout, or a word. Silence and hurrying feet!

Ah! he knew now. It was the searchers returning, a grim swaying voiceless mob with one black figure amid them. They were swarming into the court house square under the big oak where an informal trial was to be held.

He rushed forward to protest against a lynching. He could just catch a glimpse of the negro's head swaying back and forth, protesting innocence in a singing monotone as though he were already half dead.

He pushed his way roughly through the excited crowd, to the centre where Hose Norman, the leader, stood with one end of a rope in his hand and the other around the negro's neck.

The negro turned his head quickly toward the movement made by the crowd as Gaston pressed forward.

It was Dick!

Dick recognised him at the same moment, leaped toward him and fell at his feet crying and pleading as he held his feet and legs.

"Save me, Charlie! I nebber done it! I nebber done it! For God's sake help me! Keep 'em off! Dey gwine burn me erlive!"

Gaston turned to the crowd. "Men, there's not one among you that loved that old soldier and his girl as I did. But you must not do this crime. If this negro is guilty, we can prove it in that court house there, and he will pay the penalty with his life. Give him a fair trial"—

"That's a lawyer talkin' now!" said a man in the crowd. "We know that tune. The lawyers has things their own way in a court house." A murmur of assent mingled with oaths ran through the crowd.

"Fair trial!" sneered Hose Norman snatching Dick from the ground by the rope. "Look at the black devil's clothes splotched all over with her blood. We found him under a shelvin' rock where he'd got by wadin' up the branch a quarter of a mile to fool the dogs. We found his track in the sand some places where he missed the water and tracked him clear from where we found Flora to the cave he was lying in. Fair trial—hell! We're just waitin' for er can o' oil. You go back and read your law books—we'll tend ter this devil."

The messenger came with the oil and the crowd moved forward. Hose shouted, "Down by Tom Camp's by his spring, down the spring branch to the Flat Rock where he killed her!"

On the crowd moved, swaying back and forth with Gaston in their midst by Dick's side begging for a fair trial for him. A crowd that hurries and does not shout is a fearful thing. There is something inhuman in its uncanny silence.

Gaston's voice sounded strained and discordant. They

paid no more attention to his protest than to the chirp of a cricket.

They reached the spot where the child's body had been found. They tied the screaming, praying negro to a live pine and piled around his body a great heap of dead wood and saturated it with oil. And then they poured oil on his clothes.

Gaston looked around him begging first one man then another to help him fight the crowd and rescue him. Not a hand was lifted, or a voice raised in protest. There was not a negro among them. Not only was no negro in that crowd, but there was not a cabin in all that county that would not have given shelter to the brute, though they knew him guilty of the crime charged against him. This was the one terrible fact that paralysed Gaston's efforts.

Hose Norman stepped forward to apply a match and Gaston grasped his arm.

" For God's sake, Hose, wait a minute! " he begged. " Don't disgrace our town, our county, our state, and our claims to humanity by this insane brutality. A beast wouldn't do this. You wouldn't kill a mad dog or a rattlesnake in such a way. If you will kill him, shoot him or knock him in the head with a rock,—don't burn him alive! "

Hose glared at him and quietly remarked,

" Are you done now? If you are, stand out of the way! "

He struck the match and Dick uttered a scream. As Hose leaned forward with his match Gaston knocked him down, and a dozen stalwart men were upon him in a moment.

" Knock the fool in the head! " one shouted.

" Pin his arms behind him! " said another.

Some one quickly pinioned his arms with a cord. He

stood in helpless rage and pity, and as he saw the match applied, bowed his head and burst into tears.

He looked up at the silent crowd standing there like voiceless ghosts with renewed wonder.

Under the glare of the light and the tears the crowd seemed to melt into a great crawling swaying creature, half reptile half beast, half dragon half man, with a thousand legs, and a thousand eyes, and ten thousand gleaming teeth, and with no ear to hear and no heart to pity!

All they would grant him was the privilege of gathering Dick's ashes and charred bones for burial.

*   *   *   *   *

The morning following the lynching, the Preacher hurried to Tom Camp's to see how he was bearing the strain.

His door was wide open, the bureau drawers pulled out, ransacked, and some of their contents were lying on the floor.

" Poor old fellow, I'm afraid he's gone crazy! " exclaimed the Preacher. He hurried to the cemetery. There he found Tom at the newly made grave. He had worked through the night and dug the grave open with his bare hands and pulled the coffin up out of the ground. He had broken his finger nails all off trying to open it and his fingers were bleeding. At last he had given up the effort to open the coffin, sat down beside it, and was arranging her toys he had made for her beside the box. He had brought a lot of her clothes, a pair of little shoes and stockings, and a bonnet, and he had placed these out carefully on top of the lid. He was talking to her.

The Preacher lifted him gently and led him away, a hopeless madman.

CHAPTER VI

THE BLACK PERIL

THE longer Gaston pondered over the tragic events of that lynching the more sinister and terrible became its meaning, and the deeper he was plunged in melancholy.

Beyond all doubt, within his own memory, since the negroes under Legree's lead had drawn the colour line in politics, the races had been drifting steadily apart. The gulf was now impassable.

Such crimes as Dick had committed, and for which he had paid such an awful penalty, were unknown absolutely under slavery, and were unknown for two years after the war. Their first appearance was under Legree's régime. Now, scarcely a day passed in the South without the record of such an atrocity, swiftly followed by a lynching, and lynching thus had become a habit for all grave crimes.

Since McLeod's triumph in the state such crimes had increased with alarming rapidity. The encroachments of negroes upon public offices had been slow but resistless. Now there were nine hundred and fifty negro magistrates in the state elected for no reason except the colour of their skin. Feeling themselves intrenched behind state and Federal power, the insolence of a class of young negro men was becoming more and more intolerable. What would happen to these fools when once they roused that thousand-legged, thousand-eyed beast with its ten thousand teeth and nails! He had looked into its face, and he shuddered to recall the hour.

He knew that this power of racial fury of the Anglo-Saxon when aroused was resistless, and that it would sweep its victims before its wrath like chaff before a whirlwind.

And then he thought of the day fast coming when culture and wealth would give the African the courage of conscious strength and he would answer that soul piercing shriek of his kindred for help, and that other thousand-legged beast, now crouching in the shadows, would meet thousand-legged beast around that beacon fire of a Godless revenge!

More and more the impossible position of the Negro in America came home to his mind. He was fast being overwhelmed with the conviction that sooner or later we must squarely face the fact that two such races, counting millions in numbers, can not live together under a Democracy.

He recalled the fact that there were more negroes in the United States than inhabitants in Mexico, the third republic of the world.

Amalgamation simply meant Africanisation. The big nostrils, flat nose, massive jaw, protruding lip and kinky hair will register their animal marks over the proudest intellect and the rarest beauty of any other race. The rule that had no exception was that one drop of Negro blood makes a negro.

What could be the outcome of it? What was his duty as a citizen and a member of civilised society? Since the scenes through which he had passed with Tom Camp and that mob the question was insistent and personal. It clouded his soul and weighed on him like the horrors of a nightmare.

Again and again the fateful words the Preacher had

dinned into his ears since childhood pressed upon him,

" *You can not build in a Democracy a nation inside a nation of two antagonistic races. The future American must be an Anglo-Saxon or a Mulatto.*"

His depression and brooding over the fearful events in which he had so recently taken part had tinged his life and all its hopes with sadness. He had reflected this in his letters to Sallie Worth without even mentioning the events. His heart was full of sickening foreboding. How could one love and be happy in a world haunted by such horrors! He had begged her to hasten her hour of final decision. He told her of his sense of loneliness and isolation, and of his inexpressible need of her love and presence in his daily life.

Her answer had only intensified his moody feelings. She had written that her love grew stronger every day and his love more and more became necessary to her life, and yet she could not cloud its future with the anger of her father and the broken heart of her mother by an elopement. She feared such a shock would be fatal and all her life would be embittered by it. They must wait. She was using all her skill to win her father, but as yet without success. But she determined to win him, and it would be so.

All this seemed so far away and shadowy to Gaston's eager restless soul.

The letter had closed by saying she was preparing for another trip to Boston to visit Helen Lowell and that she should be absent at least a month. She asked that his next letter be addressed to Boston.

Somehow Boston seemed just then out of the world on another planet, it was so far away and its people and their life so unreal to his imagination.

But he sighed and turned resolutely to his work of

preparation for an event in his life which he meant to make great in the history of the state. It was the meeting of the Democratic convention, as yet nearly two years in the future. He held a subordinate position in his party's councils, but defeat and ruin had taken the conceit out of the old line leaders and he knew that his day was drawing near.

" I'll take my place among the leaders and masters of men," he told himself with quiet determination, " I will compel the General's respect; and if I can not win his consent, I will take her without it."

CHAPTER VII

EQUALITY WITH A RESERVATION

THE lynching at Hambright had stirred the whole nation into unusual indignant interest. It happened to be the climax of a series of such crimes committed in the South in rapid succession, and the death of this negro was reported with more than usual vividness by a young newspaper man of genius.

A grand mass meeting was called in Cooper Union, New York, at which were gathered delegates from different cities and states to give emphasis and unity to the movement and issue an appeal to the national government.

When Sallie Worth reached Boston, she found Helen Lowell at home alone. The Hon. Everett Lowell had made one of the speeches of his career at the mass meeting held in Faneuil Hall, and he was in New York where he had gone to make the principal address in the Cooper Union Convention of Negro sympathisers.

George Harris had accompanied him, supremely fascinated by the eloquent and masterful appeal for human brotherhood he had heard him make in Boston. There was something pathetic in the dog-like worship this young negro gave to his brilliant patron. In his life in New England he had been shocked more than once by the brutal prejudices of the people against his race. His soul had been tried to the last of its powers of endurance at times. He found to his amazement that, when put to the test, the masses of the North had even deeper repugnance to the person of a Negro than the Southerners who grew up with him from the cradle. He had found himself cut off from every honourable way of earning his bread, gentleman and scholar though he was, and had looked into the river as he walked over the bridge to Cambridge one night with a well-nigh resistless impulse to end it all.

But Lowell had cheered him, laughed his gloomy ideas to scorn, and more practical still, he had secured him a clerkship in the Custom House which settled the problem of bread. Others had failed him, but this man of trained powers had never failed him. He had taught him to lift up his head and look the world squarely in the face. Lowell was, to his vivid African imagination, the ideal man made in the image of God, calm in judgment, free from all superstitions and prejudices, a citizen of the world of human thought, a prince of that vast ethical aristocracy of the free thinkers of all ages who knew no racial or conventional barriers between man and man.

Harris had published a volume of poems which he had dedicated to Lowell, and his most inspiring verse was simply the outpouring of his soul in worship of this ideal man.

He was his devoted worshipper for another and more powerful reason. In his daily intercourse with him in his library during his campaigns he had frequently met his beautiful daughter, and had fallen deeply and madly in love with her. This secret passion he had kept hidden in his sensitive soul. He had worshipped her from afar as though she had been a white-robed angel. To see her and be in the same house with her was all he asked. Now and then he had stood beside the piano and turned the music while she played and sang one of his new pieces, and he would live on that scene for months, eating his heart out with voiceless yearnings he dared not express,

In his music he made his greatest success. There was a fiery sweep to his passion, and a deep oriental rhythm in his cadence that held the imagination of his hearers in a spell. It is needless to say it was in this music he breathed his secret love.

At first he had not dared to hope for the day when he could declare this secret or take his place in the list of her admirers and fight for his chance. But of late, a great hope had filled his soul and illumined the world. As he had listened to Lowell's impassioned appeals for human brotherhood, his scathing ridicule of pride and prejudice, and the poetic beauty of the language in which he proclaimed his own emancipation from all the laws of caste, the fiery eloquence with which he trampled upon all the barriers man had erected against his fellow man, his soul was thrilled into ecstasy with the conviction that this scholar and scientific thinker, at least, was a free man. He was sure that he had risen above the limitations of provincialisms, racial or national prejudices.

He had begun to dream of the day he would ask this Godlike man for the privilege of addressing his daughter.

The great meeting at Cooper Union had brought this dream to a sudden resolution. Lowell had outdone himself that night. With merciless invective he had denounced the inhuman barbarism of the South in these lynchings. The sea of eager faces had answered his appeals as water the breath of a storm. He felt its mighty reflex influence sweep back on his soul and lift him to greater heights. He demanded equality of man on every inch of this earth's soil.

" I demand this perfect equality," he cried, " absolutely without reservation or subterfuge, both in form and essential reality. It is the life-blood of Democracy. It is the reason of our existence. Without this we are a living lie, a stench in the nostrils of God and humanity!"

A cheer from a thousand negro throats rent the air as he thus closed. The crowd surged over the platform and for ten minutes it was impossible to restore order or continue the programme. Young Harris pressed his patron's hand and kissed it while tears of pride and gratitude rained down his face.

This speech made a national sensation. It was printed in full in all the partisan papers where it was hoped capital might be made of it for the next political campaign, and the National Campaign Committee of which he was a member ordered a million copies of it printed for distribution among the negroes.

When Lowell and Harris reached Boston, as they parted at the depot Harris said,

" Will you be at home to-morrow, Mr. Lowell?"

" Yes, why?"

" I would like a talk with you in the morning on a matter of grave importance. May I call at nine o'clock?"

" Certainly. Come right into the library. You'll find me there, George."

That night as Lowell walked through his brilliantly lighted home, he felt a sense of glowing pride and strength. With his hands behind him he paced back and forth in his great library and out through the spacious hall with firm tread and flushed face. He felt he could look these great ancestors in the face to-night as they gazed down on him from their heavy gold frames. They had called him to high ambitions and a strenuous life when his indolence had pleaded for ease and the dilettante-ism of a fruitless dreaming. His father had cultivated his artistic tastes, dreamed and done nothing. But these grim-visaged, eagle-eyed ancestors had called him to a life of realities, and he had heard their voices.

Yes, to-night his name was on a million lips. The

door of the United States Senate was opening at his touch and mightier possibilities loomed in the future.

He felt a sense of gratitude for the heritage of that stately old home and its inspiring memories. Its roots struck down into the soil of a thousand years, and spread beneath the ocean to that greater old world life. He felt his heart beat with pride that he was adding new honours to that family history, and adding to the soul-treasures his daughter's children would inherit.

Seated in the library next morning Harris was nervous and embarrassed. He made two or three attempts to begin the subject but turned aside with some unimportant remark.

"Well, George, what is the problem that makes you so grave this morning?" asked Lowell with kindly patronage.

Harris felt that his hour had come, and he must face it. He leaned forward in his chair and looked steadily down at the rug, while he clasped both his hands firmly across his lap and spoke with great rapidity.

"Mr. Lowell, I wish to say to you that you have taught me the greatest faith of life, faith in my fellow man without which there can be no faith in God. What I have suffered as a man as I have come in contact with the brutality with which my race is almost universally treated, God only can ever know.

"The culture I have received has simply multiplied a thousandfold my capacity to suffer. But for the inspiration of your manhood I would have ended my life in the river. In you, I saw a great light. I saw a man really made in the image of God with mind and soul trained, with head erect, scorning the weak prejudices of caste, which dare to call the image of God clean or unclean in passion or pride.

"I lifted up my head and said, one such man redeems

a world from infamy. It's worth while to live in a world honoured by one such man, for he is the prophecy of more to come."

He paused a moment, fidgeted with a piece of paper he had picked up from the table and seemed at a loss for a word.

It never dawned on Lowell what he was driving at. He supposed, as a matter of course, he was referring to his great speeches and was going to ask for some promotion in a governmental department at Washington.

"I'm proud to have been such an inspiration to you, George. You know how much I think of you. What is on your mind?" he asked at length.

"I have hidden it from every human eye, sir, I am afraid to breath it aloud alone. I have only tried to sing it in song in an impersonal way. Your wonderful words of late have emboldened me to speak. It is this—I am madly, desperately in love with your daughter."

Lowell sprang to his feet as though a bolt of lightning had suddenly shot down his backbone. He glared at the negro with wide dilated eyes and heaving breath as though he had been transformed into a leopard or tiger and was about to spring at his throat.

Before answering, and with a gesture commanding silence, he walked rapidly to the library door and closed it.

"And I have come to ask you," continued Harris ignoring his gesture, "if I may pay my addresses to her with your consent."

"Harris, this is crazy nonsense. Such an idea is preposterous. I am amazed that it should ever have entered your head. Let this be the end of it here and now, if you have any desire to retain my friendship."

Lowell said this with a scowl, and an emphasis of indignant rising inflection. The negro seemed stunned by this swift blow in his very teeth, that seemed to place him outside the pale of a human being.

" Why is such a hope unreasonable, sir, to a man of your scientific mind? "

" It is a question of taste," snapped Lowell.

" Am I not a graduate of the same university with you? Did I not stand as high, and age for age, am I not your equal in culture? "

" Granted. Nevertheless you are a negro, and I do not desire the infusion of your blood in my family."

" But I have more of white than Negro blood, sir."

" So much the worse. It is the mark of shame."

" But it is the one drop of Negro blood at which your taste revolts, is it not? "

" To be frank, it is."

" Why is it an unpardonable sin in me that my ancestors were born under tropic skies where skin and hair were tanned and curled to suit the sun's fierce rays? "

" All tropic races are not negroes, and your race has characteristics apart from accidents of climate that make it unique in the annals of man," rejoined Lowell.

" And yet you demand perfect equality of man with man, absolutely in form and substance without reservation or subterfuge! "

" Yes, political equality."

" Politics is but a secondary phenomenon of society. You said absolute equality," protested Harris.

" The question you broach is a question of taste, and the deeper social instincts of racial purity and self preservation. I care not what your culture, or your genius, or your position, I do not desire, and will not permit, a mixture of Negro blood in my family. The idea is nauseating, and to my daughter it would be repulsive beyond the power of words to express it! "

" And yet," pleaded Harris, " you invited me to your

home, introduced me to your daughter, seated me at your table, and used me in your appeal to your constituents, and now when I dare ask the privilege of seeking her hand in honourable marriage, you, the scholar, patriot, statesman and philosopher of Equality and Democracy, slam the door in my face and tell me that I am a negro! Is this fair or manly?"

"I fail to see its unfairness."

"It is amazing. You are a master of history and sociology. You know as clearly as I do that social intercourse is the only possible pathway to love. And you opened it to me with your own hand. Could I control the beat of my heart? There are some powers within us that are involuntary. You could have prevented my meeting your daughter as an equal. But all the will power of earth could not prevent my loving her, when once I had seen her, and spoken to her. The sound of the human voice, the touch of the human hand in social equality are the divine sacraments that open the mystery of love."

"Social rights are one thing, political rights another," interrupted Lowell.

"I deny it. If you are honest with yourself, you know it is not true. Politics is but a manifestation of society. Society rests on the family. The family is the unit of civilisation. The right to love and wed where one loves is the badge of fellowship in the order of humanity. The man who is denied this right in any society is not a member of it. He is outside any manifestation of its essential life. You had as well talk about the importance of clothes for a dead man, as political rights for such a pariah. You have classed him with the beasts of the field. As a human unit he does not exist for you."

"Harris, it is utterly useless to argue a point like this," Lowell interrupted coldly. "This must be the end of our acquaintance. You must not enter my house again."

" My God, sir, you can't kick me out of your home like this when you brought me to it, and made it an issue of life or death ! "

" I tell you again you are crazy. I have brought you here against her wishes. She left the house with her friend this morning to avoid seeing you. Your presence has always been repulsive to her, and with me it has been a political study, not a social pleasure."

" I beg for only a desperate chance to overcome this feeling. Surely a man of your profound learning and genius can not sympathise with such prejudices? Let me try—let her decide the issue."

" I decline to discuss the question any further."

" I can't give up without a struggle ! " the negro cried with desperation.

Lowell arose with a gesture of impatience.

" Now you are getting to be simply a nuisance. To be perfectly plain with you, I haven't the slightest desire that my family with its proud record of a thousand years of history and achievement shall end in this stately old house in a brood of mulatto brats ! "

Harris winced and sprang to his feet, trembling with passion. " I see," he sneered, " the soul of Simon Legree has at last become the soul of the nation . The South expresses the same luminous truth with a little more clumsy brutality. But their way is after all more merciful. The human body becomes unconscious at the touch of an oil-fed flame in sixty seconds. Your methods are more refined and more hellish in cruelty. You have trained my ears to hear, eyes to see, hands to touch and heart to feel, that you might torture with the denial of every cry of body and soul and roast me in the flames of impossible desires for time and eternity ! "

" That will do now. There's the door ! " thundered Lowell with a gesture of stern emphasis. " I happen to know the important fact that a man or woman of negro ancestry, though a century removed, will suddenly breed back to a pure negro child, thick lipped, kinky headed, flat nosed, black skinned. One drop of your blood in my family could push it backward three thousand years in history. If you were able to win her consent, a thing unthinkable, I would do what old Virginius did in the Roman Forum, kill her with my own hand, rather than see her sink in your arms into the black waters of a Negroid life! Now go!"

CHAPTER VIII

THE NEW SIMON LEGREE

HARRIS immediately resigned his office in the custom house which he owed to Lowell and began a search for employment.

"I will not be a pensioner of a government of hypocrites and liars," he exclaimed as he sealed his letter of resignation.

And then began his weary tramp in search of work. Day after day, week after week, he got the same answer—an emphatic refusal. The only thing open to a negro was a position as porter, or bootblack, or waiter in second-rate hotels and restaurants, or in domestic service as coachman, butler or footman. He was no more fitted for these places than he was to live with his head under water.

"I will blow my brains out before I will prostitute my intellect, and my consciousness of free manhood by such degrading associates and such menial service!" he declared with sullen fury.

At last he determined to lay aside his pride and education and learn a manual trade. Not a labour union would allow him to enter its ranks.

He managed to earn a few dollars at odd jobs and went to New York. Here he was treated with greater brutality than in Boston. At last he got a position in a big clothing factory. He was so bright in colour that the manager never suspected that he was a negro, as he was accustomed to employing swarthy Jews from Poland and Russia.

When Harris entered the factory the employees discovered within an hour his race, laid down their work, and walked out on a strike until he was removed.

He again tried to break into a labour union and get the protection of its constitution and laws. He managed at last to make the acquaintance of a labour leader who had been a Quaker preacher, and was elated to discover that his name was Hugh Halliday, and that he was a son of one of the Hallidays who had assisted in the rescue of his mother and father from slavery. He told Halliday his history and begged his intercession with the labour union.

" I'll try for you, Harris," he said, " but it's a doubtful experiment. The men fear the Negro as a pestilence."

" Do the best you can for me. I must have bread. I only ask a man's chance," answered Harris. Halliday proposed his name and backed it up with a strong personal endorsement, gave a brief sketch of his culture and accomplishments and asked that he be allowed to learn the bricklayer's trade.

When his name came up before the Brick Layers' Union, and it was announced that he was a negro, it precipitated a debate of such fury that it threatened to develop into a riot.

One of the men sprang toward the presiding officer with blazing eyes, gesticulating wildly until recognised.

" I have this to say," he shouted. " No negro shall ever enter the door of this Union except over my dead body. The Negro can under live us. We can not compete with him, and as a race we can not organise him. Let him stay in the South. We have no room for him here, and we will kill him if he tries to take our bread from us ! "

" Have you no sympathy for his age-long sufferings in slavery? " interrupted Halliday.

" Slavery ! of all the delusions the idea that slavery

was abolished in this country in 1865 is the silliest. Slavery was never firmly established until the chattel form was abandoned for the wage system in 1865. Chattel slavery was too expensive. The wage system is cheaper. Now they never have to worry about food, or clothes, or houses, or the children, or the aged and infirm among wage slaves.

" Once the master hunted the slave,—now the slave must hunt the master, beg for the privilege of serving him and trample others to death trying to fasten the chains on when a brother slave drops dead in his tracks.

" No, I don't shed any crocodile tears over the Negro slavery of the South. It was a mild form of servitude, in which the Negro had plenty to eat and wear, never suffered from cold, slept soundly and reared his children in droves with never a thought for the morrow.

" Then mothers and babes were sometimes, though not often, separated by an executor's or sheriff's sale. Now, we know better than to allow babes to be born. Then, a babe was a valuable asset and received the utmost care. Now, we have baby farms which we fertilise with their bones. I know of one old hag in this city who has killed over two thousand babes.

" What chance has your girl or mine to marry and build a home? Not one in a hundred will ever feel the breath of a babe at her breast.

" No! " he closed in thunder tones. " I'll fight the encroachment of the Negro on our life with every power of body and soul! "

A hundred men leaped to their feet at once, shouting and gesticulating. The chairman recognised a tall dark man with a Russian face, but who spoke perfect English.

" I, gentlemen, am an anarchist in principle, and differ slightly in the process by which I come to the same conclusion as my friend who has taken his seat. I grieve at the necessity before the workingmen of returning to slavery. All we can hope now for a century or two centuries, is socialism. Socialism is simply a system of slavery—that is, enforced labour in which a Bureaucracy is master. We must enter again a condition of involuntary servitude for the guarantee by the State of food and clothes, shelter and children.

"It is no time to weep over slavery. The one thing we demand now is the nationalisation of industries under the control of State Bureaux which will enforce labour from every citizen according to his capacity, for the simple guarantee of what the negro slave received, the satisfaction of the two elemental passions, hunger and love."

Again a clamour broke out that drowned the speaker's voice. A Socialist and an Anarchist clinched in a fight, and for five minutes pandemonium reigned, but at the end of it Harris was lying on the sidewalk with a gash in his head, and Halliday was bending over him.

When Harris had recovered from his wound, Halliday took him on a round of visits to big mills in a populous manufacturing city across in New Jersey.

"These mills are all owned by Simon Legree," he informed Harris," and the unions have been crushed out of them by methods of which he is past master. I don't know, but it may be possible to get you in there."

They tried a half dozen mills in vain, and at last they met a foreman who knew Halliday who consented to hear his plea.

"You are fooling away your time and this man's time, Halliday," he told him in a friendly way. "I'd cut my right arm off sooner than take a negro in these mills and precipitate a strike."

"But would a strike occur with no union organisation?"

"Yes, in a minute. You know Simon Legree who

owns these mills. If a disturbance occurred here now the old devil wouldn't hesitate to close every mill next day and beggar fifty thousand people."

" Why would he do such a stupid thing? "

" Just to show the brute power of his fifty millions of dollars over the human body. The awful power in that brute's hands, represented in that money, is something appalling. Before the war he cracked a blacksnake whip over the backs of a handful of negroes. Now look at him, in his black silk hat and faultless dress. With his millions he can commit any and every crime from theft to murder with impunity. His power is greater than a monarch. He controls fleets of ships, mines and mills, and has under his employ many thousands of men. Their families and associates make a vast population. He buys Judges, Juries, Legislatures, and Governors and with one stroke of his pen to-day can beggar thousands of people. He can equip an army of hirelings, make peace or war on his own account, or force the governments to do it for him. He has neither faith in God, nor fear of the devil. He regards all men as his enemies and all women his game.

" They say he used to haunt the New Orleans' slave market, when he was young and owned his Red River farm, occasionally spending his last dollar to buy a handsome negro girl who took his fancy.

" Look at him now with his bloated face, beastly jaw, and coarse lips. He walks the streets with his lecherous eyes twinkling like a snake's and saliva trickling from the corners of his mouth practically monarch of all he surveys. He selects his victims at his own sweet will, and with his army of hirelings to do his bidding, backed by his millions, he lives a charmed life in a round of daily crime.

" How many lives he has blasted among the population

of the multitude of souls dependent on him for bread, God only knows. It is said he has murdered the souls of many innocent girls in these mills—"

"Surely that is an exaggeration," broke in Halliday.

"On the other hand I believe the picture is far too mild. I tell you no human mind can conceive the awful brute power over the human body his millions hold under our present conditions of life."

There was a tinge of deep personal bitterness in the man's words that held Halliday in a spell while he continued,

"Under our present conditions men and women must fight one another like beasts for food and shelter. The wildest dreams of lust and cruelty under the old system of Southern slavery would be laughed at by this modern master."

He paused a moment in painful reverie.

"There lies his big yacht in the harbour now. She is just in from a cruise in the Orient. She cost half a million dollars, and carries a crew of fifty men. With them are beautiful girls hired at fancy wages connected with the stewardess' department. She ships a new crew every trip. Not one of those young faces is ever lifted again among their friends."

He paused again and a tear coursed down his face.

"I confess I am bitter. I loved one of those girls once when I was younger. She was a mere child of seventeen." His voice broke. "Yes, she came back shattered in health and ruined. I am supporting her now at a quiet country place. She is dying.

"Think of the farce of it all!" he continued passionately.

"The picture of that brute with a whip in his hand beating a negro caused the most terrible war in the history of the world. Three millions of men flew at each other's throats and for four years fought like demons. A million men and six billions of dollars worth of property were destroyed.

" He was a poor harmless fool there beating his own faithful slave to death. Compare that Legree with the one of to-day, and you compare a mere stupid man with a prince of hell. But does this fiend excite the wrath of the righteous? Far from it. His very name is whispered in admiring awe by millions. He boasts that dozens of proud mothers strip their daughters to the limit the police law will allow at every social function he honours with his presence, and offer to sell him their own flesh and blood for the paltry consideration of a life interest in one-third of his estate! And he laughs at them all. His name is magic!

" I know of one weak fool, a petty millionaire, whom Legree lured into a speculative trap and ruined. On his knees in his Fifth Avenue palace the whining coward kissed Legree's feet and begged for mercy. He kicked him and sneered at his misery. At last when he had tortured him to the verge of madness he offered to spare him on one condition—that he should give him his daughter as a ransom. And he did it.

" No, the brute power of such a man to-day is beyond the grasp of the human mind. His chances for debauchery and cruelty are limitless. The brain of his hirelings is put to the test to invent new crime against nature to interest his appetites. The only limit to his power of evil is the capacity of the human mind to think, and his body to act and endure. When he is exhausted, he can command the knowledge and the skill of ages and the masters of all Science to restore his strength, while satellites lick his feet and sing his praises—

" Risk the whim of such a man with the lives of these poor people dependent on me? No, I'd sooner kill that negro you have brought here and take my chances of detection."

Halliday gave up the task, returned to New York, and sought the aid of the greatest labour leader in America, who had arrived in the city from the West the day before.

"No, Halliday," he said emphatically. "Send your negro back down South. We don't want any more of them, or to come in contact with them. I have just come from the West where a desperate strike was in progress in one of Legree's mines. Our men were toiling in the depth of the earth in midnight darkness, never seeing the light of day, for just enough to keep body and soul together. They tried to wring one little concession from their absent master, who had never condescended to honour them with his presence. What did he do? Shut down his mines, and brought up from the South a herd of negroes who came crowding to the mines to push our men back into hell. We begged them to go home and let us alone. They grinned, shuffled and looked at their white driver for the signal to go to work. I ordered the men to shoot them down like dogs. We made the Governor issue a proclamation driving them back South and warning their race that if they attempted to enter the borders of the state he would meet them with Gatling guns.

"No, send your friend South. The winters up here are too cold for him and the summers too hot."

In the meantime Harris walked the streets with a storm of furious passion raging in his soul. The realisation of the shame and the horror of his position! He was the son of Eliza Harris who had fled from the kindliest form of slavery in Kentucky. He had a trained mind, and the brightest gifts of musical genius. Yet he stood that day at the door of Simon Legree and begged in vain for the privilege of serving in the meanest capacity as his slave! What a strange circle of time, those forty years of the past!

And then the tempter whispered the right word at the right moment, and his fate was sealed.

"There's but one thing left. I will do it!" he exclaimed.

He entered the employ of a gambling joint and deliberately began a life of crime. After a month he won five hundred dollars, and went on a strange journey, visiting the scenes in Colorado, Kansas, Indiana and Ohio where negroes had recently been burned alive. He would find the ash-heap, and place on it a wreath of costly flowers. He lingered thoughtfully over the ash-piles he found in Kansas made from the flesh of living negroes. He tried to imagine the figure of John Brown marching by his side, but instead he felt the grip of Simon Legree's hand on his throat, living, militant, omnipotent. His soul had conquered the world. Yet even Legree had never dared to burn a negro to death in the old days of slavery.

He found one of these ash-heaps at the foot of the monument in Indiana to the great Western colleague of Thaddeus Stevens, and with a sigh placed his wreath on it, and passed on into Ohio.

He went to the spot where his mother had climbed up the banks of the Ohio River into the promised land of liberty, and followed the track of the old Underground Railroad for fugitive slaves a few miles. He came to a village which was once a station of this system. Here strangest of all, he found one of these ash-heaps in the public square.

CHAPTER IX

THE NEW AMERICA

ANOTHER year of struggle and suffering, hope and fear, Gaston had passed, and still he was no nearer the dream of realised love. If anything had changed, the General's pride had added new force to his determination that his daughter should not marry the man who had defied him.

His chief reliance for Gaston's defeat was on time, and the broadening of Sallie's mind by extended travel. He had sent her abroad twice, and this year he sent her to spend another three months in Europe.

These absences seemed only to intensify her longing for her lover. On her return the General would burst into a storm of rage at her persistence. She had ceased to give him any bitter answers, only smiling quietly and maintaining an ominous silence.

He had a new cause now of dislike for the man of her choice. Gaston had become a man of acknowledged power in politics and was the leader of a group of radical young men who demanded the complete reorganisation of the Democratic party, the shelving of the old timers, among whom he was numbered, and the announcement of a radical programme upon the Negro issue.

Radicalism of any sort he had always hated. Now, as advanced by this young upstart, it was doubly odious. The General had never given much time to his political duties, but his name was a power, and he gave regularly to the campaign committee the largest cash contribution they received.

He tried in a clumsy way to put Gaston off the State Executive Committee, but failed. He saw Gaston quietly laughing at him. Then he opened his pocket book and worked up a machine. It was a formidable power, and Gaston feared its influence in the coming convention.

While this fight was in progress, and Sallie was in Europe, the destruction of the *Maine* in Havana harbour stilled the world into silence with the echo of its sullen roar. There was a moment's pause, and the nation lifted its great silk battle flags from the Capitol at Washington, and called for volunteers to wipe the empire of Spain from the map of the Western world.

The war lasted but a hundred days, but in those hundred days was packed the harvest of centuries.

War is always the crisis that flashes the search light into the souls of men and nations, revealing their unknown strength and weakness, and the changes that have been silently wrought in the years of peace.

In these hundred days, statesmen who were giants suddenly shrivelled into pigmies and disappeared from the nation's life. Young men whose names were unknown became leaders of the republic and won immortal fame.

We were afraid that our nation still lacked unity. The world said we were a mob of money-grubbers, and had lost our grasp of principle. The President called for 125,000 men to die for their flag, and next morning 800,000 were struggling for place in the line.

We feared that religion might threaten the future with its bitter feud between the Roman Catholic and Protestant in a great crisis. We saw our Catholic regiments march forth to that war with screaming fife and throbbing drum and the flag of our country above them, going forth to fight an army that had been blessed by the Pope of Rome. The flag had become the common symbol of eternal justice, and the nation the organ through which all creeds and cults sought for righteousness.

We feared the gulf between the rich and the poor had become impassable, and we saw the millionaire's son take his place in the ranks with the workingman. The first soldier wearing our uniform who fell before Santiago with a Spanish bullet in his breast, was an only son from a palatial home in New York, and by his side lay a cowboy from the West and a plowboy from the South. Once more we showed the world that classes and clothes are but thin disguises that hide the eternal childhood of the soul.

Sectionalism and disunity had been the most terrible realities in our national history. Our fathers had a poet leader whose soul dreamed a beautiful dream called *E Pluribus Unum*. But it had remained a dream. New England had threatened secession years before South Carolina in blind rage led the way. The Union was saved by a sacrifice of blood that appalled the world. And still millions feared the South might be false to her plighted honour at Appomattox. The ghost of Secession made and unmade the men and measures of a generation.

Then came the trumpet call that put the South to the test of fire and blood. The world waked next morning to find for the first time in our history the dream of union a living fact. There was no North, no South,—but from the James to the Rio Grande the children of the Confederacy rushed with eager flushed faces to defend the flag their fathers had once fought.

And God reserved in this hour for the South, land of ashes and tombs and tears, the pain and the glory of the first offering of life on the altar of the new nation. Our first and only officer who fell dead on the deck of a war-ship, with the flag above him, was **Worth Bagley, of**

North Carolina, the son of a Confederate soldier. The gallant youngster who stood on the bridge of the *Merrimac,* and between two towering mountains of flaming cannon, in the darkness of night blew up his ship and set a new standard of Anglo-Saxon daring, was the son of a Confederate soldier of North Carolina.

The town of Hambright furnished a whole company of eighty-six men, a Captain, three Lieutenants, and a Major, who saw service in the war.

When they were drawn up in the court house square under the old oak, the Preacher stood before them and called the roll from four browned parchments. They were Campbell county Confederate rosters. Every one of the eighty-six men was a child of the Confederacy. And the immortal company F, that was wiped out of existence at the battle of Gettysburg furnished more than half these children.

" Ah, boys, blood will tell! " cried the Preacher, shaking hands with each man as they left.

A single round from the guns, and it was over. The yellow flag of Spain, lit with the sunset splendour of a world empire, faded from the sky of the West.

A new naval power had arisen to disturb the dreams of statesmen. The *Oregon,* that fierce leviathan of hammered steel, had made her mark upon the globe. In a long black trail of smoke and ribbon of foam, she had circled the earth without a pause for breath. The thunder of her lips of steel over the shattered hulks of a European navy proclaimed the advent of a giant democracy that struck terror to the hearts of titled snobs.

He who dreamed this monster of steel, felt her heart beat, saw her rush through foaming seas to victory, before the pick of a miner had struck the ore for her ribs from a mountain side, was a child of the Confederacy— that Confederacy whose desperate genius had sent the

Alabama spinning round the globe in a whirlwind of fire.

America united at last and invincible, waked to the consciousness of her resistless power.

And, most marvellous of all, this hundred days of war had re-united the Anglo-Saxon race. This sudden union of the English speaking people in friendly alliance disturbed the equilibrium of the world, and confirmed the Anglo-Saxon in his title to the primacy of racial sway.

CHAPTER X

ANOTHER DECLARATION OF INDEPENDENCE

ALMOST every problem of national life had been illumined and made more hopeful by the searchlight of war save one—the irrepressible conflict between the African and the Anglo-Saxon in the development of our civilisation. The glare of war only made the blackness of this question the more apparent.

While the well-drilled negro regulars, led by white officers acquitted themselves with honour at Santiago, the negro volunteers were the source of riot and disorder wherever they appeared. From the first, it was seen by thoughtful men that the Negro was an impossibility in the newborn unity of national life. When the Anglo-Saxon race was united into one homogeneous mass in the fire of this crisis, the Negro ceased that moment to be a ward of the nation.

A negro regiment had been in camp at Independence during the war and was still there awaiting orders to be mustered out. Its presence had inflamed the passions of both races to the danger point of riot again and again. The negro who was editing their paper at Independence had gone to the length of the utmost license in seeking to influence race antagonism.

When the regiment of which the Hambright company was a member was mustered out at Independence, Gaston was invited to deliver the address of welcome home to the soldiers, and a crowd of five thousand people were present, one-half of whom were negroes.

While Gaston was speaking in the square, a negro trooper passing along the street refused to give an inch of the sidewalk to a young lady and her escort, who met him. He ran into the girl, jostling her roughly, and the young white man knocked him down instantly and beat him to death. The wildest passions of the negro regiment were roused. McLeod was among them that day seeking to increase his popularity and influence in the coming election, and he at once denounced Gaston as the cause of the assault, and urged the leaders in secret to retaliate by putting a bullet through his heart.

The white regiment had been mustered out, and their guns in most cases had been retained by the men. The negro troops were to be mustered out the next day.

Late in the afternoon Gaston had received information that a plot was on foot to kill him that night, when a negro mob would batter down his door on the pretense of searching for the man who had assaulted the trooper. The Colonel of the regiment just disbanded heard it, and that night his men bivouacked in the yard of the hotel and slept on their guns.

A little after twelve o'clock, a mob of five hundred negroes attempted to force their way into the hotel. They met a regiment of bayonets, broke, and fled in wild confusion.

This event was the last straw that broke the camel's back. In the morning paper a blazing notice in display capitals covered the first page, calling a mass meeting of white citizens at noon in Independence Hall.

The little city of Independence was one of the oldest in the nation. It boasted the first declaration of independence from Great Britain antedating a year the Philadelphia document. The people had never rested tamely under tyranny nor accepted insult.

The McLeod Negro-Farmer Legislature had remodelled

the ancient charter of the city, and under the new instrument a combination of negroes and criminal whites had taken possession of every office.

One half of these office holders were incompetent and insolent negroes. The Chief of Police was an ignoramus in league with criminals, and their Mayor, a white demagogue elected by pandering to the lowest passions of a negro constituency.

Burglary and highway robbery were almost daily occurrences. The two largest stores in the city and four residences had been burned within a month. Appeal to the police became a farce, and it was necessary to hire and arm a force of private guards to patrol the city at night. When arrests were made, the servile authorities promptly released the criminals. Negro insolence reached a height that made it impossible for ladies to walk the streets without an armed escort, and white children were waylaid and beaten on their way to the public schools.

The incendiary organ of the negroes, a newspaper that had been noted for its virulent spirit of race hatred, had published an editorial defaming the virtue of the white women of the community.

At eleven o'clock the quaint old hall, built in Revolutionary days to seat five hundred people, was packed with a crowd of eight hundred stern-visaged men standing so thick it was impossible to pass through them and thousands were massed outside around the building.

Gaston, whose ancestors had been leaders in the great Revolution, was called to the chair. The speech-making was brief, fiery, and to the point.

Within one hour they unanimously adopted this resolution:

" Resolved, that we issue a second Declaration of Independence from the infamy of corrupt and degraded government. The day of Negro domination over the Anglo-Saxon race shall close, now, once and forever. The government of North Carolina was established by a race of pioneer white freemen for white men and it shall remain in the hands of freemen.

We demand the overthrow of the criminal and semi-barbarian régime under which we now live, and to this end serve notice on the present Mayor of this city, its Chief of Police, and the six negro aldermen and their low white associates that their resignations are expected by nine o'clock to-morrow morning. We demand that the negro anarchist who edits a paper in this city shall close his office, remove its fixtures and leave this county within twenty-four hours."

A committee of twenty-five, with Gaston as its Chairman, was appointed to enforce these resolutions.

By four o'clock an army of two thousand white men was organised, and placed under the command of the Rev. Duncan McDonald, pastor of the First Presbyterian Church of the city, who had been a brave young officer in the Confederate army. Every minister in the county was enrolled in this guard and carried a musket on picket duty, or in a reserve camp that night.

At six o'clock, Gaston summoned thirty-five of the more prominent negroes of the county including two of the professors in Miss Susan Walker's college, to meet the Committee of Twenty-Five and receive its ultimatum. Stern and hard of face sat the twenty-five chosen representatives of that world-conquering race of men at one end of the room, while at the other end sat the thirty-five negroes anxious and fearful, realising that their day of dominion had ended.

Gaston rose and handed them a copy of the resolutions.

" We give you till seven-thirty to-morrow morning as the leaders of your race to carry out these demands," he said gravely.

" But we have no authority, sir," replied the negro preacher to whom he handed the paper.

" Your authority is equal to ours—the authority of elemental manhood. If you can not execute them in peace, we will do it by force."

" We must decline such responsibility unless "—the negro started to argue the question.

" The meeting stands adjourned! " quietly announced Gaston, taking up his hat and leaving the room followed by his Committee.

At seven-thirty next morning no answer had been received. Gaston called for seventy-five volunteers to execute the decrees.

Within thirty minutes, five hundred men swung into line at eight o'clock, and marched four abreast to the office of the negro paper. It was promptly burned to the ground, its editor paid its cash value, and with a rope around his neck, escorted to the depot and placed on a north bound train.

As Gaston handed him his ticket for Washington he quietly said to him,

" I have saved your life this morning. If you value it, never put your foot on the soil of this state again."

" Thank you, sir. I'll not return."

While this guard, under strict military discipline, was executing this decree, a mob of a thousand armed negroes concealed themselves in a hedge-row and fired on them from ambush, killing one man and wounding six. Gaston formed his men in line, returned the fire with deadly effect, charged the mob, put them to flight, driving them into the woods outside the city limits, and placed the town under informal but strict martial law. By ten o'clock the resignation of every city and county officer was in his hand, and the Mayor and Chief of Police were at his feet begging for mercy.

He posted a notice over the county warning every negro and white associate that no further insolence or criminality would be tolerated.

The county and municipal election was but three days off and there was but one ticket on the field. When the white men elected were sworn in, the guards went to the woods and told the terrified and half starving negroes they could return to their homes, a competent police force was organised, and the volunteer organisation disbanded. Negro refugees and their associates once more filled the ear of the national government with clamour for the return of the army to the South to uphold Negro power, but for the first time since 1867, it fell on deaf ears. The Anglo-Saxon race had been reunited. The Negro was no longer the ward of the Republic. Henceforth, he must stand or fall on his own worth and pass under the law of the survival of the fittest.

This event made a tremendous impression on the imagination of the people. It increased the popularity and power of Gaston, its intended victim.

The General was more than ever determined to destroy Gaston's power in the convention which was to meet in a few weeks. He had his candidate for Governor well groomed and he had captured the largest number of pledged delegates. There were three other candidates, but none of them apparently were backed by Gaston. The General was puzzled at his methods, and failed to discover his programme, though he spent money with liberality and exhausted every resource at his command.

A strange thing had occurred that had upset all calculations. Beginning at Independence a race fire had broken into resistless fury and was sweeping along the line of all the counties on the South Carolina border and over the entire state with incredible rapidity. Everywhere, the white men were arming themselves and parading the streets and public roads in cavalry order dressed in scarlet shirts. This Red Shirt movement was a spontaneous combustion of inflammable racial power that had been accumulating for a generation.

The Democratic Executive Committee was called together in haste and made the most frantic efforts to stop it. But there was no head to it. It had no organisation except a local one, and it spread by a spark flying from one county to another.

McLeod laughed at the address of the Democratic Committee and swore Gaston was the organiser of the movement. He determined to nip it in the bud by putting Gaston under a cloud that would destroy his influence. He did not dare to attack him for his part in the Revolution at Independence. He preferred to belittle that affair as a local disturbance.

But at an election for Congressman to fill a vacancy, the Democratic candidate had won by a narrow margin in a campaign of great bitterness under Gaston's leadership.

Charges of fraud were freely made on both sides. McLeod determined to utilise these charges, and by producing perjured witnesses before a packed court, place Gaston in jail without bail until the convention had met.

He had every advantage in such a conspiracy. The United States judge whom he intended to utilise was a creature of his own making, a trickster whose confirmation had been twice defeated in the Senate by the members of his own party on his shady record. But he had won the place at last by hook and crook, and McLeod owned him body and soul.

Accordingly Gaston was arrested with a warrant Mc-

Leod had obtained from his judge, arraigned before him and committed without bail. He was charged with a felony under the election laws, taken to Asheville and placed in jail.

The audacity of this arrest and the vehemence with which McLeod pressed his charges created a profound sensation in the state. It was rumoured that the graver charge of murder lay back of the charge of felony and would be pressed in due time. A murder had been committed in the district during the exciting campaign and no clue had ever been found to its perpetrator. McLeod knew he had no evidence connecting Gaston with this event, but he knew that he had henchmen who would swear to any thing he told them and stick to it.

CHAPTER XI

THE HEART OF A WOMAN

A WEEK after Gaston's imprisonment Sallie Worth arrived in New York from her last trip abroad. She had cut her trip short and cabled her father of her return.

She was in an agony of suspense and uncertainty about her lover. Gaston's letters had failed to reach her for a month by reason of the war which had demoralised the mail service. Her own letters had failed to reach Gaston for a similar reason.

The General hastened to New York to meet his wife and daughter and persuade Sallie to remain in the North until December. He was hopeful now that her long absence and Gaston's absorption in politics, his bitter opposition to him personally, and the cloud under which he rested in prison, would be the final forces that would give him the victory in the long conflict he had waged for the mastery of his daughter's heart.

Before informing Sallie of the stirring events at Independence and the part Gaston had taken in them, or allowing her to learn of his imprisonment, the General sought to find the exact state of her mind.

" I trust, Sallie," he began, " you are recovering from your infatuation for this man. You know how dearly I love you. I have never taken a step in life since I looked into your baby face that wasn't for you and your happiness."

She only looked at him wistfully and her eyes seemed to be dreaming.

"I want you to have some pride. Gaston has attempted to kick me out of the councils of the party, and become the dictator of the state. His course is one of violence and radicalism. I regard him as a dangerous man, and I want you to have nothing to do with him."

She was gravely silent.

"Do you believe he has been faithfully dreaming of you in your absence?" asked the General.

"Yes, I do!"

"Then let me disabuse your mind. It is not the way of strong men. He is absolutely absorbed in a desperate political struggle in which his personal ambitions are first. I have seen him paying the most devoted attentions to the daughter of our rival down east, whose influence he wants, and it is rumoured among his friends that he has proposed to her."

"Who told you that?" she asked impetuously.

"I had it first from Allan, but I've heard it since from others."

"I do not believe a word of it," she declared.

"That's because you're a woman and hold such silly ideals. I tell you, he wants you only because he knows you are rich, and he wishes to brow-beat me. Such a man will try to whip you before you have been his wife five years. I know that kind of man. Why can't you trust my judgment?"

"I had rather trust my heart's intuitions, Papa. I can not be deceived in such a question."

"Well, you are being deceived. He is anything but a languishing lover. At present he is a political tiger at bay. Unless you hold him to you by some pledge he has given, he will forget you, and marry another in two years. I am a man and I know men. I thought I was desperately in love twice before I met your mother. I got over both attacks without a scratch, fell in love with her, married and have lived happily ever since. You have overestimated your own importance to him and your influence over him."

A great fear awed her into silence. For the first time in all her struggle with her father the sense suddenly came into her heart of her dependence on Gaston's love for the very desire to live, and for the first time she realised the possibility of losing him. What if he should press his great ambitions to successful issue while she stood irresolute and tortured him with her indecision? If he could win the world's applause without her, might he not, when successful, cease to need her? Her breast heaved with the tumult of uncertainty. What if another woman saw and loved him, and drew near to him in his hours of soul loneliness and struggle, and he had learned to see her face with joy! The conviction came crushing upon her that she had not responded bravely to this powerful man's singular devotion into which he had poured without reserve his deepest passion. Had he weighed her and found her wanting in some dark hour in her absence? Her heart was in her throat at the thought!

The General watched her keenly for several moments, and thought at last he had broken the spell. He believed he could now tell her of the cloud that hung over Gaston.

"I said, Sallie, that I believed Gaston a dangerous man. I did not speak lightly. We have had terrible riots in Independence while you were absent in which Gaston was the leader of an armed revolution which overturned the city and county government. Two thousand men were under arms for a week and several were killed and wounded on both sides. The results were good as a whole, I confess. We have a decent government and we have security of property and life, but such methods will lead to civil war."

Her face grew tense, and she looked at her father with breathless interest during this recital.

" Was he in danger in those riots? " she slowly asked.

" Yes, and I expect him to be killed at an early day if he continues his present methods. A mob of five hundred negroes attempted to kill him. This was one of the causes that led to the Revolution."

She was on her feet now pale and trembling with excitement.

" Where is he? " she gasped.

" Now, my dear, it's useless to get excited. The trouble is all over and a new Mayor and police force are in charge of the city. But he is resting under a serious cloud at present. He is held in jail at Asheville on a charge of felony, and a charge of murder is being pressed."

" In jail! in jail! " she cried incredulously while her eyes filled with tears.

" Yes, and Allan believes these ugly charges will be proved in the United States court, and he will be convicted."

She did not seem to hear the last sentence.

" In jail! " she repeated, " my lover, to whom I have given my life, and you, my father, while I was three thousand miles away stood by and did not lift a hand to help him? "

" Has he not been my bitterest enemy, seeking to insult me! " thundered the General.

" No, he never insulted you, or spoke one unkind word about you in his life. Oh! this is shameful! God forgive me that I was not here! " Tears were streaming down her face.

" You hold me responsible for the crazy young scamp's career? " cried the General indignantly.

" Not another word to me!" she exclaimed. " You shall not abuse him in my presence."

The General was afraid of her when she used the tone of voice in which she uttered that sentence. He had heard it but once before, and that was when she told him she was a free woman twenty-one years old, and he had broken down. He looked at her now, fearing to speak. At length he said,

" I have engaged a suite of rooms for you here at the Waldorf-Astoria, my dear, for the winter. I hope you will enjoy the season. Let us change this painful subject."

" I do not want the rooms," she firmly replied, " I am going to Asheville on the first train."

The General stormed and raged for an hour, but she made no reply. Her mother was suffering from the effects of the voyage and took no part in this storm.

" But your mother will not be able to accompany you. Surely you will not disgrace me by visiting that man in jail!"

" I will. And when he is released I will return. I will visit Stella Holt. I shall have ample protection."

The General was afraid to oppose her in this dangerous mood, and begged her mother to try to prevent her going. Sallie sent Gaston a telegram that she was coming.

In obedience to the General's request her mother called her into her room that night and they had a long talk and cry in each other's arms.

Mrs. Worth did not try very hard to persuade her not to go. Down in her own woman's soul she knew what she would do under similar conditions, and she was too honest with her child to try to deceive her. She only made love to her mother-fashion.

" Oh! Mama," cried Sallie, burying her face beside her

mother as she lay in bed. "I am at a great soul crisis. I don't know what to do. I feel lonely, helpless and heart-sick. You are a woman. Put your dear arms about me and help me to know the truth and my duty. I want to ask you a question."

"What is it, darling? I'll answer it, if I can," she replied stroking her dark hair tenderly.

"Do you believe these stories about Charlie's character?"

"Not one word of them!" she promptly answered.

An impulsive kiss and a sob!

"Dear Mother!" she said in a low tearful voice. "And now one more. Papa has been dinning into my ears his own fickleness in love when young and the fact that he knows in a long life that love is of little importance in a man's existence. He says that I can forget and love again with equal intensity and better judgment. Can one treat thus lightly the soul's deepest instincts and still find life rich and worthy of effort?"

Her voice broke and she continued slowly and tremblingly, as she held one of her mother's hands tightly,

"Now, Mama dear, heart to heart, tell me as you would talk in your inmost soul to God, do you believe this is true? You have sounded life's deep meaning. Is this all you know of life? You love me. Tell me truly?"

"No, darling, a woman can not deny this deep yearning of her soul and live. I would tear my tongue out sooner than deceive you in such an hour."

"Sweet Mother!" she softly murmured again as she kissed her good night.

CHAPTER XII

THE SPLENDOUR OF SHAMELESS LOVE

WHEN Gaston received her telegram in jail he was seated by a window looking out through the bars on Mt. Pisgah's distant peak looming in grandeur amid a sea of smaller blue mountain waves. He read the message and his soul was filled with a great peace.

"At last! at last! These prison bars, they are good! I could kiss them. I can never be grateful enough to my enemies!"

He had taken his prison as a joke from the first, sneering at the judge who had committed him. He knew that every day he stayed in that jail he was becoming more and more the master of the people. If McLeod had tried he could not have played into his hands with more fatal certainty. Five hundred citizens of Independence had wired him their congratulations and offered him any assistance he desired, from unlimited money for defence to a delegation to tear the jail down.

He declined any assistance. He knew the storm would break over their heads soon enough, and they would be delighted to get rid of him. In the meantime he gave himself up to his thoughts about the woman he loved, and wondered what change had suddenly come over her to send him that message. He felt sure the great crisis in their life had come. What would it be? A sorrowful surrender on her part to her father's iron will and a tearful good-bye forever, or the full surrender of her woman's soul and body to the dominion of his love?

He was glad the hour had struck that should decide. He trembled at the import of her answer but he was ready to receive it.

A carriage rolled into the jail enclosure and two young ladies alighted. One of them stopped in the sitting room for visitors, and he heard the tramp of a man's heavy feet on the stairs and after it the tread of a woman like a soft echo.

The key grated in the lock, the door opened. She looked into his eyes for just an instant of searching soul revelation, saw the yearning and the grateful tears, and with a glad cry sprang into his arms.

" You do love me! " she passionately cried.

" Love you? I drew you back across the sea with my love. I knew you would come. I willed it with a power you couldn't resist."

" I never got your letters, and I was hungry to see you," she whispered.

" And I never got yours, and drew you back by the power of a great heart purpose."

" Forgive me, for being away from you when you were in danger."

" I was glad you were safe. Don't let this jail alarm you. I'll be out too soon for my good I'm afraid."

" No other woman has come into your heart to cheer it even with her friendship since I've been away, has she? "

" What a silly question. I've never looked at any other woman since the day I first saw you! "

" Tell me you love me again! "

" I—love—you, unto the uttermost, in life, in death, forever! " he whispered tenderly.

She sighed and smiled. " The sweetest music the ear of a woman ever heard! " she half laughed, half cried.

" Now, my dear, you are a full-grown woman in the beauty of a perfect womanhood. For five years and more, I have waited and suffered. My life is an open book before you. When are you going to end this suspense? You must decide now whether your father's will shall rule your life or my love?"

" Must I decide to-day?" she asked tremblingly.

" Yes," he answered. " It is not fair to torture me longer."

" Then I give up!" she tearfully exclaimed. " God forgive me if I am doing wrong! I can not resist you longer. I do not desire to,—I *will* not! I am all yours, forever—soul, body, will, honour, life—all! I can not live without you. I love you. *I love you!*—Kiss me!— again—ah, your lips are sweeter than honey! Am I bold to say it? I do not care, I am yours. Your arms are the bonds of my slavery and they are sweet!"

Gaston was trembling with the joy that flooded his being with these the first words of perfect faith and submissive love that had come from her lips. And he winced at the memory now of those hours of dissipation when he had doubted her. He tried to confess it and receive her absolution.

" My dear, my joy is too great. It is pain, as well as joy. In the dark days of our first year of separation I thought once you had forgotten me. I went away into two weeks of debauchery. Your perfect love crushes me with its beauty and purity. I must confess this wrong to you. I must not deceive you in the smallest thing in this hour."

She placed her hand over his lips, " I will not hear it. I ought to have been braver and fought for my rights and yours. I will not hear one word of humiliation from you. I love you. You are my king. I love you, good or bad. I would love you if you were a murderer on the gallows. I can not help it. I do not wish to help it. I will follow you to the bottomless pit or to the throne of God and say it without fear to devil or angel. Kiss me again!—There, do not cry—let me see your beautiful brown eyes. I'll kiss the tears away. Tears are for my eyes not yours!"

"Then you will fix the day, dear?" he softly urged.

"How soon would you like it?"

"The sooner the better."

"Then I fix to-day," she said impulsively.

"What, here, in this jail?"

"Yes, where you are is heaven to me. I haven't noticed the jail," she said soberly.

He looked at her a moment, strained her to his heart and brushed the tears of joy from his eyes.

"My beautiful queen! This hour is worth every pain and every throb of anguish I have suffered. Its memory will encompass life with a great light."

"I'll go with Stella, see Dr. Durham who is here looking after your case, have him get the license, and we will be back in half an hour!"

The Preacher greeted her with delight. "Ah! Miss Sallie, if I had known a little thing like this would have brought you back, I would have hired a jail for him long ago, and put him in it."

"Doctor, I want you to get the license and marry us now, will you do it?"

"Will I? Just watch me. I'll have the documents and be ready for the ceremony in fifteen minutes!" cried the preacher as he hurried to the office of the Register of Deeds.

Sallie ran up to Mrs. Durham's room, told her, and asked her to be one of the witnesses.

"Of course, I will, Sallie. You are the one girl in the world I have always wanted Charlie to marry."

Sallie slipped her arm around Mrs. Durham. "You don't think I am doing wrong to disobey my parents thus, do you?" she faltered. "I feel just for a moment, now that I have decided, bruised and homesick,—I want my mother. Let me feel your arms about my neck just once. You are a woman. You love me as well as Charlie, tell me, am I doing wrong?"

Mrs. Durham kissed her. "I do love you child. It is a solemn hour for your soul. You alone can decide such a question. Any intrusion of advice in such a trial would be a sacrilege. Under ordinary conditions it would be a dangerous thing for a girl thus to leave her father's roof and take this step that will decide forever her destiny. Marriage is something that swallows up life, the past, the present, the future. We seem to have never known anything else. I can only say, if I were in your place, knowing all, I would do as you are doing."

Sallie impulsively kissed her, bit her lips to keep back a tear, and held her hand.

"I know your father well," she continued. "He is a man I greatly admire. But he is unreasonable with any one who dares to cross his will. You could never get his consent now that his pride is aroused except by forcing it. When it is over, he will forgive you, and when he knows your lover as I know him, he will be as proud of his son-in-law as a peacock of his plumage."

"Oh, it is so sweet to hear just the advice one wishes in such an hour," cried Sallie. "I shall always love you for these words."

"Yes, I congratulate you on the end of your long hesitation. I know you will be happy. Any woman would be happy with the love of such a man, and he was made for you."

"Then you don't believe with Papa," she said with

a smile, " that his mouth is cruel, and that he will try to whip me in five years, do you ? "

Mrs. Durham laughed. " Yes, he will whip you, but they will be love licks and you will cry for more. Your lover is a rare and brilliant man. He is strong, rugged, resistless in will, fierce in his passions from the blood of sunny France in his veins, and masterful in life from the iron heritage of the hardier races. You have seen these traits. Wait until you know him as I do in his daily life, and you will find a wealth of patience and a depth of tenderness that will startle. I envy you."

" Thank you," Sallie interrupted. " You don't know how glad your words are to my heart. I've not seen much of that trait yet. I've been half afraid of him sometimes. Let me kiss you again."

The keeper of the jail treated Gaston with every consideration and arranged for the marriage to take place in the little sitting room where he allowed him to come on parole.

The bride wore a plain travelling dress in which she had come from New York. She had driven from the depot past Stella Holt's home, and with her straight to the jail.

Gaston thought her the fairest vision that ever greeted the eye of man as he stood by her side; for he had seen that day the soul of a radiantly beautiful woman in the splendour of shameless love. His own soul was drunk with the joy of it all and his eyes now devoured her with their intense light.

Standing there before the Preacher whom he loved as his father, and the foster mother who had wrapped his little shivering body in the warmth of a great heart that night the light of life went out in his own mother's room, with Stella Holt's sympathetic face reflecting her friend's happiness, the marriage ceremony was performed. He took Sallie's trembling hand in his and promised to love, honour and cherish her as long as life endured. And under his breath he added, "Here and hereafter—forever." And then she looked into his smiling face with her blue eyes full of unspeakable love, and in a voice low and soft as the note of a flute, gave to him her life.

And the Preacher said, "What God hath joined together, let not man put asunder!"

She stayed there with him until the gathering twilight.

"Now, I must hurry back to my father and win him. I will not come to you a beggar. My father shall not disinherit me. I am going to bring you my fortune, too."

"Oh! curse that fortune, dear! I've feared it was that keeping us apart so long."

"Don't curse it. I like it, and I am going to win it for you. You are a man of genius. Your success is as sure as if it were already won. I will not come to you a helpless pauper. I have never been taught to do anything. I should like to cook for you if I knew how, and I am going to learn how. I am going to make you the most beautiful home that the heart of a woman can dream. I'd rob the world for treasure for it. I am going to rob my dear old father. He has sworn to disinherit me if I marry without his consent. He shall not do it."

"Then, don't be long about it. You are my treasure. I can build you a snug little nest at Hambright."

"I will only ask four weeks. Now do what I tell you. Sit down and write Papa a letter telling him I am your affianced bride and ask his consent to the celebration of our marriage within three weeks. That will produce an earthquake, and something will surely happen within four weeks."

He wrote the letter, and she looked over his shoulder.

"You see, dear," she said as she kissed him good-bye,

"I love Papa so tenderly. You can't understand how close the tie is between us, perhaps some day in our own home of which I'm dreaming you may understand as you can not now," she added softly.

"Then for your sake, dearest, I hope you can win him. But I'm afraid of this plan of yours."

"Leave it with me for a month, do just as I tell you, and then I'll obey you all the rest of our lives,—if your orders suit me," she playfully added.

She returned to Stella Holt's, and Gaston went back to his jail room and dreamed that night he was sleeping in the Governor's Palace.

CHAPTER XIII

A SPEECH THAT MADE HISTORY

WHEN General Worth received Gaston's brief and startling letter, the wires were hot between New York and Asheville for hours. His last message was a peremptory command to his daughter to join him immediately at Independence.

When Sallie arrived at Oakwood the General was already there, and the storm broke in all its fury. At every bitter word she only quietly smiled, until the General was on the verge of collapse. Day after day he begged, pleaded, raged and finally took to hard swearing as he looked into her calm happy face.

In the meantime McLeod and his henchman on the judge's bench had seen a new light. The excitement over the arrest of Gaston seemed to have fanned the flames of the Red Shirt movement into a conflagration. He was alarmed at its meaning. The judge heard a rumour that five thousand Red Shirts were mobilising at the foot of the Blue Ridge near Hambright, and that they were going to march across the mountains, into Asheville, demolish the jail, liberate Gaston, and hang the judge who had committed him without bail.

The rumour was a fake, but he was not taking any chances. He issued an order releasing Gaston on his own recognisance, and left for a vacation.

Gaston returned to Hambright showered with congratulatory telegrams from every quarter of the state.

He received a brief note from Sallie saying the war was on but had not reached its final climax, as the General was now devoting his best energies to the Democratic convention which was to meet in ten days, when he expected to crush any " fool movement of young upstarts ! "

Gaston knew of his organisation but he was sure the number of delegates pledged to the General's machine was not enough to dominate the body, even if he could hold them in line.

When this convention met at Raleigh, no body of representative men were ever more completely at sea as to the platform or policy upon which they would appeal to the people for the overthrow of an enemy. The coalition that conquered the state and held it with the grip of steel for four years was stronger than ever and was absolutely certain of victory. The enormous patronage of the Federal Government had been in their hands for four years, and with the state, county and municipal officers, a host of powerful leaders had been gathered around McLeod's daring personality. Apparently he was about to fasten the rule of the Negro and his allies on the state for a generation.

When Gaston entered the convention hall he received an ovation, heartfelt and generous, but it did not reach the point of a disturbing element in the calculations of the three or four prominent candidates for Governor. General Worth had drilled his cohorts so thoroughly in opposition to him, that any sort of stampeding was out of the question.

The platform committee was composed of seven leaders, among whom was Gaston. There was a long wrangle over the document, and at length when they reported, a sensation was created. For the first time since their triumph over Simon Legree the committee was divided, and, refusing to agree, submitted majority and minority reports. The committee stood five for the majority and two for the minority.

Gaston and a daring young politician from the heart of the Black Belt signed the minority report. The majority report as submitted, was merely a rehash of the old platform on which they had been defeated by McLeod twice, with slight additional impeachment of the incapacity and corruption of the State Administration. The delegates from the Black Belt and the counties where the Red Shirts had been holding their noonday parades received it with silence. General Worth's machine cheered it vigourously, and gave a rousing reception to their chosen champion who made the presentation speech.

When Gaston rose to offer and defend his minority report, a sudden hush fell on the sea of eager faces. A few men in the convention had heard him speak. All had heard he was an orator of power, and were anxious to see him. His leadership in the Revolution of Independence and his subsequent arrest and imprisonment had made him a famous man.

" Mr. Chairman and Gentlemen of the Convention:" he began with a deliberate clear voice which spoke of greater reserve power than the words he uttered conveyed—" I move to substitute for this document of meaningless platitudes the following resolution on which to make this campaign."

You could have heard a pin fall, as in ringing tones like the call of a bugle to battle he read,

" Whereas, it is impossible to build a state inside a state of two antagonistic races,

And whereas, the future North Carolinian must therefore be an Anglo-Saxon or a Mulatto,

Resolved, that the hour has now come in our history

to eliminate the Negro from our life and reëstablish for all time the government of our fathers."

The delegates from New Hanover, Craven, and Halifax counties, the great centres of the Black Belt, sprang on their seats with a roar of applause that shook the building, and pandemonium broke loose. When one great wave subsided another followed. It was ten minutes before order was restored while Gaston stood calmly surveying the storm.

Just before him sat General Worth, pale and trembling with excitement. The audacity of those resolutions had swept him for a moment off his feet and back into the years of his own daring young manhood. He could not help admiring this challenge of the modern world to stand at the bar of elemental manhood and make good its right to existence. He was about to summon his messengers and rally his lieutenants when Gaston began to speak, and his first words chained his attention.

While the tumult raised by his resolutions was in progress he lifted his eye toward the gallery and there just above him where it curved toward the platform sat his beautiful secret bride. His heart leaped. Her face was aflame with emotion, her eyes flashing with love and pride. She slyly touched with her lips the tip of her finger and blew a kiss across the intervening space. He smiled into her soul a look of gratitude, and with every nerve strung to its highest tension resumed his place by the speaker's stand. When the tumult died away he began a speech that fixed the history of a state for a thousand years.

His resolutions had wrought the crowd to the highest pitch of excitement, and his words, clear, penetrating, and deliberate thrilled his hearers with electrical power.

"Gentlemen:" he said, and the slightest whisper was hushed. "The history of man is a series of great pulse beats, whose flood overwhelms his future and fixes its life. Like the dammed torrent on a mountain side, it breaks the conservatism that holds it stagnant for generations and floods the world with its sweep. Theories, creeds, and institutions hallowed by age, are cast as rubbish on the scarred hills that mark its course. The old world is buried and a new one appears.

" The Anglo-Saxon is entering the new century with the imperial crown of the ages on his brow and the sceptre of the infinite in his hands.

" The Old South fought against the stars in their courses—the resistless tide of the rising consciousness of Nationality and World-Mission. The young South greets the new era and glories in its manhood. He joins his voice in the cheers of triumph which are ushering in this all-conquering Saxon. Our old men dreamed of local supremacy. We dream of the conquest of the globe. Threads of steel have knit state to state. Steam and electricity have silently transformed the face of the earth, annihilated time and space, and swept the ocean barriers from the path of man. The black steam shuttles of commerce have woven continent to continent.

" We believe that God has raised up our race, as he ordained Israel of old, in this world-crisis to establish and maintain for weaker races, as a trust for civilisation, the principles of civil and religious Liberty and the forms of Constitutional Government.

" In this hour of crisis, our flag has been raised over ten millions of semi-barbaric black men in the foulest slave pen of the Orient. Shall we repeat the farce of '67, reverse the order of nature, and make these black people our rulers? If not, why should the African here, who is not their equal, be allowed to imperil our life? "

A whirlwind of applause shook the building.

" A crisis approaches in the history of the human

race. The world is stirred by its consciousness to-day. The nation must gird up her loins and show her right to live,—to master the future or be mastered in the struggle. New questions press upon us for solution.

" Shall this grand old commonwealth lag behind and sink into the filth and degradation of a Negroid corruption in this solemn hour of the world? "

" No! No! " screamed a thousand voices.

" What is our condition to-day in the dawn of the twentieth century? If we attempt to move forward we are literally chained to the body of a festering Black Death!

" Fifty of our great counties are again under the heel of the Negro, and the state is in his clutches. Our city governments are debauched by his vote. His insolence threatens our womanhood, and our children are beaten by negro toughs on the way to school while we pay his taxes. Shall we longer tolerate negro inspectors of white schools, and negroes in charge of white institutions? Shall we longer tolerate the arrest of white women by negro officers and their trial before negro magistrates?

" Let the manhood of the Aryan race with its four thousand years of authentic history answer that question! "

With blazing eyes, and voice that rang with the deep peal of defiant power, Gaston hurled that sentence like a thunder bolt into the souls of his two thousand hearers. The surging host sprang to their feet and shouted back an answer that made the earth tremble!

Lifting his hand for silence he continued,

" It is no longer a question of bad government. It is a question of impossible government. We lag behind the age dragging the decaying corpse to which we are chained.

" Who shall deliver us from the body of this death?

" Hear me, men of my race, Norman and Celt, Angle and Saxon, Dane and Frank, Huguenot and German martyr blood!

" The hour has struck when we must rise in our might, break the chains that bind us to this corruption, strike down the Negro as a ruling power, and restore to our children their birthright, which we received, a priceless legacy, from our fathers.

" I believe in God's call to our race to do His work in history. What other races failed to do, you wrought in this continental wilderness, fighting pestilence, hunger, cold, wild beasts, and savage hordes, until out of it all has grown the mightiest nation of the earth.

" Is the Negro worthy to rule over you?

" Ask history. The African has held one fourth of this globe for 3000 years. He has never taken one step in progress or rescued one jungle from the ape and the adder, except as the slave of a superior race.

" In Hayti and San Domingo he rose in servile insurrection and butchered fifty thousand white men, women and children a hundred years ago. He has ruled these beautiful islands since. Did he make progress with the example of Aryan civilisation before him? No. But yesterday we received reports of the discovery of cannibalism in Hayti.

" He has had one hundred years of trial in the Northern states of this Union with every facility of culture and progress, and he has not produced one man who has added a feather's weight to the progress of humanity. In an hour of madness the dominion of the ten great states of the South was given him without a struggle. A saturnalia of infamy followed.

" Shall we return to this? You must answer. The corruption of his presence in our body politic is beyond the power of reckoning. We drove the Carpet-bagger from our midst, but the Scalawag, our native product, is always with us to fatten on this corruption and breed death to society. The Carpet-bagger was a wolf, the Scalawag is a hyena. The one was a highwayman, the other a sneak.

"So long as the Negro is a factor in our political life, will violence and corruption stain our history. We can not afford longer to play with violence. We must remove the cause.

"Suffrage in America has touched the lowest tide-mud of degradation. If our cities and our Southern civilsation are to be preserved, there must be a return to the sanity of the founders of this Republic.

"A government of the wealth, virtue and intelligence of the community, by the debased and the criminal, is a relapse to elemental barbarism to which no race of freemen can submit.

"Shall the future North Carolinian be an Anglo-Saxon or a Mulatto? That is the question before you.

"Nations are made by men, not by paper constitutions and paper ballots. We are not free because we have a Constitution. We have a Constitution because our pioneer fathers who cleared the wilderness and dared the might of kings, were freemen. It was in their blood, the tutelage of generation on generation beyond the seas, the evolution of centuries of struggle and sacrifice.

"If you can make men out of paper, then it is possible with a scratch of a pen in the hand of a madman to transform by its magic a million slaves into a million kings.

"We grant the Negro the right to life, liberty and the pursuit of happiness if he can be happy without exercising kingship over the Anglo-Saxon race, or dragging us down to his level. But if he can not find happiness except in lording it over a superior race, let him look for another world in which to rule. There is not room for both of us on this continent!"

Again and again Gaston raised his hand to still the mad tumult of applause his words evoked.

"And we will fight it out on this line, if it takes a hundred years, two hundred, five hundred, or a thousand. It took Spain eight hundred years to expel the Moors. When the time comes the Anglo-Saxon can do in one century what the Spaniard did in eight.

"We have been congratulated on our self-restraint under the awful provocation of the past four years. There is a limit beyond which we dare not go, for at this point, self-restraint becomes pusillanimous and means the loss of manhood."

He then reviewed with thrilling power the history of the state and the proud part played in the development of the Republic. He showed how this border wilderness of North Carolina became the cradle of American Democracy and the typical commonwealth of freemen.

He played with the heart-strings of his hearers in this close personal history as a great master touches the strings of a harp. His voice was now low and quivering with the music of passion, and then soft and caressing. He would swing them from laughter to tears in a single sentence, and in the next, the lightning flash of a fierce invective drove into their hearts its keen blade so suddenly the vast crowd started as one man and winced at its power.

Through it all he was conscious of two blue eyes swimming in tears looking down on him from the gallery.

The crowd now had grown so entranced, and the torrent of his speech so rapid, they forgot to cheer and feared to cheer lest they should lose a word of the next sentence. They hung breathless on every flash of feeling from his face or eloquent gesture.

"I am not talking of a vague theory of constructive dominion," he continued, "when I refer to the Negro supremacy under which our civilisation is being degraded. I use words in their plain meaning. Negro supremacy means the rule of a party in which negroes predominate and that means a Negro oligarchy.

"I call your attention to one typical county of over forty thus degraded, the county of Craven, whose quaint old city was once the Capital of this commonwealth. What are the facts? The negro office-holders of Craven county include a Congressman, a member of the Legislature, a Register of Deeds, the City Attorney, the Coroner, two Deputy Sheriffs, two County Commissioners, a Member of the School Board, three Road Overseers, four Constables, twenty-seven Magistrates, three City Aldermen and four Policemen. There are sixty-two negro officials in this county of 12,000 inhabitants, and their member of the Legislature is a convicted felon. The white people represent ninety-five per cent of the wealth and intelligence of the community, and pay ninety-five per cent of its taxes and are voiceless in its government.

"Would a county in Massachusetts submit to such infamy? No, ten thousand times, no! There is not a county in the North from Maine to California that would submit to it twenty-four hours. Will the children of Lexington, Concord and Bunker Hill demand such submission from the children of Washington and Jefferson? No. The passions that obscured reason have subsided. The Anglo-Saxon race is united and has entered upon its world mission.

"We will take from an unprofitable servant the ballot he has abused. To him that hath shall be given, and from him that hath not shall be taken away even that which he hath. It is the law of nature. It is the law of God.

" Yes, I confess it," he continued, " I am in a sense narrow and provincial. I love mine own people. Their past is mine, their present mine, their future is a divine trust. I hate the dish water of modern world-citizenship. A shallow cosmopolitanism is the mask of death for the individual. It is the froth of civilisation, as crime is its dregs. Race, and race pride, are the ordinances of life. The true citizen of the world loves his country. His country is a part of God's world.

" So I confess I love my people. I love the South,— the stolid silent South, that for a generation has sneered at paper-made policies, and scorned public opinion. The South, old-fashioned, mediaeval, provincial, worshipping the dead, and raising men rather than making money, family loving, home building, tradition ridden. The South, cruel and cunning when fighting a treacherous foe, with brief volcanic bursts of wrath and vengeance. The South, eloquent, bombastic, romantic, chivalrous, lustful, proud, kind and hospitable. The South with her beautiful women and brave men. The South, generous and reckless, never knowing her own interest, but living her own life in her own way!—Yes, I love her! In my soul are all her sins and virtues. And with it all she is worthy to live.

" The historian tells us that all things pass in time. Wolves whelp and stable in the palaces of dead kings and forgotten civilisations. Memphis, Thebes and Babylon are but names to-day. So New Orleans and New York may perish. African antiquarians may explore their ruins and speculate upon their life ; but we may safely fix upon a thousand centuries of intervening time. On your shoulders now rests the burden of civilisation. We must face its responsibilities. For my part, I believe in your future.

" The courage of the Celt, the nobility of the Norman,

the vigour of the Viking, the energy of the Angle, the tenacity of the Saxon, the daring of the Dane, the gallantry of the Gaul, the freedom of the Frank, the earth-hunger of the Roman and the stoicism of the Spartan are all yours by the lineal heritage of blood, from sire and dame through hundreds of generations and through centuries of culture.

" Will you halt now and surrender to a mob of ragged negroes led by white cowards who at the first clash of conflict will hide in sewers?

" I ask you, my people, freemen, North Carolinians, to rise to-day and make good your right to live! The time for platitudes is past. Let us as men face the world and say what we mean.

" This is a white man's government, conceived by white men, and maintained by white men through every year of its history,—and by the God of our Fathers it shall be ruled by white men until the Arch-angel shall call the end of time!

" If this be treason, let them that hear it make the most of it.

" From the eighth day of November we will not submit to Negro dominion another day, another hour, another moment! Back of every ballot is a bayonet, and the red blood of the man who holds it. Let cowards hear, and remember this! Man has never yet voted away his right to a revolution.

" Citizen kings, I call you to the consciousness of your kingship! "

Gaston closed and turned toward his seat, while the crowd hung breathless waiting for his next word. When they realised that he had finished, a rumble like the crash in midheaven of two storms rolled over the surging sea of men, broke against the girders of the roof like the thunder of the Hatteras surf lashed by a hurricane. Two thousand men went mad. With one common impulse they sprang to their feet, screaming, shouting, cheering, shaking each other's hands, crying and laughing. With the sullen roar of crashing thunder another whirlwind of cheers swept the crowd, shook the earth, and pierced the sky with its challenge. Wave after wave of applause swept the building and flung their rumbling echoes among the stars. These patient kindly people, slow to anger, now terrible in wrath, were trembling with the pent-up passion and fury of years.

What power could resist their wrath!

Through it all Gaston sat silent behind the group of the majority of the platform committee, with eyes devouring a beautiful face bending toward him from the gallery. She was softly weeping with love and pride too deep for words.

While the tumult was still raging, before he was conscious of his presence, General Worth's stalwart figure was bending over him, and grasping his hand.

"My boy, I give it up. You have beaten me. I'm proud of you. I forgive everything for that speech. You can have my girl. The date you've fixed for the marriage suits me. Let us forget the past."

Gaston pressed his hand muttering brokenly his thanks, and his soul sank within him at the thought of this proud old iron-willed warrior's anger if he discovered their secret marriage.

The General turned toward the side of the platform; for he had seen the flash of Sallie's dress on the stairs of the balcony leading to the stage. He knew her keen eye had seen his surrender and his heart was hungry for the kiss of reconciliation that would restore their old perfect love.

He met her at the foot of the stairs and she threw her arms impulsively around his neck.

" Oh! Papa, dear! I am the happiest girl in the world. The two men of all men—the only two I love— are mine forever! "

While the applause was still echoing and reëchoing over the sea of surging men, and thousands of excited people were crowding the windows from the outside and blocking the streets in every direction clamouring for admittance, a tall man with grey beard and stentorian voice, sprang on the platform. It was General Worth's candidate for Governor. He had not consulted the General but he had an important motion to make. The crowd was stilled at last and his deep voice rang through the building,

" Gentlemen, I move that the minority report offered by Charles Gaston "—again a thunder peal of applause —" be adopted as the platform by acclamation! "

A storm of " ayes " burst from the throats of the delegates in a single breath like the crash of an explosion of dynamite.

" And now that our eyes have seen the glory of the Lord, as we heard His messenger anointed to lead His people, I move that this convention nominate by acclamation for Governor—*Charles Gaston!* "

Again two thousand men were on their feet shouting, cheering, shaking hands, hugging one another and weeping and yelling like maniacs.

A speech had been made that changed the current of history, and fixed the status of life for millions of people.

CHAPTER XIV

THE RED SHIRTS

A S soon as Gaston could leave the throngs of friends who were congratulating him on his remarkable speech and his certainty of election, he hastened to find Sallie.

"My lover, my king!" she cried impulsively as he clasped her in his arms.

"Your eyes kindled the fire in my soul and gave me the power to mould that crowd to my will!" he softly told her.

"It is sweet to hear you say that!"

"Now, my love, we are in an awful situation. What are we to do with the General storming around preparing for a grand wedding? What if that jailer gives out the news? McLeod can get it out of him if he ever suspects anything."

"Don't worry, dear. I'll manage everything. We've fixed the wedding on the Inauguration day—so you can't be defeated. We will be busy day and night getting ready my trousseau, and issuing our invitations. Papa will never dream that one ceremony has been performed already. He need never know it until we are ready to tell him."

"If he discovers it, he will swear I have tried to humiliate him, and he will never forgive it. Telegraph me if anything happens, and I will come immediately. I can't see you for weeks in the campaign, but I will write to you every day."

445

"His Excellency, the Governor of North Carolina!"
she softly exclaimed with a dreamy look into his face.
"My lover!"

"Don't make me vain. I may be the Governor, but I
shall always be the slave of a beautiful woman who came
one day to a jail and made it a palace with the glory of
her love!"

"I'm glad I didn't wait for your success."

＊　　　＊　　　＊　　　＊　　　＊

The campaign which followed was the most remarkable ever conducted in the history of an American commonwealth. In the dawn of the twentieth century, a resistless movement was inaugurated to destroy the party
in control of a state, and affiliated with the most powerful
National Administration since Andrew Jackson's, on the
open declaration of their intention to nullify the Fourteenth and Fifteenth Amendments to the Constitution
of the Republic.

There was no violence except the calm demonstration
in open daylight of omnipotent racial power, and the defiance of any foe to lift a hand in protest.

When Gaston spoke at Independence, five thousand
white men dressed in scarlet shirts rode silently through
the streets in solemn parade, and six thousand negroes
watched them with fear. There was no cheering or demonstration of any kind. The silence of the procession
gave it the import of a religious rite. A thousand picked
men were in line from Hambright and Campbell county
and they formed the guard of honour for their candidate
for Governor.

Like scenes were enacted everywhere. Again the
Anglo-Saxon race was fused into a solid mass. The result was a foregone conclusion.

CHAPTER XV

THE HIGHER LAW

McLEOD knew from the day of that outburst which followed Gaston's speech in the Democratic convention that no power on earth could save his ticket. To the world he put on a bold face and made his fight to the last ditch, predicting victory.

His secret anger against the Preacher and Gaston, his pet, knew no bounds. Chagrined at his repulse by Mrs. Durham and the attitude of contempt she had maintained toward him, his tongue began to wag her name in slander to the crowd of young satellites loafing around his office in Hambright.

"Yes, boys," he said, "the Preacher is a great man, but his wife is greater. She's the handsomest woman in the state in spite of a grey thread or two in her rich chestnut hair. She has the most beautiful mouth that ever tempted the soul of a man—and boys, my lips know what it means to touch it."

And when they stared with open eyes at this statement, McLeod shook his head, laughed and whispered, "Say nothing about it—but facts are facts!"

McLeod chuckled over the certainty of the shame and suffering that would wring the Preacher's heart when dirty gossips of a village had magnified these words into a complete drama of scandal. For all preachers McLeod had profound contempt, and he felt secure now from personal harm.

The day the Preacher first heard of these rumours was the occasion of Gaston's campaign address under the old oak in the square. He had looked forward to this day with boyish pride mingled with a great fatherly love. It would be his triumph. He had stirred this boy's imagination and moulded his character in the pliant hours of his childhood. He had told himself that day he spent with him in the woods fishing, that he had kindled a fire in his soul that would not go out till it blazed on the altar of a redeemed country. And he was living to see that day.

The streets and square were thronged with such a multitude as the village had never seen since it was built. But the Preacher was not among them at the hour the speaking began.

A simple old friend from the country asked him about these rumours. He turned pale as death, made no answer, and walked rapidly toward his study in the church where his library was now arranged. He was dazed with horror. It was the first he had heard of it. One thing in his estimate of life had always been as securely fixed and sheltered in his thought as his faith in God, and that was his love for his wife, and his perfect faith in her honour.

He closed his door and locked it and sat down trying to think.

Had he not grown careless in the certainty of his wife's devotion, and his own quiet but intense love? Had he not forgotten the yearning of a woman's heart for the eternal repetition of love's language of sign and word?

The tears were in his eyes now, and he felt that his heart would beat to death and break within him!

He saw that his enemy had struck at his weakest spot, and struck to kill.

He lifted his face toward the walls in a vague unseeing look and his eyes rested on a pair of crossed swords over a bookcase. They had been handed down to him from a long line of fighting ancestors. He arose, took them down mechanically, and drew one from its scabbard. How snugly its rough hilt fitted his nervous hand grip! He felt a curious throbbing in this hilt like a pulse. It was alive, and its spirit stirred deep waters in his soul that had never been ruffled before.

He recalled vaguely in memory things he knew had never happened to him and yet were part of his inmost life.

"Damn him!" he involuntarily hissed as he gripped the sword hilt with the instinctive power of the fighting animal that sleeps beneath the skin of all our culture and religion.

And then his eyes rested on a quaint little daguerreotype picture of his wife in her bridal dress, her sweet girlish face full of innocent pride and warm with his love. By its side he saw the portrait of their dead boy. How he recalled now every hour of that wonderful period preceding his birth—the unspeakable pride and tenderness with which he watched over his young wife! He recalled the morning of his birth, and the heart rending, piteous cries of young motherhood that tore his heart until the nails of his own fingers cut the flesh and drew the blood. How the minutes seemed long hours, and how at last he bent over her, softly kissed the drawn white lips, and gazed with tearful wonder and awe on the little red bundle resting on her breast! He recalled the tremor of weariness in her voice when she drew his head down close and whispered,

"I didn't mind the pain, John, though I couldn't help the cries. He's yours and mine—I am as proud as a queen. Now our souls are one in him—I am tired—I must sleep."

Every movement of his past life seemed to stand out in

this crisis with fiery clearness. He seemed to live in an instant whole years in every detail of that closeness of personal life that makes marriage a part of every stroke of the heart.

At last he set his lips firmly and said,

"Yes, damn him, I will kill him as I would a snake!"

He sat down and wrote his resignation as pastor of the church, left it on his desk, and strode hurriedly from the study leaving his door open. He purchased a revolver and a box of cartridges and walked straight to McLeod's office.

The speaking was over, and McLeod was alone writing letters. He looked up with scant politeness as the Preacher entered and motioned him to a seat.

Instead of seating himself, he closed the door, and standing erect in front of it, said,

"Allan McLeod, you are the author of an infamous slander reflecting on the honour of my wife!"

"Indeed!" McLeod sneered, wheeling in his chair.

"I always knew that you were a moral leper "—

"Of course, Doctor, of course, but don't get excited," laughed McLeod enjoying the marks of anguish on his face.

"But that your lecherous body should dream of invading the sanctity of my home, and your tongue attempt to smirch its honour, was beyond my wildest dream of your effrontery. How dare you?"—

"Dare? Dare, Preacher?" interrupted McLeod still sneering. "Why, by 'The Higher Law,' of course. You have been teaching all your life that there are higher laws than paper-made statutes. You have trained this county in crime under this beautiful ideal. Surely I may follow the teachings of a master in Israel?"

"What do you mean, you red-headed devil?"

"Softly, Preacher," smiled McLeod. "Simply this.

"I HAVE RESIGNED MY CHURCH—TO KILL YOU."

You expound ' The Higher Law,' for political consumption. I apply it to all life.

" There are but two real laws of man's nature, hunger and love—all others change with time and progress. These are the higher laws, in fact they are the highest laws. The stupid conventions that superstition has built around them may hold back the weak, but the powerful have always defied them. Your brilliant exposition of the higher law in politics first set my mind to work, and led me to a complete emancipation from the slavery of conventionalism in which fools have held society for centuries. There are conventional laws and superstitions about the little ceremony called marriage cherished by the weak-minded. There is a higher law of nature. The brave live this life of daring freedom, while cowards cling to forms. Do I make myself clear? "

" Perfectly so, you mottled leper. You think that because I am a preacher, I am a poltroon, and that you can play with me without danger to your skin. Well, I was a man before I was a preacher. There are some things deeper than the forms of religion, if you wish to push the higher law to its last application. You have found that quick in my soul, mine enemy! I have resigned my church—to kill you. There is not room for you and me on this earth "—

McLeod sprang to his feet, his soul chilled by the tone in which the threat was uttered. He started to call for help, and looked down the gleaming barrel of a revolver.

" Move now or open your mouth, and I kill you instantly. Sit down. I give you five minutes to write your last message to this world."

McLeod sank into his seat trembling like a leaf, with the perspiration standing out on his forehead in cold beads. Now and then he glanced furtively at the stern face of blind fury towering over his crouching form.

Unable to endure the terrible strain, he sank to the floor whining, slobbering, begging in abject cowardice for his life. He crawled toward the Preacher, reached out his hand and touched his foot.

"My God, Doctor, you are mad. You will not commit murder. You are a minister of Jesus Christ. Have mercy. I am at your feet. Your wife is as pure as an angel. I only said what I did to torture you"—

"Get up you snake!" hissed the Preacher, stamping his body with all his might until McLeod screamed with pain and scrambled to his feet cowering and whining like a cur.

"Finish your letter. You will never leave this room alive."

A long pitiful sob broke the stillness, and McLeod was looking into the Preacher's face in vain for a ray of hope.

Suddenly Gaston burst into the room trembling with excitement. "My God, Doctor, what does this mean?" he cried seizing the revolver.

McLeod sprang toward Gaston, groaning and crawling toward his feet. "Save me Gaston,—the Doctor's gone mad—he is about to kill me!"

"Charlie, I must!" pleaded the Preacher.

"No, no, this is madness. I thank God I am in time. I missed you at the speaking, and hearing a rumour of this slander I hurried to find you. I saw your study open and read your letter. I knew I'd find you here. I'll manage McLeod."

The Preacher sat down crying. McLeod had crawled back to his desk and was mopping his face. Gaston walked over to him and said with slow trembling emphasis,

"I give you twelve hours to close this office, wind up your business, and leave. In the meantime you will write a denial of this slander satisfactory to me for publication. If you ever open your mouth again about my foster-mother or put your foot in this county, I will kill you. I expect your letter ready in two hours."

Gaston took the Preacher by the arm and led him down the stairs and back to his study. In the reaction, there was a pitiable breakdown.

"Oh! Charlie, you've saved me from an unspeakable horror. Yes, I was mad. I was proud and wilful. I thought I knew myself. To-day, I have looked into the bottom of hell. I have seen the depths of my own heart. Yes, I have in me the germs of all sin and crime. I am the brother of every thief, of every murderer, of every scarlet woman of the streets, that ever stood in the stocks, or climbed the steps of a gallows "—

"Hush, I will not listen to such talk. You are a man, that's all," interrupted Gaston.

"But God's mercy is great," he went on. "I have tried to live for my people and my country, not for myself. If I have failed to be a faithful husband, this is my plea to God, I have not thought of myself, or of my own, but of others."

After an hour he was quiet, and turning to Gaston he said,

"Charlie, go tell your mother to come here, I want to see her."

When she came, and sat down beside him with quiet dignity, she said, "Now Doctor, say what you wish, Charlie has told me much, but not all. Let us look into each other's souls to-day."

"I only want to ask you, dear," he said tenderly, "just how far your friendship for this villain may have led you. I know you are innocent of any crime. I only want to know the measure of my own guilt."

"You know, John," she said, using his first name, as she had not for years, "he has always interested me from a boy, and in the darkest hour of my heart's life, when I felt your love growing cold and slipping away from me, and my faith in all things fading, he attempted to make vulgar love to me. I repulsed him with scorn, and have since treated him with contempt. You know that I kissed him once when he was a boy. I have told you all. What do you propose to do?"

"What will I do, my darling?" he softly asked, taking her hand. "Begin anew from this moment to love and cherish, honour and protect you unto death. You are my wife. I took you a beautiful child, innocent of the world. If you have failed in the least, I have failed. If you have stumbled in the dark even in your thought, I will lift you up in my arms and soothe you as a mother would her babe. If you should fall into the bottomless pit, into the pit and down to the lowest depths of hell I would go, and lift you in the arms of my love. To break the tie that binds us is unthinkable. It has passed into the infinite. Not only are our souls one in a little boy's grave, but there is something so absorbing, so interwoven with the hidden things of nature in our union that I defy all the fiends in perdition to break it. Love is eternal. And your love for me was the great fixed thing in my life like my faith in the living God!"

"Oh, John, you are breaking my heart now, when I think that I doubted your love! I could have brooked your anger, but this overwhelms me!"

"It has always been my character," he gravely said.

"Then I have never known you until now,"—and in a moment she was sobbing on his breast, the years had rolled back, and they were in the sweet springtime of life again.

CHAPTER XVI

THE END OF A MODERN VILLAIN

TWO days after McLeod's flight from Hambright the press despatches flashed from New York a startling two-column account of the attempted assassination of the Hon. Allan McLeod, the Republican leader of North Carolina, in the terrific campaign in progress, and that he was compelled to flee from the state to save his life.

Gaston was elected Governor by the largest majority ever given a candidate for that office in the history of North Carolina.

McLeod was promptly rewarded for his long career of villainy by an appointment as our Ambassador to one of the Republics of South America, and the Senate at once confirmed him. The salary attached to his office was $15,000, and his dream of a life of ease and luxury had come at last.

For six months he had been quietly going to Boston paying the most ardent court to Miss Susan Walker, whom he had met at her college at Independence. She was a matured spinster now appproaching sixty years of age, and worth $5,000,000 in her own name.

He had easy sailing from the first. He joined her church in Boston, after a brilliant profession of religion that moved Miss Walker to tears, for he had told her it was her love that had opened his eyes. And it was true.

McLeod timed his last visit to Boston so that he arrived the day the city was ringing with the sensation of his attempted assassination, and the desperate fight he was making to uphold law and order in the South.

When Miss Walker read that article in her paper she resolved to marry him immediately. She gave McLeod a wedding present of a half million dollars. He wept for joy and gratitude, and kissed her with a fervour that satisfied her hungry heart that he was the one peerless lover of the world.

CHAPTER XVII

WEDDING BELLS IN THE GOVERNOR'S MANSION

TWO days after McLeod and his bride reached Asheville on their wedding trip, General Worth received a letter which threw him into a paroxysm of rage. Sallie's wedding had been fixed for the day of the inauguration of the Governor. The invitations were out and society in a flutter of comment and gossip over the romantic and brilliant career of young Gaston, and his luck in winning power, love, and fortune in a day.

The letter was from McLeod, at Asheville, informing him that his daughter was already married, and that Gaston was simply seeking his fortune by a subterfuge, and showing his power over him by humiliating him at the last moment before the world. He enclosed a transcript of the marriage record, signed by the Rev. John Durham, and witnessed by Mrs. Durham and Stella Holt. This record was certified before the Clerk of the Court and bore his seal. There was no doubt whatever of the facts.

When the General handed this letter to Sallie she flushed, looked wistfully into his face, saw its hard expression of speechless anger, turned pale and burst into tears.

Her father without a word went to his room, and locked himself in for twenty-four hours, refusing to see her or speak to her.

On the following day she forced her way into his presence, and they had the last great battle of wills. All the iron power of his unconquered pride, accustomed for a lifetime to command men and receive instant obedience, was roused to the pitch of madness.

" If you marry him I swear to you a thousand times you shall never cross my doorstep, and you shall never receive one penny of my fortune. He is a gambler and an adventurer, and seeks to make me a laughing stock for the world! "

" Papa, nothing could be further from his thoughts. He has always loved and respected you. I assume all the responsibility for our secret marriage."

" Then sharper than a serpent's tooth is the ingratitude of a disobedient child! "

" But, Papa, I waited five years of patient suffering trying to obey you," she protested.

" I had rather see you dead than to see you marry that man now, and have him sneer his triumph in my face."

" We are already married. Why talk like that? " she pleaded tearfully.

" I deny it. I am going to annul that marriage. Felony is ground for the dissolution of the marriage tie. A ceremony performed under such conditions, when one of the parties is in prison charged with felony without bail, is illegal, and I'll show it. The lawyers will be here in an hour and I will take action to-morrow."

" Never, with my consent! " she firmly replied. She left the room, consulted with her mother, and hastily despatched a telegram to Hambright summoning Gaston to Independence immediately.

When this telegram came he was in his office hard at work on his inaugural address, outlining the policy of his administration. He was in a heated argument with the

Preacher about the article on education, which followed his recommendation of the disfranchisement of the Negro.

He had advised large appropriations for the industrial training of negroes along the lines of the new movement of their more sober leaders.

" It's a mistake," argued the Preacher, " if the Negro is made master of the industries of the South he will become the master of the South. Sooner than allow him to take the bread from their mouths, the white men will kill him here, as they do North, when the struggle for bread becomes as tragic. The Negro must ultimately leave this continent. You might as well begin to prepare for it."

" But we propose to train him principally in Agriculture. We need millions of good farmers," persisted Gaston.

" So much the worse, I tell you," replied the Preacher. " Make the Negro a scientific and successful farmer, and let him plant his feet deep in your soil, and it will mean a race war."

" It seems to me impracticable ever to move him."

" Why? " asked the Preacher. " Those over certain ages can be left to end their days here. The Negro has cost us already the loss of $7,000,000,000, a war that killed a half million men, the debauchery of our suffrage, the corruption of our life, and threatens the future with anarchy. Lincoln was right when he said,

' There is a physical difference between the white and the black races, which I believe will forever forbid them living together on terms of social and political equality.'

" Even you are still labouring under the delusions of ' Reconstruction.' The Ethiopian can not change his skin, or the leopard his spots. Those who think it possible will always tell you that the place to work this mira-

cle is in the South. Exactly. If a man really believes
in equality, let him prove it by giving his daughter to a
negro in marriage. That is the test. When she sinks
with her mulatto children into the black abyss of a
Negroid life, then ask him! Your scheme of education
is humbug. You don't believe that any amount of education can fit a negro to rule an Anglo-Saxon, or to marry
his daughter. Then don't be a hypocrite."

"But can we afford to stop his education?"

"The more you educate, the more impossible you make
his position in a democracy. Education! Can you
change the colour of his skin, the kink of his hair, the
bulge of his lips, the spread of his nose, or the beat of his
heart, with a spelling book? The Negro is the human
donkey. You can train him, but you can't make of him
a horse. Mate him with a horse, you lose the horse, and
get a larger donkey called a mule, incapable of preserv-
ing his species. What is called our race prejudice is
simply God's first law of nature—the instinct of self-
preservation."

Gaston was gazing at the ceiling with an absent look
in his eyes and a smile playing around his lips.

"You are not listening to me now, you young rascal!
You are dreaming about your bride."

Gaston quickly lowered his eyes, and saw the messenger boy who had been standing several minutes with his
telegram.

He read Sallie's message with amazement.

"What can that mean?" He handed the telegram to
the Preacher.

"It means he has discovered the facts, and there is
going to be trouble. He is a man of terrific passions
when his pride is roused."

"I must go immediately."

He closed his office and caught his train after a hard

drive. When he reached Independence he sprang into a carriage and ordered the driver to take him direct to Oakwood. What had happened he did not know and he did not care. Of one thing he was now sure—Sallie's love and the swift end of their separation.

His heart was singing with a great joy as he drove over the familiar avenue through the deep shadows of the woods, and turning through the gate saw the light gleaming from her room.

" God bless her, she's mine now—I hope I can take her home to-night ! " he cried.

She had walked down the drive to meet him. He leaped from the carriage, kissed her and asked,

" What is it, dear ? "

" McLeod wrote him about our marriage, and now he swears he will bring a suit to annul it. Leave your carriage here and come with me. If he don't send these lawyers away and receive you, I will be ready to go with you in an hour."

" Queen of my heart ! " he whispered. " You are all mine at last ! "

She called her father from the library into the parlour and stood on the very spot where Gaston had writhed in agony on that night of his interview with the General.

He started at the expression on her face and the tense vigour with which she held herself erect. His suit had not been progressing well with his lawyers. They had tried to humour him, but had declined to express any hope of success in such an action. He saw they were half-hearted and it depressed him.

" Now, Papa," she firmly said, " It will not take us ten minutes to decide forever the question of our lives. If you take another step with these lawyers,—if you do not dismiss them at once, I will leave this house in an hour, go with the man of my choice to his home, and you will never see me again. You shall not humiliate me or him another hour."

The General looked at her as though stunned, his voice trembled as he replied,

" Would you leave me so in an hour, dear? "

" Yes, Charlie is waiting there on the porch for me now, and his carriage is outside. I will not subject him to another insult, nor allow any one else to do it."

The General sank heavily into a chair, and stretched out his hands toward her in a gesture of tender entreaty.

" Come child and kiss me,—you know I can't live without you! Forgive all the foolish things I've said in anger and pride. Your happiness is more to me than all else."

She was crying now in his arms.

" Go, bring Charlie. The youngster has beaten me. I've fought a foeman worthy of my steel. It's no disgrace to surrender to him."

In a moment she led Gaston into the room, and the General grasped his hand.

" Young man, for the last time I welcome you to this house. Now, it is yours. You can run this place to suit yourself. I've worked all my life for Sallie. I give up the ship to you."

" General, let me assure you of my warmest love. I have never said an unkind thing or harboured a harsh thought toward you. I shall be proud of you as my father. I have loved you and Mrs. Worth since the first day I looked into Sallie's face."

The invitations stood. Gaston returned immediately to Hambright, and on the morning of the inauguration, accompanied by Bob St. Clare, and the Chief Justice of the Supreme Court, he entered the grand old mansion with its stately pillars and claimed his bride. The Chief Justice performed a civil ceremony, and the party started on a triumphal procession to the Capital. The General was bubbling over with pride in the handsome appearance the bride and groom made, and tried to outdo himself in kindliness toward Gaston.

"Come to think it over, Governor," he said to him after the inauguration, "it was a brave thing in my little girl marching into that jail alone and marrying her lover in a prison, wasn't it? By George, she's a chip off the old block! I don't care if the world does know it!"

"General, that was the bravest thing a woman could do. She is the heroine of the drama. I play second part."

They did not wait long for the people to know it. At four o'clock in the afternoon an extra appeared with a startling account of the fact that the Governor's beautiful bride had braved the world and secretly married him when his fortunes were at ebb-tide, and he was a prisoner in the Asheville jail.

That night when Sallie entered the Banquet Hall of the Governor's Mansion, leaning proudly on Gaston's arm, she was greeted with an outburst of homage and deep feeling she had never dreamed of receiving. When the Governor acknowledged the applause of his name, he bowed to his bride, not to the crowd.

The Preacher rose to respond to the toast, "The Master and the Mistress of the Governor's Mansion," and seemed to pay no attention to the Governor, but turning to Sallie, he said,

"To the queenly daughter of the South, who had eyes to see a glorious manhood behind prison bars, the nobility to stoop from wealth to poverty and transform a jail into a palace with the beauty of her face and the splendour of her love—to her, the heroine who inspired Charles Gaston with power to mould a million wills in his, change the current of history, and become the Governor of the

Commonwealth—to her all honour, and praise, and homage.

" My daughter, it is meet that our wealth and beauty should mate with the genius and chivalry of the South. May it ever be so, and may your children's children be as the sands of the sea!"

Sallie bowed her head as every eye was turned admiringly upon her. The General trembled, and, when the crowd rose to their feet and reëchoed, " To her all honour and praise and homage," and the Governor bent proudly kissing her hand, he bowed his head and wept.

Her mother sitting by her side with shining eyes pressed her hand and whispered,

" My beautiful daughter, now my work is done."

As Gaston strolled out on the lawn with his bride after the banquet, they found a seat in a secluded spot amid the shrubbery.

" My sweet wife!" he exclaimed.

" My husband!" she whispered, as they tenderly clasped hands.

" Tell me now who was the author of all those lies about me to your father?"

" Why ask it, dear? You know Allan wrote the last letter."

" The dastard. I was sure of it from the first. Well, he had the facts in that last letter, didn't he?"

" Yes," she answered with a smile.

They rose to return to the Mansion, roused by the stroke of midnight from the clock in the tower of the City Hall.

" From to-night, my dear," he said, with enthusiasm, " you will share with me all the honours and responsibilities of public life."

" No, my love, I do not desire any part in public life except through you. You are my world. I ask no higher gift of God than your love, whether you live in a Governor's Mansion, or the humblest cottage. I desire no career save that of a wife—your wife"—she hid her face on his breast as a little sob caught her voice, "and I would not change places with the proudest queen that ever wore a crown!" She said this looking up into his face through a mist of tears.

With trembling lips and dimmed eyes he stooped and kissed her as he replied,

"And I had rather be the husband of such a woman than to be the ruler of the world."

THE END

Printed in the United States
737500001B

9 781565 549814